Lily at War

Keith Sheather

Published in 2019 by FeedARead.com Publishing

Copyright © Keith Sheather.

The author asserts his moral right under the Copyright, Designs and Patents Act, 1988, to be identified as the author of this work.

All Rights reserved. No part of this publication may be reproduced, copied, stored in a retrieval system, or transmitted, in any form or by any means, without the prior written consent of the copyright holder, nor be otherwise circulated in any form of binding or cover other than that in which it is published and without a similar condition being imposed on the subsequent purchaser.

A CIP catalogue record for this title is available from the British Library.

Acknowledgements

I am indebted to my wife, Judith, for the unerring eye she cast over my manuscript and for the valuable editorial suggestions she made to improve the text. I want to thank, too, Gill Bowen and Elizabeth Fudge, for their copy reading and helpful comments. Finally, I am grateful to Alison Levinson for putting me right on my German language and sorting out my erratic hyphenation.

Cover designed and illustrated by Jac Jones

1

He was oblivious to the insistent knocking on the front door, and it was only Peg, his wife, shouting from upstairs that aroused him.

'Hubert! The front door …. Are you awake? Hubert! You haven't gone to sleep, have you?' The shouting and the banging finally collided in his ears and he sat up with a start.

'All right,' he said, not quite sure where he was, 'I'll go.' He stood up, poised in limbo, and then it came to him. The wireless was still on. He had fallen asleep. His cocoa lay cold beside him and there was a loud knocking at the door. He shuffled into the hall and waited momentarily before calling out to ask who was there. An agitated male voice answered, 'Mr Rood. Let me in. I've been shot.'

Even in his sleep befuddled state, Hubert Rood was alert enough to know that such a melodramatic cry in the middle of the night in wartime was to be treated with caution. Especially as their large red brick house stood in detached isolation on the edge of town. Pulling aside the blackout curtain, he tried to look through the small window in the door, but the glazing distorted the figure outside, a distortion made worse by the pouring rain.

'Who's there?' he asked suspiciously.

'Friedrich, Herr Rood. Please let me in.' The man sounded more and more frantic. Hubert looked around him in confusion, uncertain what to do. The man had an accent. He had dropped the 'Mr' and called him 'Herr'.

'Hubert, who is it?' His wife stood behind him wrapping around her a hastily grabbed dressing gown. 'What does he want?'

'He says he's Friedrich,' said Hubert, looking back through the window.

'Impossible,' said Peg sharply.

'He says he's been shot.'

'Who, Daddy?' Their daughter Lily had joined them, curious to know what the commotion was about. She heard her mother repeat the man's name. Like a gazelle she leapt past her parents and grabbed at the door handle. Peg pulled her back.

'Don't be a fool, Lily. It could be anyone out there. And we have to turn the lights out. Hubert, get the bicycle lamp.' Her husband grunted and disappeared into the scullery. Lily tried to look through the glazed window but had no more luck in identifying the man than her father.

'Is it really you Friedrich?' she asked with her nose pressed to the glass.

A strangled voice came back at her. It had become unintelligible, but she did catch a heavily accented 'Fräulein Lily …' There was no doubt in her mind and she turned to her mother with a look of panic on her face.

'It is Friedrich,' she said. 'What is he doing here? He will be in danger.' She seized her mother by the arm, her fingers digging into Peg's flesh. 'Mummy, we must let him in.'

Hubert returned with the lamp which had been specially adapted for the blackout. Metal shutters covered the lens, which, when switched on, directed the light downwards. Against her better judgement Peg relented and told Hubert to open the door. But her husband had roused himself enough to hesitate.

'Dammit, Peg. You were right, woman. He could be anyone.' He turned to Lily. 'Ask him something only Friedrich would know.'

Lily thought for a moment and then shouted: 'Friedrich, what kind of hair has Sally got?' They listened for an answer, but only heard the persistent patter of the rain.

'I'll fetch a poker,' said Hubert, decisively. Then a faint word came through the door.

'What's he say?' blustered Hubert.

'Locken,' said Lily.

'That's German,' said Peg.

'Yes.' Lily shouted again through the door. 'In English! Friedrich!'

'Curly .... red.' They all looked at each other in relief. Peg switched off the hall light. The two women were pushed into a corner by Hubert, who switched on the shuttered lamp and went to the door and opened it. The figure outside was caught in the faint beam. It teetered momentarily in front of Hubert and then crashed into his arms. The elderly man had not the strength to hold the falling weight and amid the agitated cries of the women tumbled helplessly to the floor with the stranger on top of him. Peg, alarmed that Hubert had done himself harm, attempted to push the dead weight off her husband.

'Mummy, be careful – he's wounded,' cried Lily in panic.

'Then give me a hand, girl,' said Peg, her hands clutching at two legs, 'grab his shoulders.' As gently as they could they eased the body to the floor. Hubert stirred and began to lift himself up.

'Hubert, are you all right?' asked Peg anxiously.

'Soft landings, old girl,' he said with a grin, 'but this fellow's not so good.' The three looked at the sodden figure lying prostrate before them. The man was wearing a British army officer's combat fatigues turned black by the drenching rain. He had been wearing a beret but it had come off when he fell. There was silence. The panic of the moment had passed. They hovered, each one uncertain what to do. Peg bent down.

'He's breathing, but he appears unconscious.' This was immediately contradicted by the man whispering something Peg couldn't understand. She looked up at Lily.

'I think he's speaking German,' she said staring into her daughter's fast watering eyes. Lily heard her name on his lips.

'We can't leave him here, Mummy. We've got to get him somewhere more comfortable.' Peg thought that moving him could be dangerous, until the man himself began lifting himself up.

'All right, we'll take him into the drawing room. We need to remove these wet clothes.' Peg and Lily each took an arm, while Hubert supported the man's body. As they prised him up, a kohl blackened face came into view slashed with jagged streaks left by the rain. Only the eyes showed any humanity and they winced with pain. Lily felt the man's body press against her but she was strong and athletic and could take the weight. They reached an upright chair and lowered him into it. A young woman on the wireless was wishing everyone a pleasant sleep.

'Lily,' said Peg urgently, 'get as many white sheets as you can, some clean towels and pillows and blankets.' Lily let the arm she was holding go loose and stepped back to do as her mother bade. She stared down at the red stains oozing across the white fleece of her dressing gown. She shot upstairs, her mother's words trailing behind her telling her father to switch off the wireless. In a blind panic she rushed around grabbing frantically at whatever she could find. She stumbled back down the stairs now hearing her father's voice suggesting he get some brandy. This forced a smile from her. Daddy's response to emergencies was always the drinks cabinet.

'No, Hubert,' said Peg firmly, 'hot water and soap. And lots of it.' She looked at the man slumped in the chair. 'What a mess.' She turned to Lily lost behind bundles of bedding. Her daughter stood transfixed at the sight of the figure in front of her.

'My poor darling …' She started to sob, before Peg cut her short.

'Lily, this is no time for sweet nothings. These clothes have to come off.' Peg's authoritative voice jolted her into action. She dropped the bedding where she stood and joined her mother in attending to the man's sodden jacket. Together they raised one arm at a time and gently slipped the blouson from his shoulders. Though barely conscious, the efforts of the two women caused him visible pain. With the jacket removed they looked in horror at the dark stain of blood spreading across his shirt. A primitive dressing appeared to have been applied, but it had not been enough to staunch the flow. Peg knew this had to be stopped without delay. Removing the shirt would be too painful. She shouted for scissors and told Lily to rip a sheet and fold it thickly, while she cut the shirt and vest away from the wound. Lily gagged when she saw torn flesh encircling a deep hole in his side. Peg realised a bullet must still be in him as there appeared to be no exit wound. Blood pumped from the hole. She snatched the folded sheet from a stupefied Lily and thrust it over the wound and held it firm.

'He'll be all right,' she said. She had no way of knowing this, but she needed to comfort her daughter. 'Now tear a sheet into strips.' Lily did as she was bidden and together they wound the lengths around his abdomen, binding them as tightly as they dared.

Hubert returned with a pail of steaming water and a handful of soap. Peg laid towels around the chair, grabbed another towel, wet and soaped it and began to wipe the blacking from the man's face. Lily looked on anxiously as slowly the recognisable features of the man she loved emerged from the grime smeared mask. A smile flickered across his face before pain erased it. From his lips came an inaudible muttering. Lily put her ears close to his lips in an effort to catch what he was saying. It was such a painful whisper she could only recognise the odd phrase.

'…. we …. betrayed …. waiting ….'

'Friedrich, you were betrayed?' she said, attempting to interpret what he was saying. There was a nod. 'They were waiting for you?' Another nod.

'Who, Friedrich?'

'Soldiers …. Tommies.' His face crumpled and he fell silent. Peg scanned her daughter's worried face.

'Lily,' she said, keeping their eyes locked, 'we have to get Friedrich to hospital. He will die if he stays here.' This seemed to rouse Friedrich. He started talking again.

'The others got away. I … was last out….. took a bullet. ….. I come here.' His eyes pleaded with Lily. She swung on her mother. But before she could say anything Hubert interjected.

'Impossible,' he protested, 'the man's a German wearing a British uniform. If he's found here, we'll all be arrested for collaboration and like as not shot for treason.'

'He knocked on our door in the middle of the night, Hubert,' said Peg calmly, carrying on cleaning him as she spoke. 'We can deny we know him. He will be taken to hospital. He will recover and be interned. But he will live.' To Lily her mother's cold reasoning was hateful.

'This is Friedrich you're talking about, mother,' she said, angrily. Hubert put his hand on her shoulder.

'Your mother's right, dear,' he said gently, reconsidering his position. 'It's for the best.'

'Saving your skin, both of you,' cried Lily bitterly, tears welling in her eyes.

'That's enough, Lily,' snapped Peg, sharply. 'Now wrap him in the bedding you've brought down, while I ring the hospital.' Lily wiped her hand across her snotty face and glared defiantly at her mother's back. She picked up the eiderdown that lay crumpled on the floor and draped it around Friedrich's body, pulling it lovingly about him and letting her arms tighten across his shoulders. The effort of talking had caused him to slip into semi-consciousness. She knelt beside him and nestled her head in his lap. Through the open door of the drawing room she could see her mother pick up the black receiver and start dialling.

2

Three years previously, in the summer of 1938, it was all so different. Lily was a girl of eighteen, packing her cases in readiness for an adventure she was about to take in a state of sublime innocence. Like several of her friends, she was going to spend her summer holidays at a language school in Munich. Her best friend, Sally, was already there living with a family and she was travelling out alone to join her. She was apprehensive and excited, but proud of her parents' trust in her. She had left school and had enrolled on a secretarial course in Bedford that was to start in September. But before that she was going to have fun and taste the delights of a foreign land.

She gazed down at the two bulging cases in front of her. The contents had been checked and rechecked by her mother, again and again, every item of clothing from coat to camisole methodically ticked off. As Harris, the chauffeur, struggled down the stairs with the now firmly strapped cases, Peg again asked out loud whether they had packed enough underwear.

'Yes, mother,' said Lily with exasperation and slightly embarrassed that her mother should mention such things in front of Harris. 'Yes, yes, yes!' Her father stood at the foot of the stairs hurrying the cavalcade on and watching Harris stow the two cases into the trunk of the family Wolsey. On each case new Thomas Cook labels proudly proclaimed the destination of the carrier. Hubert owned a flourishing sawmill outside Bletchley where they lived and, with it in the safe hands of his manager, could take the day off to escort his daughter to the cross-channel port at Dover.

Well recompensed by her father, porters found Lily a discrete corner of the ferry's first-class saloon and she felt very important as she settled herself on the richly upholstered seat. Other passengers smiled. A young girl on her own was a novelty, but they quickly ignored her as they became pre-occupied with their own business. After a few minutes, Lily decided she should go out on deck and see if she could see her father on the quay below. She spotted him at once and waved frantically to catch his attention. He saw her and waved back.

'You're going on a great adventure, Lily,' he had told her. 'You're going to a country emerging from a terrible defeat and forging for itself a bright new future.'

She had seen pictures in magazines lying around the house of wide roads being built that went straight as an arrow into the distance, of great concrete buildings emblazoned with flags as high as Nelson's column, of smiling marching faces, so different from the drab, colourless places that were all around her in England.

Whatever awaited her on her return, for four glorious weeks, all that would be forgotten.

The ferry's hooter sounded with a shrillness that made her jump. She leaned over the rail and watched the stevedores release the heavy mooring ropes. A shiver of apprehension came over her, as the ship imperceptibly eased itself away from the quayside. She too felt she was being cast off. She strained to keep her father in focus but soon his shambling figure was a dot in the distance. The white cliffs that at first seemed a towering wall of white chalk quickly became a shadowy line on the horizon. In no time at all she found they were slipping into Calais and she was being escorted along the platform and helped aboard the night train to Munich.

Hubert had paid for her to have a sleeping compartment to herself. She sat on the edge of the bed with her cases beside her and gazed at the opulence of her surroundings. The copper light fittings, the marquetry of the panelling, the chair and table, the china wash basin with its ceramic taps were touches of sophistication beyond anything she had seen in England. She sat and revelled in the space, before the sight of the cases on the floor pulled her out of her reverie. She heaved one onto the bed, unstrapped it, pushed the lock open and lifted the lid. Her flannelette nightdress lay on top along with her toilet bag, placed there by her ever-practical mother.

She was on the point of laying out her bed things when a commotion outside caused her to pull back the curtain at the window. She saw a group of boys shouting to each other, pushing bicycles along the platform. They wore khaki shirts and brown shorts and reminded her of scouts. They were all about the same age. She watched them with fascination and then was acutely aware that she was staring at boys with no giggling school chums around her and no disapproving parents to embarrass her. Two of the boys caught her looking at them and waved. She felt she shouldn't wave back and contented herself with a suppressed smile. But she couldn't pull herself away from the window and sheepishly watched until the last pair of legs, darkly tanned from being exposed to the outdoors, disappeared to the far end of the train. Bringing up the rear was an older man, their leader she presumed, but more military looking than any scout master she knew in England.

She went back to unpacking her case. She heard a distant whistle and the compartment shuddered into movement. She felt the shunt of the coaches and as the great steam engine took the strain, she turned once more to the window to see a now empty platform slowly glide by. Soon they were hurtling through the French countryside and in no time at all had reached the German border town of Aachen. Passport formalities were carried out with the legendary efficiency she had heard her father talk so much about.

As the train started its journey through Germany, the steward announced dinner would shortly be served and she just had enough time to pull out a suitable dress before she was being escorted to the dining room. She hoped what she was wearing would not make her look too much like a schoolgirl. She was all too aware that her clothes were dull and unfashionable, but when the head waiter, a Frenchman, took her over and saw her to a table at the end of the restaurant car with a window and a view of the whole dining area, she suddenly felt very grown up.

'Mademoiselle will be private here,' he said, placing a napkin across her lap with a flourish. She thanked him with what she felt was grown up courtesy and took the menu he had offered her.

'The special tonight is moules marinière,' he said and waited for a response.

Her French was good enough to understand what he meant, but she didn't think she wanted mussels. She thanked him, but he hovered and that unsettled her. She made a close study of the menu and hoped that would move him. It did, but as he walked off to attend to more customers, the maître du vin arrived with the wine list. Another challenge, thought Lily. Her mother had warned that she would be exposed to alcohol and that she must be very careful how much she drank.

'Too much can lead to unfortunate consequences.' She never said what these 'unfortunate consequences' were.

'Best abstain, old girl,' re-joined her father. She smiled at this. She knew all too well what drinking too much involved. She had seen a girl at school expelled for being drunk. It had disgusted her when she vomited into the bushes. But this was the continent and she had been told they even drink wine with their lunch. Perhaps a small glass would do no harm? As she pondered her dilemma, the carriage started filling up and it occurred to her that she might be asked to share her table.

A waiter brought a jug of water.

'Is Mademoiselle ready to order?' He stood over her with pad and pencil expectantly. Before she could answer he was distracted by a noise behind him. He looked disapprovingly at the group of the boy scouts

Lily had seen earlier making their way noisily through the saloon in her direction.

'Ces enfants allemands - they have no manners,' the waiter said through his teeth. Lily thought high spirits rather than rude and was pleased when three of them stopped at her table. One spoke in a German she could not understand.

'They want to sit with you,' translated the waiter curtly.

'Of course,' said Lily sweetly, 'they are welcome.'

'Danke, Fräulein. You are English?' asked one, settling himself into the window seat.

'Yes,' said Lily. 'I'm afraid my German is not very good.'

The boy laughed. 'I am Hans,' he said, continuing in English. 'This is Wilhelm' - and then he pointed to a tall blonde blue-eyed boy who stood silently beside them – 'and this is Friedrich.' Lily smiled happily as the three of them sat around her. The waiter, knowing he was not going to get an order for some time, swung on his heels and left.

'You travel alone, Fräulein?' asked Hans.

'My friend is meeting me in Munich.' Lily was careful not to give the impression she would be leaving the train alone.

'A beautiful city. Sadly we do not go there – only Friedrich.' The tall blonde boy was still sorting his legs out under the table but shot Lily a quick smile.

'Yes, in Munich is my home.'

'And you have all been in England?'

'Yes,' said Hans, 'we have been riding our bicycles. It has been very instructive.'

'Oh,' said Lily eagerly, 'our Scouts go to France.'

'We are not Scouts,' said Friedrich, with an earnestness that startled Lily. He went on to explain in the same earnest tones: 'We are members of our glorious Führer's Youth League. There are no Scouts in Germany, although I believe your Herr Baden-Powell is a great admirer of our leader.'

'It is expected in our country that we all belong to the Hitlerjugend,' explained Hans. He struggled to translate.

'Hitler Youth,' said Lily, pleased she could understand.

'Ja. Hitler Youth.'

'But weren't you on holiday? I mean why are you wearing your uniform?' asked Lily, noticing the toggled scarves they wore, the highly polished buckles that adorned their belts, the lightning flashes sewn to their shirts.

'We wish to learn much about the English, Fräulein' said Friedrich, which was not the answer Lily was expecting. She saw nothing sinister in it, but she did think it was an odd reply coming from someone her own age. But there was something about the blonde boy's unblinking seriousness that appealed to her.

'I'm going to Munich to find out about *your* country,' she said, 'and please don't keep calling me 'Fräulein', my name is Lily.'

'Ah, a noble flower,' said Hans, who had picked up Lily's mocking tone.

'Actually, I was christened Lilian.'

'Will you be staying with a good German family in Munich?' asked Friedrich with an emphasis on "good".' Another strange question, thought Lily.

'Dr Wulf Gruber and his wife. Do you know them?' Friedrich shook his head.

At that moment, the waiter returned and took their orders. He left with the same surliness as he had appeared, leaving the four to exchange further notes about themselves. The German boys would not normally be eating in the saloon, but their leader had allowed them the funds as it was their last night. Lily described the language school she would be attending. Friedrich had heard of it and apparently approved. The boys drank beer and Lily had her glass of wine. The train thundered through the evening countryside and steamed into Cologne as they were finishing their meal.

'Ah, Heimat,' said Friedrich with a sigh. Lily did not understand the word and sat sipping her coffee waiting for an explanation.

'The soul of Germany, the heart of the Fatherland, the source of our Aryan stock …. the bedrock of the German people ….'

'You do say the strangest things.' Lily looked down as she spoke, desperately suppressing the urge to giggle.

'He's always getting steamed up,' said Wilhelm, slapping his companion on the shoulder. 'Lily doesn't want to hear all that stuff that's pumped into us.'

Friedrich turned on his friend.

'You don't believe it?'

'Of course, I do,' said Wilhelm hastily, 'but not over coffee.' Lily sensed a note of panic in his voice and chipped in brightly.

'It's jolly good to be proud of your country. Daddy's always saying so. That's why he admires your Führer so much. He says our politicians have all been got at by Communists and Jews who are repeatedly running our country down.'

Friedrich looked smugly at Wilhelm.

'You see our English Fräulein understands what I say.'

Before Wilhelm could reply, they were interrupted by the steward, who looked after Lily's sleeping compartment, announcing that it was ready for her to retire. She thanked the boys for their hospitality, gave Friedrich an extra smile and left them to their banter.

In the confined space of her compartment a warm flush enveloped her, the work no doubt of the wine she had drunk, but as she brushed her teeth and slipped into her night dress, she wondered whether this was being grown up. But the rhythmic clatter of the train cut short any answer sending her into a deep and contented sleep.

3

The next morning Lily awoke to squealing wheels lurching drunkenly across an expanse of scissored rails. She pushed up the blind and saw the train crawl into the cavernous maw of Munich's railway station. Her eyes popped as she glimpsed the enormous banners hanging from the walls, a dazzling wash of red and black. They were emblazoned with symbols she only half understood. Her father had told her about the cross like swastikas but she was only later to learn what the jagged lightning gashes meant.

The station concourse heaved with a surge of humanity. In the dazzle of faces and uniforms she feared she would never find Sally. Then, there she was, waving frantically across a line of marching soldiers. Sally was shorter than Lily, freckle faced with a straggly mop of ginger red hair. She was always laughing and it was this that caught Lily's attention. To her the world was one big joke. Her diminutive figure disappeared again only to re-appear grinning as if by magic from behind a group of the soldiers.

'Lily, you've made it,' she said excitedly, pulling into view a smartly dressed, big boned middle-aged woman. 'This is Frau Gruber, whom we are staying with.'

The woman took Lily's hand. 'Hallo, Lily. Sie sind herzlich willkommen', she said kindly. Lily looked for a translation, but none came.

'We only speak German,' said Sally, 'it's the best way of learning.'

'Danke, Gruß Gott,' said Lily struggling to summon the words. Marlene Gruber smiled, took Lily's hand again, nodded to the porter who was carrying her cases and led them out of the station to a waiting car. Lily looked around but saw no sign of Friedrich.

The Grubers' house was a large mansion outside the walled city close to the imposing mass of the Glyptothek. To Lily it seemed old, but it was only built in the last century. She was to share a room with Sally on the second floor, but even at that level the dimensions were huge.

As she was unpacking her cases and carefully laying out her clothes, she turned to Sally and asked her what the Grubers were like.

'Oh, all right, a bit strict. I wouldn't want them as my parents.' She reconsidered. 'But I suppose that's understandable. They're responsible for us while we're here.' She was looking at the pile of underwear Lily was retrieving from the bottom of the case.

'Are they cotton?' Lily nodded.

'How boring, we must go out shopping. There are some simply divine French knickers in the stores.'

'But mother said ….'

'Don't be such a prude, Lily. We're here to have fun. Provided we keep out of the way of Frau Gruber, that is.' Yes, she was being treated like a grown up. It was quite intoxicating really. Then a thought came into her head.

'Sally, what's a good German?'

Sally's freckles seemed to pucker. 'They're a bit funny about the Jews,' she said choosing her words with a care that struck Lily as odd.

'Funny in what way?'

'Well, the Führer seems to want to keep the Jewish people separate from the German people. He thinks they should have their own quarters and shouldn't mix.'

Lily thought nothing of this as she had heard her father express similar views.

'But the Grubers are good Germans?'

'If you mean, do they have Jewish friends, I think no, they don't, or at least I haven't seen any come to the house. They make so much fuss about them, but they don't seem to look any different from us. Come on Lily, you mustn't worry yourself about such things. Think of all those blonde German boys we're going to meet.'

Not to mention, Lily soon found out, a string of German syntax, boring German writers and endless learning by rote. Boys had to wait. The school she and Sally attended was for girls only and if the harpy who stalked the aisles conjugating verbs ever suspected that one of those girls was imagining herself in the company of a boy, that girl's hand would not be capable of picking up the pen to write the verb she was being ordered to parse.

The first days were getting used to the German way of life. The strangest part for Lily was understanding the country's obsession with physical fitness. Strapping German boys with tanned legs and weathered faces she could admire, but she never thought that she personally was expected to be part of the regime. So, it was a surprise to her, when about halfway through the first week their teacher Frau Busch announced that the class was to have a morning of physical exercises. Sally had not mentioned this.

The girls were taken to a hall attached to the school building that doubled as a gymnasium. They were each given a set of clothes to change into. Lily looked around for a changing room. There were none. They were clearly expected to undress in the hall. Frau Busch introduced the instructor, a Frau Hutger, who was to lead them in their exercises. She was an unsmiling martinet of indeterminate age who was wearing grey slacks, a white vest and plimsolls. She spat out an instruction in German that appeared to say 'get a move on' and whose volubility echoed around the room.

A murmur of alarm spread through the new girls. Embarrassment and uncertainty about what to do gave way to a sudden discarding of dresses, skirts and blouses, but stopped short at removing underwear. Frau Hutger would have none of it. She had in her hand a short cane, which she hooked under the elastic of one of the girl's knickers accompanied by a guttural 'off'. Lily was used to the changing room at school, but this seemed very public. At least the windows were high up. Diffidently she joined the others in baring all, giggling as she did so. What they had to put on made them all even more giggly. They climbed into a pair of large white baggy pants. This was bad enough, but nothing compared with the cotton vest-like tunic that went on top. Its hem flared in a way that barely covered their backsides. Sally and Lily looked at each other and could hardly contain their laughter.

'I've seen this on Eastbourne pier in a pantomime,' said Lily.

Sally did a twirl. 'What are we, Vestal Virgins?' There was general pandemonium until the instructor called order by banging the cane against a table. They were told to fold their clothes neatly and place them against the wall. As Lily was finishing the task, she became conscious of the girl next to her. She was black, probably from Africa. Lily of course had noticed her in the class, but she had never seen so much naked black skin before. The white of the girl's tunic showed off the shiny ebony of her legs. Lily was transfixed.

'You look nice,' she said. The girl smiled. Lily wanted to say more but Frau Hutger called them to attention and they all padded barefoot into the centre of the room where they were divided into ranks of six. Using the cane as a prop the instructor whirled it around to demonstrate the movements she wanted the girls to mimic. Arms out, arms up, arms to the side, arms stretch, the litany went on uninterrupted for thirty minutes. Or longer it seemed to Lily, who never liked physical jerks at school and was now puffing violently, praying for relief. This came momentarily when they were told to touch their toes and hold their position, a posture which Lily decided was one to execute without protest and to give no excuse for that whirling cane to land on her rump.

Finally, it was over and the girls were told to strip once more and rub themselves down with towels. There were no showers. The instructor demonstrated a towel rubbing exercise which made Lily again barely able to contain her mirth and Sally suspect it was done purely for the prurient pleasure of the instructor.

Breasts jiggled and bellies wobbled to the violent sawing action of the towel.

While dressing Lily found herself next to the black girl.

'What's your name?' she asked sweetly.

'Naoomie,' the girl replied, 'I'm from Namibia. My father is in the embassy in Berlin. He wishes me to improve my German.' Lily, who had little knowledge of Africa other than that provided by her textbook geography, looked bemused.

'Many speak German in Namibia,' explained the black girl.

'What is it like – this Namibia?' asked Lily, wide eyed with wonder.

Naoomie laughed. 'Very different from here. There is sand everywhere and many wonderful animals, elephant, giraffes, zebra ….' She would have gone on but Fraülein Hutger stopped the chatter and commanded them to sit on the floor cross legged. She was joined by Frau Busch and the two stood over them, legs akimbo, canes held behind their backs like sergeant majors. The instructor started to speak in a slow, deliberate German, which Frau Busch translated. It was clearly considered important enough not to risk misinterpretation.

'Fräuleins, we are honoured that you come to our country to learn our language. Our Führer has said that a healthy body precedes a healthy mind. We in Germany are proud of our bodies and we are keen to exercise them for the Fatherland, that we may grow strong as women and productive as mothers….' There was not a flicker of irony in her voice as she carried on in a similar vein, clearly believing every word she spoke. After the lecture they all filed back to the classroom for another lesson in German grammar.

'I ache all over,' groaned Lily when they returned to the Grubers and were able to throw themselves on their beds. 'What a dragon, she's worse than Busch. You never told me about her.' She looked at Sally reproachfully.

'I didn't want to alarm you, Lily,' said Sally with a silly grin on her face.

'I do declare I thought she was going to wallop someone with that stick.

'She did last week – on the backside. The girl couldn't control her laughter and got a whack for her pains.'

'They do take things seriously.' Lily rolled over on her front and looked straight at her friend. 'Sally, when are we going to get out? I'm so bored with grammar.'

'I've spoken to Frau Gruber. She says that she and her husband want to show you around the city on Saturday.' Lily's face dropped. 'But ….,' she paused meaningfully, 'she thinks we should carry on with our studies on Sunday.' Lily let out a huge groan and rolled back in protest.

'Just joking!' laughed Sally. 'She said we were studying really hard and we could go out on our own on Sunday.'

Lily sat up and flung a pillow at her friend and missed. 'You're a horrid person. I hate you and love you.' A second pillow found its mark. They collapsed in laughter. Lily stopped as a thought suddenly came into her head.

'Could we take Naoomie?' she asked. 'She seems a jolly nice girl, but I think she's lonely'. Sally's face went serious. 'Naoomie has her own friends in another part of the city. I don't think she would be happy going out with us.' Lily asked why to herself, but said nothing. As she had so little contact with black people or understanding of them, thoughts about racial prejudices did not enter her head. She simply nodded in answer.

4

School finished at noon on Saturday to prepare everyone for mass, but, as most of those attending were not Catholic, they were excused church. The Grubers had a car and after lunch they all piled in while Wulf Gruber drove them sedately around the city pointing out the many grand buildings that came into view. Lily was impressed, much as she always was when she went to London. The long red banners she saw at the railway station seemed to dangle from every building they passed. They crossed the Marienplatz, the throbbing heart of the city. Lily gazed in wonder on the many people who criss-crossed its vast space. From walls of the old and new town halls hung still more banners. It was summer, but to Lily it seemed like Christmas had come early.

Wulf Gruber stopped the car outside an old building four stories high with soaring red-tiled gabled roofs. Sally pinched Lily.

'We're going shopping,' she said, excitedly. They piled out of the car into Oberpollinger, Munich's prestigious department store. Lily looked around her. Heavy wooden counters stretched into the furthest reaches of the shop. High ceilings allowed cardboard banners to hang down, advertising goods for sale. Racks of shelves piled with products towered over severe looking shop assistants. To Lily it all appeared a little dowdy and not the glittering cornucopia Sally had led her to expect. Still there were rows of silk stockings draped like bunting around the doyennes serving, making an ironic comment on their severely regimented uniforms.

'You have money? You wish to buy something?' asked Marlene Gruber. The girls' eyes lit up and they hungrily prowled the fashion displays. Sally bought a long straight dress in a russet coloured fabric that matched her red hair. Lily went for a hat which made her feel terribly grown up. It was wide brimmed in soft grey with a red band into which was tucked a long red feather. She was shown the way to wear it at a slant giving her a rakish look. When she saw herself in a mirror, she gave a whoop and noisily twirled around the shop attracting attention from other customers. The assistant quickly retrieved the hat and deposited it in a commodious red and white striped hat box tightly wrapped in tissue paper. Lily resigned herself to the fact that it was going to stay there until she returned to England.

Back in the car they wove among trams, often three carriages long, to reach the edge of another square. Here Wulf Gruber parked the car and they got out and walked towards what he called the Odeonplatz. Ahead of them loomed a strange edifice which Lily only caught a brief glimpse of. It towered over people, a ferocious eagle standing on a wreathed swastika, atop a great slab of black marble, to which those who passed by gave a hurried salute. Black uniformed soldiers stood to attention on either side. Lily was about to ask what it was, when Herr Gruber took her by the arm and ushered her and the others down a narrow cobbled alley that ran along the back of the grand houses that fronted the square.

'This is a short cut to square,' he explained. It didn't seem like a short cut to Lily, but she said nothing, nor was anything mentioned about the monument. Many people passed them in the alley, which was called Vickardigasse, after a Swiss architect explained Herr Gruber. Lily did one of her giggles. He was a funny little man with his balding head, circular spectacles and tweedy clothes, who clearly loved taking them around, even if neither of them understood much of what he was saying. The alley finally gave way onto the square about halfway down its south side.

'This was built by Ludwig I our great Bavarian king,' Herr Gruber declaimed in his halting English. Lily had no idea who Ludwig I was, but decided, as they strode out over the immensity of his handiwork, that, if he could build this, he must have been important.

'Look,' said Wulf excitedly, 'that building at the end.' A strange arched shape appeared. They waited for the explanation they knew was coming. 'It is a monumental loggia which Ludwig saw in Florence and had built here. Magnificent, isn't it?' He continued in similar vein until he could see his young charges were flagging. They returned to the car via Vickardigasse and drove out of the city. The Grubers had planned a small country inn for afternoon tea.

Houses gave way to grass covered fields thick with cows and punctuated by forests of conifers. They had the windows down and sucked in the fragrant air.

One smell above all assailed Lily's nostrils, the moist sweetness of wood. Timber was everywhere. Farms were built of wood. Logs were piled high in barns, tucked below house floors or strewn along the roadside.

Wulf turned off the road and pulled into a clearing. In front of them stood a monumental wooden building with a deep sloping roof that almost touched the ground. A veranda ran around the front of what was in fact an inn accessed by a wide staircase. Below the decking were sawn lengths of log ready for winter burning.

The girls felt very grand climbing the steps and entering the reception hall. They were shown to the restaurant and seated at a table that gave a view onto the garden and the forest beyond. An embroidered tablecloth with laid place settings promised treats to come. Lily who had a sweet tooth could hardly contain herself as she looked around at the sugary delights being consumed at the other tables. A smattering of swastika arm bands could be seen but otherwise most of those who ate were as informal in their demeanour as the Grubers.

'Meine Fräuleins, you like cake? We have good Bavarian cake,' said Herr Gruber. A large trolley piled with mouth-watering confections was wheeled alongside them by a tall unsmiling blonde girl. Her hair was pulled back in a beignet. She wore a simple blouse with puffed sleeves poking out from a tight-fitting waistcoat. This in turn gave way to a long grey skirt. Lily thought she looked alarmingly severe and noticed the Grubers tighten up.

'Was möchten Sie?' she asked in a flat voice that was a little off putting. Are we welcome here? wondered Lily, as the girl stared unblinkingly at them. No matter, the cakes looked scrumptious and soon she and Sally were tucking into generous helpings of apfelstrudel and raspberry torte. The raspberry cake was especially delicious. Topped with fruit, it was a triple sandwich of raspberry flavoured cake layered with cream and jam. Despite the sullen waitress it was a good end to a pleasant afternoon. Yet as they drove back into the city and she gazed out at the people thronging the pavements in what seemed almost a festive spirit, she reflected on the odd detour along the cobbled alley and the less than friendly manner of the girl at the inn and tried to make sense of them. They unsettled her and she didn't know why. But that evening all such thoughts were pushed from her mind when Sally announced that she had been told by Frau Gruber that they could go out on their own the next day. Neither said it, but both thought 'boys'.

5

Sally knew just where to go on a warm summer Sunday. It was one of her favourite places. She called it the English Beer Garden and said it was in the middle of Munich's largest park. This tickled Lily's curiosity and as they walked in the company of many other strollers, she wondered what she was going to find. Ahead of them was a large glade of cedar and linden trees and they could hear the distant strains of music and then a buzz of chatter growing in intensity as they got closer. They burst through the outer ring of trees and found themselves in an open area of long wooden tables and benches filled with people, talking excitably and drinking what seemed to Lily to be unconscionably large amounts of beer. To enforce the happy mood a brass band played rousing folk tunes and military marches.

Sally searched for free places at a table and found two at the end of one of the benches. Lily looked around her and was staggered at the size of the glasses everyone drank from.

'They're called maßkrugs', said Sally, 'They hold a litre of beer.' Lily was impressed by the strength of the waitresses who could carry five or six of these glasses at a time, all brimming with the yellowish liquid. The women had their hair fixed in traditional braids and wore long dirndl skirts and elaborately embroidered aprons.

'Does everyone here wear fancy dress?'

'They certainly like their uniforms,' Sally said, in what was virtually a whisper. Lily looked up and saw a waitress hovering over them. Sally ordered a Maβkrug.

'One for you, Lily?'

'I've never really had beer before', she said hesitantly. In fact she had never been in a pub before. The nearest she got was when her parents stopped at a country inn. She had to sit in the garden and wait for them to bring her drink out, although she did pop her head through the door. She saw her father standing at the bar and her mother sat at a table. There was a lot of cigarette smoke, but the glasses people were drinking from did seem a lot smaller than the ones here.

'Always a first time – better start with a small glass,' said Sally. Lily nodded. She wasn't certain about the taste when it came, but thought it rude not to drink it.

'What do you think about our teacher?' asked Sally.

'Bit old fashioned.'

'Neanderthal more likely. I think she was fossilised before she arrived. Best place to learn German is here.' She turned to the woman sitting beside Lily and passed a few pleasantries with her. Lily was impressed and was even more impressed with the fact she thought she understood what was being said.

She was now into her second glass and feeling a little drowsy from the warm summer sunshine, the babble of voices and the intoxicating effect of the beer. A voice in English came from nowhere and seemed to chime with the first chords of a military two step.

'Fräulein Lily, how good to see you here.' Lily jumped and looked around to see the tall gangly silhouette of Friedrich standing over her.

'I apologise for startling you, Fräulein.' He came around to where she could see him properly. He proffered his hand and simultaneously clicked his heels.

'Sally, this is Friedrich. We met on the train. He lives in Munich.' Lily rattled off the introductions with Sally, whose eyes were popping, gaping in amazement. 'He is a member of the Hitler Youth,' said Lily in conclusion.

'So I see,' said Sally, running her eyes up and down the uniformed young man. He wore a grey peaked cap, khaki shirt, grey shorts and beige socks that came to the knee. A shiny brown strap crossed his chest and clipped to the belt around his waist, adorned with a silver buckle decorated with an eagle. Missing from the time on the train were the two arm bands with their sewn-on swastikas.

'May I join ladies from England?' he asked with continuing formality. Lily concluded that most of his English must have come entirely from books.

'Of course.' She was conscious that where there had been nowhere to sit before, miraculously a space appeared beside her. And no sooner had his shorts touched the wooden seat than a waitress appeared at his side. He ordered a Maßkrug, the girls declined another.

'Munich, is gay in the sun, is it not?'

'Yes, it's grand,' said Lily, staring at his eyes that were as blue as the sky around them.

'It is a glorious time to be German. Thanks to our Führer we are one people again.' Lily looked puzzled.

'He means Germany taking over Austria,' explained Sally.

'I prefer 're-joining',' said Friedrich. 'After all the Führer was born in Austria. Now we are free. No more borders. We can cross our mountains and no one stops us.'

'How did you come to meet Lily?' asked Sally, not happy with the way the conversation was going. She had learnt while in Munich to keep clear of politics.

'On the train, silly, I told you,' said Lily.

'No, I mean, why were you on the train, Friedrich?' His beer arrived. He took a large gulp before answering.

'I was coming back from England. I had been with a group. We had been riding our bicycles.' He took another swig. 'Do you like to ride the bicycle?'

Sally said she did. She often borrowed a push bike from the Grubers.

'Then let me take you and Lily on a ride around the countryside. I could come to your house, next Saturday.' Sally looked hesitant.

'Oh, do let's,' said Lily eagerly. 'Do the Grubers have a bicycle for me?' Sally thought they did.

6

So it was arranged. Friedrich would call at mid-morning and the three would take a train out to the villages around Munich. Sally remained uncertain wondering what the Grubers would think when a uniformed young man turned up on their doorstep. She had often heard them express concern about the growing militarism among the country's youth. But to her surprise they said nothing. Frau Gruber made a picnic of bread, sausage and ginger beer which she packed into the paniers that sat on either side of the rear wheels.

Soon the three were free-wheeling down deserted lanes with tall hedges bordering fields of fast ripening corn. Friedrich behaved with exemplary correctness. Sally found him humourless and stiff, but she saw that Lily hung on his every word. They passed through well-kept villages. Friedrich announced they would stop at the next one for lunch. Lily was pleased as she was starting to feel hungry and not a little fatigued. Friedrich set a furious pace and her legs struggled hard to keep up.

Tiled roofs came into view. Friedrich turned into a narrow but well-made side road 'to find a secluded spot' he promised. They followed in single file twisting along lanes that didn't seem to be getting anywhere. Sally started to wonder whether Friedrich was lost. Then, without warning, he pulled up and wheeled his bicycle around.

'I make mistake,' he said briskly, 'we go back.' As Lily dismounted and turned herself around, she saw what she thought was the outline of a tower hidden in the trees. She also caught a glimpse of fencing with barbed wire on top. She went to ask Friedrich about it, but he was now well ahead of them frantically waving for them to follow him. They clambered on their bicycles but try as they might they couldn't catch him up. Then he disappeared from view.

Sally saw it first, the top of a large lorry coming in their direction. She shouted at Lily: 'Get in the hedge. It's too wide to pass us.' The girls flung themselves and their bicycles into the bank just as the monster hooting and flashing its lights roared by. A cloud of dust shot up and through it Lily could see two soldiers with rifles on their shoulders watching them from the tailgate. She was also convinced she could see shadowy faces staring out from the dark interior. They seemed to vanish as the lorry retreated.

Friedrich returned to help them pick themselves out of the hedge, apologising profusely for taking the wrong road.

'I make bad mistake,' he said again, 'we hurry.' Lily thought he seemed agitated. This time they kept up with his furious pedalling and only when they were back on the main road did he slow down.

'What was the name of that place?' Lily asked of Sally's back.

'Dachau,' Sally shouted. Lily's stomach rumbled but Friedrich was not going to stop. They passed through the same villages they had ridden through on their way out. He continually looked over his shoulder as if he were worried they might be followed. When they finally stopped for their picnic, it was only a brief halt and they were soon on their way to the railway station.

It was when they were standing on the platform waiting for the train that they were able to ask Friedrich what it was that he had seen that made him pedal away in such haste.

'It is a prison camp,' he said. 'My father says it is full of dangerous people and we should not go there. I forget.'

'Were those prisoners in the lorry?' asked Lily.

'I think, yes.' He was quiet for a moment. 'People who oppose the Führer must go to prison,' he said mechanically.

'But that's not right,' said Sally, 'it doesn't happen in England.'

'We have elected our Führer to do what is best for us. We have chosen him to lead us to a glorious future. If we oppose his will, we oppose the German people.'

Sally's freckles puckered as she struggled to follow the logic of what she had heard. Lily heard only her father speaking.

Before either could say any more, the train, an electric wonder of Friedrich's new Germany, glided into the station and they busied themselves with loading their bicycles into a special compartment.

'He is odd, your Friedrich,' said Sally when they were back in their room. She was lying on the bed with her legs in the air, pedalling furiously, mimicking their afternoon escapade.

'I think he's fun. He shows us places.'

'Yes, but he's so serious about his Fatherland. Do you think he believes it all?'

'I think he's proud of his country. Daddy's always saying we should be proud of ours.' Lily rolled over on her front and fixed her eyes on her friend's athletic gyrations.

'You'll tire yourself doing that and you won't be able to enjoy my surprise.'

'What surprise?' asked Sally between breaths.

'Well, Friedrich told me that Hans is coming to Munich on Wednesday and he says we should join them in the evening at a bierkeller.'

Sally stopped pedalling and jumped up and clapped her hands.

'Tickety-boo! Fun at last.'

7

Sally was surprised when Frau Gruber expressed delight that one of her young English girls had become friendly with a boy from the Hitler Youth and she showed no objection to her young charges being be escorted by boys in Hitler Youth uniforms.

'You go and have a good time,' she said waving them off with gestures showy enough to attract the attention of her neighbours. Sally thought this sudden friendliness sat at odds with the Grubers often frosty reaction to what was going on around them. She even wondered whether the house was being watched. But she put such thoughts aside as she took Lily's arm and looked forward to the night ahead.

The four sat on barrels at a wooden table in a large brick arched cellar. All around them young men and women were shouting, carousing and heel clicking. It was hot and clammy. Lily felt very grown up, especially as Sally had persuaded her to wear lipstick. She hadn't any of her own but had borrowed Sally's bright red shade. Sally put it on for her. Now she felt it pulling at her lips, making her both self-conscious and excited. Had Friedrich noticed her lipstick? She wanted him to say something, but of course he didn't. Like her he and Hans were mesmerised by the scene in front of them. As in the English Garden, waiters in embroidered waistcoats and waitresses in dirndl skirts skilfully wove around crowded tables holding aloft trays of glasses filled with foaming beer. Miraculously they never seemed to spill a drop but appeared and disappeared through a thick haze of smoke like mysterious wraiths.

'I love Munich,' said Hans over his shoulder. He turned and smiled at the two girls. 'I must find work here and marry an English girl. Then we go back to England and settle in Potters Bar.'

Sally looked at Lily.

'Why Potters Bar, Hans?'

'Beautiful English girls from Potters Bar one day come to Augsburg.'

Sally laughed. 'Lucky Augsburg.'

Lily laughed too. Friedrich pulled nervously at the crisp cuff of his shirt sleeve, not sure that he fully understood why they were laughing. He watched Lily as she tentatively sank her mouth into the beer glass in front of her. Now it was his turn to laugh as her red lips emerged in a froth of foam.

'You like our beer more now Lily?' She nodded. At that moment a small band struck up a lively Bavarian folk song and all around them people started to clash their glasses to the beat. Hans and Friedrich joined in. The girls watched happily, although Lily was concerned that the boys would spill beer down their shirts and splash the gleaming buckles of their belt straps.

'Yes, I like Munich very much,' said Hans, giving Sally's glass an extra bang.

'You will like Munich even more when you see what I have,' said Friedrich unbuttoning the flap on his shirt pocket. He pulled out a small brown envelope, opened it and took out its contents.

'What is it?' asked Lily, looking at the flimsy type-written pieces of paper in his hand.

'These,' he said, 'are passes to see the Führer ride through the centre of Munich.'

Sally and Lily exchanged puzzled glances, not certain what to make of what Friedrich had just said. Hans showed equal surprise.

Friedrich explained: 'The Führer flies to Munich airport tomorrow on his way to Berchtesgarten. That's where he stays in the summer. It's in the mountains. But he loves the city so much, he is making a special car visit to see us.'

'Why do we need tickets, Friedrich, just to wave flags?' asked Sally.

'We must protect the Führer. There are those who wish him bad. Please bring your papers.'

'What papers?'

'Your passports, I believe.'

'How exciting,' said Lily. She could go home and tell her parents she had seen Adolph Hitler. How amazed they would be. 'Sally isn't this just too super?'

'Great guns!' said Sally. Friedrich looked alarmed.

'Not guns, I hope, Fräulein Sally.'

'No, Friedrich, just an English expression,' reassured Lily with a laugh.

'That is good. I come for you tomorrow at 10 o'clock.'

'What about school?' asked Sally.

'No school,' said Friedrich, 'it is a holiday.'

'Ohne Frau Busch ….? They laughed in merriment at their awkward German. Friedrich looked uncomfortable, but they re-assured him by chinking his glass and saying how much they wanted to come. He responded with another chink and caught Lily's eye one second longer than Sally thought was necessary.

Without warning, Sally found her glass spinning out of her hand, its contents spilling across the floor and spattering her dress. Hans was on his feet, picking up the glass and helping her move away from the puddle. He offered her his cravat to wipe her dress.

'What happened?' asked a bewildered Sally looking up from sponging off the beer.

'I think they knocked you,' said Hans.

'Who?'

'Those ladies who passed us.' Lily, who had only seen the glass fall, looked in the direction Hans was pointing. She saw the backs of three women being warmly greeted by a group of men in uniform. Hans was all for going after them, but Friedrich was insistent they did nothing.

'It was an accident,' he said. 'Fräulein Sally, you are all right, no?'

'Yes,' said Sally, 'I'm fine.'

'I'm taking Sally to the Ladies,' said Lily firmly. She grabbed her friend by the hand, just as a waitress arrived with a mop and bucket to clean up the mess. Hans explained what had happened.

'Juden!' the woman muttered under breath, slopping water over the floor in disgust. The girls moved away quickly. On the way to the lavatory they cast a quick glance at the three women who had caused the disruption. When they re-emerged they hovered to get a better look.

The group was noisy and jovial. The men had their arms around the women's shoulders and waists. They held glasses of beer as they spoke. Two of the women let cigarette smoke curl from their mouths. Lily thought they looked very sophisticated. She particularly liked the one who wore a dark green dress with a pleated top and a daring hemline just above the knee. Sally said it was the very latest in fashion.

'Why did that waitress say what she did?' asked Lily, pretending to smooth her dress.

'I think they are Jewish,' whispered Sally.

'But they are blonde,' said Lily.

'Probably dyed their hair.'

'They are very pretty.' Sally said nothing but steered Lily back to the table, where they found Friedrich fuming.

'It is wrong. Those people should not come here.'

'Is there a law?' asked Sally.

'Yes,' said Hans.

'They are friends of those soldiers, are they not?' said Lily growing ever more confused. 'Why should they not come? Besides they seem to have been invited.'

'Werhmacht.' Friedrich almost spat the word out.

'German Army,' explained Hans.

Lily thought Jewish people were dark and thick featured, but these women had finely contoured faces and looked very German. She mused on this but was distracted by a commotion at the door. She could hear raised voices but couldn't see what was going on. Then like a breaking rugby scrum a gang of uniformed young men sprang at them and surged around the tables shouting and waving sticks. They wore brown shirts sporting bright red arm bands slashed with jagged lightning flashes.

'SS,' breathed Friedrich in Lily's ear. The mob of men pushed aside anyone in their way, knocking over benches and jumping across tables. Lily and Sally could see they were coming towards them and involuntarily grabbed at the boys for protection.

'They do not hurt us,' said Hans with little conviction in his voice. As if to underline his uncertainty, a stick whipped the table, inches from his arm. But the uniformed swarm moved on and surrounded the soldiers and their lady companions. Before the men could resist they were physically restrained by overwhelming numbers.

The three women received vicious slaps across the face. The one who wore the green dress was seized by the hair and thrown to the floor. As she fell her face caught the edge of a table cutting a large red gash across her temple and cheek. The blow stunned her and she lay immobile on the ground. Lily watched in horror as blood seeped from the wound and stained the green fabric of the woman's dress. The men stood over her and jeered. One kicked her hard in the stomach. Sally and several others in the hall stood and made to intervene but their companions restrained them

'They are wrong to be here,' said Friedrich.

'But they don't need to be treated like that,' protested Sally. As she spoke arms roughly lifted the woman to her feet and dragged her barely conscious out of the bierkeller. The others were similarly led away, several people spitting at them as they passed by.

'What will happen to them?' asked Lily shaken by what she had seen.

'They will be fined for coming into the bierkeller,' said Hans.

'My father tells me that there is a law that has been made,' said Friedrich. 'Jews must not come into places where Germans are.'

'You mean public places,' said Sally.

'Ja. No cinema, no café.'

'But that's awful,' said Lily.

'They go to their own places,' said Hans, trying to reassure them. Another disturbance made them look up. More uniformed men arrived.

'The police,' said Friedrich. They watched. The three soldiers were confronted by the new arrivals. Pencils and notebooks came out. Details were taken and the three were eventually escorted civilly from the premises. How very different thought Sally to what had happened to the women.

'Friedrich?' asked Lily. 'You said SS, what is SS?'

'Schutzstaffel. They guard our Führer. They make us safe.' By beating up three defenceless women, thought Sally.

'Why,' she asked, 'couldn't the police have handled it?'

'Jews are not good people. They stab in the back.' He made a gesture with his arm. 'My father says the police do not do their duty. The Führer's men act quickly.'

For the second time in a week the girls had seen something that conflicted with what they thought Germany was like and it worried them. But Lily remembered what her father had said about order and what Friedrich was saying and accepted there were times when it was necessary to be tough.

But the incident had affected the jollity of the evening. Voices were lowered, the music's tempo slowed and people began to drift home. The four friends decided it was time to go. What they had seen they put behind them, as tomorrow they hoped to come face to face with Adolph Hitler.

8

In the morning a shiny black Daimler drew up at the Grubers' residence chauffeured by a man in uniform with the now familiar black and red Nazi armband. He escorted them to the car where Friedrich sat waiting for them, his face seeming even more scrubbed than usual, his Hitler Youth uniform sharply creased and polished. Sally expressed surprise at the size of the car as she sank back into its soft leather seat. Lily could only stare in wonderment. They both wore their prettiest dresses. Friedrich stumbled over a compliment before ordering the chauffeur to drive off.

'Is this your car?' asked Lily innocently.

Friedrich shook his head. 'My father borrowed it. He said he could not have two English ladies going to see the Führer in anything but the best.'

Lily looked out of the window. There were soldiers and police everywhere. Normal life in the city seemed to have stopped. At every road junction wooden blocks and barbed wire barriers sprouted from nowhere. The working day had been suspended with few ordinary people on the streets. Those that were there were being stopped and their papers checked. Lily observed that the Daimler had no difficulty in negotiating the roadblocks. Then she noticed the Nazi flag fluttering on the bonnet. The car slid past a line of stationary buses, full of excited, expectant people of all ages. They drove to the head of the column and pulled up at a fortified barrier. Two thick set soldiers guarded the small gate that was inserted into the steel structure. When they saw Friedrich and the girls emerge from the car, their arms shot up in a Nazi salute. Lily shivered with excitement and, although she only understood a few words that passed between Friedrich and the guards, she was conscious that they were getting privileged treatment. One of the soldiers pulled a bolt on the gate and they were ushered through. A woman in uniform led them to the road edge where a space had been reserved for them to stand. For a few moments they were alone, but one by one others began to arrive and soon the whole length of the road had people standing along it, all precisely positioned by the uniformed attendants.

Lily felt a charge of electricity in the atmosphere around her. It was another hot day and everyone seemed to be in holiday mood. They clutched flags and laughed and joked. But they all stood tall, young blond men and slim beautiful women. Lily marvelled at the spectacle that unfolded before her, but it never occurred to her that it was being staged managed.

'Isn't this just too exciting,' she said. She turned to Sally. 'We should wave flags.' Sally wasn't sure.

'It is not our country,' she said.

'Sally is right, Lily,' said Friedrich, 'you just wave.'

The space behind them now started to fill up and soon the crowd stretched several rows back to the barrier through which they had come. A gaggle of schoolchildren were chirruping close by, slipped in front of the adults, while a little way off a patriotic song performed by a male choir soared unseen over their heads.

Lily wondered how long they would have to wait. When she had been to events like this in London the waiting had seemed interminable. But not here. They had hardly been put in position when a great cheer went up further down the line and a black car came into view.

The girls didn't know what to expect. A military escort perhaps? Motorcycle outriders? The German equivalent of the Household Cavalry? What they didn't expect was a single open top automobile of gigantic proportions cruising almost silently past the crowds. At the back sat two uniformed officers, while in the front beside the driver stood the figure of Adolph Hitler himself, his arm continually raised in salute. Jubilant roars of delight and endless shouts of 'Heil Hitler' scoured the air. Lily was caught up in the frenzy and found herself shaking with excitement. She tried to memorise every detail, to photograph the moment in her mind's eye so she could relay it again and again for her parents. She noticed the Führer wasn't in uniform but was wearing a light-coloured suit. But, of course, he was going on holiday. His eyes twinkled, clearly pleased with the adulation he was receiving. Was there a split second when he saw her? She liked to think he had. He looked so relaxed, at ease, his hair smoothed over an almost cherubic moon face, finished with his now famous moustache, which seemed even sharper in the flesh.

Friedrich was beside himself with excitement. His 'Heil Hitlers' rattled off like a machine gun. His arm rigid in a quivering salute brushed Lily's head. They watched the car roll on its way, the Führer's back receding into the distance, everyone straining to savour a last glimpse of their leader. Only when he vanished from sight did the noise begin to abate. But the atmosphere remained electric. People talked excitedly to each other, compared notes, hugged one another or slapped each other on the back.

Friedrich lost himself in an outpouring of German. In his excitement he lowered his arm and rested it on Lily's shoulder. She shivered at this unexpected touch and felt a strange tingle pass through her. It was an intimacy she had not experienced before. She couldn't understand what he was saying, but there was no mistaking the pressure of his fingers on her bare arm. Nor was it a movement that escaped Sally's ever watchful eyes.

Friedrich realised what he was doing and let his arm drop to his side.

'Did you see how fearlessly he rode?' he said, returning to English.

'Was that because the crowd was carefully selected?' observed Sally. Friedrich failed to pick up the caustic note in Sally's voice.

'We are only good Germans here,' he said.

What Sally was increasingly becoming aware of - the relentless separation of 'the good Germans' from the rest - never occurred to Lily. She made no indication that she understood what her friend was talking about. She only had eyes for the blonde German boy who towered over her and who now led her through the exiting crowd to the swastika-pennanted Daimler.

9

'You should have seen him, Frau Gruber,' said Lily entering the hall of the Gruber residence. 'He was so poised. You should have been there.' The German woman said nothing, only to remind them that it was school as usual the next day. Sally noted her frostiness had returned. The girls groaned at the thought of Frau Busch and skipped to their room to talk about what they had seen.

For Lily, the day had been magical, not just because she had seen the German leader in the flesh, but because she was starting to have strange feelings which she had never had before. She didn't know where they came from. She only knew that being near Friedrich made her feel warm inside. Was this love? Was this what she read about in those 'Stories for Girls' she devoured so voraciously? She didn't know, but what she was certain of was that she wanted to be alone with Friedrich. Only whenever she was with him, Sally was there too. Now she actively sought to engineer a chance meeting without Sally. But this proved impossible. Sally became weirdly possessive and clung to Lily as if she were her sister. She made sure they were booked on the same train home and never left her side for an instant.

Not that there was much chance of that changing during the week, when studies kept their noses to the grindstone. As Lily poured over the texts given to them by Frau Busch, she came to the conclusion that the literary heritage of German culture went way over her head. She wrestled with Goethe and Schiller and quickly realised she was losing the battle, but her conversational German was improving. She was pleased with this as she could now talk to Friedrich in his own language.

The day after seeing Hitler, Frau Busch got them reading bits from Nietzsche.

'He is the Führer's favourite writer,' she explained to a sea of puzzled faces. 'He says that the Aryan peoples - that's you and me - are the master race. It is our destiny through a struggle of blood and iron to lead the world.' Looking at her young charges, she had little fear that what she was saying was going to be challenged, nor did it worry her that it was a total travesty of what Nietzsche actually said. Certainly to Lily it seemed to chime with what she had heard at home.

After her declamatory introduction, Frau Busch handed out sheets of paper to translate that contained selective quotes from the nineteenth century philosopher. Lily studied the text with her usual expression of puzzlement, a rolling of the eyes and a desperate look towards Sally. Her friend was already writing. No help there. Then her eyes alighted on Naoomie, also writing furiously. It did occur to Lily to wonder if this Aryan race everyone talked about included black people. As Naoomie was sitting in their midst, she assumed it did. Having answered that, she finally got down to tackling what was in front of her. She translated: 'Men are trained for war .... Women belong in the kitchen and their chief role in life is to bear children ....' Did she agree with that? She wasn't sure, although Mummy spent most of her time in the kitchen. Then she let her thoughts drift off dreamily to Friedrich and she saw herself preparing his meals and bearing his children, while he assumed the pose of warrior protecting the family. Such romantic notions clouded her mind and brought Nietzsche down to the level of schoolgirl fiction. That at least made him palatable. Frau Busch's iron voice snapped her out of her reverie. A large crack on the table from the ever-present stick made everyone sit up.

'Tomorrow,' said Frau Busch, 'we go out to visit great art. You must come well dressed. Now I take your papers on Nietzsche.'

'Where are we going?' asked Lily when they were back in their room.

'Across the road,' said Sally dismissively.

The next day they walked in crocodile from the school to the Glyptothek, the museum that confronted the Grubers house. They were taken to the Greek section and stood before the imposing statue of a muscle-bound discus thrower. The girls tittered as they stared at the manly contours of the naked athlete. Lily's eyes like all the others roamed over the marble until they came to rest on his finely carved genitals. There were knowing looks from some and shock from those like Lily whose knowledge of the male anatomy was hazy. Is this how Friedrich would look with no clothes on, she wondered?

'Pay attention, Meine Mädchen,' said Frau Busch in sotto voce tones, trying to honour the hushed atmosphere of the museum. 'This noble example of Greek art has just been purchased by our illustrious Führer and we are privileged to have it here in our city. It shows the beauty and harmony of the human body that we should all aspire to.' Gosh, thought Lily, those rippling chest muscles would crush her if she was held by this man. He looked so powerful. While Frau Busch droned on Lily lost herself in the perfect proportions of the man's anatomy. No wonder Herr Hitler liked it. As if to echo this sentiment, Frau Busch drooled in sympathy.

'Our Leader,' she continued, 'wants us to be like the ancient Greeks and hone our bodies that they may be offered on the altar of German greatness ....' Lily only half understood the meaning of what she was saying, but she could see her teacher was becoming unexpectedly excited. In fact, so much so that the deep voice had started to rise and was getting louder and louder. An attendant in uniform appeared from nowhere and whispered something in German, which although Lily couldn't hear the exact words she knew from Frau Busch's decisive nodding that he was telling her off. Her face went red and she stood in a state of flustered silence not quite certain how to proceed. The class, bottling up their hilarity at her embarrassment, waited for her to continue. She never did. Instead she dismissed them for half an hour to explore the museum on their own, while she turned smartly on her heels and walked over to another exhibit, where Lily felt certain she saw her stamp her feet.

The girls quickly dispersed bent on taking full opportunity of this unexpected freedom. Lily found Sally and Naoomie in a tittering huddle and joined them and together the three of them walked off and found a quiet corner where they started to laugh uncontrollably until the same uniformed attendant hoved into view and abruptly put a stop to their mirth. They then wandered in silence around the array of sculptured heads, limbless torsos, and fragments of broken off anatomy. Lily was particularly struck by the feet she saw, cut at the ankle but larger than life and immaculately executed. Struggling with the German notice she was told feet were always well carved because they usually stood on a pediment at eye level with the viewer.

The girls drank in the naked men, their eyes fixed on their genitals, giving them an instant sex lesson, which in Lily's case was the most explicit she had had. How strange these Germans are? she thought, the men brazenly exposing themselves while the women are told to wear the severest of clothes. The Greeks seemed to be the same. The sculptured women wore long dresses with only a hint of breast pushing through the folds of their garments. Like many of the German women they wore their hair tied back. For the girls of Frau Busch's class, their thirty minutes of freedom in the Glyptothek were well spent.

But the next day they were to pay for it when they assembled for the last exercise class before their course came to an end. Frau Hutger had a particularly strenuous set of moves to teach them and got each girl to mimic a pose they had seen in the museum. Lily chose the discus thrower but she just was not cut out to be one. As she twirled herself round to swing the phantom plate she somehow collided with a group of girls preparing to throw the javelin. The impact sent them all hurtling across the floor straight into another group, causing one of the girls to trip and fall and the rest to pile on top of her, with Lily the last to land.

Frau Hutger was beside herself with annoyance as her beautifully orchestrated tableaux ended in chaos. She angrily struck out with her cane. Lily could see from its trajectory that it was going to make contact with her bottom. She gave an involuntary cry of pain. A hand grabbed her tunic top and hauled her to her feet amid a storm of German invective. This Lily had not the means to translate beyond the isolated phrase 'you silly girl, you make trouble....' The other fallen girls picked themselves up in silence hoping the cane wasn't coming anywhere near them. Sally looked on in horror, sorry for her friend. No one quite knew where to put themselves. They shuffled their feet and waited to see what would happen next. But Frau Hutger regained her composure and without saying any more about what had happened ordered the girls into their lines and dragooned them for another five minutes before ending the session. Lily was thankful it was over. Her bottom had started to smart and she wanted to get changed and disappear. But that wasn't going to happen. As she went to pick up her towel, Frau Busch came into the hall followed by a young man with a camera and tripod slung over his shoulder. They were told to wipe themselves with the towel but not to change out of their tunics.

'Today,' said Frau Busch, 'we take your photo. We want to show health and beauty of English girls for our director. He will take it with pride when he visits Berlin. One day our nations will stand together ....' Lily soaked in the words. Surprisingly they made her feel better. She thought of Friedrich too and she felt sure he would be uncomplaining had it happened to him. She didn't notice that Sally and Naoomie were standing beside her.

'Are you all right?' asked her friend anxiously.

'I think so. Bit bruised.'

'That was quite a whack she gave you.'

Lily smiled. 'It was a bit of a to do, wasn't it?

'You should tell Frau Busch,' said Naoomie.

'She won't do anything,' said Sally ruefully, 'she'd have used it herself, given half a chance.'

'Anyway, we must be disciplined. Frau Hutger was only restoring order,' said Lily without a trace of irony in her voice that produced odd looks from the other two.

As if to echo her words, Frau Hutger showed she had regained her swagger by brusquely marshalling the girls into rows of ascending height. Lily, Sally and Naoomie, all roughly measuring the same, were pushed into the middle row. As they adjusted their hair and brushed out their tunics, Frau Busch pointed her finger at Naoomie.

'Not you. You come and sit by the wall.' For a few moments nobody reacted uncertain what she meant. Naoomie looked down, stunned, realising it was she who was being singled out. Frau Busch repeated her order.

'You come out, please.'

Without a word, the black girl broke away from the others and quietly walked over to a chair beside the wall.

'Please stand to attention and face the camera,' shouted the instructor. The photographer focussed his lens. Several flashlights exploded and a class of English girls unblemished in their whiteness was committed to celluloid. Naoomie stared at them with moist eyes.

10

The three of them, Lily, Sally and Friedrich, stood at the tram station opposite the Grubers' house waiting to go into the centre of Munich. It was the girls' last day in the city and Friedrich was taking them on a final tour of their favourite haunts. Sally had decided she was going to have a girls' night out with Lily, but Lily insisted they accept Friedrich's offer and she reluctantly agreed.

A tram trundled into the station, brakes squealing and the folding doors hissing open. The three clambered aboard. Friedrich paid for the tickets, while the girls looked for seats. Sally steered Lily to an empty pair and got her to sit before she had a chance to protest. Friedrich ended up opposite them. Lily saw that Sally had once again managed to keep them apart. Her over attentive manner where Friedrich was concerned was beginning to irritate her. She even began to wonder whether Sally was jealous. But even if she longed for

Friedrich to be sitting beside her, she at least could see the smile on his face.

The tram clattered and banged its way along the tracks. People got on and off. The coach was hot with little ventilation. Lulled by the rocking motion of the vehicle, Lily slipped into one of her daydreams. She had been in this strange city for four weeks. She had been assaulted on all sides by its colourful vibrancy. The fashionable women, the kaleidoscope of uniforms. She loved the gaiety of the street cafes, the liveliness of the beer gardens, the raucousness of the bierkellers. All around her buildings were draped in garlands and banners creating an ever-present festive spirit, which seemed to add to the excitement she felt. And on top of it all was this handsome German boy sitting opposite her.

A disturbance at the front of the car made her look up. An old man wearing a battered homburg and tattered raincoat was trying to get on the tram but was being pushed away by the conductor. Odd, thought Lily, seeing someone wearing a coat in this heat. The man was unshaven and a piece of frayed rope doubled as a belt. He held an old case in one hand, while holding on to the door rail with the other. To Lily he looked like a tramp, but in the stream of angry German coming from the conductor, she heard the word 'Jew' several times.

'Jews are not allowed on trams, except at the back,' said Friedrich. 'He must leave.' They watched as reluctantly the old man was forced off the steps of the car. The conductor closed the door and the tram accelerated away leaving the man stranded on the pavement.

'They should have waited,' said Sally indignantly.

'Fräulein Sally, you protest too much,' said Friedrich. 'It is the law.'

'Then the law is wrong.' Friedrich looked at her and said nothing. Lily was sorry she had seen another example of bad treatment of Jewish people, but things like that happened in London. Bus drivers were always leaving people behind.

The tram carried on without further incident. She saw the store where she had bought her hat. She couldn't wait to show it off to her parents. Finally they arrived at their destination. Lily recognised it. It was near the Odeonplatz where they saw the great Nazi monument and where they came with the Grubers. This time there was no diving down the cobbled alley way as they had done earlier. Friedrich marched straight towards the edifice with the girls in tow. He stood before it, clicked his heels and gave the Nazi salute. The girls looked awkward. All around them, passers-by, men and women, were doing the same. Lily looked at the unsmiling black uniformed guards, with their slung rifles and steel helmets, and felt deeply uncomfortable. But as before, Friedrich reassured them that as they were visitors they did not need to salute.

'What is this?' asked Lily gazing in awe at the huge structure, with its ferocious eagle and colossal wreaths.

Friedrich smiled. 'It is where our glorious leader faced the forces of Jewish decadence and began his road to greatness.' Sally wasn't sure this was quite right but said nothing. 'See the date,' continued Friedrich, 'November the 9th 1923. Our Führer was leading a group of his followers on a peaceful march when he was stopped by police and some soldiers who fired guns. Sixteen men were shot.' In his enthusiasm he walked closer to the monument. The two sentries, motionless until now, moved their weight from one foot to the other. Friedrich took the hint and stopped. 'Their names.' he said, 'are on that stone. When I became a member of Hitler Youth, I took my oath to the Fatherland here.' Lily could see how proud he was. Sally looked around her and her eyes alighted on the entrance to the cobbled alley. Friedrich spotted her. His face soured.

'The Viscardigasse,' he said with disgust, 'you know what we call it - 'Druckebergergasse''

'What does that mean?' asked Lily.

'They who go down there are cowards who do not wish to honour our fallen comrades.'

'I think it means 'Shirkers Lane', said Sally, whose German was more proficient.

'Yes, that is good,' said Friedrich.

'But we ….' Before she could blurt out what she was about to say, Lily got a sharp kick in the ankle from Sally.

'Now, we go for coffee, I think,' said Friedrich who hadn't seen the blow. Lily looked daggers at Sally, but she realised it probably wasn't a good thing to mention they had been taken down the Viscardigasse by the Grubers.

They walked across the great space of the Odeonplatz, Friedrich in the lead. Lily soaked in his tall firm blonde frame and wondered how she could shake off Sally and be alone with him. Sally for her part wanted to know more about what had happened all those years ago and vowed to ask the Grubers when they got back.

Friedrich took them to Café Heck where tables covered in white fringed check tablecloths were laid out under the dappled shade of the linden trees. As they sat down on curlicue iron chairs Friedrich could hardly contain himself with excitement. This, he told the girls, was another favourite haunt of his beloved Führer. At least, thought Sally, the coffee and cake were good.

While Friedrich was catching the waiter's eye, Sally decided to go to the Ladies.

'Are you coming,' she asked Lily.

'I'm all right,' said Lily staying firmly in her seat and hoping this was her chance.

'Fine.' Sally's freckled face puckered momentarily before relaxing with a resigned smile. She picked up her handbag and disappeared into the café's dark interior.

They both watched her go. Lily felt Friedrich's hand envelop hers. She shivered at his touch and then put her hand on his. It felt awkward and intoxicating at the same time.

'You write to me,' he said almost spitting the words at her.

'Yes, Friedrich,' she said, her voice a husky whisper.

'You write in German, Lily.'

'But my words won't be right.'

'You will find the right words. I know.' Yes she would. She was sure of this. She looked at his clear blue eyes and before she knew she was saying it, the words came out.

Ich liebe dich.' She felt his hand tighten on hers. Neither noticed the waiter place a small plate in front of them nor that Sally had returned to her seat.

'When you two have finished playing games, perhaps we could pay,' she said icily.

11

'It was a rabble trying to overthrow the elected authorities.' Wulf Gruber paused for a moment and reflected on what he had said. He stood at the black marble mantelpiece of the drawing room fireplace where he had just relit his briar pipe and was answering Sally's question about what had happened in the Odeonplatz. 'This you should keep to yourself, Fräulein Sally. It is not good to say such things to others.'

'I understand, Herr Gruber,' said Sally, standing somewhat stiffly before her German host. 'Thank you for talking to me.' She had seen Wulf Gruber alone in the drawing room as she passed the open door and had plucked up the courage to ask him the question.

'At the time Herr Hitler was the leader of a gang of bullies and thugs who went around the city beating up people they disagreed with. One day he gathered his followers together and led them onto the streets in a demonstration that was clearly bent on taking over the government of the city.' Sally listened intently as Herr Gruber warmed to his subject. In between puffs on his pipe, which sent thick curls of smoke spiralling to the ceiling, he reached the dramatic conclusion of his tale. 'When they arrived at the Odeonplatz they were stopped by police and armed soldiers. Shots were fired and several were killed including four policemen. Herr Hitler escaped but was arrested two days later and was put in prison. It was ….' He paused again. 'how you say it in English? …. a dirty little scrap.' He paused again and puffed. 'But Herr Hitler is now our leader. We chose him.' He looked pained. 'We live quietly and have pretty English girls to make us smile.' He brightened when Sally smiled in response. 'Now Fräulein, you must go and find your friend, Lily. You have much packing, I think.'

'Thank you for explaining this.' He made a slight bow of his head and smiled. Sally left Herr Gruber to his pipe and began the ascent of the spiral staircase that led to their room at the top of the house. She thought about what she had heard. However Friedrich described a 'Good German', she was in no doubt in her mind that Herr Gruber was a good German. She understood too how he must feel passing that monument and how he would take steps to avoid it.

She found Lily buried deep in a mound of unfolded clothes.

'I hate packing,' said Lily in exasperation, who had little idea how to go about it as her mother always packed for her.

'Where have you been?' she asked distractedly, looking in disdain at a crumpled skirt.

'Talking to Herr Gruber,' Sally said simply, expecting Lily to interrogate her. Instead, Lily threw the skirt back onto the pile and blurted out her affection for Friedrich.

'We're going to write to each other when I'm back in England. Isn't it divine? I have a German boyfriend.' She threw herself backwards and sprawled over the pile of clothes. Sally, thankful that she hadn't had to explain her conversation with Herr Gruber, tried to show a modicum of enthusiasm, but Lily saw through it.

'What's the matter, Sally? Aren't you pleased? It's just too wonderful.' She stopped and looked curiously at Sally. 'I do believe you are jealous,' she said.

Sally's freckles reddened. 'It's not that. You're my best friend, Lily. I don't want you getting hurt.'

'Why should I get hurt, Sally?' Lily asked, a hardness creeping into her voice. She sat up and stared at her friend accusingly. Sally didn't know what to say. Lily repeated her question.

'You know …. it's not easy at the moment.' Sally stumbled to find the words.

'What isn't easy?'

'Living here.' She looked straight at Lily. 'Look, these last weeks, we've had fun. Enjoyed ourselves.'

'And met lots of people, German people, nice people – all those gay cafes and beer gardens.'

'Yes, but it's summer ….'

Lily looked confused. 'What are you saying?

'We've seen things, too. Upsetting things. The camp at Dachau. Those women we saw beaten up. The way that waitress treated the Grubers when we went for tea.'

Lily was quiet for a moment and then said: 'Friedrich says what Daddy says - we must have order.' How many times had Sally heard this from Lily.

'We've seen plenty of that,' she said sarcastically, 'Your backside for instance.'

'She was wrong.'

'Did she apologise?'

'No.'

'Because she didn't think she was wrong. And Friedrich felt the same when you told him, didn't he?' Lily was starting to look angry.

'Are you trying to say I shouldn't be friends with Friedrich?'

'No, Lily. I'm just saying that things are changing in this country and not always for the better. It will be difficult for you when you get back to England if things get worse. Being involved with Friedrich could bring you trouble.'

Lily had tears in her eyes. 'I think you are being horrid.' She threw the words at Sally. 'I hate you. Get on with your packing. I'm going to bed.' She grabbed her nightdress, put it on, threw the pile of clothes on the floor along with the case and climbed into bed, pulling the cotton sheet over her face.

Sally had never seen her friend like this before. She had hoped she could have alerted Lily to the consequences of a friendship with Friedrich, but she saw this was unlikely to happen. It upset her to think she had caused this rift and she went over and sat on Lily's bed.

'Look, Lily, I'm sorry. You're my best friend. I only wanted to help you.' She touched Lily's sheet covered shoulder. She recoiled as a head shot up from the bed.

'No you didn't,' Lily snarled, wiping a tear stained face with her hands. 'You've been trying to keep Friedrich and me apart for days. You're jealous I've found a boy and you don't want us to be together.'

'That's ridiculous, Lily. I think you should get out of bed and we can get on with the packing. The taxi will be with us early in the morning.'

'The taxi's not coming,' said Lily triumphantly. 'Friedrich is picking us up. His father still has the Daimler.' She sat waiting for Sally's reaction. When none came, she lay back in bed, turned over and muttered an oath from under the sheet. 'And to hell with the packing. I'll do it in the morning and wake you up.'

12

The two girls had lain all night bitterly regretting their words to each other. Neither had got any sleep and when Friedrich arrived early they were still putting the finishing touches to their packing. Lily popped her head blearily over the banister.

'Hello Friedrich. Sorry we are not quite ready. Been a bit of a to do. Can you wait?'

'Of course.'

'Frau Gruber's with us helping us finish. Make yourself comfortable.'

'I help,' said Friedrich.

Lily laughed. 'You can't, Friedrich,' she protested, perhaps not too convincingly. She had hardly spoken when he had bounded up the stairs two at a time and was standing beside her on the landing.

'I help,' he insisted.

'Albert will take the cases, Friedrich,' said Frau Gruber from inside the girls' room. She looked a little shocked. 'You should not be up here.'

'Then I help Albert.' He looked in at Frau Gruber as she pushed the last of Lily's clothes into a case. He blushed profusely when he caught sight of a brassiere strap hanging over the side. The German hausfrau pounced on it. She slipped it under a jumper and slapped down the lid, forcefully snapping tight the two latches. She called out sharply. Albert appeared from nowhere. She spoke to the old retainer, who nodded and picked up Lily's two cases and the hat box that contained Lily's precious purchase. She then shouted to Friedrich. The girls understood some of what she said. Clearly she had relented as a bashful Friedrich entered the bedroom and gathered up Sally's luggage. He stood at the door to let the girls go ahead of him and then followed them down the stairs. Albert and Friedrich's driver took charge of the cases, while Frau Gruber said her goodbyes. She hugged the two girls and was on the point of releasing Sally when she started to wave her hands wildly in the air.

'I had forgotten. My dears, I have something for you. Come, it is in the drawing room.' She led the way. Sally followed. Friedrich was hovering close by and when Sally disappeared through the drawing room door, he slid Lily into the adjacent dining room. Without warning he bent over her and gave her a tentative kiss. Lily stood there unsure how to react. Films she had seen at the pictures flicked into focus and before she could stop herself she had taken his head in her hands and brought his lips down onto hers. They felt firm and moist and she luxuriated in their intimacy until reality intervened and they guiltily broke away from each other. Lily heard a noise and saw Sally standing at the door.

Her friend made no comment but merely said that Frau Gruber had something for them. Friedrich slunk away to supervise the loading of the cases, while Lily sheepishly followed Sally into the drawing room. What their host produced were two antique spoons, the bowls made of copper Bavarian coins, with twisted metal handles, one for each of them 'to remember her by'.

There was little conversation in the car on the way to the station. Friedrich sat in front with his driver. The two girls sprawled on the back seat, turned from each other in deliberate rejection. Lily boiled inside. Despite Sally's denial, she continued to believe she was jealous. This gave her a guilty pleasure that of the two she was the first to make a conquest, but equally she didn't want to lose Sally's friendship. In the silence that surrounded them she watched the great glass and iron mass of Munich railway station loom up and within minutes they were standing on the concourse with Friedrich and his driver searching out porters.

They loitered awkwardly lost in their own thoughts, assailed by the furious criss-crossing of people on their way to and from platforms and the insistent noise of their excited voices soaring up into the vaulted expanse of the station roof. In this blur of hurrying bodies they were only half aware of seeing Friedrich accost a porter who was in the act of helping a couple with their bags. When the man saw Friedrich's uniform, he dropped the bags, leaving the couple standing. The woman smartly dressed in a suit and hat put her arms out to protest, but her companion hastily restrained her.

'I have man,' said Friedrich returning with the porter. Neither said anything about how he had obtained the service. Minutes later the driver appeared with a second porter. The two men escorted the girls to the ticket barrier. Friedrich obtained a platform ticket and went with them to where the train to Calais stood steaming in readiness. They passed the great engine that had brought the coaches into the platform still panting from its exertions. Lily was in awe of these monsters and quickened her step as she went by. Sally walked ahead in sullen determination to distance herself from Lily and when they reached their coach she climbed aboard with the porters and the luggage, leaving Lily standing on the platform with Friedrich.

He took her hands in his. 'You write,' he said earnestly, repeating his plea of the day before. Her eyes moistened as the warnings from Sally filled her head. Are we so different? she asked herself. Why should living in separate countries affect how we feel about each other? She was certain she loved Friedrich and wanted to be with him whatever happened.

'I'll write,' she said tenderly. Sally's voice made her turn. She was gesticulating madly from the window of their compartment. The train was about to go, a message reinforced by a guard in polished uniform passing by. Lily broke away and hurried to the steps of the carriage door. At the top she swung round and blew Friedrich a kiss, her accompanying words lost in the shrill whistle of the engine announcing its departure. But he couldn't mistake their meaning.

'I thought we were leaving you behind,' said Sally cuttingly as Lily entered the compartment. Lily ignored her, climbing onto one of the bunks to put her head out of the window. Friedrich stood below waving.

'I love you,' shouted Lily in her best German. Friedrich stood to attention and gave her a salute. 'Good Lord,' thought Sally in amazement, 'the boy's off his head.' To Lily it was an endearing token of love. She hung out of the window trying to reach Friedrich's outstretched arm, but the train was too high.

There was a second whistle from the engine and the coach jolted into movement nearly toppling Lily from the bunk. She clung on as the train eased itself along the platform, great gasps coming from the engine as it built up steam. Friedrich followed for a while but soon became a dot in the distance.

'Lover boy gone?' said Sally sarcastically. Lily rounded on her, her face contorted in an uncharacteristic snarl.

'Just cut it out, Sally. I've listened to you and I've made my mind up. I love Friedrich and I'm going to stay loving him.'

'Okay Lily.' Sally went to her knees and held her arms out in a gesture of submission. 'Pax.' she said, declaiming the word as if she were on the stage at school. Lily, still holding onto the window, laughed at her ridiculous pose. The train lurched violently as it went over points and Lily lost her grip on the window. She fell on Sally and the two rolled over in a heap. A mass of red curls filled Lily's face. She grabbed a handful and pulled with a furious tug. Sally yelped with pain but returned the blow by seizing Lily's hair. They went at each other like cats pulling with such strength that it felt as if their hair was being torn from its roots. Each hoped the other would give way. Neither did. Then the farcical situation got the better of them and they collapsed on the floor in fits of laughter.

The door of the compartment opened - they hadn't heard the knock - and the attendant put his head in. The sprawled bodies at his feet caused him to widen his eyes somewhat but he went on to announce solemnly that lunch was served in thirty minutes. The girls looked up, let go their hair and nodded sheepishly. Lily's hair had fallen over her face and she could hardly see the attendant through the tangled strands. She was only aware of a pair of uniformed trouser legs turning sharply and leaving her field of vision. She crawled to a sitting position and stared into Sally's rapidly reddening face.

'Pax,' she said, offering her hand.

'Pax,' Sally replied taking Lily's hand in hers. The two gazed at each other solemnly for a few moments then broke out in more fits of laughter.

'Cripes,' said Lily looking down at herself, 'what a mess we're in. We've got to get a move on if we're going to have lunch.' They stood up smoothing down dresses and trying, unsuccessfully, to straighten hair. They looked aghast at the dirt on their clothes and in Lily's case a badly scuffed shoe.

'Back to the drawing board, old girl, as my father would say,' said Lily, scrambling to lift her case onto the bunk. She sprung the catches, opened the lid to release an exploding pile of clothes that upset Frau Gruber's careful packing and dived in to retrieve a blouse and skirt she knew were near the top. Climbing out of her dress she raced to the basin only to find Sally already there. She had no hesitation in giving her a friendly jostle. Sally, a flannel over her face, smiled. Lily twirled a curl of Sally's hair around her finger. 'Pax,' she whispered. She was happy. She was best friends again with her best friend.

13

They got to the restaurant in time for the lunch sitting and the first person they saw was the attendant who had disturbed their cat fight. He stood impassively to let them pass, his face betraying no sign of what he had seen. The girls tittered as they slid by and finally broke into laughter on entering the heavily carpeted dining car. Their noisy arrival caused passengers already seated to look up and an unsmiling maître d' carefully sat the girls on a table by themselves. So different, thought Lily, from the solicitous treatment she had received on the way out.

'I don't think they approve,' she said, leaning over and whispering in Sally's ear.

'Stuffy lot,' said Sally. 'Hans would liven them up.'

'And Friedrich ….'

'If he gave that salute of his he would,' said Sally mockingly and in return got a cuff over her ear for her remark.

'He's serious, but he's also a poppet.' Sally was spared answering by the waiter arriving to take their order. They chose soup of the day followed by pork chops then settled back to enjoy the passing Bavarian scenery.

The restaurant car filled up, but as they were half-way through their soup, two late comers arrived, a woman and man, who looked like a married couple. There was a sudden hush, spoons fell on bowls and knives and forks laid on the table. All eyes were on the couple with everyone waiting to see where they would be sat. The maître d' looked around him for an empty table, but he could see none. He pondered the problem for a few moments and finally his eyes came to rest on the two girls.

'Meine Damen,' he said with a sycophancy he had not shown before, 'may these people sit with you. There is no other table.' In his reference to the couple, Sally felt his German was cold, even bordering on rudeness. But she in unison with Lily gestured to the pair to sit down.

'Thank you Meine Damen. You are most kind,' said the woman hovering at the seat beside Lily. Lily waited for the chair to be pulled out, but no one came. In the end the man did it for her and then sat down himself.

'The soup is good,' said Sally, 'potato and leek, I believe.' There was a flicker of a smile from the woman but she and the man both had an aura of intense melancholy about them. While Sally spoke, Lily studied their features. The woman was in her forties probably. She seemed very thin. The lime green suit she wore hung loosely about her, designed for a fuller figure which she must have had when she first bought it. It was also wearing thin in places, the result thought

Lily of much use. Her face was wan, devoid of make-up and lipstick, emphasising sunken cheeks and a prominent nose. But she did have beautifully coiffured hair, that was curled about her face in a way that reminded Lily of Vivien Leigh, the only defect being a number of white strands appearing in the curls. Something Lily at first didn't notice was a faint black mark that spread from the corner of her mouth to halfway up her cheek. She also wore gloves which when she removed revealed red scars across the back of both hands.

The man was similarly thin and gaunt looking. His posture was hunched and the charcoal striped suit he wore with its shoulders and large lapels made him look even more wizened. His hair was thinning on top, offset by a small moustache. Like his companion his clothes had seen better days. As Sally bumbled on about the menu, Lily wondered who this sad couple might be.

The waiter arrived to take the order. At the same time, the man opposite threw down his napkin and strode over to them.

'You're not going to serve these two, are you?' he said in a sharply hostile voice. The waiter put his pad down.

'Yes, sir,' he said nervously.

'Can't you see they are Jews? They shouldn't be here.'

'I thought ….' Before he could say more the maître d' arrived.

'What's the problem?'

'Sir, these people are Jewish.'

The maître d' turned vehemently on the couple, angry that he had been caught out. When asked whether they were Jews the couple made no answer, merely rose from their seats and submissively left the restaurant car. The maître d' shook hands with the man who had intervened, knowing that he had been saved from a serious mistake. The two girls fell silent, horrified at what they had seen. For Sally it was confirmation that the future was not good, for Lily it only added to a growing confusion in her mind. She could not believe that Friedrich would have acted like the man opposite who first apologised for causing them discomfort and then sat down with a triumphant expression on his face.

'That was awful. How can they be so unfeeling?' said Sally thrusting her soup bowl from her and staring stiffly out of the window.

'I'm sure Daddy will have an answer if I ask him.'

'Oh Lily you are such a dreamer,' said Sally sweetly, still with her face against the window. The wooden houses, the rolling fields, the herds of cattle flashed by and the rest of the journey to the border with France was without incident.

The next day after a fitful sleep the girls watched the train steam into Calais station and towards the awaiting ferry and the last leg of their long journey home.

Having been incarcerated for two days, they quickly had their luggage stowed and went up on deck to drink in great gulps of the salty sea air. There was little wind and they went for'ard with the prospect of a calm crossing. The ferry was very crowded and there seemed to be many families who were carrying what household goods they could manage.

'They must be fleeing Germany,' observed Sally.

Lily thought of the wonderful time she had had and found it difficult to believe that people were wanting to leave Germany or that they might be forced to do so. She watched children clambering over seats, adults gathered in silent huddles. Above them smoke poured from the great red stack and the deck on which they stood throbbed with the pounding of the engines, a turmoil of steam and noise that must have chimed with their emotions.

Lily turned from the deck and looked out to sea. Beyond the turbulence caused by the bow wave the Channel was as calm as a pond. The sun shone on the water creating a blue mirror like effect broken only by a gentle swell. But they were not alone. A flotilla of craft, large and small, dirty coastal tramp steamers and fishing boats, sailed across their path in such numbers Lily feared they might have a collision. At one moment they were so close to a passing liner Lily could read the name.

'The Bremen,' said a voice behind them, 'it's on its way to America.' Lily looked round to find the couple from the restaurant car standing a few feet from them. They were as sallow and hunched in the open air as they were inside. Their drab shapeless clothes contrasted sharply with the bright floral colours of the girls' dresses. They made an odd quartet.

'We tried to buy tickets on that,' said the man in precise if halting English, 'but they refused us. They said it was for Germans only.'

'We are Germans, Bertold,' said the woman almost spitting the words out.

'Ah, yes my dear,' he said taking her arm in his as if to humour her, 'in your heart it is so.' She shot him a pained expression which made him turn away from her. 'It is a beautiful ship is it not?' The four gazed out at the great vessel as it sliced through the water. It was bigger than anything Lily had seen. In the sun its white superstructure shone with an almost ethereal glow. They were so close to it they could see the passengers crowding the deck rails and waving joyously. Above them two orange funnels poured out clouds of black smoke.

'I am Bertold Hartmann,' said the man introducing himself with just the suggestion of heel clicking born no doubt of long habit, 'and this is my wife, Magda.'

'How do you do,' said Lily with equal formality.

'You were very kind to us in there,' said Magda, 'I want to thank you.'

'It was awful, asking you to leave like that,' said Sally, her eyes half on the couple and half on the Bremen.

'Ah, we are used to it,' sighed Bertold.

'You are used to it. I will never be used to it. When they treat us like pigs,' said Magda bitterly.

'That is why we go to America - to Michigan. We have uncle there. We hope for a better life,' said Bertold.

'But not on that', said Lily also gazing at the disappearing liner.

'No, sadly. We go first to England, then board a boat from Laeverpool,' he said, mispronouncing the word.

'Liverpool,' said Lily correcting him.

'Ja, so.'

Sally still looking at the Bremen seemed puzzled.

'I can't see the Nazi flag.'

'No,' said Bertold, 'it is flying the colours of the old imperial Germany. We have two flags.'

80

'So the world feels better when they see it,' interjected Magda, cuttingly. 'Oh, that's good. All's well. The old Germany is still there. These bastards can't be as bad as all that.'

Berthold put his hand gently on his wife's shoulder as her face seemed to lose its pallor and contort into an ugly red mask.

'Don't humour me, Bertold,' she snapped. 'They've stolen everything from us.' Magda's language shocked the girls. They turned from the ship and stood rooted to the spot not quite sure where to look. Magda was not consoled by Bertold's touch. 'Look at all these people,' she continued furiously. 'Why do they only carry one case? Because they've had everything taken from them. We have nothing. They took our house, they stole our business. To them we are not human. We're just rubbish to be thrown out ....' Tears were welling up in her eyes and she collapsed sobbing into Bertold's shoulder. He wrapped his arms around her and looked at the girls with moistened eyes.

'It is the strain of leaving,' he said quietly. 'Please forgive us. Come Magda we go below.' With that he held onto his wife and the two shuffled away across the deck.

Lily and Sally were left speechless. Behind them in the distance they could see the Bremen about to disappear over the horizon, while ahead of them rose a great stretch of white chalk cliffs.

14

The family Wolsey stood in the parking area of the dock, Lily's father leaning against it waving at them as they came out of the terminal. Harris, Hubert's chauffeur, hunted around for a porter while Hubert walked across to the girls, giving Sally a hearty handshake and Lily an affectionate kiss.

'You look pretty good, old girl, considering ....' he said taking their small cases from them.

'Considering what, Daddy?' asked Lily with a sideways wink at Sally.

'A month eating with those foreign johnnies.'

'We were in Germany, Daddy.' she protested. 'Look at me.' She pinched her waist to show him she had put on weight. 'The cakes were divinely scrumptious.'

'And the beer, Mr Rood, did wonders for our complexion,' added Sally, knowing how easy it was to poke fun at Lily's father.

'Damn right. That's why you went. Come back with a glow, eh?' He half laughed at his own joke before opening the door of the car for the girls to get in.

'Where's Harris?' he said looking around him. 'Can't be that difficult to get a porter.' Sally smiled remembering how Friedrich had just helped himself to somebody else's porter in Munich. Eventually Harris emerged out of breath accompanied by two porters and the girl's luggage with the brightly striped hat box sitting in pride of place on top.

'What the devil's that?' spluttered Hubert.

'Be patient Daddy,' said Lily brightly. 'Wait 'til we get home.' Hubert huffed. 'Oh do be careful,' she shouted to the men as one of them tried to squeeze the hat box into a corner of the trunk. It wouldn't go and Lily ended up nursing it on her lap as Harris manoeuvred the car out of the dock buildings and through the congested streets of Dover.

All the way home on the long drive to Bletchley, Lily and Sally vied with each other to describe all that they had seen and done. A veritable chatter of headlines echoed around the car, but not wishing to cause Lily's father any more splutterings they were careful to avoid all mention of physical exercises, short tunics and misplaced canes. Nor did Lily talk about Friedrich. Much as she was bursting to tell her parents everything, she thought it better to keep quiet about it for the moment as she wasn't certain how they would respond. A friend, yes, but a real boyfriend? She thought they weren't ready for that yet.

Their chatter subsided when they noticed Hubert had dozed off and they could see that Harris, sitting passively at the wheel, was no audience. They stared into the driving mirror and when they caught Harris looking at them they grabbed each other and collapsed in a heap of giggles. Why, wondered Lily, were there so many unbending adults around? The frozen faces of Frau Busch, Fräulein Hutger, the assistant at the department store, the waitress at the inn rose up and hovered like ghosts before her. To erase the horrors she tickled Sally, deliberately provoking more giggles. This led to her friend squealing and flailing her arms, which instantly woke Hubert.

'Stop it Lily. You know I'm ticklish.' Sally slapped playfully at her friend, extricating herself from a tangle of limbs. Seeing that Hubert had woken, Lily turned to him. 'Daddy we met Mr Hitler.'

'Met!' exclaimed Hubert craning his neck in surprise.

'No not met exactly. We didn't shake his hand. He was passing us in his car. He was going on holiday. He has a place near Munich.'

'Berchtesgaden.'

'You know it?' asked Lily impressed.

'No, silly girl,' chuckled Hubert, 'I've read about it. Anyway, what did you think?'

'He seemed so relaxed and in command. He stood in an open car and waved. People were so excited.'

'I'd like to have been there. I must tell everyone at work. My daughter has seen Herr Hitler.' Sally looked at him askance. I doubt they'll receive that news with enthusiasm, she thought. Harris flinched momentarily. 'And Daddy,' continued Lily excitedly, 'I do think he caught my eye.'

'That's wonderful, my dear. It's something you will always remember.' He beamed at her before turning back to face the road. Harris gave them all a fleeting quizzical look before resuming his impassive posture.

They reached the Thames and drove onto the car ferry at Gravesend. Lily and Sally took advantage of the break to stretch their legs. They clambered up the iron staircase that gave access to a passenger promenade area. Above them the tall thin funnel belched out black smoke as the vessel rode the choppy waters of the Thames estuary, causing them to hold onto the rail tightly to keep their balance. They stared at the approaching industrial landscape of Tilbury on the opposite bank.

'Sad to think it's all over,' said Lily wistfully. 'It was such jolly good fun.'

'No more school though,' said Sally.

'That's true.' Lily was quiet for a moment lost in her own thoughts. She hoped Friedrich would write. She would, but she thought boys weren't good at it. She must encourage him, she told herself. But she was worried. All around her people were saying such bad things about what was happening in Germany. Even Sally. She wanted Friedrich, but she didn't want to lose Sally. The ferry gave an unexpected roll which brought her back to more immediate concerns.

'What do you think Secretarial College will be like?' she asked. The two girls had both enrolled on a secretarial course which started in Bedford in a fortnight's time. Now they had left school they felt they should be getting some work qualification and learning to type seemed the best option. Especially, as Sally had pointed out, they could put it 'with our German and we could go places.'

'Oh, it'll be fun. New friends.'

Lily watched the cranes of Tilbury docks grow taller as the ferry approached the incoming bank. She turned and looked at Sally with sudden alarm in her eyes. 'We'll always be friends, won't we?' Sally put her arm around Lily's waist and hugged her tightly.

'Of course,' said Sally softly, 'always.' Lily smiled contentedly and let her face nuzzle against her friend's curls.

A figure stood behind them. Harris had come up the ladder. He startled them and they let their arms drop to their sides.

'Your father said you should come down,' he said with obvious disdain. They nodded and followed him to the car as the ferry's reverse engines edged the vessel to the landing stage. Back in the car they sat and watched the endless streets of London pass before them. Lily missed Munich's cleanliness, its open-air cafes and soaring banners. These streets were so drab and colourless. After what seemed an eternity they reached Bletchley and Hubert dropped Sally off at her house in the centre of town. Lily watched from the car as her friend's curls seemed to dance when she turned to give her a farewell wave. From the heart of Bletchley the Wolsey drove north and eventually nosed its way slowly down a narrow drive until it reached the front of the Roods' large red brick house. The car scrunched to a halt on the gravel and before Harris could leave his seat, Peg had opened the rear door and half pulled, half lifted Lily into her arms.

'Thank God, you're back safely,' she said, hugging her daughter tightly. As always Peg's motherly concern grated with Lily, especially at this moment when she thought she was coming back sporting the poise of a grown woman.

'Of course I'm home safely.' She spoke a little too harshly and quickly regretted it. 'Mummy, why shouldn't I be?' Her tone softened. 'It was fun.' Her mother pushed her away and held her at arms-length.

'My word, look how you've filled out,' she said not certain this was a good thing. She let her eyes roam over the body of her daughter noting the thicker waist, the fuller hips and beneath the delicate fabric of the summer dress the blossoming breasts.

'It looks like you had a good time.'

'Divine, Mummy,' and without stopping for breath, Lily repeated like a scatter gun the stories she had told her father. Peg listened intently until she got distracted by Harris in the process of lifting the cases out of the car.

'Take them up to Lily's room, will you Harris?' He muttered something inaudible under his breath and went to retrieve the hat box.

'No, leave that,' shouted Lily. Harris gave a scowl and shuffled off.

'Ah, we shall now learn the secret of what's in that box,' said Hubert joining them. 'The little minx has kept mum about it all the way from Dover.'

'You must wait a little longer, Daddy'. She suddenly had a desperate need for the lavatory. 'I'm going upstairs to freshen up,' she said gaily and skipped off, leaving her parents standing.

On the stairs she met Harris coming down. She needed to go to the bathroom and didn't want to talk to him. But he stood in front of her in a way that was almost threatening.

'Best be careful what you say about 'im, Miss,' he said, whispering to avoid being overheard.

'Who?' She fixed his red blistered face with a hard cold look. She had never liked Harris.

'Your Mr Hitler,' he said sourly. 'People won't take too kindly to hearing what you said in the car.'

'That's impertinent,' she snapped. 'You don't know what you are talking about. I've been over there for a month, remember.' She would have said more but the need to pee got the better of her and she walked away. What he had said unsettled her. Were people really being so hateful about other people's opinions? After she had washed and tidied her hair, she felt better, and ran down into the drawing room where her father had his head in a newspaper and her mother was pouring tea. On a small Victorian occasional table sat the striped hat box.

'The moment has arrived,' chuckled Hubert, putting his paper down in expectation. In a dramatic flourish Lily walked over to the table and flounced herself beside it. She lifted the lid of the box with studied precision and triumphantly took out the grey felt hat with its red band and jaunty red feather. Peg clapped with excitement.

'It's lovely, darling.' Lily put it on her head at the rakish angle she had been shown in the shop and paraded around the room like a model from Vogue.

'Good heavens, the girl's grown up,' spluttered Hubert.

'Isn't the feather just too chic,' simpered Lily in as sultry a voice as she could muster, recalling how they said such things in the movies. The three collapsed in laughter.

15

Despite Lily's fears, Friedrich kept his promise and wrote regularly. In fact, the couple exchanged letters almost every day. Lily was like a sprite about the house and when questioned by her parents she merely passed it off with how gay all the young people were in Munich and how much fun she had going out with them. But Peg, certainly, suspected there was more. It quickly came to a head just before Lily was to start college. Hubert was home recovering from a bout of flu. He sat reading the paper when Lily bounced in.

'Has the post come today, Daddy?'

'In the hall, Lily, where it always is.' But he was talking into space. When he looked over his shoulder, he saw a flash of skirt disappearing through the door and Peg, holding a tray of coffee, almost knocked over.

'Another letter?' she asked of her husband.
'Yes.'
'That's one nearly every day.'
'Do you think it's a boy, Peg?'

'Of course it's a boy, Hubert. She wouldn't be living on some distant planet if it wasn't.' Peg put the tray down on the table and sat, or more accurately, flopped on the sofa beside Hubert. He looked at the frown on her brow.

'You're worried about this, Peg?'

'She's still very young and I assume he's ....' She hesitated.

'German?' finished Hubert.

'Don't get me wrong. I'm pleased for her. After all that's partly why we approved of her going to Germany.'

'To get a husband,' laughed Hubert. Peg gave him a mocking slap.

'You know what I mean. We want our two countries to stay friends. But if it doesn't go as we hope they could be in serious trouble.'

'It'll blow over,' said Hubert. 'Chamberlain is a sensible fellow and he's got that crackpot Churchill on the back benches where he belongs. It is going to work out. Believe me.'

'I hope you are right,' said Peg doubtfully. She got up and poured their coffee. Sitting back down beside Hubert she glanced over at the headline he had open before him.

'The Sudetenland, I've read a lot about that recently. It's a part of Czechoslovakia, isn't it?'

'Yes, but unfortunately a lot of German people live there and it appears Mr Hitler wants to make it part of Germany. Mr Chamberlain is flying out next week to try and patch things up. He's going to meet Mr Hitler at Berchtesgaden ....'

'Berchtesgaden! Who's going there, Daddy?' Lily had come back into the room. She was holding an open letter and her face looked fit to burst.

'Mr Chamberlain, next week. There's a bit of a to do on over there at the moment ….' Hubert stopped when he saw Lily's face.

'What's the matter dear?' asked Peg.

Lily could contain herself no longer. 'Mummy, Daddy,' she said excitedly, 'wonderful news. Friedrich says he wants to come to England and he wants to stay with us.'

'Friedrich?' her parents chorused from the sofa with pretended puzzlement.

Lily waved the letter. 'I met him in Munich. We got on famously.'

'And he has been writing all these letters to you?'

'Yes. We like each other very much.'

'Is he from a good family?' asked Peg anxiously. Hubert looked at her not considering this to be a matter of concern at this moment.

Lily hesitated suddenly realising she knew little about Friedrich's family background. He had never spoken about it and she had never asked. Eventually she said: 'He is very smart. He wears a uniform almost every day. People respect him. They even salute him. And he's kind, Mummy.' Peg smiled.

'I'm sure he is very nice,' she said.

'What uniform?' asked Hubert.

'Hitler Youth,' replied Lily. 'It is like our scouts.' Then another thought came to her. 'When we went to see Herr Hitler, Friedrich came in a special car his father had borrowed. It was very big and swish and it had Herr Hitler's flag on its bonnet. We felt very important.'

'And what does Frederick's father do?' persisted Hubert.

'No, Daddy. It's Friedrich.' She formed a guttural explosion at the back of her mouth. Then she considered what Friedrich's father did do. But of course she didn't know. Hubert suspected the obvious. If they were riding around in a large car it could only mean one thing, that Friedrich's father was an official in the Nazi party. For most people in Britain this would be a cause for concern, but Hubert was quietly pleased. His long-time sympathy with what Hitler was doing, his pleasure in seeing him build a strong Germany made it a source of pride for him that his daughter was being courted by the son of a Nazi officer. In the past he had even supported the British fascist party by clandestinely giving them funds, although their recent violent activities had disenchanted him. He hoped that a peaceful accommodation could be made with the German government. It was this romantic notion that now infatuated his daughter.

'I would like to meet your Friedrich,' he said beaming at her and making every effort to pronounce his name correctly. Lily hugged him from behind and kissed his cheek.

'When is he coming?' asked Peg. 'And will he be alone?'

'He says next June.' She looked down at the letter to check what Friedrich had written. 'He will be joining the army then but wants to have a holiday touring England. He will be bringing his bicycle.'

'That's a long time to wait,' said Hubert. 'Don't get your hopes up dear. With the political situation being what it is, it may not be possible for him to come at all.'

'Oh Daddy, I know he'll come.' Nothing was going to deter Lily from her optimism.

'If he does come,' said Peg, 'we will do everything to make him welcome.'

'Mummy, you're a darling.' She bounced onto the sofa and gave her mother a kiss almost upsetting the coffee cup Peg was holding.

16

Nine months went by against a backdrop of an increasingly worsening situation abroad. Neville Chamberlain's efforts to appease Hitler looked doomed to failure. Whatever was offered, the German Chancellor always seemed to want more. Hubert Rood was starting to feel less bullish about peace. He was worried too about how war would affect his business. His thriving sawmill depended on imports and if a German blockade came about it would cause him problems. He was the younger son of a country family that had fallen on hard times after the Great War, but with the small amount of money bequeathed him he had, through hard work, determination and financial drive, built up a thriving business. He considered he possessed qualities that until recently he saw being exhibited across the Channel. Now this love affair was starting to unravel and he was concerned as to where it might lead. He brooded on the deepening crisis as he looked down from his office and watched great lengths of tree being sliced into sections in a cloud of dust and wondered for how much longer he would be sitting there. He thought too of Lily on her first day at secretarial school.

But for the moment international disputes were far from Lily's thoughts. She stood with Sally on Bletchley station waiting for the train to take them to Bedford. They had bought themselves suits and were wearing heels and each sported a hat, although not the fashion statement Lily had brought back with her from Munich. They felt smart and important in the company of other workers but hadn't expected the rush that would happen when the train finally steamed into the station. Doors banged and clanged as people jostled each other for a space. The girls were left standing. A voice shouted from one of the carriages.

'Hey you two get in. There's space here'. A bespectacled dark-haired woman in a black beret was leaning out of a window and opening a door to let them on board. They scrambled into the carriage as the whistle blew and the train started to move. Sally wiped her brow sinking into a spare seat.

'Phew! Thanks.'

'First day?' asked the woman, who although older was probably still in her early twenties.

'At Secretarial School?'

'Yes.' How did she know they were going there, wondered Lily? The woman could see the perplexity on Lily's face and laughed.

'I teach at the school and there are always new girls waiting at Bletchley on the first day of term.' She held out her hand. 'Clara Meadows', she said pleasantly. They introduced themselves.

'Can you type?' They shook their heads. 'Well I shall be teaching you, as I'm taking the beginners class.' She spoke well but her voice had a slight North London accent.

'We've been learning German,' said Lily, eager not to appear dim. Clara Meadows raised an eyebrow.

'Have you now,' she said. 'And where did you do that?'

'In Germany …. this summer,' went on Lily without a thought of the consequences of what she was saying and forgetting what Harris had said to her earlier. Sally wished she'd shut up. She cast around her fellow passengers, two men with their heads in their newspapers and an elderly woman who had taken out some knitting from her bag. No one seemed to have reacted to Lily's remarks.

'Well,' said Clara tactfully, 'today we will be typing in English.' Before Lily could say anything else the train shuddered and braked to a stop at a station. Two people squeezed into the remaining seats and the carriage descended into silence. Lily's eyes scanned the different papers her fellow passengers were reading. They all seemed to condemn what Hitler was trying to do and in one there was even a suggestion there might be war between Germany and England.

Seeing it in bold print unnerved Lily. In his letters to her Friedrich never mentioned the troubles in Europe. He was always so correct and polite. Even his protestations of love continued to be stiff and reserved. Perhaps he didn't want to worry her. Now seeing those headlines she saw the possibility that they might be separated by war. It was a reality that hit her forcibly for the first time. And what's more Friedrich could be killed. He talked about becoming a soldier. In his latest letter he said he had volunteered and would be joining up in June. He gave her lots of detail of all the exercises his Hitler Youth group were doing. It was already like military training, he said. Now she realised, if war broke out, they would be fighting on different sides. They would be enemies. She got suddenly very angry. Why, she said to herself, couldn't these silly men stop acting like children and make up?

She looked out of the window. The train was steaming between a forest of chimneys all belching thick smoke. They were passing the huge brickworks that dominated the outskirts of Bedford. In the yards mountains of bricks lay piled up awaiting delivery around the country. It was an awesome sight and, as the train rattled and shuddered over rails leading to a patchwork of sidings, Lily could never imagine what a big part these works were going to play in her life.

They arrived at Bedford station and the girls accompanied Clara Meadows to the school. On the way, Clara turned to Lily.

'I don't think you should talk about being in Germany in public.' She caught Lily's freckle faced friend looking at her warily. 'People can get the wrong idea. Everyone's very twitchy at the moment.'

'I know what you mean,' she said, 'but we did meet some nice people in Germany.'

'I'm sure you did,' said Clara, 'I'm sorry I must have sounded like a bossy parent. Not a good way to start.' They both gave her nervous smiles. She pointed ahead.

'We're almost there.' A large Victorian institutional looking building came into view. 'The typing school's round the corner and has its own entrance, but you have to register in the main hall first. I'll see you later.' With that she walked off and left them at the steps. These led to a soaring and rather intimidating portal that was sucking in a steady stream of students. They followed cautiously and were accosted by a man in uniform who directed them to the registration desk.

Just as Clara had said they were told to go back out of the building and around the corner. They joined a group of about twenty other women in an ante room attached to the side of the typing pool. Through the glass doors they could see returning students pouring into the hall and sitting at desks. The windows only provided a partial view of what was going on, but Lily could see Clara Meadows in her black beret with her back to her checking numbers. She pointed her out to the others: 'There's Miss Meadows. She's going to be our teacher.'

''Ow'd you know that? 'asked a short frumpish girl in an ill matching suit standing beside Lily. 'You got blinking sixth sense?'

'No,' laughed Lily, missing the sarcasm, 'she was on our train. Found a seat for us. Jolly sporting of her, I thought.'

'We got teacher's pet 'ere, 'ave we?'

'Lay off 'er, Lil,' said another older girl from behind.

'That's my name,' said Lily eagerly, again missing the resentful tone of the first girl. 'I'm Lil, too. Actually Lily.'

'Lord luv a duck. A toff and 'er tart.' The woman thought this funny and gave a laugh that had the throaty croak, which Sally thought had probably been brought on by smoking. Lily smiled awkwardly, not sure how to react. Sally jumped in to save her friend.

'That is a co-incidence. I think you must both be Lillian. I'm Sally,' she said brightly.

'Pleased to meet, I'm Lil Bates,' said the one called Lil who then turned to her friend, 'and this is Ag, short for Agatha.'

The woman smiled. 'I like your freckles, love, and them curls.'

'All natural,' said Sally sweetly. Ag was the opposite of Lil, tall and willowy, with sharply etched features that if seen in the right light could pass as beautiful.

None of them noticed a tiny girl as young as Lily and Sally watching the exchange with interest. She had a sallow complexion, sharp pinched features, tired sunken eyes and jet-black hair hanging in loose lifeless strands about her neck. Where everyone else in the room wore business suits, she was dressed in a grey sweater that had been darned in several places and a shapeless skirt that hovered around her ankles. Even when the doors opened and they began to be ushered into the hall she kept her eyes on Lily.

The group moved steadily out of the ante room. In the crush Sally whispered in Lily's ear. 'Steer clear of those two,' she hissed. Lily nodded. In the press of people pushing through the narrow entrance, they instinctively held hands to stay together. The noise hit them the moment they got into the hall. The older students were already working through their exercises. The sound of hundreds of metallic keys being pressed in rapid fire movements was deafening. Assistants ushered them to the back of the hall which was quieter and told them to find a typewriter and desk. With a wary eye on where Lil and her friend Ag were going, Sally guided Lily and herself in the opposite direction. They found desks side by side and sat down. Lily stared in awe at the huge machine in front of her, bristling with cogs, levers and keys. She was wondering how she was going to manage when a voice made her look up.

'Hello love. Thought we'd come and join you.' The round red faces of Lil and Ag beamed down at them. Lily swallowed and gave Sally a fleeting look of scarcely disguised irritation.

'Of course,' she smiled sweetly.

'We might get some tips seeing as 'ow you're teacher's pet.' Lil gave Lily a smirk as she sat down beside her.

'Hardly,' said Lily, 'I can't type.'

'But that's what we're 'ere for, 'ain't it darling?' The two sniggered. If this was going to go on, thought Sally, they were going to have to do something about it. But for the moment their attention was diverted by the tiny girl who had watched them earlier coming to sit in front of them and then one of the assistants called everyone to attention.

Clara Meadows still wearing her black beret emerged from a side room and addressed her class.

'Welcome, ladies. I'm pleased to see you all at the start of our new class for beginners. My name is Miss Meadows and I shall be instructing you this term.' As Clara got into her stride, Lily's thoughts drifted back to Germany and she chuckled to herself to think that here she was again in a regimented line of desks. As she listened she mischievously superimposed Frau Busch on Clara's face. But Clara carried no stick and unlike Frau Busch she seemed like a poppet.

'The first thing you must remember, ladies, is posture. You will be spending many hours sitting in front of a typewriter and to avoid aches and pains you must sit correctly.' To illustrate her point, she sat down at a desk and pulled herself up to an erect position and began typing.

Lil leant over and whispered to Lily. 'Why'd she keep that beret on? Do we call her comrade or something?'

Lily shook her head, both to say no and in the hope of shutting her up.

'Remember, Ladies, you must sit above the keys so you can push down on them hard. But more of that later. First look at the keys and tell me what's strange about them?'

'Can think of other things I'd rather be pushing down on,' muttered Lil under her breath. The remark made Ag give a dirty laugh, while Lily blushed at what she thought Lil meant. Sally lost her patience.

'If you don't shut up. we'll move.'

'Suit yourself, darling,' said Lil unperturbed. She and Ag gave each other conspiratorial looks, but finally turned back to Clara who sat at her desk waiting patiently for an answer to her question. A voice from the far side of the group spoke up: 'The keys are not in alphabetical order.'

'Well done. Can someone read out the first six letters, please.'

The tiny girl in front of them answered. Her accent was husky and to the others sounded foreign.

'Q.W.E.R.T.Y.'

'Thank you. QWERTY is the system we use. As you see the letters are spread over the keyboard and were designed to stop pairs of letters like 'th' being close to each other. This prevented keys jamming.'

Lil leaned over once more: 'What's she talking about?'

Lily hissed back: 'I'll show you when we break. Do please shut up.' Her vehemence shook Lil who apart from responding with 'hoity toity' settled back in her chair. For the rest of the lesson there was no further interruption.

When they broke for tea, Lily was as good as her word and sat with Lil and Ag and tried to help them. Sally said she would save some tea and went off into the refectory area at the back of the hall. She managed in the crowd to get two mugs and some biscuits and located a small table in the corner of the room. To her surprise the tiny girl with the husky voice appeared, almost as if she was waiting to way-lay her.

'Can I sit with you,' she asked.

'Of course,' said Sally, who, although she wasn't tall, towered over the girl. When they were seated the girl seemed to go down to the level of the table. Sally was certain her legs never touched the floor. The girl introduced herself.

'My name's Yakova Marcuson.' Sally stared at the big sunken eyes that looked up at her and wondered who she was. She shook hands and gave her name.

'They were unkind. They treated you badly' she said mysteriously.

'Who?'

'The two girls who were talking to you.' Sally laughed.

'They were annoying, but nothing worse.'

'I know what is like to be tormented. It is horrible.'

'Where are you from.' Sally assumed with her accent that she wasn't local and she was intrigued by the earnest weight she was putting on a trivial encounter.

'From Austria.' She took a sip of tea and cast her eyes down as she did so. 'I am a refugee,' she continued without looking up. 'I live with my uncle in Bedford. My mother and father were arrested and taken to a camp. I hid but I could see my father being put into handcuffs and beaten around the face.' She stopped. Sally thought she was going to cry, but she carried on. 'They pulled the rings from my mother's fingers. One they couldn't get off so they smashed the finger with a bar to make it fall off. Then they pulled her into the street by her hair.'

Sally sat in silence. The voices around her that she had been able to identify as audible individuals became a background murmur isolating the two of them in a sudden intense relationship. Sally had to pinch herself that a stranger would divest themselves of so personal and horrible a story with barely a nodding acquaintance.

'How did you escape?' she asked matter-of-factly.

'As I said, I hid and then managed to find friends of my parents who got me to England.'

'You speak good English.'

'We spent holidays with my uncle.'

'Why were your parents arrested?'

'We're Jews.' She spat the words out as if she was disgusted by them. 'They also thought my parents were Bolsheviks.' Sally wasn't sure who Bolsheviks were but she thought they were probably communists. 'They have been harassing us for years. We can't vote. We can't study law or medicine. We can't go to the cinema. Our shops get smashed. They burn our books. We can't sit in the park.' She paused. Tears started to fill her sunken eyes.

'Don't upset yourself, Yakova' said Sally gently, 'it's not like that here. It is only banter. The sort of thing you get at school.'

'But you must be careful. It happens so quickly,' said Yakova, returning to her former earnestness. Sally still couldn't see how burning books squared with Lil's sarcasm. But the horror of Yakova's outburst had alarmed her. She was more than ever convinced now that there was something rotten at the core of German life. Yet she was grateful that Lily wasn't with them to hear what Yakova had said. Her friend was dancing on air and counting the days to Friedrich's arrival. She just couldn't prick the bubble.

'Thank you for confiding in me, Yakova. I know it helps sometimes to talk to strangers.' She looked down at the soulful figure in front of her and found she couldn't even begin to understand the torment she must be suffering. The girl was silent now. Sally sat draining her cup, the babbling chatter of voices erecting a wall around them. Finally Sally broke the silence by asking why she was on the typing course.

'My uncle is paying for me. I hope to get a job in England.'

'Like us.' She saw Lily pushing her way through the crowd.

'That took some time,' said Sally as Lily plonked herself down in a fluster. 'Sorry, I think your tea's cold.'

'It's liquid at least. I'm parched.' Hardly had she put her mug to her lips than a bell rang to summon them back.

'Darn it. Oh well at least Lil's happy,' she said cheerily getting up with the mug still in her hand for a last slurp.

'Lily, this is Yakova,' said Sally. Lily smiled an acknowledgement but was more interested in telling Sally about her triumphant encounter with Lil.

'She's my friend for life. She and Ag were really grateful when I put them right on the keys.' They were now hemmed in by the others and Lily had to talk over her shoulder. 'I think they've got the hang of it now.' They reached their desks, but there was no Lil and Ag.

'Gone to powder their noses, I expect,' said Lily cheerily. Yakova settling in her seat twisted herself to look back with a bemused expression. 'You say powder their noses?'

'She means they've gone to spend a penny.' said Sally by way of clarification.

'Ah, yes, I understand,' said Yakova. 'You English have such quaint words.'

Lily leant over to Sally and whispered in her ear. 'I don't think Ag can read very well. That's why they are having trouble, although Lil seems pretty smart to me'

'How did they get on this course then?'

'Ag's a barmaid and Lil calls herself a hotel skivvy. They saved their earnings, they said. Lil's boss said they needed girls in the office at the brick works who knew the ropes. The family have been working there for generations, so she thinks she qualifies. Ag goes to reading classes, too, Lil tells me.'

A guttural voice behind them cut short further explanation.

'Lav's a bit of a posh squash,' guffawed Lil. 'Missed our tea. Did you get yours, Lily darling?'

'Yes, thank you.' As the two sat down, Sally looked at them with more curiosity in the light of what Lily had said. She couldn't see their arms as they were hidden by the suit jackets, but Lil's hands did have a roughness about them as if hardened by manual work. And she was now conscious that Ag's make up was more thickly applied than normal.

The class was called to order and the typing began. Keys clattered, carriages returned with a clang, completed paper ripped from rollers. The sound was discordant and relentless. Clara Meadows and her assistant roamed the aisles encouraging, helping and cajoling. Then the end of day bell rang, the noise stopped, and the excited chatter of female voices took over amid scraping chairs and a rush for the door. Lily and Sally said goodbye to Lil, Ag and Yakova and joined the stream of people hurrying to the station. This time the train was waiting for them and they easily found a seat.

'I'm so tired,' said Lily yawning and pressing herself into the leather. 'I didn't realise that pushing keys all day could be so wearing. And I ache all over.' She shifted her body to make herself more comfortable. The whistle blew causing her to switch her eyes to the platform. She could see Clara Meadows running up the steps. She jumped to her feet and pulled at the heavy restraining strap on the window. It released the frame bringing the window down with a crash. She stuck her head out and shouted.

'Miss Meadows, we're here.' The carriage jolted violently. 'Hurry'. Lily found the door handle and went to open it.

'Don't!' shouted Sally in alarm. 'The train's moving.' But it was too late. The door flew open and swung back with the forward advance of the train. Clara was now alongside and with the door open she was able to drag herself into the compartment. She sat down panting heavily. A man pushed Lily out of the way and with a superhuman effort managed to pull the door shut. He turned to Lily who sat chastened by what had happened and spoke to her with some severity.

'I wouldn't do that again, miss,' he said. 'You could earn yourself a hefty fine if they caught you.' Lily looked sheepish

'He's right, Lily,' said Clara not having it in her heart to be angry. 'You should have left me on the platform. But thank you.' She turned to the man. 'And thank you, sir.' She gave him a warm smile and he beamed back in response. He was slightly older than Clara, thought Lily, and his smart suit and leather briefcase gave him the air of a regular office worker. After her thank you he appeared to ignore Clara, yet as the engine ahead puffed into its stride, both Lily and Sally noticed the two taking sly looks at each other.

'How was your first day?' asked Clara, settling back in her seat.

'Fine, miss,' said Sally.

'Bit tiring. Sitting for so long,' added Lily.

Clara laughed. 'You'll get used to it.'

'But we did make some friends.'

'So I saw. You met Yakova.'

'She has a funny voice,' said Lily. 'Do you know where she comes from? I didn't get a chance to ask her.' Before Clara could reply the train clattered into the station serving the massive brickworks. They were all distracted by the banging of doors and the press of workers waiting to board. Sally was grateful. She continued to be worried as to what Lily's reaction would be when she learned about Yakova's background.

But for the moment the spectacle of the brickworks occupied their attention. Like a dense pine forest, chimneys rose from the brick producing sheds sending clouds of smoke into the sky. Lily thought they looked graceful, their thin elegance heightened by the low-slung buildings from which they sprouted. Two workers climbed into their compartment. They brought with them a distinct odour which smelt to Lily like bad eggs. She wrinkled her nose in protest which made Clara laugh. She leant over and whispered in Lily's ear.

'Sulphur fumes. They cling to everything around here.' Lily studied the two men. They looked weary, their faces and jackets speckled with flecks of clay, making them look as if they had been inflicted with a disease. Neither spoke, but one pulled out a hand rolled cigarette from his pocket and lit it, filling the compartment with a noxious smoke that mingled with the sulphur. His companion, to the relief of everyone, released the strap on the window a couple of notches, letting in a welcome draught of fresh air.

The train shuddered once more into motion and passed an enormous hole, the size of which made Lily gasp.

'They call it the 'knot hole'. It's where they excavate the clay,' said Clara. Lily watched, as they passed by. Colossal machines were dredging up mounds of the tacky substance and depositing it on conveyor belts which disappeared into the long sheds.

It seemed that everyone had forgotten Yakova Marcuson. Sally was grateful for the diversion and certainly by now it was obvious that Clara was more interested in the man from the office than anyone else. In fact when they arrived at Bletchley she gave the girls only a cursory good-bye before dropping back with the pretence of looking at a notice. When they reached the ticket barrier and handed in their tickets, they took the opportunity of looking round to find Clara in conversation with the young man.

'All in a day's work,' said Sally brightly as she skipped off home with a cheery 'see you tomorrow!' Lily had ridden to the station in the morning and went to retrieve her bicycle from the shelter. As she undid the padlock, Clara and the young man walked by without a word. It made her think instantly of Friedrich and as she rode home she wondered whether there would be a letter waiting for her.

17

There was, but it was different. Yes, Friedrich professed his love in his usual halting way. Yes, he described his activities in the Hitler Youth. They were on an all-night exercise in the woods outside Munich. They blacked their faces and had to avoid being captured. He was successful although he said there were some scary moments. Yes, he talked proudly of his father and his work in the service of the Fatherland. But for the first time he wrote about unrest in the country. Everyone in Munich, he said, was talking about the trouble in Czechoslovakia. 'German people in the Sudetenland,' he wrote, 'are being attacked. Our Führer has said this must stop. He says the land there is part of Germany and he has asked for it back. If this doesn't happen there will be war.' Lily stopped reading at this point and considered the significance of Friedrich's words. She didn't understand how everything could change so quickly when only a few weeks ago she was having such fun and now people in Friedrich's country and here in her own were talking of going to war. Perhaps if fighting happened it would be over quickly and Friedrich wouldn't be involved. But would she see him in the summer? All the events of the day vanished from her thoughts and she sank into a state of melancholy. She let the letter slip to her side and she moped around the upstairs rooms. She could hear her mother in the kitchen preparing supper. Her father would be back any minute. In fact she thought she could hear the car on the gravel. She was in her parents' bedroom which had a view over the drive. She saw Harris get out of the car and open his employer's door. He, she thought, would be the first to kill Germans if he got the chance. It was all so dreadful.

She went back to her room and got out her writing materials. She had to get a letter off to Friedrich by tomorrow's post. She sat at her dressing table with a blank sheet of paper in front of her. She wasn't sure what she was going to write. Then she saw his blonde tanned features looking up at her and she wanted desperately to hold him. She unscrewed the fountain pen she had been given for her eighteenth birthday and began to write. Sadness dripped through the ink onto the page:

'Dearest Friedrich,
> All this talk of war really upsets me. People mention it a lot here too and I think, why can't our politicians grow up ....'

The nib hovered over the page as she considered what to write next. She was going to say: 'They're acting like children and need their ears boxed.' But she didn't think Friedrich would understand. Instead she simply wrote:

> '.... and sort things out peacefully. I started my typing class today. It was great fun, although a bit like school still. We

met our teacher on the train. She is really nice although she wears this black beret all the time, indoors and out. No one knows why. I will ask her one day ....'

She was interrupted by her mother calling her from downstairs announcing that supper was ready.

As she sat in front of a plate generously filled with a large helping of steak and kidney pie, potatoes, vegetables and lashings of gravy, she suddenly realised how hungry she was. Her knife sliced the brittle crust of the pie and she dug out a rich mess of meat which went straight into her mouth, a dribble of gravy escaping down her cheek, her gloomy thoughts momentarily banished.

'How'd your day go, old girl?' asked Hubert, without looking up.

A throttled reply came out of Lily's mouth as she masticated a piece of steak.

'You shouldn't talk with your mouth full,' said Peg.

'Can't you see the girl's starving.'

When the battle with the steak was over and it had gone down her throat, Lily wiped her mouth with a napkin, put her knife and fork on the plate and gave them a brisk summary of her day.

'You were a long time in your bedroom,' was Peg's only comment.

'Well, you saw I had a letter from Friedrich,' said Lily intimating that staying in her bedroom was the obvious response. She picked up her cutlery and started eating again. This time she attacked the food with more delicacy and sat quietly while her parents discussed their day.

Peg noticed her daughter's silence and asked whether anything was wrong. Lily didn't answer her mother directly but turned to her father.

'Daddy, Friedrich says there may be war. Everyone's talking about it over there. He's never written like this before.'

Hubert continued eating and dismissed it with a wave of his hand.

'It'll blow over. They're talking like that here. The sawmill's full of loose talk. Bloody commies.'

'Language dear.'

'You mean communists?' asked Lily.

'Agitators. Troublemakers. I should get rid of the lot of them. But I can't. Rules you know.' He blustered and puffed. He was beginning to get agitated.

'You must leave all that to Nixon. He's in charge now, dear.' Peg sought to calm her husband. Although he still owned the sawmill, he had handed over the running of it to Alan Nixon, a bright young man who had been his second in command. Yet Harris still drove him to work each day. Peg tried to persuade him that he didn't have to do it, but without success. He could never leave the fresh smell of newly sawn wood. He always said that when they cut him open it would not be blood that came out but sawdust.

'I tell them,' he said, talking as if he were addressing his work force, 'no one wants a war after the last one. They'll sort it out. You'll see.'

Lily wanted to believe her father. She had trusted everything he had said up to now. But niggling doubts had begun to bubble up in her mind. Sally was upset by many of the things that happened to them. Lily wanted to believe Friedrich when he said there were many enemies wanting to destroy Herr Hitler's efforts to protect his people. But she wondered whether the methods he was using were right. Were the Jews so evil they had to leave the country they were living in? The Hartmanns they met on the train seemed nice people. In fact rather ordinary. Why were they dangerous? But then Friedrich and her father were probably right when they said people should live separately. They would have no need to fight each other if they each had their own country. Lost in thought Lily only distantly heard her father announce that Mr Chamberlain was going to Munich tomorrow to see Herr Hitler. Munich! At the word, her eyes shot up.

'Thought that would get you Lily,' laughed Hubert.

'Is that really so?' she asked excitedly.

'Seems so,' he said reading the newspaper he had in his hand. Peg had cleared away the first course and was serving out a cold trifle.

'That's wonderful news,' said Lily. As soon as supper was over, she raced back to her room to complete her letter to Friedrich. Words poured out of her in her excitement to tell him not to worry. There would be peace and they would be seeing each other. Her pen gushed ink as her love for him expressed itself in flowery sweet nothings.

18

The next day she rode to the station with a light heart. As she pushed her bicycle past the newspaper billboards, she glanced at the headlines imprisoned behind lattice frames. All spoke hopefully of Chamberlain's mission, proclaiming their message in gargantuan letters. '*Chamberlain Flying To See Hitler Today. Let's Try To Find A Peaceful Solution*', said one. On the train, along the street, at their desks, in the canteen, all spoke with growing optimism that the talks would bring peace.

'And about bloody time,' said Lil over a mug of thick tea. 'I'd knock their 'eads together if I was out there.'

'War would be worse for my people, yes' said Yakova. The five, who sat together in the typing pool, now sat at a table in the canteen during their morning break.

'Where do you come from?' asked Lily.

'Austria. But it is not nice there now, I think. I live here with my uncle.' Lily said nothing. She was going to say that Austria had beautiful mountains and lovely lakes like Germany, but caught Sally looking at her very oddly. Then, she suddenly tumbled to the fact that Yakova, with her name and dark features, might be Jewish.

'In Bedford?' she finally said.

'Yes, close. I walk here.'

'Can't see what it's to do with us?' chipped in Ag.

'Well,' said Lil, 'you can't 'ave someone walking into yer country without so much as a by your leave.'

'But I don't even know where this Suden ....' Ag stumbled over the name.

'Sudetenland,' said Lil helpfully.

'Where is it then?'

'Well, it's part of yer Czechoslovakia. Like 'ere. Bedfordshire is part of England, init?

'And this Hitler wants it for 'imself?'

''Cos it's full of Germans.' Given Lil's lack of apparent learning, Lily found this crude illustration of the events instructive. Was this how most English people saw the crisis? A mix of incomprehension and a sense that English fair play was being violated. Lil reminded her of a younger version of Old Mother Riley whom she listened to on the wireless.

'Yes, we must resist,' said Yakova. 'See what has happened in my country, when nobody did?' Lily was about to ask what she meant when the bell rang and they were swept up in the rush to return. Back at her desk Lily pounded the keys of her typewriter as if she were in a trance. She barely saw the text in front of her. Her mind was in Munich. Would Friedrich see Mr Chamberlain arrive? She remembered him pointing out Herr Hitler's residence in the Princeregentenplatz and how she thought it looked quite ordinary standing amid a grand theatre and large stone mansions. She hoped so much that all would go well.

Then, about halfway through that morning session she got her answer. The bell rang and the insistent clatter of metal keys slowly died away. An expectant silence fell on the assembled hall. One of the instructors jumped up onto a table and made a brief announcement.

'I have just been told,' he said excitedly, 'that Mr Chamberlain has returned from Germany with a peace agreement. I have been given this to read to you. It is from his speech. He spoke with a deliberate sense of drama. "We regard the agreement signed last night and the Anglo-German Naval Agreement as symbolic of the desire of our two peoples never to go to war with one another again." He waved the paper he held in the air, a gesture Chamberlain had himself made only a few hours earlier.

The typing pool broke out in an uproar. People leapt from their chairs, clapped and frantically hugged each other. Lily felt Sally's arms around her squeezing her with uncontrolled delight. Lily kissed her friend with tears streaming down her face.

'He will be able to come now, won't he?'

'Yes, Lily.'

It felt as if the world had been lifted from her shoulders. Typing was impossible. In fact an extended lunch break was allowed. The excited hubbub carried on unabated. As they were queued up waiting to be served, Lil who was standing behind Lily suddenly said,

'You and Sal want to join me and Ag for a drink after we finish? To celebrate like?'

'A drink?' said Lily turning around in surprise.

'Yeah, at the local boozer. There's one up the road - The Bricklayers Arms.' Lily had never been across the threshold of a public house in England before, but it was kind of Lil to ask and she didn't want to upset her by refusing and getting another 'stuck up bitch' hurled at her.

'We'd like that. I'll ask Sally.'

Sally had planned to go out with another friend that night but she thought a later train would still get her home in time. Besides it would give them an excuse to leave. Like Lily she was still wary of Lil and Ag.

The four of them walked the five hundred yards to The Bricklayers Arms. Ag lifted the brass latch on the door, resplendent with an oval stained-glass window and decorative brass plaque with the word Saloon written on it, and led them in. Lily held her breath. She wasn't sure what she was going to find. Her first impression was a dimly lit space with a number of wooden tables and chairs spread around, some occupied, most empty. Then, at the back she saw the glint of glasses and bottles lining shelves with the balding figure of the barman standing in front of them with his arms on what she assumed was the bar. Before him rose the tools of his trade, four fine china handles topped with brass fittings with which he pulled the beer from hidden barrels. As the girls came in he looked at them with a quizzical expression which had 'where are the men?' written all over his face.

'Hello ladies,' he called out, deep suspicion in his voice. Ag nodded and then deliberately ignored him. As a barmaid herself she took instant charge, directing them to a round table in the corner away from the other customers, all male, whom she could see from the way they stared at them were the sort of frequent customer who felt they owned the place.

'What will it be for you two, then?' she asked as they sat down. 'Lemonade?'

'We have had beer,' said Lily brightly. Ag looked at her with raised eyebrow. 'Yes, in Germany.'

'You have, have you?' said Lil, instantly curious. 'When was that?'

'A few weeks ago,' continued Lily disarmingly.

'Then it's light mild all round, Ag,' said Lil. Ag nodded and went off to the bar to place the order. Lil was silent. The girls looked around them. Lily thought the place rather drab. The stained varnish of the woodwork and the faded yellow patterned wallpaper gave the room, despite its grand name, a decidedly neglected feel. The only bright spot were the shelves behind the bar with the line of bottles reflected in a mirror behind them. Ag came back with four glass tankards of beer, which she skilfully laid on the table without spilling a drop.

'Do you work here?' asked Lily

'Gawd no. Mine's a spit and sawdust hole. Not posh like this.' Lily could hardly imagine what that must be like. Ag raised her glass.

'To peace. And thank God for Mr Chamberlain.' The others lifted their glasses.

'To peace.'

'And to Friedrich!' said Lily silently to herself.

'Down the hatch, my darlings,' said Lil taking a long draft. Lily took a sip. It was sweeter than what she had tasted in Germany, smoother and less bubbly, and much warmer. Ag could see she was slightly hesitant.

'Don't you like it Lily?'

'It's different …. warmer.'

'They don't have beer like this in Germany?' asked Lil.

'No,' said Sally, 'it's served cold.' Lil wrinkled her nose. A man in his thirties came into the Saloon. He wore a flat cap, tie, an ill-fitting tweed jacket and non-matching trousers. Lily's eyes followed him to the bar. He sat on a stool at one end. Lily saw that the barman handed him a tankard of beer without him having to ask for it. He put the glass to his lips, noticed the four girls, touched his cap and raised the glass in their direction.

'Regular,' said Ag. 'Don't catch his attention.'

'What were you doing in Germany?' Lil asked eyeing the two girls through her glass.

'We were on a German language course,' said Sally who thought it best if she answered the questions.

'Why on earth did you want to do that? You some Nazi sympathiser or something?

'Several girls from our school had been before. We were learning German anyway,' said Sally matter-of-factly.

'Fuck me. You meet all sorts, Ag.' She turned to her friend gave her a wink and turned back again.

'What were they like?'

'Who?'

'The bloody krauts.'

'Ordinary like us. We met lots of nice people.'

'I read them Nazis are knocking everyone around. Kicking the shit out of Jews. You didn't see any of that?' Sally thought on her feet. No point in denying what they saw, she felt.

'There were some nasty incidents, yes. But most of the time people were going about their everyday lives.'

'There were wonderful open-air cafes,' interjected Lily. 'That's when we drank beer - in the beer gardens - under the trees with the band playing.'

'Can I buy you a drink, ladies?' They were so engrossed in their conversation they hadn't noticed the man, whom the barman had called Reg, sidle up to them. Ag glared at him.

'And what makes you think we want another drink? Our glasses empty, are they?' Her voice was hard and steely.

'Back to your stable, lover boy.' Lil said this without even looking up. The man doffed his cap and shuffled back to the bar. Sally and Lily sat in awe of the way the two girls handled the interruption. They looked at each other with suppressed mirth. Lily looked back at the man who was now engaged in conversation with the barman and felt momentarily sorry for him. He must, she thought, be lonely. Ag had no such sympathy.

'Got to treat tossers like that like the pathetic losers they are.'

'Do you think he overheard us?' asked Lily anxiously.

Lil gave one of her coarse cackles. 'Like we were fifth columnists or something!'

'Still,' said Sally, 'it's perhaps best if we don't say too much about our time in Germany.'

'I think so, dear,' said Lil. She looked at the clock above the bar. 'If you two are going to get the next train you had better hurry.'

'Cripes.' Lily jumped to her feet. 'I hadn't noticed the time.' She rummaged in her handbag. 'What do we owe you for the drinks?'

'Go on love. Buy us one next time.'

'There will be a next time,' said Lily. 'It's been topping.' She and Sally raced for the door crashing into a group of young people from the college coming in.

Lil looked at Ag. 'Those two are innocents abroad heading for trouble if they are not careful. You on tonight Ag?'

'Eight o'clock. That's if I get the bugger to pay me.' They swallowed their beer dregs and left, watched by Reg.

19

The next day was Saturday. Lily felt exhausted after her first week at the typing school and decided she was going to have a lie in. When her mother came in to pull the curtains,, she pretended to be asleep and after Peg had tip toed out she curled herself into a ball luxuriating in the chance to be idle. When she finally emerged yawning and stretching, she found cold breakfast on the table and her mother busying herself in the kitchen. She helped herself to a bowl of cereal and watched the energetic shape of her father pass to and fro across the window as he mowed the lawn. Peg came in and huffed at the sight of her daughter sitting unwashed in her nightdress and open dressing gown.

'I hope you are going to tidy yourself up for lunch, young lady.'

'Yes, mother,' said Lily wearily, that old irritation rising up. She heard the mower outside stop and moments later she heard a kerfuffle in the scullery as her father removed his gardening boots. Hubert appeared at the dining room door in his socks. He wore a thick Argyll jumper, corduroy trousers and a pair of gloves which he was in the process of removing when he saw Lily at the breakfast table. He beamed.

'So you've managed to get up, you sleepy head. Plenty of work to do in the garden.'

'Where's Harris?' She scrunched a piece of cold toast as she enquired after the chauffeur who also helped around the house doing odd repair and gardening jobs.

'Let him go today. Had to go into Bedford.'

'I'll come out later, Daddy. Got to spruce up a bit.' This was aimed at her mother who had followed Hubert in with a duster in her hand. She didn't need to dust. They had a cleaning girl come in twice a week. But Peg was always complaining that she missed what was in front of her and never went behind anything.

'Heavy week, was it?' Hubert looked down at the slumped figure of his daughter.

'Rather, Daddy. It was the endless typing. Those keys are awfully difficult to push down. You have to hammer them. It makes the arms hurt.' She was sounding sorry for herself. 'And look at my fingers!' She held up her hands in a dramatic flourish. 'The tips are black and blue!'

'Well I've got a suggestion that'll take your mind off it,' Hubert said with a grin. 'Why don't we all go to the pictures tonight?'

Lily perked up. 'That'll be lovely, Daddy. What's on?' He picked up the local newspaper that lay on the table and leafed through it.

'Let's see? At the Studio they are showing "The Adventures of Robin Hood". That's got Errol Flynn. Lots of dashing around. It's in colour too.'

'Who's Maid Marian?' asked Lily knowledgeably. Hubert studied the advertisement in front of him.

'I suppose it's Olivia De Havilland.'

'She's a bit soppy,' said Lily. Peg wasn't sure about this choice.

'What's on at the County?' she asked.

'"Bringing Up Baby". I think it's a comedy. Something about a baby leopard, it says here.'

'Who are the stars?' asked Lily.

'Cary Grant and Katharine Hepburn.'

'Then it is a comedy,' said Lily, again displaying her knowledge of the film world, gleaned from the gossip magazines she had read at school. 'Is it in colour?'

'No, I don't think so,' said Hubert.

'Then it's got to be Robin Hood,' said Peg. 'A bit of colour will be good for us. Anyway the County's a flea pit. The projector's always breaking down.'

Hubert didn't tell them but he also had another reason for wanting to go. It was likely that the Newsreel would be showing pictures of Chamberlain at Munich. These days the news films were almost as popular as the main feature.

And he was right. With Harris still away, he drove the car into Bletchley and, after he had parked it and the family had walked around to the front of the cinema, they found a large queue emerging from the theatre foyer. Saturday night was always busy but tonight seemed especially crowded. The cinema ran continuous performances during the day but had a break for the evening audience.

The Studio was a new cinema. It had only opened two years before and its red bricks still felt as if they had just been laid. It was a single storey building and looked from the outside like the gatehouse of a castle. All seating in the auditorium was on one level. Hubert paid a shilling each for the tickets which were the most expensive in the house and gave the three of them an uninterrupted view of the screen. They just managed to find seats together and sank into their plush red unworn upholstery. The large proscenium curtains were still closed and Lily sat staring at them with the eager anticipation she always felt at the start of a film show. But it was only minutes before the lights went down and the large screen was revealed.

Lily was soon lost in the flickering images in front of her. Over her head the projector beam danced in a rising cloud of tobacco smoke. She smelled the sickly-sweet aroma of her father's pipe as he sat contentedly puffing and watching the advertisements being shown on the screen. Then came the cartoon. She smiled at the sadistic antics of Tom and Jerry as they dealt ever more devious humiliations on each other. But what made her sit up along with most of the audience was the screeching cock announcing the arrival of Pathé News. The headline title proclaimed: 'Peace In Our Time'. She was all attention as she gazed at the scene unfolding before her. There was the Prime Minister on the tarmac at Hendon Airport waving a piece of paper to an applauding crowd.

'See that plane behind him,' whispered Hubert in Lily's ear,' that's the Lockheed Electra. Not been flown before. Made of aluminium.' She bowed to her father's technical knowledge and cast an admiring glance at the shiny surface of the plane, before quickly returning to Chamberlain, the man who had brought peace.

The pictures then flashed back to the previous day when Chamberlain met Hitler. They showed

Chamberlain arriving at Munich airport and driving through the centre of the city. Lily clapped with excitement.

'Sally and I were there,' she said in a voice that was audible to all around. 'That's where we saw Herr Hitler. And look that shop …. that's where I bought my hat.' Hubert patted her arm, hoping to lower her voice. 'Isn't it exciting, Daddy?'

There was an irate voice from behind. 'Can you keep quiet, miss!' Lily put her hand to her mouth and gave a complicit grin. She said no more but watched in rapt silence as the film showed Chamberlain meeting Hitler in his apartment in the Prinzregentenplatz. The two were sat on comfortable sofas around the fireplace of the modestly furnished room. The film then cut to Chamberlain outside No 10 Downing Street and recorded what he had to say.

'My good friends.' There was a deep hush in the auditorium, the silence only broken by the muffled clatter of the projector. 'For the second time in our history, a British Prime Minister has returned from Germany bringing peace with honour. I believe it is peace for our time.' Lily thought how tired he looked. She wondered whether he was close to crying. 'We thank you,' he went on, 'from the bottom of our hearts. Go home and get a nice quiet sleep.' There was a loud roar and the rest of the newsreel went unwatched as people clapped, shook each other's hands and generally expressed relief at what they heard.

After this euphoria, the rest of the evening was an anti-climax to many in the cinema. But Lily sat back and let the ensuing derring-do sweep over her. She gripped the arms of the seat as Errol Flynn, brightly costumed in Lincoln green, fought his way through countless arboreal perils. In the climactic scene, when he clashed swords with Basil Rathbone on the spiral staircase of the great castle, it was not Errol Flynn she was looking at, but Friedrich. And when Robin Hood kissed his Maid Marian at the end, it was she and Friedrich embracing each other on the screen.

The lights came up to a stream of excited chatter.

'Great stuff, old girl,' said Hubert his eyes twinkling with pleasure.

The three of them turned to go when Lily noticed that a man in front of her was looking in her direction. He had not been there when they arrived, she was sure of that. He must have slipped in after the film had started. She recognised him. It was the man in the pub, the one the barman called Reg. He fixed her with an unblinking stare. She ignored him and followed her parents out. But he had unnerved her enough to have her look behind several times on the way back to the car.

20

But the optimism of Munich was short lived. People soon began to feel peace was slipping from their grasp. The situation in Europe far from improving got worse. Sally and Lily stood dejected as one of the other girls in the typing pool showed those around her a report from the front page of that day's newspaper. It was a description of what was to become known as Kristallnacht, Since September they had been hearing many stories of unrest in Germany. It was now November and this was by far the worst incident. The girl read out the headlines: 'Looting mobs defy Goebbels. Jewish homes fired, women beaten.'

'Bloody animals,' said one of the group.

'That Hitler's not fit to run a country,' said another.

'They're little better than gangsters,' said a third.

'They have to be stopped.' It was Yakova who had come up to find out what the huddle was about. She saw the two-inch high headlines blazing out at her, and the photograph of a burning building. 'They have done terrible things in my country. Now they are doing even more horrible things in their own country. They are evil. They are the devil.' There was a murmur of agreement. Lily wanted to say something, but she now held her counsel. The mood of her typing companions, and many others she had met recently, would not have allowed them to listen kindly to anything favourable she might say about Germany. She must now wait for Friedrich, to get him to tell her what was really going on. Sally looked at her friend wary of anything she might say and ready to pounce if she saw her lip so much as quiver. Lil, who had also joined the group, watched Lily with equal concern.

'You'll get yourself roughed up if you start blabbing where you've been,' she warned Lily later when they were at lunch.

'Yes, I know,' said Lily sadly. 'It's all so awful.'

'You've just got to forget the place, love,' said Lil kindly. 'I know they can't be all bad, but my Dad says they did vote that Hitler into power.'

'How does he know?'

'Well, he talks to people at work, see. Tell you what, love, why don't you come and have tea with us? It's Saturday tomorrow.' Lily said she would like that and asked whether Sally, who was still at the servery, could also come.

''Corse.'

So it was arranged and the two girls took the train into Bedford and a bus to the area where Lil lived. It was a jumble of red brick terraced houses, most of them facing straight onto the street, all well looked after, but worn down with age. Having asked several people, they finally located Lil's house. Lily banged the polished knocker on the brown painted door. It opened to reveal a round red faced woman looking exactly like an older copy of Lil.

'You must be Lil's friends. Welcome to Black Tom.' Not only did she look like Lil, she sounded like her too. She smiled in a friendly way and ushered them inside shouting as she did so.

'Lil, your friends from the typing school are here. We're in the parlour.' Mrs Bates turned to the two girls. 'Let me take your coats, love.' Lily eased herself out of the belted coat she was wearing while taking in every detail of the room she was in. It was small, neat and sparsely furnished. There was a rather battered dresser against the back wall with china ornaments, mainly of animals, behind the glass doors. A table with a green fringed cloth sat in the middle with four plain wooden chairs. In the window and along another wall four armchairs were neatly arranged each with what looked like hand crocheted cushions.

There was a crash at the door and Lil burst in arranging her dress.

'Sorry,' she said breathlessly, 'been having forty winks. Dad's not here. Back shortly. We can have some tea, can't we Mum?' Mrs Bates went out and Lily heard her clattering around next door. She had wondered why everything was crowded into one room. It was, she now realised, the only room. The other was the kitchen.

'Sit down, loves. Take the comfy chairs. You found us all right?' Lil yawned, her sleepiness still with her.

'What is Black Tom?' asked Sally.

Lil gave one of her hoarse laughs. 'It's what we call this place. Black Tom's an old highwayman what was hanged hereabouts. They say his ghost prowls around at night. I've never seen him although Ag says she has. But she was in 'er cups at the time.'

Mrs Bates returned carrying a wooden tray with a china tea pot, cups and saucers, a milk jug and a plate with a slice of Madeira sponge cake on it, which she placed on the table. Lily spotted chips on the rim of two of the cups and the spout of the tea pot had an ugly brown stain down its length. Before she could pour Mrs Bates' attention was drawn to the front door. Her husband had arrived back home.

Len Bates was a swarthy faced man, with dark curly hair. His short stature combined with the muscle-bound look of one accustomed to hard physical labour made him seem as if he were hewn from a single block of stone. Like so many men Lily had observed recently, his clothes betrayed the red stain of brick dust, even though today was his day off. He removed his cap and overcoat, hung them on a peg in the small entrance hall and came into the parlour with a welcoming smile on his face.

'So these are the young ladies you been working with Lil? he said sitting down on a chair at the table. Lil introduced them.

'Pleased to meet you, lassies. Lil here says you been helping her with the typing.'

'Just the theory, Mr Bates. Lil's good with the keys,' said Sally, anxious for them not to think they were being over helpful.

'Did she tell you she wants to come and work in the office at the brick works?'

'Yes.'

'Skivvying in a snotty hotel's no place for my daughter,' he said decidedly.

Mrs Bates momentarily stopped the conversation while she served tea to everyone. Lily tucked into the Madeira cake.

'Did you make this?' she asked brightly.

'Yes, I made it, dear,' said Mrs Bates pleasantly.

'It's jolly scrumptious,' said Lily her boundless enthusiasm knowing no irony. But Sally saw the looks on the faces of the others.

'Did the meeting go well, Dad?' asked Lil quickly.

'Well attended, yes, but the revolution is not coming tomorrow with this war hanging over our heads.' Sally picked up on the word 'revolution', which passed Lily by, but said nothing. She realised the family were probably the lefties their fathers had talked about who wanted what they called a socialist revolution. She wondered what the meeting was about, but she didn't think she should ask

'Do you think there will be war, Mr Bates?' spluttered Lily through the cake crumbs in her mouth.

'If this maniac carries on the way he is, no question of it.'

'What do the men think of it?' asked Lil.

'They're gloomy. It'll be the draft for them. Won't be no jobs.'

'Why's that, dear?' asked Mrs Bates, 'I would have thought bricks would be needed.'

'House building will stop. Got better things to do than be putting up houses in wartime. Brick making won't be a reserved occupation. It'll be the army for them.'

'Is brick making hard, Mr Bates?' asked Sally, anxious to get the talk away from war, which was only going to upset Lily.

'It is. You got to dig out the clay, press it and then cut it into bricks, which you shovel into huge furnaces where the temperature is as hot as the earth's core. Then when the bricks is cooled they have to be heaved out of the ovens and put on lorries. But it's good work. The boss is better than most.' He turned to Lily. 'I hear your dad's a boss, Lily? That right?'

'He owns a sawmill.'

'Well, he'll lose the lads.'

'Perhaps it won't come to that.'

'Lil says you saw him when you were over in Germany.'

'You mean Herr Hitler?' asked Lily. Sally groaned - more questions.

'Yes, what's he like?'

'We saw him when he was in Munich. He was going on holiday.' Len looked disbelieving. 'People cheered him. I think he smiled at us. He seemed very pleasant.'

'He doesn't seem very pleasant when he's ranting away with all those crowds,' said Mrs Bates with a sense of disgust in her voice.

'But he's not ranting all the time,' protested Lily. 'He seemed very relaxed when he met Mr Chamberlain.' Sally noticed the time on the clock that sat above the dresser. An hour had passed and she decided now was a good time to leave.

'Can I spend a penny, Mrs Bates?' asked Lily suddenly.

'Of course, dear. Lil'll show you where to go. It's in the back yard.' The two girls went out and moments later Lil returned.

'Thank you very much for the lovely tea, Mrs Bates,' said Sally getting out of her chair.

'That's a pleasure, dear. Anyone who helps our Lil is a friend.'

'She's a bit wrapped up in him, your Lily,' said Len sharply.

'She can seem like that sometimes. She has a friend she's fond of in Germany, so I suppose she wants to see the best.' The moment Sally said this, she regretted it. Neither had spoken to anyone about Friedrich, now without thinking she had betrayed Lily.

'Please keep this to yourself,' she said limply, knowing she was having to trust people she didn't really know.

'Lucky her. Either way she'll be all right.' Lil spoke with a heavy sarcasm in her voice Sally had not heard since they first met.

Lily returned. They collected their coats, said their good-byes and made their way back to the railway station.

'Do you know,' said Lily when they were out of earshot of the house, 'their lavatory is outside. It has no running water and you pee into a bucket with ash in it. It's a bit smelly.'

'Not everyone lives like us.'

'I suppose.'

'You can see why Lil wants to better herself.'

'What was that about revolution?' asked Lily as they got within sight of the bus stop.

'You did notice. I think Mr Bates is a lefty.'

'A communist?'

'Perhaps. A socialist at least. I think that was a trade union meeting he had come from. They can't meet at work, so they meet in pubs and places.' Sally's understanding of politics was much more developed than Lily's, yet the last weeks had caused her to doubt

134

that she really knew what was going on. Lily was impressed, nonetheless.

They didn't have long to wait for the bus. They climbed to the top deck where they were the only passengers.

'Lily, I've got a confession to make.' Her friend looked at her and wondered what she was going to say. 'When you were outside, they asked me again about Germany and I told them about Friedrich. I'm sorry, Lily.'

Lily looked at her feet while she tossed about in her head what Sally had said. 'I don't care,' she said finally. 'I want people to know about Friedrich. I want to shout about him to the heavens and to hell with what people think. We shouldn't have got into this silly war anyway.' The strength of her feelings betrayed in this outburst alarmed Sally and she felt she had to do everything she could to protect her friend from herself.

The bus pulled in at the station. They could see the train waiting for them. As Lily climbed down the stairs, she recalled the words Len Bates had said to them when they left. 'There will be war, mark my words.'

21

Len Bates was right. On March 15th Hitler's troops marched into Czechoslovakia. Two weeks later Chamberlain gave assurances that Britain would defend Poland if Hitler attempted to invade that country. Britain and Germany seemed on a collision course. Yet history would record that in the first months of 1939 more Germans visited Britain than at any time during the decade. Among them was a tall blonde boy in shorts and short sleeved shirt walking his bicycle heavily laden with bulging panniers off the Harwich ferry on a hot June day. The rucksack he wore on his back and the other bags on the bicycle were thoroughly searched by the customs officers, but they found no Nazi regalia, nothing to incriminate or link him with the regime. He was free to embark on his touring holiday of England.

His first objective on clearing the port area was to find a telephone box. He parked his bicycle beside some railings and pulled open the heavy door of the bright red box. He had in his hand a scrap of paper on which he had written instructions on how to use a

British public telephone. First he counted out the correct money. It was the amount he was told was needed for a long distant call. He put coins one by one into the slot and as instructed picked up the receiver. A female voice asked him for the number he wanted to call.

'Bletchley 428,' he said.

'One moment please.' There was a pause. He heard distant noises as connections were made.

'Push Button A,' instructed the operator finally. He looked around him and saw a round steel projection with a large letter A beside it. He gave it a firm push and heard the loud clatter of the coins dropping down.

'You're through, caller.'

It was Peg who picked up the phone. Lily was out doing some shopping and Hubert was at the sawmill.

'Hello,' she repeated, trying to catch the barely audible voice at the other end. 'Who? I can't hear very well. Can you speak up?' She continued to struggle but eventually grasped who it was.

'Friedrich,' she said delightedly, 'how wonderful to hear you. Where are you dear? Harwich? Well that's not far away……. We'll be seeing you soon then ….?'

'Four days!' Lily was beside herself with anger. When she got in laden with groceries, her mother said she had just missed Friedrich.

'Where is he?' She dropped the bag she was carrying with a loud thump and pushed her mother onto the sofa. She sat down beside her ready to hear Peg say that Friedrich would be coming down the drive any minute.

'He's in Harwich. It was a bad line but I think he said he wanted to tour around on his bicycle before he came to Bletchley.'

'He can do all his touring when he gets here,' said Lily sounding irritated. 'How long will he be?' When Peg told her, she exploded.

'How can he take so long?' He's only here for a week. He has to report to his barracks by the end of June.' She couldn't understand it. For the first time in their relationship she felt angry and betrayed. If he really loved her, he would come straight to her. Did he love her?

'How can he be so cruel?' She tore herself from the sofa and swept upstairs to bury herself in her still unmade bed. Peg looked on bemused. After half an hour of silence from her daughter, she went up to see what was going on. Lily, as she knew, was nothing if not mercurial and she found her, not as she expected lying with her face in the pillows but sat up in bed reading a book.

'Four days will soon go by,' she said resignedly as her mother came in.

'He seemed such a nice boy. So polite,' said Peg.

'You will like him, Mummy.'

'I'm sure I will.' She stood over her daughter. 'Come on, let's make this bed.' Together they pulled the sheets, puffed the pillows and tidied the eider-down.

Lily counted the days. They didn't go as quickly as she expected. Now that her first year at typing school was over, she had nothing to do, except the odd errand to the shops. Sally had gone off on holiday with her parents. 'A few days,' she said, 'twiddling my thumbs in Felixstowe.' Well, said Lily to herself, she was twiddling her thumbs in Bletchley. Time dragged. Even helping Harris in the garden had no effect. But at least being outside in the warm sunshine was pleasant.

'We should be digging more of this up to grow vegetables,' the chauffeur said as he tended the roses, with Lily weeding nearby. 'If that Hitler of yours has his way he'll try and starve us for sure.'

'You still think it will come to war?' Her trowel wrestled with a particularly obstinate clump of grass.

'No doubt about it,' he growled. 'It's just a matter of time.' He clipped the dead heads off a rose. 'You got your gas mask yet?'

'Yes. The ARP warden delivered them last week.' She giggled. 'Sally and I tried them on. They aren't very nice to wear. The rubber kept clinging to our faces. They are very tight and difficult to breathe in.'

'That's the point,' said Harris, 'it keeps the gas out being tight. The gas gets filtered through that bit in the front.'

'Any way it made me feel woosy.'

'You'll be pleased you got it when they start chucking gas bombs at us.'

'Sally said we looked like Martians.'

'Better live Martians than dead ducks,' said Harris gloomily, moving to another rose. When he had finished, he stood up full height and stretched, surveying his domain.

'Them gates at the end of the drive.'

'What about them?'

'They'll be wanting them for scrap. Build Spitfires. Country needs all the metal it can get.'

'That would be a shame,' said Lily, 'but if it has to happen ….' She let the words hang in the air, stung by what Harris said next.

'Your fellow from Germany still coming, is he?' She stopped what she was doing and looked at him strangely.

'How'd you know? Who told you?' she asked sharply.

He spluttered and cut off three dead roses before he answered. 'Your mother I think.' She didn't believe him. He'd been snooping she felt sure. She would check with her mother later.

'Can you keep it to yourself, please. There's no law to stop him coming, but we don't want to advertise it.'

'You're right, miss. Mum's the word.'

'I think I've finished now. I'm going indoors.' She instinctively felt she wanted to get away from Harris as quickly as possible. He made a cursory flick of his hand to his forelock and carried on with the roses.

'No dear, I never told him,' said Peg, when Lily questioned her. 'I expect he overheard us talking at some time. As you know he has to come in to see Hubert about arrangements.

'Well, I think we should be careful what we say about Friedrich.'

It remained sunny into the afternoon and Lily took a book and went to her favourite spot in the garden, a leafy arbour where Hubert had slung a wicker seat. She curled up on it and opened the book. It was a German romance which she had brought back with her. But she had hardly read the first paragraph before confused thoughts flooded into her head. She wasn't clear where her life was going. Can you love, she asked herself, a person for themselves and ignore the time and place in which they live? Has she been living in a fool's paradise all along? She loved being in Munich. She had such a happy time and she did love Friedrich. But she and Sally saw things that they both felt uncomfortable with and could they really brush them under the carpet? Sally had done her best to open her eyes, but she refused to see, preferring, for Friedrich's sake, to believe the best about his country. Now back in England, those niggling doubts, barely perceptible at first, had grown and besieged her. Arrows had been shot at her by person after person trying to make her see sense. Harris, Miss Meadows, Lil and her dad, Yakova - each in their way had pierced her certainty.

She looked down at the German text in front of her but saw none of the words she had been reading. Her mind was in a turmoil. The sheltered life she led had left her unprepared to cope with cruelty, but the encounter with the Hartmanns on the journey home she found very unsettling. They seemed such ordinary people who could do no harm to anyone, yet they had been cruelly treated. To have had their business, their house, all their possessions taken from them just for being Jewish upset her terribly. She looked through the foliage of the arbour and saw the red brick walls of Fenny Way burning in the sunshine. Birds sang, insects buzzed, there was even a gentle breeze in the leaves. How would she feel if she were told to leave all this? If someone came one day and told her and her parents they no longer belonged here? And only be allowed to take two suitcases? She wondered what she would put in hers. She couldn't think how a lifetime, even a short one like hers, could be packed into two small boxes.

What does Daddy say about all this? He had taught her that being strong and firm was the way forward. But he had been much quieter about affairs in the country in the last few months. Was he as confused as she was? When he got home she would ask him.

'Damned if I know, old girl. Thought that Moseley fellow would show us the way, but he's turned out to be nothing but a street agitator.' Hubert tucked into his supper and took a few moments to answer Lily's question. 'Best to lie low and see how the wind blows.'

'But if war breaks out, how can we support two countries?' asked Lily, sensing she was not going to get a clear answer.

'Can't. I continue to run the mill, you get a job, Peg keeps the house going. As I say, we lie low.'

'Does that mean we abandon any support for Herr Hitler?'

'I don't think it would be advisable to talk about him at the moment,' said Peg who had been silent until now. 'It is best if you keep your views to yourself.'

'But I can't abandon Friedrich.'

'No, dear, but keep him to yourself.' How do you keep the person you love to yourself? She saw the conversation was going in circles. The simple truth was that her parents were caught in a vice of their own making. Their support for Germany and the new Reich could only be resolved in one way. They would have to move to Germany and that they would not do, even if they could manage it. It was, realised Lily, all bluster and make believe. At the end of the day they were English and they would stay English. They had sent her to Germany to learn the language and she had come back having fallen in love with the country and a German man. Her parents had only seen the fantasy. She was stuck on the spike of reality, hung out to dry, with no-where to go except reject the man she loved. All this flashed through her mind like a thunder bolt. She looked at her parents and in that moment hated them for what they had done to her. For all their protestations of support and endearment she knew she was now on her own

22

Friedrich arrived a day earlier than expected. The summer sunshine continued and Lily was with Harris in the garden, when she heard the squeak of the gates and saw a tall figure push himself diffidently around the crack he had made between the panels. A bicycle followed him. When she saw who it was she threw down the trowel she was holding, ripped off her gardening gloves and flew down the gravel drive.

'Friedrich, you have come,' she shouted excitedly. She ran to him and would have fallen into his arms except he never let go of the bicycle.

'Lily, I come early,' he said. 'It is all right, no?'

'Of course, Friedrich. And put that bicycle down.' He did as bidden, laying the machine gingerly on the grass beside the gravel. Now, she thought, there was no excuse for him not to kiss her, but he still held back, his eyes going beyond her to the figure of Harris standing four-square at the end of the drive, watching them with a scowl on his face. Lily looked over her shoulder.

'Ignore him,' she said. She was several inches shorter than he was and, as he was making no effort to bend to her level, she strained upward and brought her lips to his. He smelt sweaty from his exertions but she didn't care. The pent-up emotions of the last weeks boiled up inside her and burst forth like an exploding geyser. She grabbed him hungrily and sunk her lips into his.

'I've missed you,' she said huskily. He started to uncoil and his arms seized her in a tightening clinch.

'I miss you too, Lily.'

'Careful, Friedrich, you're squeezing the air out of me.'

He let go. 'Sorry,' he said bashfully.

'Come, you must meet Mummy. She's in the house.' She gave a broad smile as she watched him pick up his bicycle. He had bulked out and his face seemed more care worn and tanned. Lily took his hand and they walked slowly up to the house.

Peg made an immediate fuss of her visitor. She feasted him on coffee and cake and told him to sit in the most comfortable chair, despite his shirt showing damp stains of sweat and his bare legs touching the fabric. Something Lily observed she would never have been allowed to do.

'Have you been to England before?' asked Peg perching herself beside him.

'Yes, I come with comrades.'

'That's how we met, Mummy. On the train. He was with other scouts. Although,' she said hastily with a conspiratorial wink at Friedrich, 'I mustn't call them scouts.'

'Of course,' said Peg, caught in a fluster. 'I remember. Silly me.'

'Your country …. it is very, how you say it? ….. green,' said Friedrich missing Peg's embarrassment.

'Yes, but now June is here it will start to turn brown. More cake?' Friedrich was still finishing his first piece, but nodded politely. Peg cut a great slice from the triple decked chocolate confection that sat on the plate in front of her. Lily was aghast at its size. Her mother must have purchased it in secret. It was as sumptuous as anything she had eaten in Bavaria.

Peg smiled to see it pleased her guest. She turned to her daughter.

'Lily, is Harris around?'

'I think he is finishing in the garden.'

'Fetch him will you dear and ask him to take Friedrich's bags to his room.' Lily assented but knew the chauffeur would not be pleased. She found Harris in the tool shed, tidying up before going home for his lunch. He lived alone in a small cottage two miles away.

'My mother has asked if you would carry Friedrich's bags up to his room before you leave.' She spoke with as much courtesy as she could muster. Harris grunted, but did not dissent. When he must have thought he was out of earshot she heard him mutter under his breath 'fucking kraut'. In the society she inhabited it was language she rarely heard and she wanted to tackle Harris, but thought the better of it and merely stood and watched him go.

'Harris seems out of sorts today,' said Hubert when he got in from work. 'Heat got to him?' He was removing his jacket when he saw Lily grinning like a Cheshire cat.

'Come and see who's here, Daddy,' she said. He didn't have to guess and walked straight into the lounge to find Friedrich sat on the sofa in earnest conversation with his wife. The moment the young German saw him, he leapt to his feet and stood upright clicking his heels. He had bathed and now wore a clean shirt and trousers.

'Herr Rood, it is a great pleasure to meet you.' Hubert was bowled over by the formality but greatly flattered. Here was the clean-cut young man he had always envisaged for his daughter and confirmed him in his opinion that German youth were receiving a proper upbringing.

'Lily has told us much about you, Friedrich. I want to thank you for looking after her in Munich.'

'It was an honour, sir,' he said still standing to attention.

'Sit down and tell me about your journey. Did you have any problems getting here?' If he had he didn't say, but once again enthused about the greenness of the countryside.

'Which we must explore tomorrow,' said Lily excitedly. 'We will go for a great bike ride and I will show you all our lovely lanes and by-ways. It will be such super fun. Can we do that, Daddy?'

'That I do want,' agreed Friedrich.

'I think that would be all right, eh Peg?'

'As long as you take care, Lily,' said the ever cautious Peg.

The two young people grinned at each other and then sat politely batting the questions that came at them as if they were on a tennis court. Lily felt warm inside and was quietly amused to see her parents vie with each other to make a fuss of Friedrich.

Hubert wanted to know every detail about life in Germany. His insistent questions got Friedrich's halting English tied in knots and he often beseeched Lily to help him out. In the end Peg took pity and intervened.

'Enough Hubert, give the boy a rest. It is time you went and cleaned up before supper.'

'Sorry, Friedrich, rather got carried away. You and Lily go and have a walk in the garden.'

'Your parents like me, no?' said Friedrich as they reached the furthest point of the acre of land that was attached to Fenny Way.

'Yes, they do.' She held his hand and they looked back to the house barely visible through the shrubbery. 'But I'm sorry for the endless questions from Daddy. He is such an admirer of Germany and all that you have achieved. It's like when the food's good. You want to savour every morsel.' He looked confused. Lily tried to translate, but her efforts were so pathetic that the two of them collapsed in laughter.

'But tomorrow, we will escape their clutches. Come, Friedrich, supper awaits.' She yanked him forward and together they ran through the garden in high spirits.

Peg had cooked a celebratory meal of pork chops in a béarnaise sauce with duchess potatoes and minted peas. Hubert offered Lily and Friedrich bottles of his best ale.

'Lily tells me you drink a lot of beer,' he winked as he snapped the serrated top off with a bottle opener.

'In the summer we have many beer gardens,' said Friedrich.

'Sounds my sort of place.'

'You drink too much beer, Hubert. You don't need encouragement,' said Peg jokingly.

Hubert ignored this and raised his glass.

'A toast to peace.'

The others raised their glasses.

'Prost,' said Lily, and smiled at Friedrich, 'to peace between our countries.'

'Yes, we live together, well.'

'I hope so,' said Peg, 'now tuck in, Friedrich.' He looked at her questioningly.

'A funny English expression, 'explained Lily. 'It means enjoy your food.'

He laughed. 'Ja, I will.'

Conversation stopped as the four of them 'tucked into' Peg's cooking. Friedrich savoured the pork chop and looked appreciatively at Peg.

'Is good,' he said with a civility that enforced Peg's already confirmed view of him being a very upright young man.

'Lily tells me you're joining the army,' said Hubert spearing some peas.

'Hubert,' scolded Peg, 'Friedrich doesn't want to be reminded of that while he is on holiday. It will come all too soon.'

'The boy's proud of it I'm sure,' replied Hubert, not to be deflected.

'Yes, it is honour for me,' said Friedrich, 'I join soon to serve the Fatherland.'

'Good boy. Let's hope it doesn't make us enemies.'

'Daddy, that's not funny.'

'Only joking, old girl.' Friedrich laughed again. He'd been told about English humour, always meaning the opposite of what was said.

'So where do you think you will be going tomorrow, Lily?' asked Peg changing the subject.

'Oh, just around the lanes, like we did in Munich.'

The evening passed pleasantly, Lily and Friedrich pleased that Friedrich had hit it off so well with her parents. Hubert described his life at the sawmill and explained proudly how it had been failing when he had bought it and that he had built it up into an expanding and thriving enterprise.

'And your parents, Friedrich, what do they do?' he asked in turn.

'My mother, she is in the office of the Party. She does what Miss Lily is learning.'

'Just Lily, Friedrich. You do not need to say Miss.' This formality might seduce her parents but Lily was beginning to find it a little wearing. 'So, she is a typist?' Her words came out harder than she intended, but she didn't think he noticed.

'Yes.'

'Your father?' Hubert felt he was on a roll and kept the questions coming.

'He is - how you say it - employed in a printing works in Munich. He does also work for the Party. He had a letter from Herr Goebbels praising papers he made.' Hearing the name of the notorious Nazi leader, Joseph Goebbels, the Reich Minister for Propaganda, introduced so matter-of-factly into the conversation gave Peg a cold shiver. Hubert on the other hand enjoyed the frisson of this unexpected contact with someone he had read so much about, while Lily wasn't sure who Goebbels was.

'He writes the speeches for Herr Hitler and controls what is written about the government,' explained Hubert.

'He is an important person, then,' said Lily. 'Your father must be very proud, Friedrich.' The clock struck ten o'clock and before Friedrich could reply, Peg stepped in.

'If you two young ones are going to be racing around the country tomorrow, you had better get an early night. Friedrich, would you like to go up first?' She gave no opportunity for Lily to accompany him. He stood up at once, clicked to attention, thanked them again for allowing him to stay and bade them all goodnight.

'What a polite young man,' said Peg again after he was out of earshot.

'I knew you would like him, Mummy,' she said. 'I'll go up now.'

'Wait a minute Lily.' Peg waved her down as she was half-way out of her seat. She fixed her with a steady look. 'We do like him, very much,' she said earnestly, 'but, remember, we may soon be at war and he will be your enemy. You mustn't get too close to each other. At least until we see what is going to happen.'

'But I thought you wanted me to find a German friend. You've always said how much you admire the German way of life.'

'We do, old girl,' said Hubert, reaching for his pipe. 'All a bit tricky at the moment, though.'

'Come on Lily, let's go to bed.' Peg held out her hand to her daughter, who demonstrably refused it. She gave her father a kiss and then followed her mother upstairs. If she had the thought of going into Friedrich's room, Peg's transparent chaperoning tactics forestalled any hope of that. She stood on the landing until Lily had come out of the bathroom and gone into her room. She hovered for several minutes within earshot until she was certain her daughter wasn't going to slip out and then went back to join her husband.

Lily refused to let her parents' caveats get between herself and Friedrich. After she had undressed, brushed her teeth and slipped into her nightdress, she sat at the dressing table and let her mind drift over all the things she was going to do tomorrow. In the same dreamy state, she climbed into bed, wrapped the sheet around her and switched off the light. She lay there in the warm evening darkness and let her body relax in the delicious knowledge that the boy she loved was only two doors away. Was he lying there with the same feelings for her, she wondered? She wanted to call out, to holler at the top of her voice. Her hands brushed across her breasts. Her body tingled. She heard the floorboards creak on the landing. Friedrich? Alas it was her mother followed moments later by her father. Sadly she knew Friedrich was too correct to come searching for her.

23

The next day dawned bright and clear. Lily was up with the lark and rushed to the window with the hope of seeing Friedrich already in the garden. Her expectations that his German fitness regime would have had him indulging in early morning press ups were dashed by his clear absence from view. She did her own stretching and breathed in the heady perfume from the many flower beds that were coming into bloom. She expected the bathroom to be occupied, but it was free and she quickly did her ablutions, before racing back to the bedroom to find her cycling clothes. She put on an aertex shirt, stepped into white shorts and fished out from a tangle of clothes squashed into a drawer a suitable woollen V neck sweater which she flung over her shoulders. Thus attired she went out into the hall and stood for a moment. There was movement in the kitchen. Her mother was already up and cooking breakfast. Otherwise all was strangely quiet.

Then the devil caught her. She seized the handle on the door of Friedrich's room, turned it and burst in.

Her boyfriend was lying prone on the bed, fast asleep, but to Lily's horror above the bedclothes and in the buff. She stared at the naked body that had lost its gangly boyishness. Her eyes roamed over the developed shoulder muscles, the well-turned buttocks and tree like thighs. She stood transfixed. Then a smell of bacon jolted her back to reality and she hastily retreated before she was seen, tip toeing into the hall as quietly as she could, closing the door behind her.

She then gave it a loud bang. 'Wake up sleepy head. Breakfast is ready.' She rattled the handle and then walked down the stairs, Friedrich's nakedness looming like an apparition in front of her.

'Sleep well dear?' asked her mother, tidily dressed in a wrap-around apron, busily cracking eggs into a frying pan.

'Very,' lied Lily, who had spent a large part of the night tossing and turning and dreaming of today. 'Daddy not down?'

'Says he wants to see you off.'

'We're only going for a bike ride, Mummy.'

'I think it's an excuse to see a bit more of Friedrich. Where is he by the way?' The eggs hissed and spattered in the pan.

'Isn't he down yet?' asked Lily with feigned surprise. She picked up the bread knife and started cutting slices for toast. 'I thought he would be out in the garden by now.'

'I think, Lily dear, he's still in bed. Don't you think you should rouse him?'

'Oh, he'll be down,' said Lily innocently. Her mother gave her an askance look. They were interrupted by a noise of a door opening upstairs and the figure of Friedrich, now modestly towelled, crossing to the bathroom, followed seconds later by Hubert fully dressed descending the stairs.

'Won't be able to do that in the army,' he puffed, entering the kitchen and poking around.

'What, Daddy?'

'Lie in.'

'But it's not eight o'clock yet.' Hubert tutted and kissed both of them on the cheek. Moments later Friedrich came bounding down the stairs, flustered and still half dressed, several of his shirt buttons undone and the shirt tails still hanging out of his shorts. Lily felt embarrassed that he was not presenting the image of the smart young man of the day before. She thought he could have spent a few more minutes tidying himself before he emerged. But neither of her parents noticed or if they did they showed no concern.

'Eggs and bacon, Friedrich?'

'Is good smell. I sleep too long, no? I'm sorry.' He looked crestfallen.

'You needed the rest, Friedrich, after all that touring. Now go and sit down with Lily and have your breakfast.' Peg's words were uncensorious and put Friedrich at his ease.' Despite the bountiful evening meal Lily and Friedrich both felt ravenous and tucked into the fare Peg put before them. She poured cups of tea as they ate.

'Don't forget to pack your raincoats. The forecast says we might get thunderstorms later in the day.'

With a full breakfast inside them, they felt ready for the road. They wasted no time in packing their saddlebags and with the day promising to heat up they brought along several water bottles. Heeding Peg's advice they also packed waterproof capes. But it was the collection of notebooks, maps and pencils that went into Friedrich's basket that made Lily query whether he was taking too much.

'Do you need all those? I know where I am going you know.'

'It is for my notes tonight,' he said disarmingly.

'Well, you're carrying them. Come I'll race you to the road.' As she spoke she had slipped her leg through the frame of the bicycle and had pushed herself off, pedalling furiously to give herself a head start. Friedrich was left behind, politely waving to Peg and Hubert who stood at the front door.

'She is happy, Hubert,' said Peg turning to her husband. I only hope the future isn't going to dash it for her.'

'Damn bad business, I agree.' Hubert had the newspaper in his hand. 'I'm afraid Herr Hitler has his eye on Poland. He wants to join up the bits of Germany that are separated.' He showed Peg the headline as they watched the two young ones disappear.

It took Friedrich a lot of effort to catch up after Lily had wrong footed him, but soon they were freewheeling side by side along deserted summer lanes. The hedgerows were thick with foliage and ablaze with the reds and mauves of wildflowers. Everything was so overgrown that in places the lanes were reduced to a single track. The pair played a dangerous game of cat and mouse racing to overtake each other, hurtling around blind bends while ringing furiously on their bells. They whooped and yelled casting the cares of a violent world to the winds.

Any stiffness between them was rapidly vanishing. On a number of occasions Friedrich held back deliberately to admire the seductive swing of Lily's rear on the saddle. In turn Lily's thoughts returned again and again to her bedroom intrusion.

Their love was turning physical and both desired a tangible contact. At the top of a hill, sweating and gasping, they stopped for water. As she gulped down the reviving liquid, Lily edged her bicycle closer to Friedrich and when she was within touching distance casually bent over and kissed him with her cold wet lips. He backed away like a startled rabbit and then recovered by seizing her around the waist and, while both stood astride their bicycles, he hugged her in a tight embrace.

'I love you, Lily,' he said.

Lily pulled herself away. 'I love you too,' she whispered. 'Come, I'll race you to the bottom of the hill.' Before he could answer she was away and she had swept over the cross-roads and up the opposite hill before she realised he was not behind her. She looked back. Friedrich had stopped. He had a map in his hand and was marking it with a pencil. He had done this at other junctions and it was beginning mildly to irritate her.

'We'll never get anywhere, if you keep stopping,' she shouted. 'Trust me, I know where we are.'

'I know, Lily. It helps my English. I write down these funny names.' When he saw her disapproving look he put the map away. She couldn't understand how writing Furzton helped his English, but her annoyance soon evaporated as he pounded past her and was out of sight before she could remonstrate further. He was now a dot in the distance, but she wasn't going to let him get ahead and pushed herself to catch up. When she finally did so, she found him standing outside a pair of imposing iron gates. She stopped, got off her bike and struck him playfully several times between panting breaths.

'You are a brute to make me pedal so hard.'

'I like to watch you ride,' he said in a way that Lily thought flirtatious. She laughed and the two stood silently staring at the gates and a disappearing drive.

'I'm getting hungry,' she said, when she had recovered her breath. 'Let's find some lunch.'

'Where this does it lead?' he asked. 'A house at the end, no?'

'Yes, Wilfred Park. Mummy and Daddy have been guests there. I went with them once.'

'We see it?'

Lily looked doubtful.

'It's a private house. You can't just go flying up the drive.' His eyes pleaded. 'Oh, come on then.' She turned her bike towards the gates. 'I don't suppose Lord Hervey will mind. He'll probably remember me.'

'I like your big houses. They are so ….?' He struggled for the right word.

'Lived in?' offered Lily.

'Ja, lived in.'

'And threadbare …' Her words trailed behind her as she eased herself around the small opening she had made in the unlocked gate. Her memory of the interior was of furnishings and décor that had seen better days, but it was a fun party that she had attended. She had worn her first grown up dress and Mummy had fixed her hair especially for the occasion.

The drive followed a curving path with large yew trees on either side. These gave out finally to reveal a grand house fronting an ornamental lake. As they emerged within view of the entrance, two figures stepped out into their path. They wore tweed suits, sported wide brimmed hats and held double barrel shotguns, broken in the crook of their arms. Lily slammed on her brakes anxious not to run them down.

'Are you part of Captain Bradley's shooting party?' the taller asked with studied courtesy.

'We've come to see Lord Hervey,' said Lily, improvising quickly, as the second and meaner looking of the two started to give them questioning looks.

'The house has been sold. Lord Hervey does not live here anymore,' said the first.

'And if you are not part of Captain Bradley's party, you're trespassing,' said the other, removing the gun from his arm. 'Please turn around and leave.' His voice had an edge of menace about it.

'We do not wish to stay,' said Friedrich stung by the man's tone.

'You foreign?'

'Dutch,' said Lily, thinking on her feet. 'He is visiting from Holland.' Something about the man's threatening behaviour told her it was wise to lie. She looked over his shoulder towards the house. The men and women standing around the entrance were dressed more like office workers than tweeded sportsmen and looked ill prepared for a scramble through hedgerows. 'We're going,' she said and motioned to Friedrich to follow her along the drive. Neither looked back.

They pedalled furiously to put a healthy distance between themselves and the house. Neither spoke until they had found a country inn, ordered food and drinks and, as the sun was now at its zenith, found a shady table in the garden.

'Your beer is too warm for me,' said Friedrich, 'but I shall like it soon.' Lily sipped her lemonade and laughed.

'Not as warm as I felt back there.'

'I think they shoot birds, no?'

'Perhaps. They seemed a bit odd though. Everyone's so jumpy nowadays.'

A woman arrived with their food. Friedrich had sought Lily's advice about what to order and they both ended up eating meat pies with gravy, potatoes and peas. Friedrich looked curiously at the bottle that was put on the table with the plates.

'Brown sauce,' explained Lily. 'You put it beside the vegetables. But not too much,' she warned as Friedrich was about to let flow a torrent. The exercise had made them ravenous and they quickly demolished the food.

'Is good,' said Friedrich washing the last morsels of pie down with the dregs of his beer. Lily yawned and nearly toppled from the bench on which she sat. They laughed and enjoyed the luxury of each other's company. War seemed a distant prospect.

'Do you think your country will go to war?' asked Friedrich suddenly.

'Daddy hopes not.' She looked him in the eye. 'But Friedrich, I don't think he believes that.' Her face crumpled. 'But it can't happen, can it? War, I mean. Why look at us, how could we fight each other?' She let her hand pass over his.

'It is true,' he said. 'We are great nations and must stay firm together.' He took her hand in his and squeezed it hard.

'Why does your leader want Poland? I saw a headline in Daddy's paper.'

Friedrich took the small notebook that was in his shirt pocket. 'I show you,' he said opening it up to a blank page. He took a pencil and deftly drew a sketch map of Germany and Poland. He then set about explaining the situation as he saw it.

'Our lands are split. Here is Germany and here is Germany. And this is Poland.' He pointed to a corridor of Polish land that separated the two German parts. 'We are divided. It is wrong. Our Führer says we must be given the land back or we will take it.' As Lily examined the scratchy pencil lines she could see how it would make German people aggrieved.

'Perhaps Mr Chamberlain will go back to Germany and sort it out.'

'It would make me happy.' The two sat in silence with their thoughts. Friedrich picked up his notebook and started to sketch. Lily watched people in the garden go about their business and wondered how many of them were feeling afraid. They all looked so normal and untroubled. She looked over to Friedrich.

'What are you drawing?'

'The sign.' He pointed to the inn sign above them. 'The signs of your taverns amuse me.' She looked up. A very large fox loomed over an unwitting hen. It looked ready to pounce. Its red tongue lolled from its mouth in gleeful anticipation. Around the two figures the artist had painted fierce looking brambles adorned with blackberries. Was the sign telling them something, wondered Lily? And why was Friedrich so interested in it? She watched his agile movements shade in the drawing. He was certainly a good artist. She never knew this until now. How little we know of each other, she reflected?

'Lily Rood, what a surprise!' A heavily accented voice made her turn. It was Yakova Marcuson. She stood arm in arm with a dark-haired young man.

'A surprise indeed,' said Lily, unscrambling herself from the bench. 'Friedrich, this is Yakova who is on the typing course with me.'

Friedrich stood up, sharply to attention, giving a firm bow.

'It is an honour to meet Lily's friend.' Yakova reacted awkwardly to hearing another accent.

'Friedrich's from Bavaria', said Lily brightly. 'He's staying with us for a few days.'

'I come from Austria,' said Yakova.

'We are cousins,' laughed Friedrich.

'I don't think so,' replied Yakova, with cold wariness in her voice.

'But yes, our countries are now one,' went on Friedrich earnestly. Yakova had no answer she wanted to make at that moment and she shifted her eyes to Lily and suddenly realised she hadn't introduced her companion. It spared her the embarrassment of having to reply to Friedrich.

'And this is Daniel. We met in Bedford. Daniel is in the navy. He has leave so we have a day out.' Lily and Friedrich shook hands.

'Where did you meet?' asked Yakova.

'In Munich. Last summer,' said Lily gaily. 'Friedrich is joining the army when he returns.'

Daniel had never met a German and here was one on his own soil.

'What is your unit?' He would find out all he could. He had little success as Friedrich didn't know.

'It will be the Waffen SS,' was all Friedrich could say.

'So warst du in der Hitlerjugend?' asked Yakova icily. With Sally not telling Lily about Yakova's past, she was taken aback by the steely tone of her voice, which was obvious to all even though she was speaking in German.

'Ja,' replied Friedrich simply.

'Daniel, we must go or we won't get any food.' She steered his arm towards the inn. 'Good-bye, Lily. See you next term.'

The two watched them go off.

'She not like me,' said Friedrich. 'I think she a Jewess. She hate me'

'Why do you say that darling? She doesn't hate you. She's a dear.'

'I see her eyes. They hate.'

'Come Friedrich, you're imagining it.' Lily took his hand and they walked to where they had left their bicycles.

'And besides, it's rude to go on about it,' she muttered almost to herself as they undid the padlocks. 'Germans don't like Jews and Jews don't like Germans. There's an end to it. Don't let it spoil our day Friedrich.'

'Yes, Lily. I'm sorry.' He swung his leg over the bicycle and pedalled off shouting over his shoulder. 'I ride faster.'

'Oh, no you don't,' she shouted with equal force and raced after him. But the meat pie lay heavily inside her and the thought of riding home on a full stomach proved too much. With great effort she caught up with Friedrich, who chivalrously reduced his pace when she got closer. Taking advantage of his act of gallantry, she shot ahead. Then, without warning, she veered off through an open gate into a field of ripening wheat. She threw down her bicycle and collapsed in the verge that ran between the hedgerow and the waving crop. She lay flat on her back, spread eagled in the long grass, feeling the blades caress her bare legs. She gazed up at the approaching Friedrich, with the quiet satisfaction that she had beaten him here.

'This is heavenly,' she sighed letting her head fall back into the cold sward. She closed her eyes and breathed in the scent of wild flowers and exhaled their heady aroma. She lay there in a magical darkness until she became aware of his presence. She willed herself to keep her eyes shut and await his body coming down beside her. But when she opened her eyes, he was standing astride her, his blonde hair shining against the blue sky, his eyes seemingly feasting on her outstretched body. He hovered uncertain what to do. She gave a smile that could only be described as seductive. Its charm had the desired effect and he dropped to his knees beside her. They lay perfectly still for several minutes, the buzz of insects and a distant lark being the only sounds that interrupted their breathing.

From his horizontal position Friedrich could see the firm flesh of Lily's thighs pushing through the long grass. He felt an unexpected stirring and unable to hold himself back any longer, he rolled over onto Lily and began kissing her. Lily's response was one of alarm. She hadn't expected this and she began to get frightened. She had heard about a man's arousal. Her friends had sniggered about it at school. But she wasn't too certain what it meant. The image of the Greek athlete she had seen in Munich flashed through her mind. A sense of panic gripped her. She struggled under the weight of his body and fought to extricate herself.

'No, Friedrich. Please!' she said, wriggling from under him and scrambling to her feet. 'It's too early. We must wait.' She fixed his crumpled face with an imploring look. She shivered. While they had lain there, the sun had gone behind a thin veil of cloud and a slight chill crept into the air. He had been rejected. She could see that. But she was frightened. She walked away to collect her thoughts, swiping at the flower heads as she went.

Dejected and angry he lay in the grass and watched her disappear. Clouds started to build up, giant cumuli, white and fan shaped at the front but trailing a dark threatening mass behind. He watched them grow fascinated by their evolving formations like an advancing army jostling for position. They were disciplined. For a moment his discipline had slipped. He now regretted it. Lily was right. It was too early. He picked the head of a thistle that hovered above him and deliberately squeezed it in his hand until the prickles punctured his flesh. He must stay in control.

A sudden cry from Lily broke his reverie and he was on his feet running to her.

'I saw all these flies,' she said with some agitation, pointing at the hedge she was standing against. 'Is it alive?' He followed her finger to a small bird huddled in a tuft of grass with a swarm of black flies clinging to its feathers. Friedrich squatted down beside it. He broke off a twig and gently prodded it. The drooping lids opened.

'It's alive,' said Lily with relief.

'It's sick. It cannot support itself,' said Friedrich.

'We could take it home and nurse it?'

'No,' said Friedrich sharply. He stood up and without warning brought the sole of his shoe crushing down on the bird. Lily shrieked. Flies encircled her. In the grass a mess of bone, feather and blood lay where the bird had sat.

'Why did you do that?' she asked, her tremulous words barely audible.

'It would not live. If a creature is weak it is better it does not live.' Lily could not understand what Friedrich was saying. Tears welled up in her eyes. Putting her hand to her face she turned and walked abruptly back to where they had lain their bicycles.

A flash rent the sky followed by a crack of thunder. The storm was almost on them and they had no time to say more. They hurriedly donned their waterproof macs and hoped they could get home before the rains came. But they were out of luck. Within minutes large splashy drops of cold water began to hit their faces, quickly followed by an approaching deluge. The thunder rumbled overhead. Everywhere went dark. An oncoming car nearly ran them over. Any tears Lily had on her face were washed away by the driving rain that was blinding them both.

'We must find shelter,' she shouted. 'It is too dangerous to carry on.' Friedrich nodded in agreement. But it seemed shelter was nowhere to be found and they rode for several minutes until they were rescued by a dark shape looming up in front of them. It was an open hay barn. A gate led to it. Friedrich tried to undo the latch but it was padlocked. They had no choice but to leave their bicycles against a hedge and clamber over. Lily went first and agilely swung her legs across the top bar, which impressed Friedrich. Not to be outdone though, he vaulted over in a single leap.

They went inside. The barn was mostly empty and, apart from a few places where water was pouring in, dry. They looked at each other's bedraggled figure and creased with laughter. Fortunately they had got their waterproofs on in time and when they removed them only a few damp patches showed. But Lily's nicely waved hair now hung in dripping rivulets. They sat down together with their backs against a hay bale and listened to the rain pounding on the tin roof above, sounding, said Friedrich, like a fusillade of continuous rifle fire.

The storm temporarily blotted from Lily's thoughts what Friedrich had done but it began to weigh on her mind again.

'It looked so pathetic,' she said.

'Sometimes we are cruel to be kind. I stop the wretched creature suffering more.' She knew this had been often said to her while she was in Germany, but she found it difficult to accept. He could see she was still upset.

'I'm sorry. This I should not have done in front of you.' She half smiled, but what he had done worried her. They sat together in silence lost in their own thoughts, until the rain stopped, the clouds passed over and the sun emerged flooding the barn with warmth. They felt it on their bare legs, a heartening caress that got them back on their feet. But they had stiffened up and found it difficult to move.

'Gosh, riding in that rain has taken it out of me,' said Lily tentatively trying her limbs. A bit of stretching got them working again. But they were less athletic climbing the gate and Lily had to be pushed over, a task Friedrich was eager to perform. He himself fell across the bars, now too stiff to vault it. They picked up their cycles and rode off.

'We must hurry. It is getting late. Mummy will be worried.'

24

Lily was right. As they rode down the drive, Peg was at the door to welcome them.

'Did you get terribly wet, dear? It was such a frightful thunderstorm,' she said anxiously, as they pedalled up to her. Lily reassured her they were fine and had found shelter.

'You have a visitor, Lily.' A mop of tousled hair emerged from behind her mother.

'Sally!' cried Lily seeing her friend. She threw down her bicycle and ran to greet her.

'Lily, my flowers,' shouted Peg, too late to save the handlebars scything the heads off a rose.

'How was Felixstowe?' asked Lily hugging Sally. Peg watched helplessly as the spinning back wheel of the bike chopped up some petunias and scattered the petals across the drive.

'Full of pebbles,' said Sally. Both girls were oblivious of the mayhem around them and it was Friedrich who came to the rescue. Sally caught sight of him retrieving the bicycle from the flower bed.

'Is that Friedrich? You've got here?' She sounded surprised. Maybe she hoped he would have gone back before the end of her holiday or that he wouldn't have come at all.

'Fräulein Sally, you are bonny.'

'Friedrich, where did you learn that word?' Lily chortled wondering what on earth he was going to say next. His awkward translations so often produced unintentional humour.

Friedrich flushed and clicked his heels in embarrassment. 'I have much pleasure to see you Fräulein Sally.'

'And you Friedrich,' said Sally sweetly. Now he was here she didn't want to upset him.

The dinner table buzzed with exchanges about their time in Munich. Then Sally dropped a bombshell.

'I've just got this letter.' She pulled a much-crumpled envelope from a pocket in her dress. Lily saw at once that it had a German stamp on it. She thought it was probably from the Grubers as she knew Sally had intended to write to them.

'Well?' Lily sat waiting for an explanation.

'It's from Hans.'

Lily's eyebrows rose. 'When did you start writing?'

'I didn't. It was on the mat when I got back from Felixstowe.'

'What does he say?' asked Lily eagerly.

'He wants me to write to him. He says he likes me and wants to be my friend. Like you and Friedrich, he says.'

Lily looked at Friedrich. 'What have you been saying to him?'

He smiled sheepishly. 'I say I like Lily very much. We are friends.'

'No we are not,' said Lily indignantly, wishing Friedrich would be more open, 'we are in love. Anyway I thought Hans was going to marry a girl from Potters Bar?'

'Which is not so far from here, Lily,' Sally reminded her. Lily did not miss the hint of irritation in her voice. It meant she was serious, which, thought Lily, was a bit rich after all her attempts to split her and Friedrich up. But she let it go.

'I'm joking,' she said, 'Hans is a nice boy. Will he be joining the army like Friedrich?

'He's not into that sort of thing,' said Sally firmly.

'What do you mean .... that sort of thing?' asked Lily sharply.

'You know …. guns.' She hesitated. 'Beating people up.'

'Now wait a minute, Sally. Are you suggesting Friedrich does this.' She was getting angry.

'No, of course not,' said Sally, quickly, 'but you get drawn into things over there, don't you?'

The conversation was going too fast for Friedrich to understand every word but he got the essence of what was being said and he struggled to find the right words to refute what Sally was suggesting.

'I do not hurt people, Fräulein Sally.'

'No, I know you don't Friedrich,' she said as sweetly as she could.

'Now young ladies, no spats over the dinner table.' Hubert sought to defuse the situation, while Peg offered more tea.

'I'm pleased you have heard from Hans, Sally.' Lily leant over and touched her friend's arm. Sally responded with a smile.

'You know who I saw at Felixstowe?' she said sounding less aggrieved.

'Who?'

'Lil. She was arm in arm with her mum and dad walking along the prom. Wanted to know how you were getting on with your German fella and hoped we would be seeing each other again in September.'

'Who's Lil?' asked Hubert.

'She's at the typing school with us,' said Sally.

'She's fun. I think she thought we were a bit stuck up at first,' said Lily. 'Her dad's a bit of a communist I think.'

'Probably only a trade unionist, Lily,' corrected Sally.

'Plenty of those in my place,' said Hubert gruffly. 'Troublemakers the lot of them.'

'Oh, but Mr Bates was a sweetie,' said Lily.

'You always see the best in people, dear. Not everyone is what they seem.'

'Yes, Mummy.' Lily winced. Here she was again getting irritated with her mother and her endless pleasantries. But she resisted her feelings spoiling the enjoyment of the ice cream, which Peg had conjured up from the serving trolley beside her. Conversation stopped while they all tucked into the generous helpings they were given. Then as she scooped up the last scraping from her bowl, Lily remembered she had something she was going to ask Sally.

'You remember, Sally, you were going to write to the Grubers? Did you ever do it?

Sally paused in finishing her ice cream and gave her a worried look. 'Yes,' she said seriously, 'several times. But I've got no reply. On the last occasion the letter was returned. When that happened, I decided to make a telephone call. It was a stranger who answered. He said the Grubers had never lived there.'

'How odd,' said Lily.

'Perhaps you got the wrong number.'

'No, it was the one I used before and I even wrote it down again before we left,' Sally assured them.

'The Grubers are good Germans, I think,' said Friedrich.

'There must be some simple explanation,' said Hubert. 'Perhaps Friedrich can call upon them when he gets back to Munich.'

'Yes, that is possible.' Silence ensued, broken only by Peg collecting up the dirty dishes. The sound of spoons on china grated on their ears as they each reflected on what Sally had said. When Lily got Sally to herself, she confronted her friend.

'Do you think something has happened to the Grubers?'

'I hope not,' said Sally, 'but I think life has become difficult for anyone who has Jewish friends.'

'I do hope they are safe. They are such nice people. Friedrich called them good Germans'

'You know, Lily, that means Friedrich thinks they are loyal supporters of his Fatherland. Well we know they are not.' Sally looked around her.

'Where has Friedrich gone?'

'He asked Daddy if he could go somewhere quiet to write up his notes. I think he is in the study.'

Sally took her arm. 'Let's go in the garden.' Her voice had an edge of urgency. Lily giggled at her friend being so conspiratorial, but allowed herself to be taken far away from the others. The two walked to Lily's arbour, which as she knew was screened from the house. The storm had cleared the air, which had become thick with the scent of jasmine. Whatever else she thought of Harris, his green fingers were not in doubt. Again she told herself how much she loved this spot. If Friedrich ever proposed to her this is where she hoped he would do it.

They settled on the seat and Sally turned earnestly to her friend. 'You laughed at me when I said I was friendly with Hans. This is true, but I do not intend to pursue it. With war coming we would be enemies and I could not face that.' Lily was about to protest. 'No, don't say anything Lily. I know you and Friedrich are deeply in love and I've tried to get you to break it off. But I know I can't do this and so I want you to know that I will give you both my blessing.' Her voice started to break up and Lily's eyes moistened. Sally continued more haltingly. 'It is a road to heartache you are both going down, but I love you for it.'

Lily could contain herself no longer. She pulled Sally to her and hugged her tightly. They held each other for what seemed an eternity, enjoying the tightness of their embrace. Lily was so thankful that Sally had accepted their relationship. To have gone on knowing her friend was still unhappy would have pained her deeply. In fact she could not have borne it. Now after what Sally had just said, her resolve had the strength of granite. For a time she let her head nestle in the luxuriant thickness of Sally's curls. When she slowly pulled back she found their faces almost touching. A wave of happiness overcame her and without thinking she kissed her friend spontaneously on the lips. Sally responded with a much more passionate kiss. Her lips were moist and giving and seemed to engulf Lily and for a brief moment she felt the flicker of her tongue. She had no idea what was going on, but she sensed they were sealing an indissoluble bond.

'Thank you,' was all she could say. They sat there quietly, hand in hand, listening to a distant buzzing of bees. Lily felt the lingering wetness of Sally's lips on hers and savoured its sweet sensation. What did it mean? Could she love both Friedrich and Sally? That was impossible, she told herself. Sally was her friend. But, yes, she did love Sally, but in a different way. It was all so confusing. To take her mind off it, she turned to the Grubers and asked once again whether Sally thought they were all right.

'When that woman spoke to me from the Gruber house, her words, Lily, were chilling. I know it was the right number. I rang it many times before we left Munich. I didn't make a mistake.'

'So you really think something has happened?' Sally nodded. 'How awful. I'm sure Friedrich will be able to help when he goes back.'

'Of course.' She patted Lily's hand. She shivered and gave herself a hug. 'It's getting chilly. Shall we go in.'

'No, you go Sally. I will stay here a little longer. It is such a lovely evening now the storm has gone.' She let her hand trail out as Sally got up. 'Thank you for everything,' she said again as her friend let go of her hand.

Sally smiled and walked back to the house. She was going to join the Roods when a scratching noise from the study made her pause at the door. She saw Friedrich sat at a desk furiously shading in with a pencil a drawing he had just made. Beside the sketchpad lay a pile of maps, several unfolded and a notebook. Curiosity got the better of Sally and she walked in.

'You travel prepared, Friedrich. All these maps.' He hadn't seen her until she spoke, but he showed no reaction.

'Ah Fräulein Sally,' he turned to confront her, 'I wish to write what I see.'

'I wonder you weren't stopped in the port carrying all these into the country.'

'I bought here.'

She came around to stand beside him. 'What are you drawing?' she asked bending down for a closer look.

'It is - how you say - an inn.'

'It is very good. I wish I could draw like that. Is it where you had lunch?'

He nodded.

'Well, Friedrich,' she said making a coquettish exit, 'you certainly won't be getting lost.'

25

'A pint of stout and a pint of best.'

'Coming up guv'nor.'

He leant against the bar drooling over the squelch the pumps made as they gushed amber liquid into the glasses.

'On the slate, Alf?' asked the barman, slicing the head of the stout and pushing the two glasses across the counter.

'That's right, Charlie. Got an important bloke with me.' He nodded to a suited gentleman sat in a quiet corner of the Lamb and Flag. The barman had already noticed him.

With care, to avoid spilling any of their contents, Alfred Harris lifted the glasses and walked across the floor to his companion and gently lowered them to the table. He sat down and raised his glass.

'Well here's to you Eric. Down the hatch, eh!' The two chinked glasses and quaffed a quantity of beer.

'So, Alf, what do you want to see me about?' The man, who faced Harris, wore an ill-fitting grey suit with barely discernible stripes. His white shirt had seen better days and the blue tie that hung around his neck had several food stains down it. Yet he had the air of someone who carried a position of authority.

'It's like this.' The chauffeur leant forward and spoke in a whisper. 'We being so close to war, there's a lot of talk around at the moment as to how we should report anything suspicious. Well, I reckon there's something suspicious going on where I work.'

'You mean at the Roods' place?'

'Yes. They got a Jerry staying with them.' The man raised his eyebrows. 'Come over a few days ago on a bicycle. It's the girl. She met him in Munich when she was staying there last summer. Says she's in love with him.'

'Could be that's the truth, Alf,' said the man taking a notebook from his inside pocket, 'on the other hand it may just not be.' He started writing notes.

'There's more,' said Harris, not certain he was making his point. 'It's what they say. It's the way they talk about Hitler.'

'How?'

'Well, it's like they admire him.'

'Doesn't your employer own the sawmill over near Moreston?

'That's right. I run him there everyday.'

'I've met some of his workers. They say he has outspoken views on how the country should be run.'

'Bloody fascist he is.'

'Well, this isn't Germany. People have the right to their opinions even if they are obnoxious.'

'She met Hitler.' This got his attention.

'Who?'

'His stupid cow of a daughter.' The man wrote at length.

'Tell me more.'

'She met him when she was in Munich. All over him she was.'

'Her name?'

'Lily. Short for Lilian.' The man made a note. Harris looked at him, now pleased with himself.

'You're a policeman. Do you think they could be fifth columnists?'

'Unlikely,' said the man, 'but I've made a note and I will be letting my guv'nor know. As you say we can't be too careful. One question, though Alf, why are you so bitter about them? Don't they give you a good living?'

'Work's difficult to come by, ain't it? You get what you can. But Harris this, Harris that …. Being kicked around like some whelp of a dog. It's the women. That stuck up bitch of a wife and her skinny daughter going on about how marvellous it all is over there. And we about to go to war. If I had my way they'd be rounded up along with all the other foreigners.'

Sergeant Eric Wilks of the Bedfordshire constabulary nodded, then put his notebook away and concentrated on draining the dregs of his stout.

26

It was in the arbour that Friedrich proposed, as Lily had hoped. It was his last day before returning to Germany. She knew something was afoot when he had disappeared for over an hour the previous evening. She asked her mother where the men were. Peg's answer was suspiciously non-committal. Now she sat on her favourite seat curled up with her German romance waiting for dinner time. He came up behind her with the stealth of a deer and put his hands over her eyes.

'I catch you Fräulein Rood,' he laughed, holding her tightly and giving her no chance to see him. She made a token effort to struggle when she felt her head being turned. But he was too strong and she submitted to whatever he was planning.

'Take your hands away, I can't see.'

'No Fräulein, you wait.'

She waited, getting more aroused by the shuffling noises she could hear. Finally he removed his hands. She laughed at the sight that confronted her. Friedrich was on one knee gazing up at her like a fairytale prince.

'Friedrich, what are you doing?' She knew perfectly well what he was doing, but she protested nonetheless. Friedrich took her hands in his.

'Lily, will you marry me?' No words of endearment. Just a bald request.

'My parents. We have to ask them, first.'

'I ask,' said Friedrich triumphantly. 'Your father say yes.'

'So that's where you were last night. Closeted with Daddy. What did he say?' she asked eagerly.

'I knock on door of study. I click heels and ask.' That must have been a shock for Daddy, she thought.

'Just like that?'

'Ja. But he ask have I money. Herr Schulz, I say, important in Party. My father, he look after us.'

'And was Daddy happy with that?'

'Yes but he worried our countries go to war. He ask us to wait, but he is happy for us to marry one day.'

'Oh, Friedrich that's wonderful,' said Lily, grabbing his blonde hair and yanking it with all her might. 'Now get up and kiss me properly.' He obeyed, if only to release the pain. His kissing, as ever, was enthusiastic, but it didn't have that delicious sensation that she got from Sally's wet lingering encounter. Perhaps men were different and their passion came from below. Which is where she now went with Friedrich pulling her to the ground and rolling on top of her. Her skirt shot up baring both legs. His hand appeared out of nowhere and crawled up her thighs, about to find its way into her knickers, when fear seized her and she pushed him away.

'Friedrich, I haven't answered your question,' she cried. She extricated herself from under him, stood up and straightened her skirt. 'You asked me to marry you and,' she said teasingly, 'I haven't said yes.' He looked up at her from the ground, a shadow crossing his brow. She laughed.

'Don't worry, dearest Friedrich.' She held out her hand to pull him up. 'I do say yes, with all my heart.' She heaved him to his feet and the two sat back on the seat. 'I'm so happy.'

He fumbled in his trouser pocket and held up a ring. It was plainly designed and made of gold.

'I put this on,' he said, taking her left hand. 'In Germany first we put the ring on the left hand and then when we marry we change to right hand.'

Lily thought it was different in England, but she didn't defer, allowing him to slide the simple band onto her fourth finger. She held it to the sun. The rays burnished it with a radiance that seared her eyes. She was beyond herself with joy. This time she wet her lips and forced herself on Friedrich.

There were celebrations all round over dinner. Toasts were made. Questions asked. For Peg a deep unease clouded her enjoyment of the evening. Fortunately the couple had postponed any wedding in whatever country until the political climate improved. To her that was sensible, but she could see they weren't too sure themselves. After dinner Lily and Friedrich walked once more in the garden. An evening chill had descended and Lily shivered, not because she had forgotten a cardigan, which she had, but because of a fear that was beginning to gnaw away at her. Friedrich felt her shudder and took off the light blouson he was wearing and put it around her shoulders. She squeezed his hand more tightly as they walked.

'You will stay safe, Friedrich.'

'Of course, Lily dearest. When our Führer has got what belongs to us, he will stop. I will not fight because it will be over and we will have peace.'

'I do hope so,' she said doubtfully.

'And then, Lily dearest, we will be married. I know a little church in the forest. You will love it. We will cut down a tree and then we saw it together outside the church.' She looked at him oddly. He laughed. 'It is an old German custom. The girl has wood to bring. It is a ….?' He searched for the right word. Lily wasn't sure but suggested 'dowry'.

'Ja, dowry.'

'So I am valued in so many logs?'

'You make fun?'

'Don't be so serious, Friedrich. I'm teasing you. You have to get used to our English humour.' She wrapped her arms around him. 'It's a lovely thing to do,' she said softly. 'I will practise my sawing.'

'You joke again! But I like your joke.' They took another turn around the garden and went in to share their last evening together, not, as Lily would hope, alone, but with Hubert and Peg sitting with them, chattering excitedly about their engagement and fantasising on future plans. With all that hung over them, Lily found this difficult to take. She excused herself and went up to bed. She hoped Friedrich would knock on her door and give her a goodnight kiss. She sat fully clothed on the edge of the bed and waited. She heard him come up the stairs, but correct as ever he went into his room and closed the door. Lily stomped to her feet, tore off her clothes, put on her nightdress and crashed out to the bathroom. Nothing. At that moment, had Friedrich appeared, she would have thrown something at him. She didn't. Weary, afraid and neglected, she returned to the bedroom, did her hair and climbed into bed. But sleep didn't come.

It was almost dark outside and through the open window she could smell the jasmine on the night air.

She lay tossing and turning, thoughts good and bad whirling around her head. She saw herself in a floaty white dress with a braid of wildflowers in her hair being showered with rice and being given a sharpened saw to cut into a log. But every time she brought the blade down the log rolled away. She went forward and it rolled away again. And again, until she was deep in the wood. The trees loomed over her, dark and threatening. And still the log rolled on. She looked for Friedrich. They should be cutting the log together. But he was not there. She was alone. A sound made her look up. Men, hundreds of them, were coming towards her. They were in uniform. Soldiers. But their uniforms were torn and bloodstained. Several were being carried on stretchers. As one passed, she looked down. It was Friedrich. His arm was in a sling, his face was smashed and bruised and his blonde hair was streaked with blood. Was he alive? She couldn't tell. She looked down at her dress and hands. They were blood red. She woke with a cry. She had dozed off and had slipped into a dream. Her nightdress was soaked with sweat and she found herself crying into her pillow.

She was frightened. She got out of bed. Moonlight was pouring in through the window. She crept to the door and quietly opened it. She went out onto the landing and stood still listening for her parents. There was no sound coming from their room. On tiptoe she moved silently to Friedrich's room and very gently turned the handle. She pushed the door open and slipped in. He was still awake reading one of his notebooks with the light of the moon.

'Lily, you should not be here,' he said emphatically. 'Your parents do not want it.'

'Friedrich, I can't sleep. I'm worried,' she cried. 'Let me lie beside you. I want you to hold me.'

'Lily, it is not approved.' She stood over him. Moonlight lit up the flimsy cotton of her nightdress. As if he were looking through a veil, he could see the sharp contour of her breasts and her nipples pushing through the fabric. He melted. She pulled the thin coverlet back and slipped under the sheet beside him. She felt his warm body through the pyjamas he wore and she lay herself against him silently waiting for his arm to be put around her. Eventually it was and they let the moon's beams coming through the open window flood around them.

'We must pull the curtains,' she whispered at length. He rolled out of bed and did as she asked him.

'Now we sleep,' he said climbing back beside her. He lay with his back to her and soon she heard his deep breathing. It was a comfort to be with him, but tears streamed down her face at the thought of his going tomorrow. Eventually she cried herself into a fitful slumber.

The next morning Peg caught sight of her daughter coming out of Friedrich's room. But she said nothing. When she was certain Lily was securely ensconced in the bathroom she called out that she was going to make Friedrich a hearty breakfast to see him on his way. She was as good as her word and when the German came down he found a plate of fried eggs, bacon, sausages and fried bread waiting for him.

'To give you energy for that long journey to Harwich,' said Peg beaming at him as he tucked into the feast.

'Weather dry, old man,' said Hubert already adopting an affectionate address for his future son-in-law. 'Should have a good road.'

'Yes, Herr Rood,' said Friedrich, through a crunching mouthful of fried bread.

After breakfast Lily helped him pack the panniers and saddlebag on his bicycle.

'So many notebooks, Friedrich. You've added to them,' she said stuffing the last into a corner of one of the panniers.

'I write about your beautiful English Heimat. I read when I not with you. It makes me think of you,' he said bending down and kissing her. 'You write often, Lily.' He gave her another more forceful kiss, mounted his bicycle and pedalled off, turning as he went to give the three of them a hearty wave. She twisted the gold ring on her finger and strained to see the last glimpse of him as he disappeared through the gate. No one said anything but they were all thinking the same thing. Would they ever see Friedrich again? Lily stood like a statue, staring at the empty drive. She heard her mother and father go back into the house. She didn't know how long she remained there, but when she turned to go in she found Harris behind her.

'I'm going to get some cut flowers for the house. Do you want to help me?' He probably meant well, she thought, but she couldn't miss the accusing sneer on his face.

'I have to go in, Harris.'

'As you wish, Miss Lily.' He watched her return to the house. Once there, her mother lost no time in asking the question that was foremost on her mind.

'I hope nothing happened last night, Lily?'

'What do you mean, Mummy?' asked Lily innocently.

'You know. Between you and Friedrich. I saw you coming out of his room, young lady.'

'I just went in to wake him up.' A little white lie she thought would do no harm. Her mother snorted but left it there. Lily picked up her German novel and escaped into the garden before any more questions came. In the distance she could see Harris with an armful of gladioli.

27

The hoped-for improvement in relations between Germany and England never came. Throughout the rest of the summer the crisis between Germany and Poland worsened. It was clear that Adolph Hitler was bent on invading Poland and as Britain had resolved to defend the sovereignty of Poland war seemed inevitable. Lily prepared to go back for her final year at secretarial school yet she saw all around her preparations for war. Leaflets from the government started to drop through the letterbox on a whole host of subjects from blackout to vegetable growing. In the air aircraft multiplied and military vehicles were a frequent sight on the roads. When she went into Bletchley to meet Sally at their local tea shop, she found railings disappearing from the municipal park, brown tape criss-crossed over shop windows and posters splashed over walls and fences. But most disturbing of all was the daily testing of the air raid sirens.

'I can't tell which one is the warning and which is the all clear,' said Lily wolfing down a piece of cake as she and Sally sat in the window of the tearoom looking through the tape and listening to the banshee moan of the siren.

'You will when it's sounding in earnest.'

'Do you think they'll use gas?' Their gas masks sat on the window ledge beside them.

'They say it's possible,' said Sally, 'but I hope not.' Neither could foresee the day when the simple ritual of partaking of good quality tea and richly decorated cakes would be a thing of the past. 'Have you heard from Friedrich?'

When Lily told her of their engagement, she was pleased for them, but full of foreboding. She smiled at the simple ring Lily showed her, which seemed so typical of Friedrich.

'Yes he wrote a letter on the ferry and posted it in France. But I haven't heard from him since. I suppose it's difficult if he's in barracks.'

'You could try and make a telephone call.'

'That's possible.'

'Pictures on Saturday? There's a rumour they might close the cinemas.'

'Then we'd better make the most of it.' They signalled to the waitress for the bill, paid their dues, pecked each other on the cheek, slung their gas masks over their shoulders and went their separate ways. Lily undid the padlock of her bicycle and rode home, her spirits lifted after seeing Sally.

In fact the next day a letter did arrive from Friedrich. It was in the morning post and she ran upstairs to read it. As her eyes took in its contents, she felt increasingly confused. There were no sweet nothings, little about what he was feeling or doing. But most oddly it was all in stiff formal German, which Lily found difficult to translate. They always wrote to each other in the other's language. She always found his eccentric turn of phrase endearing. Now he hadn't tried.

'Couldn't old girl,' said Hubert through a cloud of tobacco smoke, when she told him about it later. 'All hush hush now, you know. If he's in the army, his letters will be censored. Can't say where he is or what he's doing.'

'I suppose. But they don't censor him saying he loves me, do they?'

'Just being careful.' Lily had an idea. She remembered what Sally said earlier.

'Daddy, can I make an overseas call to Friedrich.'

'Well if he's in his barracks he won't be at home,' said Hubert, reasonably.

'But his mother will be there. It would be lovely to talk to her. Friedrich said he would tell his parents when he got back to Germany about our engagement. He said they would be proud.'

'You can try. Probably all right at the moment but there is talk of cutting off all connections with Germany.'

'Thanks Daddy.' She picked up the phone that sat in the hall and asked for the international operator. When she gave the number there was a long pause but she eventually got connected. A female voice answered in German. Lily said who she was and that she was asking after Friedrich. Her German was greatly improved and she knew she was being understood, but the woman whom she assumed was Frau Schulz sounded cold and distant. She explained that she and Friedrich were engaged.

'Frau Schulz, ist Lily. Ich bin mit Friedrich verlobt.' The woman did not deny that she was Friedrich's mother but said Friedrich knew no English girl and if he did he would soon forget her. He had gone to fight for the Fatherland. Lily could understand the words but not the sense of what she was saying. Then the woman launched into a sudden rant which was unintelligible to Lily. She shouted into the phone and finally slammed down the receiver with the words 'Englische Hure!' Lily burst into tears. She ran upstairs and opened up her dictionary. She had nasty feeling inside her about what the word meant. When she found it, her fears were confirmed. 'Hure' translated as 'whore'. She flung herself onto the bed and buried her face in the pillow. It's not possible, she cried to herself, there must be some mistake. Friedrich would never let his parents think she was bad.

'Perhaps it's their way of distancing you from each other to stop you getting hurt,' said Sally as she listened to Lily's outpouring in the tearoom the next day. Lily had rung in a terrible state of distress and they arranged to meet for coffee.

'But why did she have to be so horrid?' said Lily tears streaming down her face as she spoke about it. 'What do you think Friedrich said to his parents?'

'Well, if he hadn't spoken to them before getting back to Germany, it would be a bit of a shock.' This was just the situation that Sally wanted to avoid with Hans. But to say so, would be no comfort to Lily. Instead she wanted to be as reassuring as possible. But words eluded her. She simply held Lily's hand and said she was sorry. The two sat in silence and drank their coffee until the siren broke their reverie.

'Ouch that noise!' Lily put her hands over her ears. 'I'm sure I'm going to like Friedrich's mother when I see her,' she said eventually,' but for now I'm going to put her out of my mind and wait for his next letter.' Sally smiled. It was what she loved about Lily, her irrepressible spirit. If something knocked her down she would bounce back and get on with life. She reminded her they were going to the pictures on Saturday night.

'They're showing one of the Thin Man films at the Studio,' said Sally.

'I love them. He's so suave,' drooled Lily. 'I wish Friedrich could be a bit more like Dick Powell sometimes.'

'And Myrna Loy wearing all those gorgeous gowns.'

'And those dinky hats she puts on.'

'She's got that perky little nose.'

'No problem when they're smooching then!' At that they started to giggle and for a flash Lily forgot herself and imagined they were tumbling around in their Munich room.

28

Lily and Sally stood waiting for the train to arrive. It was Thursday August 31, the first day of secretarial school. Unbeknown to them Adolph Hitler was to issue that afternoon Directive No. 1 ordering the invasion of Poland to start at 4.45 am the next day. Overhead a squadron of bombers from a nearby airfield rumbled skywards. Lily watched them as they took off and thought how frightening they looked. The noise from their propellers shattered any quiet there was. They seemed like primeval beasts looking for forage. That they were the RAF gave her some comfort but had they been the enemy they would have been more frightening than anything she could imagine.

On the fence opposite colourful posters newly pasted stared at her. They were not adverts for soap powder or holidays beside the sea as they used to be. They were official exhortations wanting to control people's lives. One in particular caught her eye. A railway engine, similar to the one they were waiting for, steamed into the station. Two business men in hats holding umbrellas and briefcases were talking to each other as they stood on the platform. The driver was pointing furiously. From the stack billowed clouds of smoke and the sounds 'Sh..Sh..Sh..Sh'. At the bottom of the poster in bold letters was the slogan 'Careless Talk Costs Lives'. She thought of all the people she had talked to. There was Yakova at the pub, and Lil ….. Particularly Lil.

She and Friedrich had taken a trip to Bedford and on the spur of the moment she had decided to call on Lil on the off chance she was in. They took the bus to Black Tom. Friedrich was all eyes, taking in the huddled red brick streets that contrasted so strikingly with the grandeur of Munich. Beryl Bates opened the door.

'Lily, how nice to see you,' she said with surprise. 'This your young man then?' She looked at Friedrich's tall blonde figure with curiosity. Lily introduced him and they both saw the sudden black look she gave them.

'Cor, I never met a Jerry before.' She recovered quickly and a welcoming smile returned. 'Lil's not here at the moment, but she'll be back shortly.'

'We'll come back, Mrs Bates.'

'No,' she said hastily, 'come in. I'll put the kettle on.' She ushered them inside and sat them down, while she busied herself in the kitchen. Friedrich looked around taking in the cramped conditions and sparse furnishings. It brought back memories. Lily wasn't to know that it was an environment he was very familiar with. He had never talked about his life before his father's elevation to the Party. But in his early years poverty and the struggle to survive were constant companions. Before Beryl Bates could complete her task there was a rattling at the door and Lil burst in.

'Back Mum!' she shouted not seeing their guests at first. Lily noticed her dress which she deduced was some sort of uniform.

'You got visitors, Lil' returned Mrs Bates from the kitchen.

'Lily!' exclaimed Lil, now seeing her friend sitting in the parlour, 'what you doin' here?'

'Come to see you, Lil. Friedrich and I were in Bedford.' Lil who had hardly noticed Friedrich until now stared in wonder at the blonde young man who filled the chair he sat in.

'Friedrich?' She stared wide-eyed. 'This your fella from Germany?'

'Yes,' said Lily proudly. Friedrich leapt to his feet, almost toppling the chair over in the process, clicked his heels and bowed.

'Pleased to say hello.'

Lil was bowled over. 'Blimey, they really do it! I've seen it in the pictures.' He blushed. Lil, not backward in coming forward was soon all over Friedrich. She asked so many questions he quickly became confused about what they all meant.

'What you going to do when you go back?' she asked.

'I join the army,' said Friedrich who at least understood that question.

Lil looked at him all eyes. 'I'll bet you'll look good in uniform. You're a lucky beggar, Lily, picking up this golden boy.' She gave Lily a wink and jabbed her finger in Friedrich's arm. He looked embarrassed and to avoid his blushes Lily quickly changed the subject.

'What's the uniform you're wearing Lil. It's very smart.' She looked Lil's grey dress up and down, picking out the white collar and matching white buttons. It seemed like a waitress's uniform, which Lil confirmed.

'I've been doing breakfast at the hotel during the summer. Have to give mornings up when we start back, but I expect I'll be able to do some evenings.'

'It's very pretty.' Lil shrugged her shoulder. Yeah, she thought, if you don't have to wear it and be ogled at by smarmy reps eating their marmalade toast while trying to get a hand round your waist.

'What colour's your uniform, Friedrich?'

'Grey.'

'Like me. Can I borrow him for the night Lily? We'd make a good pair, 'im being so tall and me being a little 'un.' Lily laughed, not quite sure, as she often wasn't with Lil, whether it was a joke or not. Mrs Bates saved the day by arriving with a tray of tea and biscuits.

'Do they drink tea in Germany, Friedrich?' asked Lil, slopping liquid from her cup and slurping it out of her saucer.

'We have tea for breakfast.'

'Bet your Adolph fancies a cuppa then? You met him?' Before Lily could say anything Friedrich had described their seeing Hitler in Munich. Lil was eying him strangely. 'You're not a Nazi, are you?' she asked slowly.

The colourful drawing on the poster was obliterated by the real engine bringing Lily's train into the station and snapping her back to the present. She had regretted Friedrich's indiscretion the moment he made it and it must have increased the lurking suspicion Lil had about Lily's loyalty. At the time she never betrayed it but went on burbling about Friedrich as if he was some kind of freak.

'Come on Lily. We'll not get a seat,' shouted Sally, pulling her friend towards an empty carriage.

'Have you seen Miss Meadows?'

'She's with some new girls. We've got another teacher.' They pulled themselves into the compartment, flung their gas masks into the luggage rack and sat down, wondering to themselves how much longer they would be doing the journey.

How she got the information, none of them knew as it hadn't been on the wireless, but at their morning break, Yakova broke the news that Germany had invaded Poland. They sat in silence for a few moments taking in the implications of this.

'That's it then,' said Ag, 'we'll be at war before the week's out.'

'Lily, do you think your fella's mixed up in this?' asked Lil.

Yakova chipped in speaking slowly and icily. 'Yes, Lily, exactly where is your friend? Has he gone back to Germany?'

'Yes, Yakova,' returned Lily sharply. 'But I don't know where he is?'

'Handsome bloke, that one,' said Lil, trying to lighten this sudden tension. 'Pity he's on the other side.'

'You met him?' asked Ag.

'Yeah. Lily dropped round a few weeks ago.'

Ag expressed surprise. 'Bet that was a how-do-you- do for your Dad?'

'He was at work,' said Lil quickly. 'And what about you, Yakova? Don't you have a bloke in the forces?'

'In the Navy. He's at sea now, but I don't know where.'

'Well, it's going to give us girls a spin with all these boys appearing in uniform,' said Lil giving one of her cackling laughs. The bell interrupted their banter and they all filed back into the typing pool and began their dictation exercises, one reading for the other. Sally sat on Lily's desk and read a passage from a financial report while Lily typed.

Later as they were putting their cases over the typewriters, a voice cut through the chatter that broke out with the end of the session.

'He's bloody going in!'

'Who?' asked another voice.

'Adolph. He's going to invade Poland' Again, how the man, who couldn't be seen from where Lily sat, had this information, no-one knew. But it was unsettling to hear.

'Just like Vienna. It's going to be hell,' muttered Yakova, under her breath. Lily heard it and looked at her.

'But it must have been nice living in Vienna, Yakova?'

'Until the Nazis forced me out,' she said ruefully.

'What happened to you in Vienna, Yakova? Why were you forced out?'

'Sally not tell you?'

'No.'

'I tell you later. It's time to go home.'

'No,' said Lily with a ferocity that surprised Yakova. 'Tell me now.'

Yakova, who had risen to leave, resignedly sat back down and told her what she had told Sally. When she came to describing how her mother's ring was removed, Lily could see how much Yakova must loathe the people who had ill-treated her mother and she knew at once that the hate directed at Friedrich when they met was real. At the time she had dismissed it as nothing, but she could see now how naïve she had been.

'Come on, you two, time to move,' said a teacher mopping up the stragglers. Lily thanked Yakova and without another word got up and hurried after Sally.

'Why didn't you tell me?' she said accusingly when she finally caught up with her friend.

'Tell you what?'

'About Yakova.'

'What about Yakova?'

'About what happened to her in Austria.' Sally's face showed a flicker of guilt, but this quickly vanished.

'I didn't want to hurt you, Lily.' She looked across at her friend as she spoke. 'I'm sorry. I was wrong.'

Lily had her eyes down on the ground. 'Friedrich and I must face these bad things together.' She mumbled the words so quietly Sally barely heard them. She was grateful, though, that Lily was finally confronting the reality of her predicament, something Sally knew in the end she couldn't run away from. Neither spoke further and together they walked to the station.

The gloom she felt had also infected her parents. When she got home, they were in sombre mood.

'I think the British Ambassador is going to ask Mr Hitler to withdraw his plans,' said her father, without conviction.

'And if he doesn't?' asked Peg, knowing full well what the answer would be.

'It'll be war,' said Hubert. And where is Friedrich now, wondered Lily? With no word from him since he left, he could be trudging through Poland at this very moment. Lily lay back on the sofa.

'Got to face up to it old girl,' puffed Hubert, 'we're in a bit of a pickle and life's going to be very difficult.' You bet it is and for me most of all! she thought to herself. Her father looked over at her. 'Your mother and I have been having a bit of a talk recently.'

'Yes, Daddy, what about?' Her voice sounded sharp. Her father's 'little talks' never boded well. She watched. If he put out his pipe a serious matter was on the agenda. A cloud of smoke rose to the ceiling. It's coming, she thought. He removed the stem of the pipe from his mouth, carefully knocked the bowl against the ashtray and emptied the contents. It was done with great deliberation, a long-practised ritual which gave him time to think.

'If the war's going to come,' he said at last, 'the quicker it's over the better.'

'Meaning?'

'Meaning, we need to support the war effort.'

'So that means,' said Lily sensing she was going to get angry, 'that we pulverise Germany into submission with the likelihood of killing my fiancé in the process.'

Peg chipped in. 'Lily dear, we don't have a choice. Not after all the nasty things Mr Hitler has been doing.'

'Fact is, old girl, although we admired all he did once, things have changed. He's become a bully. And Mosley's men in this country are little more than street thugs.' She couldn't believe what she was hearing. It was a betrayal of all that they had stood for, all that they had told her she should be standing up for.

'How could you!' Her face became wet with tears. 'You told me what a wonderful country Germany was. You sent me there to learn the language, but I did more than that. I fell for the place and I fell for the people. Friedrich came into my life and I can't just shut the door on him.'

'We're not asking you to Lily,' said Peg herself getting riled, 'we're always going to be there to support him ... and you.'

'Are you? When you betray your principles.' Her words cut into them. 'And us.'

'That's enough Lily,' shouted Peg. 'We're on opposite sides and we have to face that fact. If we show disloyalty here we could be arrested and go to prison.'

'Don't be so silly Mummy. We have a right to our opinions. You're always saying that. The problem is you've changed your opinions. You have put me in a trap and left me.' Her face was contorted with anguish. 'What am I to do?' she asked pleadingly. Then she went quiet and spoke almost in a whisper. 'I'm not going to see him again, am I?'

'Of course you will dear.' Peg put out her hand but her daughter recoiled at the touch. Her mother's reassurance was hollow and she knew it.

'I'm going to take a tour of the garden,' said Hubert rising from his chair. 'You coming, Lily?' She shook her head.

'Hubert, make sure you put a jacket on. It's getting chilly these days in the evening.' Hubert winked at Lily, but she ignored him, staring at the floor. Denied her conspiratorial wink in return Hubert shuffled out of the room.

'Well if you are going to sit there and sulk, young lady, I'm going to do something useful like make your supper.'

'Don't bother, Mummy. I'm not hungry. I'm going to my room.' She got up and without looking at her mother, she climbed the stairs. She had hardly reached the top when an overwhelming sense of weariness overcame her. She felt utterly drained. She threw herself onto the bed fully clothed and within seconds had fallen asleep. The day had taken its toll.

29

Sunday 3rd September 1939 dawned warm and sunny, but the situation in Europe was far from bright. Germany had been given an ultimatum to withdraw from Poland by 11 o'clock that morning. The nation prepared for the Prime Minister's broadcast to be given shortly after the deadline had expired. To the exasperation of the two women Hubert was having difficulty tuning in. Reception in the area was often patchy and he frantically twiddled the knobs to try and locate a signal.

'Oh, for goodness sake, Hubert, you should have done this earlier,' cried Peg getting more and more irritated by the discordant noises coming from the receiver.

'I'm trying, old girl. Heard something then.' He made some fine-tuning movements with the dial and a broken voice became audible. It settled down at what were the last words of a BBC announcement …. 'broadcast by the Prime Minister, the Right Honourable Neville Chamberlain, MP.' There was further shushing noise, but finally the familiar voice of the first minister, sounding even more grave than usual, emerged hesitantly and lugubriously from the wireless.

'I am speaking to you from the Cabinet Room at 10 Downing Street.' All three strained to catch every word, virtually embracing the bakelite cabinet as they did so. 'This morning the British Ambassador in Berlin Neville Henderson handed the German government a final note stating that unless we heard from them by 11o'clock, that they were prepared at once to withdraw their troops from Poland, that a state of war would exist between us.' Lily felt her heart turn to ice. 'I have to tell you now that no such undertaking has been received, and that consequently this country is at war with Germany.' For Lily these chilling words were a death sentence. She and Friedrich were officially enemies and any contact between them would be a treasonable offence. As the Prime Minister's voice intoned on, she stood numb with disbelief. As with death, she knew it was coming, but its moment of arrival was still a shock.

The broadcast was followed by announcements stating that cinemas and places of entertainment were to be closed, that the blackout was to be strictly enforced, that gas masks were to be carried at all times. No one heard them. They stood looking at each other. For once Peg said nothing, for which Lily was grateful. She couldn't have borne a fatuous comment from her mother. Hubert played with the dials of the wireless and finally turned the set off. She winced. No, Daddy, she thought, don't say it please. He caught her frowning at him. He shrugged and went to the window. Peg couldn't take the pregnant atmosphere any longer. She said she was going to make a cup of tea and disappeared into the kitchen.

Seconds later she was driven back by the sinister wail of the air raid siren coming from the centre of town. Even where they lived its plaintive note could be clearly heard. It galvanised Hubert into action.

'Cellar everyone and bring your gas masks,' he shouted. They ran to the scullery where the boxes were kept. Lily began to open hers, but her father stopped her. 'We'll put them on down below.' The door to the cellar was accessed from the kitchen. It was not really a cellar, but a stoke hole for the coal. But the new boiler Hubert had recently installed was smaller and used less coal, so part of the area had been cleaned up and could be used for storage. It also had a small electric light which Hubert switched on after he had firmly closed the door.

In the pale light shed by the bulb, Lily looked around her. A small heap of coal sat beside the boiler, which was turned off during the summer months. In the cleaner part, pieces of furniture were jumbled together alongside some wooden crates which the three of them now used to sit on. All the time she had lived in the house she had rarely been down here. What a perfect place to have hidden herself and Friedrich had she thought about it. Now she was listening to her father's sergeant-major-like instructions to put on the gas masks. Although they had all practised it, he insisted on showing them again.

'Hold your breath and stretch the sides out. Stick your chin into the hole and pull these straps over your head as far as they will go.' He demonstrated until his face disappeared behind the mask and a half-choked voice spluttered from within. However many times she saw people wearing the mask she always burst out laughing. Now it was her turn to look ridiculous. But worse the mask was uncomfortable to wear. It clung to the cheeks and smelt unpleasantly of rubber.

The three of them sat looking like aliens from an H.G.Wells fantasy and waited for the all clear. It never came. Alarm spread silently between them until Peg pointed to the door to the cellar. She gesticulated with a muffled voice and put her hands to her ears. Of course they wouldn't hear the all clear down here, would they, thought Lily? She rose from her box and climbed the stairs. She cautiously opened the door and looked into the kitchen. Everything appeared to be normal. She crept to the window and looked out. She could see nothing in the sky. The others joined her and together, still with their masks on, they tentatively put their heads around the front door. Standing on the other side of it, about to knock, was Harris. He was wearing the uniform of an Air Raid Warden. His gas mask box was slung over his shoulder.

The three of them pulled off the clammy rubber masks, gasped for air and gazed wide-eyed at Harris.

'All clear over, Harris?' asked Hubert struggling to sound authoritative.

'About half an hour ago, sir,' he said flatly. 'False alarm apparently.'

'Right.' He took in the uniform. 'Good to see you're doing your bit, Harris.'

'Got accepted last week, sir.'

'No doubt,' said Lily with barely disguised sarcasm, 'you'll be keeping us on our toes.'

Harris gave a smile. No, she thought, that was a sneer. 'We've all got to muck in now, miss,' he said, his words grating in her ears. Doubtless his new-found authority would be held over them. She withdrew back to the house and packed her gas mask, still smelling of rubber, stale breath and sweat, back in its box.

The next day, Lily and Sally stood on Bletchley railway station as usual. Most regulars were there too. There had been no more air raid warnings, but the mood on the platform was decidedly sombre. The cheerful inconsequential chatter and the friendly banter were absent. No one spoke. All were immersed in their own thoughts.

The mood was broken by the snorting approach of the train. People prepared themselves to board. But the advancing engine gave a warning whistle that it wasn't going to stop. The station master shouted for everyone to stand back. With a shrieking hiss of steam and the pounding thrust of its pistons the mighty behemoth thundered past shaking the foundations of the station. From the carriages it pulled in its wake, a myriad of faces looked out at those standing on the platform. Some waved excitedly, others pressed their faces to the window, squashing their noses against the glass, many looked lost and confused. They wore caps and berets, their gas masks slung over their shoulders and large name tags hung from their necks. One little girl wore a brightly coloured mask that had been designed to look like Mickey Mouse.

'Children being evacuated from London,' whispered Sally, as they watched the tiny 'rodent' disappear. How awful thought Lily to be uprooted from your home, from your mother and father, to be delivered into the arms of strangers, however well-meaning those strangers might be. They looked so young.

Lily saw the children again when they finally got to Bedford. The evacuee train had upset the schedules. Their train crept into the station half an hour late and then lurched on a halting progress to its destination. When they left the station Lily could see the children ahead of her. They had been herded into the cattle pens that were adjacent to the marshalling yards. They stood bewildered and forlorn waiting to be collected and taken to safety in the villages around. Some were well-clothed, others had patches in their jackets. A crowd of adults stood in front of them. Lily watched as one woman pointed to a little girl, walked up to her and took her by the hand. Together they walked away.

'They're choosing who they want,' said Sally as they walked past. 'The well-dressed go first and you're left with the slum kids.'

'Is it really going to be that bad, that all these little ones have to leave their parents?'

Sally shrugged. 'No one knows. But it seems we're not going to give up without a fight.' As they walked along the wooden fencing, Lily felt an urge to grab a child and take it back home with her. But it would hardly be welcomed by her house-proud mother. Both of them looked in horror at a group standing on their own. They were shabbily clothed, the girls in stained and torn dresses, the boys with frayed shirts and heavily darned pullovers. Snot ran down their upper lips. Their hair was greasy and unkempt. Who, asked Lily, would take these? She fished in her handbag and to her surprise found a handful of sweets. She pushed them through the fence into the hands of the nearest girl.

'For you to share,' she said. The others were on the girl at once, but she cannily curled herself into a ball and carefully passed out a sweet one by one. Lily and Sally laughed and then left them to their fate.

Arriving at the secretarial school, they were quickly aware that it was not going to be business as usual. Students and staff were standing around in huddles. No one made any effort to sit at their desk.

'They're going to close us down,' said Lil coming up to Lily and Sally.

'But why?' asked Sally in surprise. 'Won't they need secretaries?'

'No one to teach us, apparently. Staff are being called up for other duties.' The bell started ringing and the principal of the school came into the hall with her deputies. It was a rare sighting. Lily could only remember having seen her once. She was tall, middle fifties probably, her hair tightly permed. She waited for silence.

'Ladies,' she began which caused an outbreak of tittering. She waited again, for this to subside, and continued. 'The governors of the school have decided that, as many of our teachers are being called to help the war effort, we will not be continuing with this term's tuition. From today until further notice this school is closed.' She went on to talk about arrangements for reimbursing fees, but this got lost in the loud murmuring that spread through the assembly especially among those who had not picked up on the rumours. She waited until the hubbub subsided and went on. 'With many of us being called now to do our duty, the governors feel you will want to serve your country to the best of your ability. Our men folk will be leaving their jobs to join the forces. You ladies will be asked to take their place. What you have learned here will equip you to do this with confidence. We wish you luck and God speed.' A spluttering of applause from the teachers prompted a greater applause from the students.

'Blimey, it sounds like we're off on the ocean wave,' sniggered Lil. 'Splice the main brace girls!' There was hearty laughter from those around Lil, but most of the gathering silently stood and watched the principal's party leave, uncertain what to do. Finally small groups began to slink off. Lily and Sally shook hands with Lil, Ag and Yakova, promising to stay in touch, and then listlessly made their way back to the station and the start of their new life.

30

The man who called himself Reg walked into the sorting office of Bedford's Royal Mail headquarters. It was several weeks since war had been declared and, although hostilities had been confined to a few engagements at sea, Britain remained on high alert. It was men like Reg who were now tasked with the job of keeping the country safe. He was one of the many undercover agents working for MI5, the country's top-secret counter espionage agency.

He walked between the sorting area, watching as he did so the piles of mail being skilfully distributed to their appropriate bins or letter racks. What information would they be revealing, he wondered? No detail was too small. Things overlooked by most people he had the nose to sniff out. Without knocking he walked into the supervisor's office. The man, a cheery figure in a fawn overall, greeted him jovially.

'Hello, Reg. I was expecting you.'

'What have you got?' asked Reg, going straight to the point.

'Not much. With the postal service to Germany shut down, we only get a trickle. Stuff that's gone through France usually.' He paused for a moment. 'But I do have one thing for you.' He bent down and opened the bottom drawer of his desk. He pulled out a few tatty files and then extracted a dirty white envelope. 'Got a German stamp. Posted in Munich.' He handed it to Reg. 'Must have slipped through with the last post and got caught up somewhere.'

Reg studied it carefully. His eyes lit up when he saw the address.

'Miss L Rood, Fenner Way, Bletchley. All carefully written in English.'

'You know Miss Rood?' asked the supervisor, knowing he wouldn't get much information out of the man in front of him. Reg nodded.

'Got a bloke in Germany has she?' His fishing provoked no response.

'These girls. See a blonde fellow and they go head over heels. Silly muts.'

'I will take this,' said Reg. 'I'll return it in a day or two.'

'Keep it as long as you like,' said the supervisor. 'Hope you get something from it.'

Reg returned to his small terraced house in Bedford, where he lived alone. He'd had a cat, but along with thousands of others had had it put down rather than subject it to being gassed.

Removing his jacket and cap, he walked straight into the kitchen, fitted a whistle attachment to the spout of the kettle and boiled up some water. Tea was not in his mind. That could wait. He wanted to generate a good head of steam. When the kettle started to whistle he took the envelope and carefully slid the seal across the steam. He did this several times until he felt confident the glue had softened. Then, very gently, he took the edge of the flap and peeled it away. There was no tear and the envelope could easily be resealed with the recipient unsuspecting that it had ever been opened. Pleased with his success he rewarded himself with a cup of tea and sat down with it to read the letter.

He pulled the flimsy paper out of its envelope and unfolded it. This was always the moment he enjoyed, being privy to what the sender had written before it reached its destination. It gave him a strange contact with the writer that excited him. He was about to read thoughts and intimacies that were meant for one eye only. Reading it was as if he was colluding with the writer. What would he be sharing he wondered? Probably not much of significance, but he felt a shiver of anticipation as he started to read.

The usual endearments. That was to be expected. They were engaged. He didn't know that. A fact to be considered. A tightening of the knot between them could have consequences. He read on. He hoped to hear from her before starting his posting. He was being sent to …. Unfortunately they had censored the letter and had cut out the name. Most likely somewhere in Poland as there was a reference to it later on. He did get through the fact that he had been issued with a submachine gun. The model was an MP35. Reg remembered that this was solely used by the SS. So this young man was likely assigned to the Waffen SS. To get into these divisions you had to be a member of the Nazi Party. Friedrich, Reg assumed, was a Nazi and possibly a fanatical one.

He paused his reading and pondered on his conclusion. These two have been caught by the war. What lies and distortions has she absorbed from their relationship? Now they are separated, which way will she go, he asked? Will she lose interest in him or will she become more deeply attached by the separation? The latter probably and if so will she pose a danger? He remembered how enthusiastic she was when he sat behind her in the cinema. He decided however to leave her alone for the moment and keep her under observation.

He took a mouthful of tea, went to a drawer in the sideboard and took out an ordinary jar of glue which had a red rubber dispenser at its end. He carefully returned the letter to its envelope and laying it on a sheet of blotting paper squeezed some glue onto the edge of the flap. He smoothed it out with the dispenser and pressed it tight to reseal it. The next day Reg Fuller returned it to the Royal Mail centre where it was bundled up and delivered by the postman through the letter box of Fenner Way.

31

When she saw the German stamp Lily gave a whoop of joy. But this was quickly tempered by the knowledge that the letter, posted before war broke out, had somehow been caught up in a backlog of undelivered post. She learnt little from it except of course that he still loved her. Most odd though was his mention of leave. This must have coincided with her ringing Germany, yet his mother had said he was not there. Now she would never know whether she had been deliberately lied to. She held the letter to her. She had it and that was a comfort.

Britain had become an island again in every sense of the word. All communications with Germany were cut off. She knew the chance of hearing from Friedrich again while the war lasted was unlikely. The most she could hope for was a quick resolution to the conflict or the hope that a stalemate happened that brought both countries to the negotiating table. To this end she joined her parents in throwing herself wholeheartedly into the war effort. Together they faced the restrictions imposed on them with good humour. At first they were minor irritations that hardly impinged on their privileged routines. The effect of the black out that had come into force the moment war broke out was mitigated by the evenings still being light. But as the days began to draw in, car accidents and pedestrians colliding with trees and lamp posts became a common occurrence. People and objects became festooned with white strips to help them show up in the dark.

'Look what I've bought,' said Peg one afternoon returning from a Saturday shopping expedition. She unwrapped a small parcel and revealed a pair of gloves which she proudly put on. The top was black and the bottom white. The other two laughed as she waved and wiggled her hands like a demented minstrel. 'Perfect for winter when I have to walk home in the dark after all that jam making.' Peg's contribution to the war effort was to enlist with the Women's Institute which had a centre close to Fenner Way. Autumn fruit was being picked and turned into jars of jam to supplement future food supplies. Hubert became more hands on at the mill as one by one his able-bodied men left to join up, while Lily quickly found herself a job at the Bletchley branch of the National Registration Office. This was a newly formed department created to issue everyone with an identity card.

'I'm not sure which is more tedious, bashing keys or stamping ID cards,' said Lily wearily sipping coffee with Sally in their usual tearoom. 'It all seems so pointless, nothing's happening. What are you up to?'

'Secretarial work,' said Sally in a non-committal way.

'Doing what?'

'I'm in an insurance office on the way out of the town.' Lily looked at her. She wasn't sure that she believed what she said. War made people cautious, even your best friend.

'How are your mother and father coping?' asked Sally hastily changing the subject.

'Frenzied, I think is the word. Daddy's having to do more work than I've seen him do for years. And you should see Mummy. It's a scream. She comes back every day covered in scratches. She's picking blackberries at the moment for jam making. She's convinced we're about to be invaded.'

'She may be right. They say our boys are over in France now but there's not enough of them. Germany's going to be breaking out soon that's for sure.' Sally always knew more than anyone else but was an insurance office the place to find this sort of information? Lily doubted it.

'Well, I must get back,' said Sally, putting on her coat. 'You too I expect, Lily. Same time next week?' Lily nodded. They paid the bill and Lily watched Sally's curls bounce down the street, while she returned to her office to find a queue outside the door. The rush to get the compulsory ID card had accelerated. People had been getting into trouble for not having one, being threatened with fines by the police and overbearing ARP wardens.

Lily pushed through the crowd and raised the hatch that gave access to her desk.

'Thank goodness you're back, Lily,' said her colleague looking at her with relief. 'I've been rushed off my feet. I'm dying for a cuppa. Hold the fort will you?' The girl got up from her seat and Lily sat down. She looked at the line of faces staring at her through the grill.

'Who's next?' Lily prepared herself for the rush. She took a blank, buff coloured card from the pile beside her, opened it up and filled in a number at the top. She looked at the woman facing her.

'Name,' she said curtly, knowing that if she was going to process everyone efficiently there was no time for pleasantries.

'Ethel Becket.'

'Address.' The woman gave it and Lily wrote it down both on the card and a ledger that sat beside her.

'Sign here.' She pushed a pen into the woman's hand and swung the card round for her to make her mark. The rubber stamp fell on the required space.

'Don't lose it,' she warned and called the next in line.

A younger woman with a child came up to the grill. 'About time,' she grumbled, 'thought you would have more doing this. I got to get back to work.'

'There's a war on you know,' said Lily learning to give the stock reply to every complaint. She filled in the details. The woman hesitated over the address.

'I'm only there for a week or two. We're from London.'

Lily wrote it down. 'When you move you've got to come back here and fill the new address in. And he needs his own card,' she said pointing to the little boy who gazed up at her. She winked at him. 'What's your name?'

'Alfred,' he said importantly.

'Well, Alfred, I'm going to give you and your mummy this card. You must never lose it.' She looked up at the mother sternly. As they made eye contact she caught sight of a man in the corner of the office looking in her direction. When she got a clearer view over the woman's shoulder, he abruptly turned and left.

32

Christmas 1939 was one of relative plenty. The Roods like most people had saved enough to have a modest Christmas dinner that included turkey and trimmings, but stormy conditions were not far away. January saw the country covered in a thick blanket of snow. What Adolph Hitler had so far failed to do, the weather achieved. Britain was paralysed.

What was worse the snow coincided with the start of rationing and Lily's office had been requisitioned by the Ministry of Food to issue ration books. Lily pulled her bedroom curtains back and looked out. What she saw horrified her. The snow lay thick around the windowpanes and mountainous drifts filled the driveway. It was going to be a tough struggle to get to work, but at least it was within walking distance.

Peg had made a breakfast of eggs and bacon which she put in front of Lily as if it was going to be her last. 'Get this down you, my girl,' she said pulling two slices of fried bread from the frying pan and putting them beside the two eggs and four rashers already on her plate, 'you'll need it now we're going to have to tighten our belts.' Lily's stomach wasn't sure it was ready for such a feast, but when she saw the snow outside she decided she needed fuel to get through it.

'When do we get our ration books?' asked Peg pouring two cups of tea, one for herself and one for Lily.

'We're starting to issue them tomorrow. That's why I have to get in today, to help sort them. These are tasty, Mummy.' She had dipped a piece of fried bread into the yolk of one of the eggs.

'Fresh from Mrs Hibbert up the road. Make the most of it. It may be your last. Everyone will be after them now. Can't see the hens producing to order!' It was a thin joke and Lily grimaced.

'We'll manage.'

Hubert emerged as she was putting on her coat. 'You take care, old girl. No chance of me getting in today.'

'Keep warm, Daddy.' She wrapped a thick woollen scarf around her neck and put on gloves and a brown felt hat along with her winter coat. In the hall lobby she donned wellington boots and, waving goodbye to her parents, she trudged out into the snow, making slow progress as she slipped and slithered through the drifts. But at least it had stopped snowing. Once out of the drive and on the road walking got easier. A half-hearted attempt had been made to clear the snow but it still lay thick on the pavements. At least here there was less danger of stepping into unexpected holes.

A few cars drove by, most going at a snail's pace. When she could she walked in the tyre tracks stepping smartly back onto the pavement when she heard a car behind her. At this rate, she thought, she would be in the office more or less on time. Until, that is, she heard a car coming faster than she considered safe. Worse, another car was coming in the opposite direction. She looked round. The car was almost upon her. She scrambled onto the pavement to let it go by. There was enough room for the cars to pass each other going slowly but not at speed. The inevitable happened. The car behind her applied its brakes, but too hard, and spun out of control on the slippery surface, narrowly missing her and hitting a tree. Lily screamed and fearing for the driver she ran round to the other side of the car.

'Are you all right?' she asked anxiously.

'Caught the side. No harm done.' The other car had managed to stop and the driver joined them.

'Is he all right?'

'I think so,' said Lily. 'He's lucky.' They opened the door and helped the man out. Lily was thankful he was able to stand without apparent injury. She couldn't think why he was looking at her strangely. Then she recognised him.

'You!' she exclaimed as she took in the identifiable features of the man she had seen in the pub, the cinema and most recently in her office.

'Why are you here? Are you following me?' she asked indignantly.

The man chuckled. 'And why should I be doing that, miss? I only wanted to offer you ladies a drink in that pub.' He held out his hand to introduce himself. 'It's Reg Fuller, miss.' Before Lily could answer, they all heard an insistent whistle coming towards them and a thickset policeman half ran into sight, managing despite his bulk to stay upright on the snow. He had his pocket book out and his pencil in hand when he saw the crashed car. He pointed first to the other car.

'Whose is that? We need to get it moved. It's causing a hold up. Is it driveable sir?' When he ascertained that it was, he asked the driver to draw up on the opposite pavement. When the car was clear of the centre of the road, he importantly waved the traffic on, then turned back to the others.

'Is anyone hurt?'

'No, officer,' said Reg quickly.

'Were you a passenger, miss?'

'No,' said Lily with a sense of triumph in her voice. 'I saw it happen.'

The policeman nodded and hovered with his pencil. 'Can you describe, miss, exactly what you saw?' She did so with relish making it sound that she was in jeopardy from Reg's speeding car. The other driver supported what Lily had said. The policeman finished his note taking after Reg had confirmed there was nothing wrong with the mechanics of the car.

He looked Reg in the eye. 'It seems like a case of dangerous driving, sir. First though I will need to see all your ID cards,' an instruction which set off a rummaging for the necessary documents. The policeman carefully examined each one in turn. Lily noted that Reg had his in a leather wallet. It was also a different colour to hers and the other driver's. She also noticed that the policeman showed a sudden deference when he was shown it. She couldn't be certain but if she had to guess it was some sort of warrant card. Immediately the policeman's attitude changed.

'Well, sir,' he said, addressing Reg, 'in view of the fact that no one is hurt and only minor damage done to the tree and given the slippery conditions, I'm prepared to take no further action. Damage to your car, sir, is a matter for you and your insurers.' Lily seethed. Who was this man keeping track of her actions and being let off a blatant act of dangerous driving? Was he working for the security services and was she really being watched. Why her? Did they think because she was engaged to a German that she was dangerous and a threat to the country? It alarmed her and made her realise that in time of war anyone can come under suspicion.

She made a hasty departure, deciding it would be imprudent to linger. When she got to the office she was over an hour late, but her supervisor was grateful to see her, however late. They spent the day preparing the books and receiving the instructions on how they were to be used.

'People will grumble and complain,' said the supervisor, 'and you need to be firm. You will tell them how they have to register with a shop to secure their ration. They can't go shopping around for a bargain. And when they hand their token over, that's it. No more of that commodity for the rest of the week.'

'And even if you have the money to pay for it you won't be able to get it without a coupon.' Lily continued, explaining how the ration book worked to her parents. Hubert thumbed through the flimsy pages, each divided into coupons marked with the words 'bacon, butter and sugar', the produce they represented.

'How much sugar do I get?' Hubert had a sweet tooth.

'12oz,' said Lily, '4oz of butter and 4oz of bacon.' Peg looked aghast.

'We'll never manage on that,' she said.

'You must do, Mummy, hoarding will be a serious offence.'

'Well, I hope you enjoyed your breakfast this morning.'

This was just the start. Other foods quickly joined the list as news from the continent got more grim and submarine warfare intensified. At the beginning of April, Germany occupied Norway and Denmark and the next month German troops invaded Holland. It looked only a matter of time before France was threatened.

33

On the day Norway capitulated, Lily was on her way to the office to face another day of queues when she noticed a small group of men, women and children gathered at the railway station. They had bundles and cases with them and wore coats and hats even though it was a mild day. She felt she had seen this before, perhaps in the newsreels at the pictures, refugees fleeing from invading armies. It was a conviction enforced in her mind by the wire fence that separated her from the station yard. As she got closer she could see clearly the solemn and dejected faces of the group. No one spoke, even the children stood in silence. Two of the adults looked familiar. Her face widened with surprise.

'Herr Hartmann,' she shouted with sudden recognition. Her voice made a man standing near the fence look up at her. He looked mystified. But it was him, she was certain. 'It is me, Lily Rood,' she said. 'We met on the ferry crossing to England.' Her excited voice had alerted the others in the group including the woman standing next to him and faces became animated with curiosity.

'I thought you were going to America.' Before he could answer, she had leapt off in the direction of the gate. 'Wait there, I'm coming round.' She half ran into the station yard and came face to face with Berthold and Magda Hartmann advancing to meet her. It was only slowly dawning on the couple who Lily was.

'You were kind to us,' said Magda, beginning to remember.

'But, why are you here?' asked Lily confused.

'They put us in prison,' said Berthold, resignedly.

'What! They can't.' Then she remembered hearing on the news how all those of German and Italian nationality were being interned.

'But you're escaping from Germany. I don't understand. And why aren't you in America?'

'Our papers were not right,' said Berthold. 'We stay in England while they sort our papers.'

'We wait too long,' said Magda. Lily remembered how she looked like Vivien Leigh. Then her face was thin and bruised, now Lily could see how beautiful she was, with her face filling out and showing off her finely sculptured features.

'The war starts,' added Berthold, 'and we cannot travel to America. Now - how you say it? – they intern us.'

'But you are Jewish,' protested Lily. Berthold hurriedly put his hand on Lily to stop her saying more. 'We are German,' he said quickly, looking around him anxiously. No one seemed to re-act, so he hoped her remark had passed unnoticed.

'Where are they taking you?'

'Man island,' said Berthold.

Lily laughed. 'You mean the Isle of Man.'

'Ja. That is so.'

'That's terrible. I'm sorry.' Lily shifted herself and suddenly had a thought. 'Look, I'm sure they won't stop you writing.' She opened her handbag and took out a small notebook. She scribbled something down. 'Here is my address. Write to me and tell me where you are.' The couple smiled and thanked her. A train whistle was heard in the distance. Two policemen accompanied by station staff suddenly appeared. One blew a whistle.

'Right everyone, move onto the platform. Your train's coming in.' Magda grabbed Lily and hugged her. She was crying. Berthold said nothing but shook hands. Lily stood and watched as they disappeared into the station building. She caught a final glimpse of them on the platform until clouds of belching steam obscured them from view. What an ironic fate having escaped the threat of incarceration in one country to be put into captivity in a country they thought was a safe haven. How could Friedrich demonise people so put upon and abused? He must come to see it is wrong. She waited for the train to leave and only after the last carriage had rolled out of sight did she realise how long she had stood there and that she was now late for work. How strange she thought were the twists and turns of war.

Twists that were quickly to get more intense, when on 13th May, German panzer divisions swept into France. Hubert had his ear glued to the wireless as the announcer, whose voice kept fading, described how the German general 'has come tearing out of the hills with seven armoured divisions totalling over 2000 tanks giving the French cavalry a severe mauling.'

'Horses against tanks. It's bloody hopeless,' he spluttered. Lily sat with her legs curled up on the sofa only catching strangled snatches of what was being said. She got the distinct impression now that her father had wholeheartedly come onto the British side. She wondered whether Friedrich was now in France. But he wasn't a tank commander and so he wouldn't be in the thick of battle.

'Is it bad, dear?' asked Peg, who liked to humour her husband with an obvious question.

'If they go on like this, they'll be in Paris in days. Got to give it to them, they're top-notch strategists.'

'Which is why you were so dazzled by them, Daddy.' Hubert puffed and shifted in his seat.

'Until they went bad.' He pushed his ear back to the radio. 'Now let me listen.'

The next day Lily decided to cycle to work. As she rode along the streets, she sensed a growing panic among people, confirmed when she got into the office. Everyone was talking about the Germans coming. Several of the women had husbands or boyfriends in France. What news they could glean was that the British troops were being trapped around Dunkirk.

'They're going to be slaughtered,' said one woman close to hysteria, 'Jerry never shows any mercy.' This was not the time, decided Lily, to share her concerns about Friedrich.

That night Hubert came back from the sawmill with some astounding news.

'Old Charlie. He's nearly sixty. He has a motor launch he runs with his brother at weekends. Moored at Morden. He told me today he's been asked to take it to Dunkirk to get some of our lads off the beaches. Bloody marvellous.'

The rescue that saved the British Expeditionary Force was considered a miracle, an army saved from the jaws of disaster. It did much to strengthen the resolve to fight on.

In the BBC's news bulletin of June 4th the announcer described the riotous scene in Parliament when the Prime Minister, Winston Churchill, vowed that 'we shall fight on the beaches, we shall fight on the landing grounds, we shall fight in the fields and in the streets, we shall fight in the hills; we shall never surrender.'

'That's the spirit,' said Hubert.

A spirit which meant a further tightening of the belt for everyone. Meat, tea and cooking fat went on the ration list. Petrol coupons were so restrictive that Hubert could barely go to his office and back before he ran out of fuel. A punitive tax on luxury goods put silk stockings and cosmetics out of reach for most people and made their wearing seem unpatriotic.

'Girls are drawing lines up their legs to make it look like they've got seams,' said Sally with a laugh. 'You need a steady hand.'

'But you don't get ladders,' answered Lily. Life was changing fast, but there was a growing bond that was tying people together. Groan and gripe they might but at least everyone was in the same boat. For the moment at least. And everyone was doing their bit.

That evening there was a knock on the door. Lily answered it. Two boys in smarmed down hair and side partings stood with a home-made wooden cart between them. They both wore boy scout uniforms.

'Any pots and pans, Missus?' asked one pointing to a pile of kitchen utensils already in the cart. Lily wasn't sure what they meant.

'We're collecting for Spitfires,' said the other proudly. 'Haven't you heard?'

'No.'

'They want to turn kettles into kites. That's what our scout master says. He's a squadron leader and he knows everything.'

'Does he? Wait here and I'll see what I can do.' She turned and disappeared inside. The boys waited patiently. A few minutes later Lily returned with two old saucepans, a leaking bucket and several old knives.

'This do?' she asked throwing the pieces with a clatter into the cart.

'Thanks, Missus.' The boys touched their forelock with a wink and then picked up the arms of the cart between them, which Lily thought must be getting heavier with each visit.

'One thing …' They stopped to listen to what Lily was going to say. '…. If your scout master is a squadron leader why isn't he flying planes?'

'Too old, Missus. He was in the last war.'

'I see,' she smiled. 'Good luck with the collecting.' She doubted it was going to make much difference, but every bit helped, she told herself as the two boys heaved their load out of sight.

If collecting aluminium utensils was a symbolic gesture, there was nothing symbolic about the capitulation of France. The pictures in the newspapers of Adolph Hitler cavorting before the Eiffel Tower sent a chill through the nation's heart. Every country around Germany, with the exception of Switzerland, had succumbed. Britain would be next. Germany's preparation for invasion began in August when waves of Stuka dive bombers targeted shipping on the south coast around Dover. Britain's fighter planes were scrambled in response.

'Hurricanes and Spitfires against Messerschmitts,' said Hubert, explaining to Peg and Lily the finer points of what became known as the

'Battle of Britain'. The nation held its breath as day after day, night after night, hundreds of planes engaged with each other in a deadly joust for the supremacy of the skies.

The nightly news bulletins had the Rood family huddled around the wireless set straining to catch every detail through the crackling airwaves. The commentators often made the conflict sound like some macabre cricket match.

'Last night,' declared an excited BBC voice, 'we had the best of the fighting, shooting down 46 of their planes, to our 14.'

Hubert gave a triumphant whoop. 'Bloody good show.' Lily winced as she thought of the young men dying in those exploding fireballs.

The bulletin finished. Hubert crossed over to his chair and took out his pipe. Lily went out into the kitchen to collect a glass of water. Peg went to the window half expecting to see vapour trails spiralling across the sky. There were none. What she did see were black clouds.

'It will rain tonight,' she said.

Lily too stared out of the window. Not a minute went by when she didn't think of Friedrich in peril. Was he in France waiting to make the dangerous crossing to Britain? Perhaps he was in Paris living in safety and comfort? She could hardly imagine the reality that was to crash that night into their lives.

34

Peg said nothing in her 999 call that would reveal Friedrich's identity. So when first the police arrived and then the ambulance, they were astonished to find a British officer lying with a bullet wound in his side. But it wouldn't be long before the truth came out and they had to have a watertight story.

Lily watched the stretcher carrying Friedrich out into the drenching blackness distantly conscious of her mother speaking sharply to her.

'Go upstairs, Lily, and wash your face. Your tears will arouse suspicion. We can't do or say anything that will connect us to Friedrich or we are all done for.' Lily was taken aback by the authority with which her mother spoke. In all this it was she who took control not Hubert.

'We must expect a call any time,' she finished ominously.

In fact it came seconds after Lily had gone to the bathroom and it came in the form of a burly military policeman and two armed soldiers. They ushered the

Roods into the drawing room, making them stand, while they waited patiently for a summoned Lily to come downstairs. The policeman stood looking at each one of them in turn, without saying anything. He wore the three stripes of a sergeant on his arm, the distinctive red cap with its prominent peak and a white bandolier attached to a white belt, from which hung a pistol holster, also white. His silence unnerved Lily. She had dried and powdered her face and stood passively, hoping her nerves wouldn't show.

'Why do you think the man showed up here?' asked the policeman at last. It was a relief to have a question.

'We've no idea, sergeant,' said Hubert politely observing the man's rank.

'Perhaps he saw a chink of light,' suggested Peg. 'He was wounded and needed help.' There was another pause. Peg wrapped her dressing gown tightly around her. She wasn't too happy that both she and her daughter were being questioned in their night clothes. She shifted her weight.

'May I sit down please?' The sergeant nodded. Hubert and Lily remained standing.

'He was off course.'

'What do you mean?' asked Hubert.

'You don't know?' He looked at them closely.

'Don't know what?' asked Lily.

'The man isn't British.' The three made a pretence at surprise. A little too obviously, thought the sergeant.

'Who is he, then?' asked Hubert. 'The fellow was wearing a British uniform.'

'He's a German.'

'Good lord, a fifth columnist!'

'How did he get here?' asked Peg in horror. 'Have the Germans landed already?'

'We think it was a small raiding party that had been put ashore on the east coast. At least that was the direction they ran off in. Except our wounded friend. He took an altogether different route. He came south.' He paused and looked them in the face, alert to any sense of betrayal. He thought he saw a flicker of movement in Lily's eyes. He turned to her.

'Miss, you have no idea who this man is?'

'No,' she said firmly.

'You've never met him before?'

She hesitated, fatally. She wanted to say no hoping the lie would absolve them all. The man's disbelieving face told her otherwise.

'Yes.' She glared at Peg to silence her.

'Yes, what?'

'I've met him.'

'Where?'

'Munich.' The man waited. 'I was on a language course with a friend. He was with some German boys we met in a bierkeller one night.' She tried to sound as casual as possible and not make too much of her meeting with Friedrich. She thought it better not to mention the train.

'So he did know about the house?' The sergeant had a sense of triumph in his voice.

'I suppose so. I wrote him a letter when I got back to England. He would have got the address from that I imagine.'

'And a lot more besides.'

'What do you mean? That I've been helping the Germans?'

'Have you?'

'Of course not. The man was wounded. He had an address. It was his chance to get help.'

'Convenient for him. If I were wounded in a strange country in pitch-black, in pouring rain, I doubt I could just hove up on a friendly house.' He paused again, to let his words sink in. 'Unless of course I had help.'

'That's ridiculous,' protested Lily. 'I've done nothing that could be of help to the enemy.'

'We shall see, miss.' He nodded to the two soldiers with him, who jumped to attention. 'I'm afraid I am going to have to ask you to come with me.'

'Am I under arrest?' asked Lily in alarm.

'No, but we are detaining you for further questioning.'

'This is absurd,' said Hubert. 'She's done nothing wrong.'

The sergeant ignored him. 'Miss, the soldiers will escort you to the vehicle outside.'

'Now wait a minute!' Peg who had been quiet throughout leapt forward. 'You can't take her dressed like that. It's indecent. Let go her go and change for goodness sake.'

The sergeant nodded.

'I'll come up with you, dear,' said Peg.

'No madam,' said the sergeant firmly. He instructed one of the two soldiers to accompany Lily upstairs. She led the way. She could hear the heavy tread of the man's boots behind her. When she got to the bedroom, she hesitated fearful of having to change under the man's gaze. But he sensed her embarrassment and solved the problem for her.

'It's all right, miss, I'll look the other way.' He swung smartly on his heel in the direction of the landing. Her day clothes lay across a chair. She made sure the soldier really had averted his gaze before she removed her dressing gown and nightdress and began putting back on what less than half an hour ago she had taken off. As she pulled her dress over her head she looked at the nape of the soldier's neck. It seemed to twitch. She felt uncomfortable being so close to another man. Her hands were shaking as she fumbled with the buttons. The soldier was equally embarrassed as he turned back while she was adjusting one of the last pair of stockings she possessed.

'Sorry, miss,' he said apologetically, but his blushes lacked conviction.

'It's all right,' said Lily, 'almost done.' As she slipped into her shoes, she pulled a small case from under the bed, which she intended to fill with clothes.

'No case, miss, handbag only.'

'But …. why can't I?' She was about to argue that she needed a change of clothes, but surely she told herself she would be back tomorrow when this terrible mistake was sorted. So she said nothing, but grabbed her handbag and put into it a tooth brush, a hair brush, a sanitary towel and a change of knickers.

35

Hubert and Peg were told to sit on the sofa as the soldiers led their daughter away. Lily found herself being bundled into the back of a military vehicle, with the two soldiers squeezed beside her. The MP got in the front. The driver was an ATS sergeant, a woman's army volunteer.

'Where to?' she asked.

'Bletchley Police Station.' Lily was surprised to hear this. She assumed she would be taken to an army camp. But of course they were going to take her to the nearest place to ask their questions. They would soon see she had nothing to tell them.

The vehicle's engine started up, the windscreen wipers sprang into life and they crawled off, wheels crunching down the drive. The rain beat on the canvas roof and percolated through the many holes in the flimsy sides. Even though she had managed to put on a light coat before she left, the dampness started to chill her. She was grateful for the proximity of the two men who sat motionless beside her. No one spoke. In the black-out, the driver edged along at a snail's pace.

They finally arrived at the darkened police station. The woman driver gave Lily a penetrating stare as she pulled the front seat forward. She watched stonily as the two soldiers helped Lily down and manhandled her up the steps. Inside the gloom continued. What was probably drab before the war was now even more so. The entrance hall and desk were lit by a single bulb. A few cautionary posters hung from the walls. The place echoed with the stamp of heavy boots. A policeman emerged from a side office as prisoner and escort entered.

'What have we here then?' He looked surprised at this late intrusion and even more so at the presence of a red cap, who rarely associated with civilian policemen. He was pleased to see though that he held equal rank.

'She's to be held here until morning,' said the military sergeant. 'She will be collected at first light.'

'What's she done?'

'We suspect her of collaborating.' That was the first time Lily had heard the word used and it made her suddenly very frightened. She wanted to speak out, but wisely held her counsel.

The policeman introduced himself as Duty Sergeant Wilks and said that he would be booking her in. He looked at the young woman facing him across the desk and realised he knew her. In fact he had been told about her by the man who was employed as her family chauffeur.

'This is the Roods' daughter,' he said, pleased with himself for having recognised her. 'She's been someone that's already come to our notice.'

'Well she's in trouble so keep a good eye on her.'

'I'll book her in at once.' He lifted a large black ledger from under the desk and importantly opened it up, wielding a pen over an empty page.

'Full name?'

'Lilian May Rood.' As he wrote he saw that the military policeman and the two soldiers still hovered behind Lily. Even the woman driver had crept into the entrance hall to watch the proceedings. It was for all of them a moment of great curiosity to be in the presence of a possible spy.

'You don't have to stay, she'll be safe with me,' said the policeman.

'We'll wait 'til she's locked up.'

'Suit yourself.' He continued writing up Lily's details.

'She got anything to do with that shooting I been hearing about? Seems some Jerries have landed. Told they've gone to ground.'

'That's right,' said the red cap carefully, not wanting to give too much away.

'Can't tell who your enemy is, can you?' He looked Lily in the face. 'Nice young girl like you. You should be ashamed.' Lily felt her head start swimming. She grabbed the edge of the desk and gripped it tightly. She mustn't faint. She bit her lip. As her head swirled she heard a distant voice.

'Empty your pockets, miss. I need to see your handbag.' His voice brought her to her senses. She looked up. His teeth protruded slightly giving him a permanent smirk. She put her handbag on the desk. 'I've only handkerchiefs in my pockets,' she said defiantly, pulling out two pieces of lace fabric. He rummaged through the contents of her handbag and pulled out a manicure set. He put this in a drawer. 'No sharp points allowed in the cells.' And handed the handbag back to Lily.

'Righty-ho, miss, this way.' The soldiers jumped to attention as Sergeant Wilks picked up a ring of keys and motioned Lily to follow him. Making a great show of jangling the keys he led her to the back of the police station where a steel gate gave on to a narrow corridor. It was dimly lit. He fumbled around to find the right key to undo the lock and when he eventually succeeded he made Lily walk in front of him until they reached the end of the corridor, the military following in close order.

'Not many residents in tonight, miss,' he said laughing at his own humour, 'so you should get a quiet night. Your fellow guest is in for being drunk and disorderly, but he's out cold so he won't be troubling you.' He looked for another key that fitted the large steel door they stood opposite. Before he turned the lock he reached for a blanket that hung on a nearby hook and threw it at Lily.

'You'll need this. It'll get cold in there.' As he spoke he turned the key and pushed the door open. It grated on its hinges. From the outside he switched on a single light bulb. Its faint glow revealed a sparsely furnished room painted a dirty cream. It contained a wooden bed frame with a mattress, a single chair and two buckets, one filled with water, the other empty. Beside them was a container with a bar of soap in it.

'You have five minutes to sort yourself out, miss, and then the light goes off.' He ushered her into the cell and without ceremony banged the door shut. Satisfied that their prisoner was safely locked up, the military did a smart about turn and left. As their footfall faded, Lily found herself alone with her thoughts and the grave situation she now found herself in.

The cell was small but lofty and as the sergeant said radiated a chill. Above her there was a narrow window but it had been blacked out and when the light went off it would be pitch black. The coat she wore offered little protection and so overcoming her distaste for the grubby blanket she held in her hand, she wrapped it around her and sat down on the bed. Blanket and mattress exuded an odour of sweat and worse. She took out from her handbag a bottle of scent and generously sprayed it around her face and neck. She luxuriated in its penetrating sweetness and found she could lie back on the pillowless bed.

The bulb flicked off and the cell was plunged into total darkness. There was not a chink of light anywhere. Lily felt helpless and abandoned. She shivered with fright as to what might happen to her. Did they really think she was a spy? That was unbelievable. In the light of day she would surely be able to explain everything. Would she be interned because she had a German boyfriend? She thought of the Hartmanns and how easily they had been rounded up. And they hated Adolf Hitler and everything he stood for.

And what of Friedrich? What had he been involved in? Was he an advance guard for the invasion? Dressed in British uniform he must have been on some espionage mission that went wrong. What was his objective, she wondered? His obsession with writing down everything in his notebook, the map details, the drawings of buildings, all began to make sense. Even then as he was declaring his love for her, was he spying? Was he using her? The thought paralysed her with fear. If she was a pawn in his game, did he really love her?

She couldn't control herself any longer. She burst into tears. Long choking sobs wracked her body. The perfume lost its potency and she became wrapped in a cocktail of sweat, tears and urine. How long she cried she had no way of knowing. The watch she wore was invisible in the darkness. Eventually the convulsions subsided and settled to a rhythmic sniffing, sufficient for her to regain her control and start thinking again.

If Friedrich was betrayed, who did it? There was any number of people who knew of his being in England with her. They had made little secret of it. Several who met them had no love of the Reich. Harris, for instance? He had never disguised his feelings. Then there was everyone at the secretarial school. Yakova? She had shown hostility at the pub. Lil and Ag? No she couldn't believe they were involved. Then there was that man who called himself Reg. He was always snooping around as if he was some kind of official spy. He might have his suspicions about her, but he couldn't know of Friedrich's plans. And what about Sally? No, she wouldn't want to subject her best friend to the inevitable hatred and pain that would be heaped upon her if Friedrich was betrayed. They loved each other too much.

And how did Friedrich get here? Was he parachuted in or did he land by boat? None of those who met him on his summer visit could have known what he was planning. Perhaps he didn't know himself. She lay in the darkness and tossed these thoughts around in her head. She came to the conclusion that the most likely explanation for the debacle was that careful as Friedrich must have been, he or one of his men made a mistake and they were reported by a stranger who became suspicious. Whatever mission he was on, it was highly dangerous, foolhardy even and doomed to failure. Once more head gave way to heart. She couldn't really conceive he didn't love her. As she lay there tussling with her demons, the knowledge that he was once more close to her gave her some solace. Whatever reckless enterprise he had been engaged in, she was relieved it had been foiled. He was now a prisoner of war, safe in some military hospital and in her own country. For the time being at least he wasn't going back to Germany. Now she must stay strong. She soaked one of her handkerchiefs with scent and placed it to her nose. It comforted her and she slipped into a fitful sleep.

36

The military wing of Bedford Hospital was on standby for casualties from the air battle that was going on. So far they had received none and the medical staff were surprised and not a little shocked that their first wounded patient was a German soldier posing as a British officer. But their Hippocratic oath ensured they did their professional best to tend him successfully. The military, too, were insistent that he was speedily treated as they needed to question him as a matter of urgency.

A captain and four soldiers tore into the hospital as soon as they got the call.

'He must be put under close guard at all times.' The captain stood stiff and tried to pull rank.

'We have to operate. He has taken a bullet,' said the surgeon assigned to treat the wounded man. 'We cannot allow you into the operating theatre.' The captain huffed but accepted the inevitable.

The operation was a simple one. The bullet had made a clean entry into the side and done little internal damage. It was extracted under anaesthetic and within an hour Friedrich's wound had been dressed and bound and he was moved to a solitary room with two soldiers standing guard beside his bed. He lay in a half-dozed state and drifted off in his mind to the moment he was called to serve his country in a way he least expected.

He could hear their voices now, crude and offensive. They sat under an elm tree checking and re-checking their rifles. His unit, part of the Waffen SS infantry division, was camped near Ypres waiting to go forward into France. The burly leader of the group spoke as he tested the release mechanism of his gun.

'You tasted one of these Belgian floozies yet, Friedrich?'

'Don't tease the lad, Heinrich. You know he's still a virgin.' Friedrich blushed at first, and then winked knowingly. If he was going to hold his own when the subject got around to women, as it always did, he had to bring his experience with Lily into the conversation. The wink passed the test.

'You'll be having a lot more by the time this war's over,' said the leader. 'They're all around, riper than Bavarian plums.'

'Always the boaster you are, Thomas.'

'Got something to boast about, haven't I?' He aimed his finger at his crotch and gave a dirty laugh. 'I had one this morning in fact. Found her in a field outside the camp. There she was her rump to the sky picking cauliflowers. When she stood up, she had this long black hair. Didn't take much to get her on her back. I reckon the uniform did it. Bloody hell she had thighs like an ox though. Fucking did for my balls. It was heaven.'

Was this really true, wondered Friedrich? Did the girl really give herself so easily? Didn't she put up a fight? Friedrich always felt uneasy listening to such stories. Like his companions he came from a working class background and like them had joined the Hitler Youth. Their fanaticism and devotion to the Führer had given them the chance to serve in the Waffen SS. For this group at least it had gone to their heads. Friedrich felt he was different. He remembered that although his father had been elevated to a position of power in the state's bureaucracy, he had passed onto his son a level of civilised behaviour. His current companions had none of that. They were going to bully and take what they wanted from the people they conquered, firm in their conviction that they were the superior race.

'Are Belgians Aryans?' asked George, the quieter of the group.

'I don't think so,' said Heinrich.

'Then we can rape their women?'

'Spoils of war, George,' said Thomas. 'Fuck the lot of them, I say. Make good German babies.'

Friedrich was tiring of this gutter talk and would have walked away when the sound of a motor bike caught his attention. A military despatch rider came into view, throttled back when he saw the group and shouted out.

'Private Schulz!'

Friedrich looked surprised. 'That's me.'

'I'm to take you to HQ. Hop on board.' The mouths of the others fell open. Friedrich took his jacket from the tree where he had hung it, put it on, slung his rifle over his shoulder and climbed on the pillion of the motorbike. He shot a fleeting smirk at his companions as they rode off.

The headquarters of the division's high command was a requisitioned Belgian country house. It stood some way from the main camp and Friedrich found himself being raced along narrow lanes and across open country. He had not been on a motorbike before and the speed, with which the goggled, helmeted man, to which he clung, hurtled him forward, excited him. In his mind it was Lily who was riding the bike, her delicate body that he clung to, her hair that flew into his face.

He moaned and turned and cried out in pain. A nurse came into the room and soothed his brow.

'He's dreaming,' she said to the soldiers who guarded the bed. 'Nothing to worry about.'

They reached the half-timbered mansion through massive stone walls. The motor bike pulled up below an ornate staircase that led to the main entrance. A soldier appeared and ordered Friedrich to follow him. He was clearly expected. He was escorted into the entrance hall and up a staircase. The soldier knocked on a door marked 'Commandant'. A voice bade them enter. Not knowing what this was all about, Friedrich was feeling decidedly nervous. The soldier opened the door and they walked into what once might have been a sumptuous drawing room but was now a grand office. Several officers in uniform were busily pouring over charts and maps scattered on tables. At the end behind a large desk, of the kind Herr Hitler might have possessed, sat an imposing figure in the full regalia of a senior SS Waffen officer. He looked up as the two men entered the room.

'Is this the private from Munich?' he asked Friedrich's escort.

'Yes sir. Private Schulz, sir.'

At the mention of his name Friedrich saluted with a 'Heil Hitler' and stood to attention with great ferocity.

'At ease, Schulz.' The man at the desk stood up and introduced himself as SS Gruppenführer Kruger, the divisional commander. Friedrich relaxed at the man's unthreatening manner.

'They tell me you've recently been to England.'

'Yes, sir. Last summer.'

'And you took notes and kept maps of where you travelled.'

'Yes, sir. I told the officer when I came back.'

The Gruppenführer nodded. 'Come here and look at this.' He unrolled a map he had in front of him and invited Friedrich to examine it. It was in German and not very well drawn, but he recognised what it depicted.

'It's the middle part of England, sir.' He paused uncertain whether to go on. But the Grupenführer clearly expected him to say more and he explained that he had better maps in his possession.

The Gruppenführer put his finger on an area and made a circular gesture. 'Where is this?' he asked. The names were in German but Friedrich was able to translate.

'I toured on my bicycle in this area.'

'Good. We have a mission for you, Schulz, that is both dangerous and of vital importance to our plans for invasion. We want to give the English a fright. Make them believe we have landed.' The Gruppenführer took a pen and made a large cross just south of Northampton. 'Here they have built a large munitions factory. We want you to guide a small band of saboteurs from the east coast, landing somewhere here.' He made a ring with his pen. 'And get them across country undetected so that they can blow up the factory. The English, we understand, have removed all road signs so it is the utmost importance we have someone in the party who knows where he is going.' He stopped to allow Friedrich to take in what he had heard. When he said nothing, he proceeded. 'We're promoting you to captain in the English army. But don't get any ideas. It's just for show. You'll have an experienced officer with you posing as an explosive expert. The team you are taking is highly trained in espionage. Your job is to get them safely to their target. How good is your English?' Not very good at all, thought Friedrich, remembering how Lily often laughed at his efforts. Could he pass as an Englishman? Possibly if he practised. The Gruppenführer sensed his hesitation. 'Well?'

'I speak it well, but with an accent,' he lied. 'But I will practise. The English have odd ways of speaking which I have learnt.'

'The trick then, Schulz, is not to get into conversation. You're on a route march. Always look as if you know the way, even if you don't. Best of all, steal a vehicle. Saves the walking.'

'The English have many narrow lanes,' said Friedrich. 'We need to use these and walk at night. We will be spotted doing it any other way. It would be too dangerous to use a vehicle.'

'How long will it take you to walk?'

'Five nights.'

'Very well. You will be called to join your team in seven days' time. I don't have to remind you that this is top secret. No talk to anyone else, least of all members of your own unit. Is that clear, Schulz?'

Friedrich stood to attention again and clicked his heels. 'Yes, sir.' His unit, he knew, would be too involved with moving into France and the anticipation of deflowering its women to be interested in the espionage activities of their virgin comrade.

The soldier at his bedside was under orders to write down anything the prisoner said in his drugged state or in moments of consciousness. Nothing made much sense but seemed to consist of route directions jumbled and incoherent, as if the wounded patient was struggling to plot a journey along roads that were not familiar to him.

37

The light in the cell came on at six o'clock. Although it shed little brightness, to Lily, who had spent the night in ink black darkness, it was blindingly dazzling. She put her hand over her eyes until she accustomed herself to the faint glow of the bulb. Then she slowly roused herself. She had slept fitfully and now her body ached all over. The skin on her face felt strangely tight and her lips tasted salty. The tears she had gushed in the night had dried on her face. She knelt down and cupped her hand in the bucket of water and threw it over her skin. She revelled in its refreshing coldness. Now her bladder told her she was desperate for a pee and she hoped they might have a lavatory she could attend rather than use the bucket. But she told herself this was unlikely. She pulled the lid off the bucket and squatted over it.

The noise she made must have attracted the attention of whoever was on duty outside. The grilled spy hole slid open with a loud grating noise and two eyes appeared at the slit. Seconds later there was a jangle of keys and a policeman appeared carrying a tray containing a mug of tea, a bowl of porridge and a slice of toasted bread with no butter. She looked at it disdainfully. The policeman could see what she was thinking.

'Can't waste our butter ration on prisoners,' he said turning to leave. 'Eat up, they'll be coming for you soon.' Lily realised she was hungry and fell on the food.

The constable was right. She had only just finished the toast, when the cell door crashed open and the ATS woman who had been the driver yesterday stood at the threshold.

'Out!' she bawled. Lily, wobbly on her feet, stumbled into the corridor. But she had no time to linger. Two soldiers frog marched her from the police station to the back seat of a car, painted in camouflage colours.

'I have to collect my handbag' she protested.

'You won't need it where we're going,' said the woman getting into the driver's seat. 'They'll keep it at the station.' Lily hadn't really noticed the woman yesterday, but now saw she carried three stripes. She was addressed as Sergeant Berwick and she appeared to be in command. Lily took a close look at her. She was in her thirties she reckoned with a weathered face that was hard and unflinching. She felt instinctively that she wouldn't be getting on with her. The two soldiers beside her in the back were portly, middle-aged and seemed to be filling more space than they needed to. She felt their bodies squeezing against her which as the journey progressed became more and more suffocating. Another woman, a corporal they called Rush, got into the front passenger seat and they were off.

Sergeant Berwick pushed the car faster than she had the night before. As they sped at times above the official limit it occurred to Lily that they were being given special treatment. The car was saluted, beckoned through red lights and escorted around hold ups by policemen on motorbikes. It soon became apparent that the car's path was being cleared to avoid it having to stop. All because they thought she was a spy.

The heat in the car got intolerable.

'Can we have the window down?' asked Lily as politely as she could. 'I need air.'

'Sorry,' said Berwick. 'Against regulations.'

'Then I've got to take this coat off.' She started to wriggle out of the coat she was wearing. It was difficult because of the bulk of the two men leaning against her.

'Can you gentlemen give me some room, please?' There was silent shuffling and a sharp look back from the driver. Before she could intervene, Lily had slid the coat off. She gave the soldiers a nod of her head.

'Thank you.'

Her dress was in disarray and she hurriedly smoothed it down over her legs. She could see the lance corporal's eyes looking at her through the rear mirror. She gave her a smirk and flicked her eyes back to the road.

To have asked where they were going would have been fruitless. But there were clues. The sun was still low in the sky and was on her left-hand side, so she assumed they were driving south, which both surprised and alarmed her. Surprised because she thought there was an army camp not far from where she lived. This seemed the obvious place to be taken. Alarmed because the odd spirals in the sky told her the battle was still raging in the direction they were heading. This thought was suddenly reinforced by a roar of fighter planes going low across their path, so low in fact she could see the pilots.

'Hurricanes', said Rush. 'Distinctive engine noise. Early morning sortie. Good flying weather.' They all watched the planes start to climb and disappear. They looked so fragile, thought Lily. She felt suddenly grateful Friedrich was lying in a hospital somewhere.

The journey seemed endless. She started to doze off from lack of sleep. Her head lolled and fell against one of the soldiers. He let her lie there and she relaxed as if she were in a cocoon. How long she was asleep she didn't know, but when she came to she felt a hand creeping up her knee and working its way between the buttons of her dress. The hand belonged to the other soldier. The one she was leaning against was aimlessly looking out of the window. The hand had now reached her thigh and, as the soldier played with the silkiness of her stocking and curled his finger around a suspender strap, he put his finger to his lips to quieten her. She sat up with a start and as she did so a voice barked out from the front.

'Private Higgins, you will bring yourself to order at once or I'll be booking you for misconduct to the prisoner.' The soldier pulled his hand away and sat upright putting as much space as he could between himself and Lily.

'Yes, Sarge.' The man sounded suitably chastised and said nothing more. His companion sniggered to himself while Lily now realising what had been happening looked understandably shocked. She was grateful for the sergeant's intervention. She didn't know that the intervention only came when she had started to wake up.

The car pulled off the main road and drove along a curving drive to reach a large turreted Victorian mansion. It looked forbidding, the kind of building, thought Lily, that you read about in a Brontë novel. The car scrunched to a halt on the gravel in front of the house. Higgins and Rush leapt out and stood guard over it. The third stayed with Lily. The sergeant came around to the back door.

'Out Rood.' She almost shouted the words. Lily looked at the house as she shuffled herself from the car in response. It didn't look like a prison, but all the windows were heavily curtained and covered in blackout. She felt a twinge of alarm.

'Corporal Rush and Private Higgins, you know the drill. Take her to reception and wait for me there.'

'Yes, Sarge.'

Rush gave Lily a sneer. 'Prisoner, follow me.'

Lily remembered. 'My coat. It's in the car.'

'Leave it,' said Rush brusquely. 'You won't be needing it.' It was still early in the day and her thin summer dress gave her no protection from the autumn chill. Goose bumps appeared on her arms. Her coat not only gave her warmth, but it was hers and its familiar fall about her person was part of the identity they were taking from her. She was quickly led into the front hall of the house. Outside everywhere seemed deserted, but once inside Lily was confronted with a hive of activity. Civilians and military criss-crossed the hall space, carrying large files and papers, emerging and disappearing into rooms on either side, once living rooms now offices.

'Up,' said Rush as the two soldiers took the stairs at a lick and walked into a large room at the front of the house. It was empty but for a small desk, a small cupboard and a single chair. Beside the desk sat a laundry basket.

'Prisoner to stand in the middle of the room with hands behind back and wait,' shouted Rush.

'Where are we?' Lily asked casually.

'Prisoner to remain silent,' she said nastily in her ear. She could shout and cajole as much as she liked, but Lily instinctively felt neither had the authority to touch her.

She asked again. 'What's the name of this place?'

'Somewhere you're not going to forget in a hurry, you dirty little collaborator,' snarled Higgins, resentful at being caught out in his secretive fondling. 'Betraying your country makes you worse than a whore. You should be shot ….'

'That's enough Higgins.' He was interrupted in his tirade by Sergeant Berwick coming into the room. 'You may stand down.' Higgins saluted and left. Berwick turned to Lily.

'While you are here, Rood, you answer to me and Corporal Rush and you do as you are told.'

'Am I under arrest?' A question she had asked earlier and now asked again. As before there was no response.

She persisted. 'What is this place?'

'You do not ask questions, Rood and you will find it best if you don't speak until you are spoken to.' Threats she could take from bullies like Higgins, but Sergeant Berwick's manner was altogether more ominous and sinister. She stood in silence and watched Corporal Rush go to the cupboard and pull out what seemed to be a pile of clothes. She sized Lily up and decided what she held was suitable and placed them on the desk.

'Watch, jewellery, any adornments you are wearing,' snapped Berwick, 'put in this bowl.' Lily took off her earrings and the simple necklace from around her neck.

Berwick noticed the gold ring on her left hand. 'That too.'

'It's my engagement ring.'

'Take it off.' It's only a ring, she told herself. Friedrich was in her heart not on her finger. She slid it off and laid it carefully in the bowl.

She was then ordered to remove all her clothes and put on what had been brought over from the cupboard. The room was warm, but when she stood naked in front of the two women her teeth were chattering. She hurried to cover herself up by grabbing the clothes on the desk. At the top of the pile was a pair of knickers. She went to put them on but recoiled in disgust when she realised they were male with buttoned flies down the front.

'We don't get many women prisoners. That's all we have,' said Berwick. Lily resigned herself to the humiliation. She stepped into the pants which at least stayed up and then put on a navy-blue cotton suit. It was a size too large and made her look as if she was wearing overgrown pyjamas. For her feet they had given her a pair of slippers, also a size too large. To keep them on she had to walk with a demeaning shuffle.

Once dressed they offered her the chance to use the lavatory, which she accepted gratefully. She was thankful to see it was not a bucket but a proper closet with a wash basin. She was now starting to feel hungry but there was no sign of food and she knew better than to ask.

Berwick led the way and Lily followed her along the landing of the house to a room at the far end. She knocked on the door. A voice from inside bade them enter. Lily shuffled through the door into a small room with a desk at the far end. The windows as with the rest of the house were blacked out. The room was lit by a single bulb hanging by a flex from the ceiling. The bulb was very bright and lit up the room. She was told to stand in front of the desk, with her legs apart and her hands behind her back. She was positioned so that her face was level with the bulb effectively preventing her seeing the man behind the desk. She could see none of his features but could just make out that he was writing.

Berwick thrust her face into hers and spat instructions out like a machine gun. 'Rood, you are to look at the wall at all times. You are not to look down. You're to ask no questions and you are to answer truthfully at all times.' Droplets of spittle landed on her skin. Her breath smelt of bad onions. The light was blinding, but through the glare she fixed her eyes on the fading Victorian wallpaper that decorated the room.

'Full name?' The voice was bufferish, a warmer version of her own father. It could be a favourite uncle speaking.

'Lilian May Rood.'
'Year of birth?'
'1920.'
'Month?'
'February.'
'Day?'
'Wednesday 4th.'
'Where were you born?'
'At home.'

'Where was home?'

'Fenner Way, Bletchley.'

'What is your middle name?' The questions, mindless and repetitive came at her through a miasma of deflected light, yet delivered quietly and politely as if asking what her name was and where she was born for the n'teenth time was perfectly normal rational behaviour. It took its toll. Standing still in one position required concentration. Her thighs started to ache. She wanted to rub her nose. She wanted desperately to turn away from that damn light.

'Keep your head up Rood.' Berwick's voice roared in her ear, a jolting contrast to the man's measured voice.

'May?'

'What is your first name?'

'Lilian.'

'What is the name you normally use?

'Lily.'

'Which languages did you learn in school?'

'French and German.'

'Which did you like best?'

'I don't remember.'

'Odd, Miss Rood, not to have recall of that.' He paused before she could answer. 'You are *Miss* Rood? Not married?'

'No.'

'So what do people call you?' She wanted to scream. She felt it was a technique to wear her down. But she didn't need it. She was already in a state of near mental collapse. Now her head started to swim. Her body seemed to be leaving the ground and she struggled to stop her legs from buckling. Without success. She found herself falling and was caught by Berwick, who shouted in her ear.

'You were told to stand Rood. Get up, woman.' She struggled to her feet. As she did so, she saw him. He sat looking at her unblinkingly through a pair of circular spectacles. He had a round face that reinforced the avuncular impression she had got from his voice. He was probably in his mid-fifties, slightly balding, and dressed in the regulation suit of a civil servant.

'That will be enough for today,' he said, putting his pen into his pocket. 'We will carry on tomorrow.' His calming voice gave her the courage to speak.'

'Why am I here?'

'That is for you and me to find out,' he replied with studied opaqueness. He turned to Berwick.

'Please take Rood to the attic room.' Berwick saluted. 'Yes sir.' She and Rush put themselves either side of Lily. As they reached the door, the man called out.

'Being a modern girl I'm sure you are not afraid of ghosts, but they tell me the attic room is haunted. My name by the way is Sir Montague Daventry. I wish you a good night.' He permitted himself a brief smile.

38

The bed was rolling violently. He felt he was going to be sick. He soon discovered he was no sailor, but they assured him the crossing would be short. He clung to the bed rails and looked at where he was. From his bed he could see the five of them sprawled over the bottom of the well of the S-Boat as it sped across the North Sea. For the last week he had been intensively studying his notes and cross-referencing them with the maps he had and the maps he had been given. He marked the objective and began to memorise in his head the intricate web of lanes and by-ways that he would have to lead them along to avoid the main roads and towns. He recalled how often Lily had quizzed him about his note taking and joked that he was more interested in maps than her.

Why was he doing it? To help the Fatherland of course. Hadn't he been encouraged to do this at his Hitler Youth meetings. 'Keep your eyes open, observe where you are, report back on what you have seen' had been the mantra of his instructors. Even on that first cycling tour of England their leader had urged them to take notes and he, Friedrich, had been particularly zealous in doing this. Had he now to make the choice between Lily and the Fatherland? In his mind, there was no choice. Germany was going to be triumphant and he was going to marry Lily. They were going to be part of the 'thousand-year Reich' and live happily in the glorious new world it promised. And he was now playing an active part in making it happen.

It felt strange wearing a British Army uniform, the more since his elevation to captain. He looked across at the sleeping form of his real commander, SS Sturmbannführer Helmut Weber, a major in rank but now demoted to sergeant. He was a tall thickset professional who was not only an expert in explosives but also skilled in the art of survival. Friedrich was conscious that his role was to navigate the group and thereafter to watch and learn. The other four, Fischer, Mueller, Koch and Beck, were all chosen for their prowess in espionage. They had been around much longer than he had and he envied their ability to sleep, something he found himself unable to do.

They were crossing in a fast motor torpedo boat, but its speed didn't lesson the danger they faced. The captain told them the sea was peppered with British patrol boats and they may have to take avoiding action at any time. They sailed without lights, relying on instrumentation to keep their course. Friedrich thought of Lily tucked up in bed. He shivered from cold and wet and desperately wanted to hug her. He realised their objective, a large weapons factory, was not so far from where she lived, but even if their mission was successful he doubted there would be any chance to see her.

They left Zeebrugge in the early evening and it was planned they would be off the coast of Essex before first light. All seemed to be going smoothly when there was a sudden abrupt change in the engine noise. The motors started to go in reverse and then stop altogether. Friedrich's sleeping companions began to stir.

'What the fuck's going on?' asked Helmut Weber.

'I think an enemy ship's been spotted,' said Friedrich. This was confirmed seconds later by the crew passing through telling everyone to stay down and keep quiet. From the small porthole they could see a large warship approaching on the port side. It was a fair way off and was not using search lights. The captain fortunately had seen it in time.

'British frigate,' whispered one of the group. They watched anxiously, bucking and rolling uncomfortably in the wake of the passing vessel. As it receded the danger appeared over, when suddenly a powerful light blazed from the stern and caught them like a paralysed animal in its beam.

'Bloody hell, they've seen us,' cried Weber, 'Keep down lads.' There was a deep roar beneath them and the whole craft vibrated violently as the captain switched on the engines and at full throttle set a course away from the direction the frigate was sailing. The S-Boat was fast but not so fast it escaped the shells fired from the rear guns. Explosions erupted around the motorboat, one so close it tossed the craft into the air, but miraculously it escaped serious damage. At full speed the 'S' Boat was able to make good its escape and headed south.

'It's taking us back to Zeebrugge,' said a surprised Friedrich.

'The captain's making them believe we are on a routine patrol. He'll change course when we're out of sight.' Weber proved correct and soon they were on their way again. There was a lot of shipping around but they always stayed far enough away to escape detection. As the motorboat settled into a steady cruising speed, Friedrich realised this was the first time he had actually been under fire. In Belgium his unit had missed the fighting and only arrived to see the aftermath. He wanted action and hoped it would come soon. It had and it had happened so quickly he hadn't been aware of the danger. But now he looked at his hands and found them shaking.

The first chink of light appeared in the east and with it a russet hue crept over the darkened sky. They saw the flat line of the Essex coast smear across the horizon. They were at the end of the first part of their journey. The S-Boat dare not go any further for fear of being sighted. They were at the estuary of the River Crouch and they had been told it was likely to be heavily defended with pill boxes and mines. But it did have extensive reed beds, ideal for concealing an inflatable boat.

The rubber dingy was being lowered into the water as Major Weber led his team onto the deck. Within minutes they were hoisting themselves over the rail and scrambling down a rope into the rocking craft. Friedrich struggled to keep balance as he helped the others manhandle the equipment and supplies into the well of the boat. Safely stowed, they seized their paddles and pushed off. No word was spoken. The captain had warned them how voices carried in the dawn stillness.

Despite the brightening in the east, it was still relatively dark. They could just make out the land ahead of them and in the middle of it, the mouth of the estuary. They kept their paddling to the minimum, just enough to propel themselves forward. Major Weber sat in the prow holding in the water in front of him a long wooden pole to which was attached a soft rubber ball. It was his invention and was designed to probe for mines. He explained to his doubting comrades that if they ran into a mine he could gently deflect it with the rubber ball and ease it safely around the boat. It was put to the test almost as soon as he put the pole in the water.

Corporal Fischer spotted it first.

'Something in the water ahead, sir,' he said in alarm. A metal object bobbed directly in their path. Weber pushed his pole out and made contact. Everyone held their breath. The major did just as he described and coaxed it around the dinghy. As it passed them there was a stifled and relieved chortle. The object was a floating beer barrel.

There were no more scares as they eased the dinghy into the reed beds away from an ominous looking pill box they could see further up river. A beam of sunlight lit up the land around them. It was momentary but they knew they had to get the dingy and themselves out of sight at once. With the sun spreading over the flat landscape they could not avoid being spotted. They heaved the boat out of the marshy water and pushed it between some tall bulrushes below the riverbank. A path passed above them but at a distance and so, unless someone made a point of coming over to where they were, it was perfectly concealed.

'Right lads, this is the hard part,' said Major Weber. 'We have to stay here all day. Try and get some kip. We'll work in four hour watches. No talking and the minimum of noise.' They each carried a heavy haversack, packed with food, explosives and a groundsheet. Only Friedrich was different. He had no explosives. Instead he had his maps and notebooks.

The dinghy was large enough for five sitting but could only cope with two sleeping. The groundsheets were laid between the reeds for the others. Friedrich drew first watch. Weber carved out a lookout in the bank camouflaged with foliage which gave a clear sighting of the path. As morning light came up so did the people. Friedrich was surprised to see how many used the path. Farm labourers and young women on their way to work. Children skipping to school. Even the odd military man. But all were too set on their purpose to deviate from the path. More dangerous were the planes that flew over. Could they be spotted from the air? Friedrich hoped their uniforms would blend with the rushes. How strange it was to be back in England, now an enemy, whereas only months before he had been a welcome guest. Strange too to look at the planes and know they were bent on killing his fellow countrymen. But this was Lily's land. These were her people walking on the footpath. One day though they would all become united under the leadership of his glorious Führer. A tap on the shoulder from Fischer told him his watch was over. He returned to find Mueller and Koch playing cards. He took out his groundsheet and lay down on it hoping to go to sleep which he eventually did, dimly conscious of frustrated mutterings from his card playing comrades.

The day passed without incident and as darkness fell the group made good their knapsacks, ensured the dinghy was secured ready for their return and with Friedrich leading, map in hand, they climbed onto the bank and set off along a deserted path. Friedrich's attention to detail navigated them safely onto the by-ways, but as the night wore on his obsession with checking and cross checking every junction began to cause friction among the others.

'Schulz, do we have to stop for so long at every fucking crossroad,' complained Fischer as Friedrich crouched in a hedgerow to study the map with the aid of a torch. He shielded the light with his arm as he looked up at Fischer.

'I have to be certain,' he said. 'These English roads twist and turn in unexpected directions. If we take the wrong one it could lead us miles out of our way.'

'Well, fucking speed it up then.'

'Easy Fischer,' broke in Weber, 'the lad's got to be careful.'

'We go this way,' said Friedrich finally, switching off the torch and walking confidently along the lane that appeared to be going in the wrong direction. But it wasn't long before it veered back again on the right course.

'See what I mean. You can't be too careful.' He looked at Fischer who said nothing, but he felt smugly pleased with himself.

Despite Friedrich's caution they made good progress and by the early hours had covered more than ten miles. They were feeling pleased with themselves when Beck who was in the rear suddenly whispered urgently.

'Someone's coming.' There was an instinctive urge to look round. Major Weber knew this was their first real test.

'Eyes forward all of you and keep marching,' he ordered. 'And Beck, remember to salute whoever it is.'

'I think it's someone on a bicycle.' They marched steadily. Friedrich's heart was pounding. A raucous singing broke out. The temptation to look was overwhelming, but they held their nerve. The owner of the bicycle was weaving all over the road as he came alongside them. He was clearly and opportunely drunk. He swerved towards them and then, as with drunks, he righted himself at the last moment. Beck saluted.

'I salute you, my brave lads.' It was an action too far. He wobbled uncontrollably and crashed to the ground. Beck and Weber rushed to him and got him back on his bicycle without having to say a word.

'I thank you and the best of the night to you.' They watched him as he rode off singing at the top of his voice.

'I hope they are all as easy as that,' said Weber. 'We'll wait here for a while. We don't want to run into him again.' They propped themselves against a wall and stood easy.

'What's that?' Koch shook himself.

'What's what?' asked Mueller.

'Water. There it is again. It's fucking raining.' Before they could get their groundsheets out of their knapsacks, a deluge hit them and the rest of the night's march proved hard and uncomfortable. As dawn broke several people passed but in the pouring rain took no notice.

'We must find shelter,' shouted Weber through the downpour. 'Keep your eyes skinned.' Friedrich spotted a barn in a field. A track led to it and they took a chance they wouldn't be seen. They reached it safely. It was open all round and stacked with newly bound hay.

'We can't stay here, sir,' said Fischer. 'It's too exposed.'

'If we move to the other side we're away from the road,' said Weber. 'We stay here, at least until the rain stops.' They found some dry bales and flopped on them exhausted.

It was Beck who spotted it. He had first watch. In the distance, on the other side of the field, he could see a copse of pine trees. He could just make out, with the binoculars he carried, a tiled roof. With further examination he decided there was a ruined building there. He pointed it out to Weber.

'It looks derelict, sir. It could be what we want.'

The others joined the two men.

'Problem is,' said Weber, 'there are people passing in that lane all the time. It's going to look suspicious seeing a patrol of soldiers crossing a muddy field for no reason.'

Friedrich interjected. 'If we wait, sir, that lane will clear.' Weber looked to him to elaborate.

'These lanes are used by people going to and from work. If we wait an hour it will become deserted.'

Friedrich was right and by nine they considered it safe enough to make the dash to the copse. It had also stopped raining. What Beck had seen was indeed a ruined building, a shepherd's hut possibly. It was a single room and had most of its roof intact. It gave shelter and a place to sleep. Also, beyond it was a neglected orchard with welcome apples hanging from the trees.

'How far have we walked, Schulz?' asked Weber staring at 'the captain' studying his map.

'Twenty-five miles.'

'Fucking feels like it,' said Fischer, removing his boots and socks and examining his feet.

'That's good,' muttered Weber. 'We're on course. Get your sleep, lads.' The team needed no urging and soon were all prostrate except the man on watch.

The next day and night followed the course of the first and steadily they edged their way to their objective. Midway through the third night on the road, Friedrich stopped at a crossroads as normal and disappeared with his torch and map. While they were waiting Weber gashed a tree with his knife as he did every time that they stopped.

'Why do you do that, sir?' asked Beck.

'So we can find our way back, you stupid fucker. If we get out of this, we won't have time to ponce around with maps.' As he spoke Friedrich emerged from the bushes with a worried expression on his face.

'Sir, I think we've taken a wrong turning. I'm not sure where we are.'

Weber looked at him as if a thunderclap had struck.

'You've got to be joking, Schulz. Are you telling me we're lost?'

'I think so, sir.'

'Can we re-trace our steps?

'I think we went wrong yesterday.'

'You're kidding! How the fucking hell did that happen?'

'I must have taken a lane that was going in the right direction, but actually wasn't.'

Despite the darkness, Friedrich could feel the growing anger gripping his commander and that he was at the centre of the firestorm coming. He needed to think on his feet.

'I could ask someone as soon as it gets light. There are isolated farmhouses around here. Even the British could get themselves lost. Knocking at the door would seem perfectly normal.'

Weber was silent. With no signposts to help them, it would be a risk, but seemed the only option.

'Your English better be up to it, Schulz.'

39

If the attic was haunted, no spectre worried Lily. As soon as her head hit the pillow she was asleep. The room they had taken her to contained only a bed, but it did have a wash basin and a chamber pot. There was no bed linen on the mattress and pillow. But this didn't worry Lily who now had been so exhausted by the day's examination that such niceties as a pillowcase and sheet were of little concern

She didn't know what time they woke her. As her watch had been taken, time was approximate. But she did know it seemed like the middle of the night when they pulled her off the bed and dragged her to the toilet.

'You won't get another chance, so make the most of it.' Through her sleep-addled head she dimly heard Rush's voice. She now knew enough of her situation not to waste any opportunity given. When she was ready they took her back to her room to allow her to wash herself. The cold water cleared her head. Then after a meagre breakfast she was led shuffling down the stairs to the room she had been in the day before. Sergeant Berwick was there when Rush opened the door. She was ordered to sit on the upright chair that had been placed in front of the desk. Her interrogator from yesterday was not there. She sat in silence, a sleepiness still weighing heavily upon her. Twice her head lolled and twice she received a sharp clip around the ear from one of the soldiers who stood behind her. How long they all waited she had no idea, but finally there was a general muttering of 'good mornings' and Sir Montague Daventry came in, dressed as yesterday, in a dark suit. Without a word to Lily he sat down, pulled papers and a notebook from the briefcase he carried and studied several of the pages in the notebook. Who was he, she wondered? Whom should she fear most, him or the two women behind her? His eyes still on the notebook, he addressed her without preamble.

'Rood, you said you didn't know which of the two languages you learned at school was the one you preferred. Is that right?'

'Yes.'

'Why then did you go to Germany?'

'My best friend had gone earlier. Others had gone the year before.'

'It's true isn't it that your father was enthusiastic in his support for what was going on in Germany and that he encouraged you to go.'

'He often spoke of the achievements of Herr Hitler, yes.'

'Which were?'

'How everything there was so much more ordered. He talked about the new roads, the modern buildings. Yes, he liked the country.'

'When you went – it was to Munich, wasn't it?'

'Yes.'

'When you got to Munich, did you find it was true?'

'Yes.'

'No questions in your mind? You must have seen some things that didn't seem quite right? It was the summer of 1938 wasn't it?'

'Yes.'

'Jewish people were being persecuted. Did you ride on a tram?'

'Yes.'

'Jews couldn't ride on the same part of the tram as Germans. Was that right?'

'Yes.'

'Didn't that seem wrong to you?'

'Friedrich said ......' Before she could answer he looked up from his notebook and looked at her, his twinkling eyes had the hardness of steel.

'Ah, Friedrich, the German boy with whom you became infatuated?' No, she told herself, not infatuated! But how did they know about what she felt for Friedrich? Unless ...... Harris? They've spoken to Harris!

'I met Friedrich like the others. We all met boys. Girls meet boys.'

'But it went further in your case.'

'What do you mean?'

'I suggest your besotted adulation for this boy blinded you to what was going on in Germany and that you were swept away by what he told you and that you became an ardent supporter of the Nazis to the point where you were prepared to collaborate.'

'No!' Her voice rose and she almost levitated but checked herself before she received another blow from behind. 'It is not true.'

'But you admired Adolph Hitler. You met him I believe.'

'No, not in the sense of being with him. We saw him once when he drove through Munich.'

'With tickets provided by the Nazi Party, driven there in a party car.' Her eyes watered. He was twisting everything.

'You were a silly little girl swept off her feet by the razzmatazz of all those uniforms and banners. You weren't alone. There were lots of girls like you, but they all saw sense and didn't betray their country.' Lily burst into tears.

'It's not true,' she sobbed. 'I betrayed no one.'

He fumbled in his briefcase and drew out a small round box. He opened it and placed what was inside on the desk in front of her. It was Lily's ring.

'This is what you took off your finger yesterday.'

Lily's shoulders shook with her sobs. She used her sleeve to wipe away the tears, but the sight of the ring convulsed her.

'Can you tell me what it means?'

Barely audible she said it was her engagement ring.

'You are engaged to this man? When did that happen?'

'When he came to England last summer.'

'When you helped him gather maps and plans of everywhere you went. Information that was going to be of great help to the enemy.'

'It wasn't like that ....' She blustered, seeing the trap he was leading her into. 'He did sketches and collected pictures, but I thought it was only as a record of his trip.'

'How naïve can you be, Rood? With war almost certain do you think a fanatical Nazi was doing all this for the fun of it?'

'He wasn't fanatical. We were in love.'

'Yes, it was love that blinded you to what you were doing. And was it love that made you go out there onto those Essex beaches and meet him as he and his gang of saboteurs landed?'

She looked at him disbelieving.

He went on. 'And was it love that made you take them by the hand and lead them to that munitions factory?'

'But that's ridiculous. What are you talking about?'

'Your saboteurs were spotted in British Army uniform and a woman was with them. It could only have been you.'

'No,' Lily screamed. 'I knew nothing of it until Friedrich knocked on our door, wounded.'

'You are lying.' He dismissed her protest and wrote a note to himself before fixing Lily with a steely gaze.

'Rood, I advise you to tell me everything you know about the operation if you wish to escape the hangman's noose.' Hearing his words Lily collapsed.

40

They approached the farmhouse with caution. From some yards off they watched and waited, hidden behind a stone wall. Friedrich advised doing nothing until the morning 'rush hour' was over. From the house there emerged at different times an elderly man who set off into the fields and then a tousle-haired schoolboy who was waved off by his mother. As he walked down the lane he greeted a passing tractor pulling a cart with several passengers. The driver of the tractor pulled into the yard beside the farmhouse to say something to the mother before carrying on into the fields.

'They are women,' observed Beck.

'Yes,' said Friedrich. 'They work on the farm. The men are in the army.'

'We have the Jews for that,' laughed Mueller.

After a space of time had elapsed with no more activity Weber reckoned that everyone had gone to work and that the only person in the house would be the boy's mother. They decided to risk it. Weber went ahead with Friedrich. The others lingered in some trees at the entrance on lookout.

Friedrich pulled an old bell chain, heard it clang inside and waited. After a few moments the door opened and the woman they had seen earlier stood on the threshold. She was in her thirties and now, in close up and despite the dowdy wrap-around apron she wore, she appeared attractive in a weathered kind of way. Her look of surprise at seeing two soldiers standing there quickly gave way to a friendly smile.

'Hello, can I help you?'

Friedrich who had been practising his accent all night knew exactly what he was going to say. First he saluted and then in cut glass tones explained they were lost.

'We were on exercises and our unit got separated.' He kept his words to a minimum, but she didn't appear to notice anything odd. Friedrich relaxed.

'Where are you going?' she asked.

'Northampton,' said Friedrich.

She looked at Weber, perhaps because he had said nothing. 'My word, you are lost.' Her eyes stayed on Weber. Was he half asleep, she wondered? He didn't appear to hear what she said.

'I see you have a map. Why don't you come into the kitchen and lay it out on the table.' She turned and ushered them into the house. Their boots clattered on the stone-flagged floor. Friedrich took in the room. On one side tall cupboards rose to the ceiling and beside them sat a large blackened range. Under the window looking onto the yard was a china sink with wooden draining boards. Iron utensils hung from hooks although many hooks were empty. In the middle stood a very large wooden table onto which the woman invited Friedrich to lay out his map. As it unfolded, to his horror, he saw some words that he had written in one corner. They were in German. He hurriedly put his hand on them and hoped the woman hadn't seen them. She studied the map and after a few moments got her bearings.

'You are here,' she said, pointing to open country between two small towns. She put a finger on a black mark that indicated a building. 'This is our farmhouse. I'm afraid you have a long way to go, officer.'

Friedrich looked closely at the location she had highlighted. He was confused. Even though they may have come too far south, this put them more than half way back to where they had started. *She had seen the words.*

'You must be mistaken.'

She looked straight at Weber. 'I think you have all come from a long way away. Am I right?' Weber looked uncomprehendingly.

Friedrich knew the game was up and they had to take a direct approach.

'Sir,' he said. 'She's lying. She knows who we are.'

Weber gave a roar and without warning leapt at the woman and gave her a brutal slap across the cheek. She fell backwards onto a chair.

'We have no time for this, Schulz. Tell her if she doesn't say us exactly where we are, it will be the worse for her.'

Friedrich turned to the woman nursing her bruised face and asked her again.

'Germans. You're Germans. Never.'
'Are you alone here?'
'No. My husband will be back soon.'

'Madam, you lie,' said Friedrich harshly. 'We've been watching the house. Your husband is not here. If you don't tell us the truth, he ….,' and he pointed to Weber ominously, '.... will hurt you.' She said nothing.

'Sir, she won't say.' Weber went to the door and called the others into the house.

'Fill the sink with water,' he shouted. Fischer jumped to it. Weber grabbed a towel and soaked it.

'Mueller and Beck, lift her up and hold her.' He looked straight into her eyes and held the wet towel in front of her face.

'Schulz. Tell her it's her last chance.'

'Please tell us where we are,' he pleaded.

'You want to kill us. Why should I help you?' She looked defiant, but Friedrich could see she was shaking with fear. He turned to Weber and shook his head. Weber put the wet towel over the woman's head and pulled it tight around her neck. She struggled but Mueller and Beck held her by the arms.

'Bring her over to the sink,' shouted Weber. They dragged the protesting woman across the kitchen and stood her against the china edge of the sink. Without ceremony Weber pushed her towel-covered head into the water and held it down for what Friedrich thought was an eternity. The woman, a farmer's wife, was strong and fought fiercely against the overwhelming sense that she was drowning. But the three men were too much for her and she went limp. Weber pulled her head gasping and dripping out of the water. He twisted the towel so tightly Friedrich thought the poor woman might suffocate. Unconcerned Weber thrust her head back down into the water and held it there for an even longer time. Friedrich had never been present when someone was being tortured. It wasn't pleasant, but he told himself it was necessary.

Finally Weber removed the towel, grabbed the woman's hair and pulled her head out of the water. She spluttered and coughed violently, her face puffed and contorted. If the two soldiers hadn't continued holding her she would have fallen. Water ran down her face, her hair hung in lank rivulets. She looked beaten into submission. Weber nodded to Friedrich.

'Show us where we are, please.' He spoke quietly, almost gently. They led her back to the table. Water dripped on the map with a patter. She put her finger on the farmhouse. It was a good twenty miles from where she had originally pointed.

'You fucking bitch.' Weber swore violently and struck her again across the face. 'You fucking English have got to learn who your masters are.'

'What do we do with her, sir?' asked Fischer. 'Do we kill her?'

'Killing her leaves a body and that tells them we've been here.' Weber thought for a moment. 'We'll take her with us. She's not going to be missed straight away. Clear the mess up in here and we'll be off.' He looked back at the map, sodden patches dotted over it.

'How far are we off course?'

'Thankfully, only by a few miles,' said Friedrich, relieved that they had lost only half a night. 'She can be useful to us. We didn't plan it but having her with us means we don't have to go asking questions.' Weber grunted.

'Right lads, grab what food you can and let's get out of here. We'll have to risk the road until we can find some shelter.' There was a scurry of activity. The woman, released by Mueller and Beck, slumped on a chair, her will to fight extinguished. She watched the soldiers shouldering their rifles and thought they were just going to walk away. She hadn't understood that they were going to take her with them. She shouted when Beck took her by the arm again.

'You're coming with us,' he said gruffly in German. She looked at Friedrich for an explanation.

'You have to come with us,' he said.

'Not like this,' she said, alarmed. 'I need to get a coat and put something on my feet.' Friedrich passed the message to Weber.

'She comes as she is,' he said brutally. 'I grew up without shoes. These peasants are going to have to learn a few privations. She walks as she is.'

'But sir,' pleaded Friedrich, 'it will slow us up if she can't walk properly.'

'Very well, Schulz, you look after her.'

Friedrich told her to get what she needed. She removed her apron. Fischer's eyes caught the shape of her figure and he gave her an admiring glance. Friedrich noticed it and for her own sake told her to hurry. She grabbed a coat hanging on the back of the kitchen door, along with a bag and went into the scullery where a pair of wellington boots stood. They were out of earshot of the others and while she was putting the boots on, Friedrich took the opportunity to speak to her in English.

'You've got to keep up or they will kill you. You will work with me in showing them the way. If you try to deceive us again it will be very unpleasant for you.'

'You're everything we were told about you. Sadistic pigs.' She spat at him. Friedrich ignored the remark although it made him seethe. What they had done to her was necessary because of her stupidity. He wondered how Lily would have acted in the same circumstances.

'What is your name?'

Half an hour ago she wouldn't have said. Now she replied meekly, 'Edith Lambert.' She wanted to put a brave face on things, but inwardly she was frightened to the core. She didn't need the coat she wore as the day was mild, but it disguised her shivering body.

41

Lily woke from her faint to the smell of roast meat. Hands sat her up and she saw that her interrogator had ordered lunch. As he tucked wolfishly into a plate of sliced lamb, mashed potatoes and sprouts generously laced with a thick gravy and spiced with mint sauce, he continued his questioning. No mention was made of her fainting only that treason carried the death penalty.

'They don't draw and quarter you anymore, but the monarch still has the right to behead a traitor and hanging can be pretty distasteful.'

She had recovered enough not to be fazed by his bullying tactics, however courteously they were delivered.

'I'm no traitor. I can see now I acted stupidly, but I wasn't part of Friedrich's mission.'

'After he left England in 1938, you never had further contact from him?'

'One letter. It arrived after war had broken out, but was posted before.'

'And what did this letter say.'

'That he loved me,' she said defiantly.

'Nothing else?'

'Only vague references to his being in the Waffen SS and that he was going on leave before his posting.'

'To where?'

'He never said.' She looked at the food being consumed in front of her. The sight of it was making her feel ill. He nodded to one of the soldiers. Rush brought in a small glass of water which she put in front of Lily, who took it thankfully.

'Excellent lamb this. Probably the last we'll get if your pals have their way. You know they've started to bomb London?'

'No, I didn't know,' said Lily weakly.

'Hundreds already killed. Your own people. And you're helping in their destruction.'

Lily was stung. How dare he say this! She was not a traitor.

'Why did you not admit to knowing Private Schulz the moment he knocked on your door?'

'Because I didn't want Mummy and Daddy getting into trouble.'

'I put it to you that your house was a prearranged refuge for the saboteurs to escape to?'

'No!' She almost shouted the word so incredulous was she.

'But things went wrong when Private Schulz came in wounded and you had to call the hospital?'

'That's not the way it was at all. I had no idea Friedrich was in the country and that he would come knocking on our door.'

At that moment Rush came in with a dish of rhubarb crumble doused in custard. Its salivating aromas made Lily gag and she hurriedly took a sip of water. Sir Montague thanked Rush and started with great deliberation to eat the dessert.

'You were saying … ?' he asked between mouthfuls.

'I was saying,' she said with great emphasis, 'that I was as surprised as anyone when Friedrich knocked on our door. Is that so strange, given his mission had gone wrong and he was wounded and needed help? Who would he have turned to?'

'Quite.' He wiped his mouth on a napkin and pushed the empty dish away from him. There were traces of crumble still in it. Lily teetered on the point of grabbing the dish and scooping up the crumbs, but Rush leant forward and picked it up.

'You were besotted with everything German, weren't you?'

'I liked much of what I saw, yes.'

'And you didn't disguise your feelings?'

'How do you mean?'

'I mean you expressed your tainted views in public. In the pub, for instance. And the cinema. People heard and noted.' That man who was always following her. So he was a spy!

'So when a woman is seen in the company of five German infiltrators masquerading as British soldiers is it any wonder that we make the obvious connection?'

'But you are wrong.'

'We shall see.' His eyes twinkled with a gimlet gaze. 'Sergeant Berwick take the prisoner back to the attic.' Without further ceremony the session abruptly ended. Lily was told to rise. When she did so she felt weak and wobbly. No one helped her, but she managed to steady herself by holding onto the chair. She waited a moment and then shuffled off towards the door. Locked in her room she collapsed on the bed.

Would they feed her? She hadn't even got water. The bucket beside the wash basin hadn't been changed since the morning. She lay and thought about everything that had been said. Who was this mystery woman? It wasn't her. How could it be? It was a bluff to trap her. Why did they need to do that? Perhaps they thought there was a wider conspiracy and she was the key. She had certainly acted in a foolish way and her indiscretions had caught up with her. But that's all they were, indiscretions. But they were bad enough. She could see she was in deep trouble. Would she go to prison? She shivered at the thought of it. As she lay there thinking this through there was a rattling of the lock and Rush came in bearing a tray of meagre food. But to Lily starved all day, the slice of cheddar cheese, the chunk of barely buttered bread and the large apple was a feast.

'Get some rest, traitor, we start again tomorrow.' She ignored the remark. Her mind had targeted the food and within minutes she had demolished it. She ate with a speed she later regretted as she was soon curled up with a crippling stomach pain that blotted from her mind all thoughts of her perilous predicament.

42

He struggled to see the shapes that blurred in front of him. They were talking, but he only caught snatches of what they said. He did hear the word 'questioning' but while he strove to process its meaning his mind fell back on the image of their race across open fields in a search for shelter, praying that they would not be seen. Edith Lambert gamely kept up with them, Friedrich's warning ringing in her ears. They eventually found an old quarry that had in it derelict bits of rusting machinery. It provided some cover and they were out of sight. Fischer drew the short straw and was on first watch, the others spreading their ground sheets and within minutes of hitting the ground all except Edith were asleep.

Fischer had no English and he signalled to the woman to sit down close to where he had positioned himself as a lookout. It was a warm autumnal day but after the rain the ground was wet. Edith removed her coat and placed it against some rocks to create a seat.

Fischer grinned at her, but she resolutely looked the other way.

The watch was two hours and its yawning emptiness soon began to be a burden on Fischer's self-control. He flitted his eyes from fields to the suggestive outline of Edith's figure. But as time went on his eyes lingered longer on the curves of her body than they did on the expanse of the countryside. Finally he could hold himself in no longer. He decided to chance his luck. He laid his rifle down and pretended to walk away from her. Then like a panther he was on top of her. Before she could make a sound, his hand was over her mouth. He managed to get the other hand around her waist, allowing him to slide her from a sitting position to a recumbent one. She was strong. He felt her powerful body move under him as she struggled to release herself. But this merely aroused him more. He fumbled under her dress and found the fabric of her knickers which he started to pull down.

The knife flashed in front of his face. A voice snarled in his ear.

'Get up corporal or I'll cut it off.' Weber stood over the couple, his face red with anger. Fischer stood up smartly and rearranged his shirt.

'She's enemy, sir, spoils of war,' he protested.

'You disgust me Fischer. You're a stain on Germany. She's our prisoner, not an animal.' By now the commotion had woken the others. Friedrich opened his eyes to see Fischer doing up his flies and Edith smoothing down her dress.

'If anyone else is thinking of molesting this woman, I want you to know that I shall be reporting Corporal Fischer on our return.' What return? wondered Friedrich.

'Beck, continue with the watch,' ordered Weber. Beck got up and with a smirk took up the position Fischer had vacated. Edith, shaken from the attempted rape, put herself between a jagged rock and Beck.

The rest of the day passed without incident. Friedrich had the watch after Beck. Still heavy with sleep he came to sit beside Edith. He opened his knapsack and pulled out some bread and a tin of beans he had taken from her larder.

'Eat?' He broke the bread and offered her half, while he cut open the tin with his knife. He doled out the beans onto the bread. The two ate without speaking.

'You're a strange people,' she said when they had finished the food. 'Your leader? He tortures me, then he defends my honour.'

'He's a professional soldier. He does what he has to do to get things done.'

'And Fischer?'

'He lost control.'

'He's a brute. He had his eye on me from the moment he first arrived. And you? Are you a Nazi?'

'We all are,' said Friedrich with a hint of pride in his voice.

'What are you doing here?'

'I can't say.'

'It's the start of the invasion, isn't it?'

'We only want to bring order to your country as we enjoy it in Germany. We are the same people. We should live together.'

'God, you really believe your own propaganda, don't you?' She laughed with disbelief. 'You won't win you know.'

He shrugged and changed the subject.

'Where is your husband?'

'Fighting.'

'He leaves you on the farm?'

'That's right. We all pull together now. That's what your Führer has done. He's got our dander up and we're bloody well going to give him the hiding of his life.' She was getting excited and Friedrich was not understanding everything she said.

'You have old man and woman on farm to help?'

'You were bloody watching. Yes, my old dad and local girls.' She heard voices in the distance and kept talking hoping they would be heard. But Weber had heard them too. He had Edith by the throat and his hand over her mouth.

'Get down,' he hissed to Friedrich. He took Edith to the lip of the quarry and made her look over the top. When he was certain she had seen who was talking, he dragged her back to the quarry floor. With one hand still over the woman's mouth, he brought one of her arms up behind her back. She winced with pain.

'Schulz, ask her what she saw. No funny business or I'll break her arm.' Her eyes were wild with fear. Weber gave her the chance to speak.

'Two boys. There is a school not far from here. They're using the fields as a short cut home.' She looked pleadingly at Weber. 'Please don't hurt them.' Friedrich explained to Weber. The major threw Edith into Friedrich's arms.

'Hold her and keep your hand over her mouth. The rest of you, backs against the wall.' The voices, laughing and joking got closer. Friedrich pressed Edith hard against the stone rock of the quarry face and leant against her. It felt strange, her soft body warm under his. Lily flashed before him, but this was another man's wife! He had no time to muse further. The boys were upon them. The soldiers sank into the rock and held their breath. Edith's eyes tilted upwards above Friedrich's hand, straining to see the top of the quarry. The two boys appeared momentarily on the skyline, but as they must have passed this way every day, they only gave the quarry floor a cursory glance and failed to see a squad of 'British' soldiers hidden at the bottom. They drew back and went on their way, their voices fading into the distance.

Weber asked Edith whether there would be more coming. Friedrich relaxed his hand and interpreted for Weber.

'She thinks not,' he said. 'She says houses are mainly isolated farmhouses around here.'

'Nevertheless, we should be extra vigilant.'

But Edith proved right and no one else came. As soon as dusk descended the squad struck camp and with Friedrich back in the lead they set off for their fourth night on what they hoped would get them within striking distance of their objective. At junctions Friedrich consulted both map and Edith as to which way to go, careful to double check for any treachery on her part. But her fear of what Weber could do to her, persuaded her not do anything foolish. In her mind she would bide her time until she felt it was safe to act.

They made good progress. As they got nearer to their objective, Friedrich estimated that Lily's house was close and he suddenly felt a desperate longing to peel off and see her. But a streak of light appearing in the eastern sky jolted him back to the task in hand. They were now on a lane he felt confident would lead to the edge of the munitions factory. Weber ordered them to take cover and they found a ditch that screened them from the road. He and Beck would make a reconnaissance of the area and report back at first light.

The others were to stay hidden in the ditch under Fischer's command. Friedrich worried for Edith, but apart from a few leering glances, Fischer left her alone.

Weber was as good as his word and he was back before the sun had appeared over the horizon. He described the layout. They had stumbled on the least protected part of the complex. There was a guard tower that would pose little problem and two perimeter fences which would be easy work for the wire cutters.

'We also saw an old building that we can shelter in,' he said, 'so let's get some kip.' He led them across the stubble of a wheat field to an isolated barn. This looked as if it had been derelict for a long time and, as they discovered, its roof gave a good vantage point for keeping watch on the factory.

They settled down for the day but only Edith got any sleep. The others were sprung for action and busied themselves checking their kit and their weapons. They only carried English arms, Lee Enfield rifles and Browning handguns. Weber had toyed with the idea of bringing a dismantled German machine gun which could be assembled at the target location, but had decided against this. Their mission was one of secrecy and speed with little need for anything other than hand weapons. But they did check with great care the explosives and detonator mechanisms.

Beck, who had first watch, reported that the guard tower was unmanned during the day. He talked it over with Weber about making a daylight entry and hiding up inside the perimeter fence.

'There are soldiers already inside the factory. We could easily pass unspotted, sir.' It was certainly an attractive notion and one that would avoid killing a guard. But in the end Weber considered it too dangerous and stuck to the original plan.

'Guard's gone into the tower, sir,' whispered Koch as he climbed down from the final watch.

'Right, let's get ready.' Knapsacks were heaved onto backs, pistols checked, knives felt. Weber turned to Friedrich.

'You stay here, Schulz, and guard the rifles.'

'But, sir ….' He began to protest but was quickly cut short.

'You've done your job. You're not trained for espionage. You stay here and cover our backs when we get out.' He paused and turned to Edith who was sat on the ground close by. 'And dispose of her.' A chill went through Friedrich, who looked down at the seated woman and was thankful she couldn't understand what was being said. He watched the men depart with a heavy heart and wished he was with them.

'Why aren't you going?' asked Edith.

'I'm to guard the rifles,' he said glumly.

'Am I to be killed?'

'Why do you say that?'

'It was the way you reacted when he pointed his finger at me.'

Friedrich had looked forward to the moment when he would make his first kill for the Fatherland. He assumed it would be in the heat of battle, helping to do his part in destroying the enemy. It would be noble and glorious, just as his teachers had taught him. Now he had been asked to kill a woman in cold blood. Could he do it? He had been taught to treat women honourably. But he had been given an order and he had never disobeyed an order. He had never even thought of doing so. To disobey an order leads to chaos and social breakdown. What is more, she's the enemy.

'Yes,' he said meekly, 'I am going to kill you.'

'How will you do it, Private Schulz? You can't use a gun. That would be heard. Use your hands?'

'Be quiet.'

She continued to taunt him. 'Slit my throat? That would be messy. Knife in the back when I'm turned the other way?'

'Frau Lambert, please be quiet.'

'Have you killed before? You look so young.'

He walked up to her and angrily slapped her across the face. She laughed at him. He slapped her again. In disgust he turned away from her taunting face and looked in the direction of the others. He could just make out their figures approaching the fence.

Mueller, the strongest of the squad, made easy work of cutting the outer wire. With his gloved hand he pulled back the linked sections and they all slipped through. When they were certain the guard in the tower was looking the other way, they crept along the fence until they were underneath the structure which lay inside the outer fence. Fischer, a practised assassin, shinned up one of the tower's legs. He unsheathed a knife, put it in his mouth, waited his moment until the guard looked towards the factory and in one movement vaulted the wooden balustrade, put a hand over the guard's mouth and sliced his knife across the man's throat. The body went limp and he let it down gently. He gave the thumbs up to the others and climbed back down the tower. Mueller cut a hole in the second fence and they were quickly inside the factory precinct.

Weber signalled to them to spread out and for each to seek a vulnerable position to place his explosives. Fischer, Mueller and Koch were to locate the fuel dumps, while Weber and Beck were to try and infiltrate working areas. Success seemed within in reach, when a voice out of the darkness suddenly addressed Weber.

'Soldier, what are you doing here? Can I see your authorisation?'

Weber didn't wait to see who it was but took his pistol from his holster and fired three shots in the air. It was a prearranged signal to the others to abort. Then he and Beck turned and dived into the darkness running with accelerated speed back towards the fence. From the shadows emerged a large number of armed men. They streamed after the retreating Germans. Mueller and Koch were at the hole in the fence almost simultaneously. Fischer came soon after. A violent explosion erupted behind him. High into the air shot a massive fire ball, its colliding colours of red, orange and yellow expanding like a kaleidoscopic mushroom. It stopped everyone in their tracks. Fischer at least had managed to detonate his explosives before they were discovered. Bullets whistled around them, several ricocheting off the wire. They just managed to get through the first hole safely. Mueller pushed the wire back and with superhuman effort tied the cut sections together. Luckily the pursuers weren't too certain in the darkness where the hole was and, when they found it, their difficulty in prising the wire apart gave the Germans valuable breathing space. Several climbed the fence and huge lights were switched on to illuminate the area, but the saboteurs had made it through the second fence.

Friedrich heard the rifle fire and knew things had gone wrong. He stood outside the barn with the guns in a pile at his feet. He strained to see what was happening. Weber's burly frame was the first to come into view. He could hear him shouting. When he reached Friedrich, he was breathless with running. Through great gasps came a stream of oaths.

'They were fucking waiting for us. Give me a rifle.' Friedrich handed him one. 'We were fucking betrayed.' He pulled the safety catch and turned the barrel on the oncoming soldiers. The others had joined him and took their rifles.

'We'll give them a volley and then run. Schulz, try and hold them off to give us time to get to the other side of the lane.' Friedrich swelled with pride until he realised what he was being asked to do. But he had no time to think further. The shouting in the distance was getting closer.

'All right lads, take aim,' said Weber. Friedrich looked through the sights of his rifle and saw a group that had got through the fence steadily advancing. He fixed on one of the men.

'Fire!' A fusillade roared out. Friedrich saw several figures fall. He had no idea if he had shot one. Weber gave the order to pull out. As he turned to run he shouted over his shoulder.

'Schulz, did you kill that woman?'

'Yes, sir,' said Friedrich.

'Good man.'

Friedrich was suddenly on his own with more soldiers coming towards him. He readied himself to face them. It never occurred to him that Weber regarded him as dispensable and was prepared to sacrifice him. His only thought was how best to defend himself. There were low lying bushes in front of him which gave him some cover. Crouching behind them he let off a succession of shots that had the effect of stopping the advance. It gave him the chance of retreating. As he reached more bushes he fired again and then reloaded. He continued to do this until he ran out of bushes and found himself in the stubble field. He had no choice now but to run for it. He zigzagged as he had been taught, but he must have been seen as bullets started flying close by, their deadly pinging sound ringing in his ears. He could see the lane ahead with more cover and thought he had made it, when he felt a thump in his side followed by a sharp stab of pain. He had been shot. He saw the gate only feet away and fell through it, his rifle flying from his hand. He hurt but could still function. Pulling himself to his feet, he crossed into the field opposite and looked for the ditch the squad had lain in that morning. He found it and dropped down wrapping as much foliage as he could find around him.

Whispered voices were getting closer, but he was saved from discovery by the arrival of vehicles in the lane. The soldiers coming across the stubble field ran into the men pouring off the tailgates of the trucks. In the general melee, Friedrich was forgotten. He lay still and blind to what was going on. He could hear orders being shouted and the tramp of men fanning out across the field. The trucks moved off and soon everything went quiet. He hoped that Weber and the others had enough of a head start to elude the chase. Now he had himself to attend to. The pain in his side intensified, the initial numbness wearing off. With difficulty he removed his knapsack and rummaged around for the medical kit they had been given. He couldn't see anything in the dark and realised he had to chance his torch. He ran the beam down his side. A sticky redness oozed through his clothes. He had to staunch the wound quickly or he would lose too much blood. He took off his jacket and lifted the sodden shirt. He saw where the bullet went. He found some dressing and pushed it hard against the wound, wincing with pain. He wrapped a bandage around his waist and put his coat back on. He needed medicine and to his relief found some pain killers in the medical box. He washed them down with water. He was so thirsty that he consumed the entire contents of the bottle.

The self-administered first aid gave him the resolve to move on. Lily's house was less than ten miles away. He knew he could make it. As he pulled himself out of the ditch it started to rain. He told himself he had done the right thing.

'She's alive,' he said. The soldier who was guarding him put down his book. 'I didn't kill her!' His voice became agitated. A nurse came over to soothe him. The soldier intervened.

'He's starting to talk, nurse. We've got to write down everything he says.' The nurse protested but the soldier had moved to his bedside and put his head close to him.

'Who's alive, lad?'

'I didn't kill her. You see,' his eyes started to roll, 'I was told to kill her. But I didn't. I saved her.' His arms waved frenziedly.

'I really must protest,' said the nurse. 'Can't you see he's agitated?'

'He wants to speak,' said the soldier. 'Let him.' He bent over Friedrich. 'Who you talking about lad?' he asked gently. Friedrich looked at the soldier and suddenly realised where he was.

'No one. It was a dream.'

43

Rush produced a pair of handcuffs which she screwed onto Lily's wrist and locked the bolt tight. They were heavy and uncomfortable, but Lily said nothing. She had learned not to complain.

'We're going for a little spin, Rood. Follow me.' The corporal walked out of the building to a waiting army car with Lily shuffling behind, her hands pinned in front of her. Sergeant Berwick was already in the driver's seat. Lily was pushed into the back beside Rush. They had barely settled themselves before Berwick had put her foot on the accelerator and they sped off with the tyres screeching on the tarmac. What the urgency was Lily could only speculate as she knew she wouldn't get an answer if she asked. She tried to locate herself as they raced through villages, but all the signs had been removed. She noticed they avoided large towns and the countryside they passed through had no identifiable landmarks. The only thing she could work out for certain from the placing of the low sun was that they were driving north.

Berwick made a signal with her hand. They had been travelling for what Lily estimated was about forty minutes. Rush pulled out from her jacket what Lily mistook to be a paper bag.

'Sorry, love,' she said, 'got to do this. Orders.' What she had in her hand was a black hood which she placed swiftly over Lily's head. The musty hairy fabric covered her face and blotted out her vision. She sat trying to work out from the car's movements any clue as to where they were going. She was still in the process of doing this when the car came to a sudden halt. No one spoke.

She was pulled from the vehicle and roughly led by the arm across a hard surface that gave way eventually to a more flexible one. The person holding her, presumably Rush, made no allowance for her shuffling gait and manacled wrists and at times she felt herself falling. She was clearly inside a building. Sounds changed, but there were no recognisable voices. The dragging suddenly stopped. Her arm was released. Rush's voice, muffled through the hood, told her to sit. She was wary of the order and for her caution got a hand on her chest pushing her backwards. She landed on a seat. The hood was ripped off and she blinked from the bright lights that dazzled her. Rush advanced with a key and unlocked the handcuffs.

'Sit and don't move,' she said as if she were talking to a dog. By now Lily had no intention of disobeying an order and prolonging her custody. She sat quietly rubbing her wrists, bruised by the heavy handcuffs, and watched Rush leave, demonstrably banging and locking the door behind her.

The room was devoid of furniture except for the chair Lily sat on. What was unusual was the number of lights. Besides the central fitting there was a bulb on each wall creating an almost shadow free space. Why was she here? What was the purpose behind the elaborate secrecy? Had she not told them everything she knew? What more were they expecting to drag out of her? She heard voices outside, but they were too indistinct to decipher.

By now she realised waiting was part of the technique to break an inmate, but she was determined to stay strong. In this timeless void there was nothing to measure time's passing. How long she sat, she had no idea, but eventually there was a rattling at the door as a key turned and the door opened.

She saw the wheels first, then the frame and finally the full shape of a hospital trolley. On top lay a recumbent man, his head propped up by several pillows, his face turned from where Lily sat. One hand was handcuffed to the frame of the bed. Two elderly hospital orderlies guided the trolley round until the man was facing Lily. She recognised him at once but was lost for words at seeing him. The men left and locked the door behind them. She could see he knew who she was, but his face was drained and immobile.

'Friedrich, darling, it's me Lily.' She sat with several feet between her and the trolley. Then she realised all of a sudden that they were alone. There was no one to stop her getting up. No one to pummel her in the back or slap her around if she moved. She raised herself and walked over to the trolley and took Friedrich's hand.

'This is wonderful. They have let me see you.'

He looked at her, his eyes barely comprehending. 'Lily, is it you?'

'Yes, my love, it is me.' She bent over and kissed him on the forehead. 'How are you, how is the wound?' He said nothing but pulled his hand from under hers and gripped her wrist. He tried, with no success, to pull himself up.

'I didn't kill her, Lily. They ordered me to, but I saved her. I will be shot if they find out.'

His eyes looked wild. His face had become animated in a way that frightened her.

'What are you saying, Friedrich?' Her voice was anxious and uncomprehending. 'Who are you talking about?'

'The woman we took hostage. When we got to the munitions factory, they left her with me. I was told to cut her throat.' There was an audible gasp from Lily. He looked at her in anguish. 'I should have killed her. It was my duty, Lily.' He gripped her even harder until she winced. 'I've betrayed the Fatherland. She should have been put down. We were betrayed.'

'Who was this woman, Friedrich?' Lily was fearful. This was not her Friedrich. The drugs they had given him were producing delusional ravings.

'A farmer's wife.'

'Calm yourself Friedrich and tell me how you are. How is your wound? Is it healing?'

'Yes.' He lay back and seemed to respond to her soothing. 'They say I was lucky. No organs hit.'

'That's good. It was a brave thing you were doing. What was your mission?'

He looked at her strangely. 'I haven't talked,' he said quickly. 'I will not talk.'

'No, of course not. But you can talk to me.'

He settled back in his pillows. His breathing had quietened. He started slowly then it came out in a torrent as he relayed to Lily all that had happened.

'It was an important operation, Lily,' he said with great pride in his voice. 'The orders came from the top, perhaps from the Führer himself. He wanted his most loyal men to strike a blow at the heart of England. It was going to sap the morale of the enemy. And I had been chosen, Lily. Me who had only been in the Waffen SS for a short time. But ….' He grabbed Lily's arm again and looked beseechingly at her, '…. not a word of this to anyone.'

She eased his grip and took his hand in hers. 'No, trust me darling,' she said softly. She would have to be strong when they interrogated her again. She now knew too much and as Friedrich poured his story out, it frightened her that he had done so. But he seemed unconcerned.

'Are your family well?'

'They are doing their bit.' she said. 'Daddy's joined the Local Defence Volunteers. It's called the Home Guard now. But they are so short of weapons they have to parade with wooden rifles.'

'No defence if we land, eh?' He laughed. 'And Fräulein Sally?'

'She's working as a secretary. She doesn't say much about it. In fact she's a bit secretive. But enough talk. They'll be back in a moment.' She stood up, bent over and kissed him. As their lips touched she felt an overwhelming love for him. He responded by grabbing her hair with his free hand and trying to pull her head towards him. She winced and gently released the pressure by taking his head in her hands. They kissed passionately. His wound made him groan whenever their bodies touched, but he ignored it. Lily felt his hand stray through the top of her pyjamas and find her breasts. He stopped suddenly.

'Lily, why are you dressed like this?' In his ravings and in his need to tell her everything, he hadn't noticed the prison uniform she was wearing.

'Because you knocked on our door, they think I was part of your operation, that I am a spy or collaborator.'

Friedrich looked stunned. 'Are they prison clothes?'

'Yes.'

'But they are wrong. You do not know of our mission. It was secret.'

'I know, but they have arrested me. It will be all right. It was a mistake.'

'But now I tell you all.' He looked at her in alarm. He knew all too well what happened to people arrested in Germany. 'Now you know, they will force you to say.'

'No,' said Lily, 'I will keep our secret.'

'They will torture you,' said Friedrich with growing horror. 'They can do terrible things to you.' She had heard of the methods used by the Gestapo in Germany, but she assured him this did not happen in England, although as she spoke she wasn't sure how much more she could take of Berwick and Rush's 'gentler' methods.

'But I am pleased you know, Lily. Now we fight together for the Fatherland.'

'Don't say that, Friedrich. I fight for my country now.'

'But you will lose. Wooden rifles against the might of our great army.'

'We are enemies, Friedrich. We must stay enemies until this war is over. I don't think you understand the spirit that is here. People are going to do everything they can to stop you. Even dying.'

'Will you die, Lily?' he asked, almost beseeching her to say no.

'Yes, darling, if I have to.' He couldn't understand her. He thought he was engaged to a girl who was in thrall to his Führer, and now she wanted to stop everything he stood for. The pain in his side gave way to an uncontrolled anger. In her mind, Lily saw the flies, few at first and then gathering in number until they consumed him. He shouted hysterically, his arms flailing at the flies that flew like a plague around him.

'Someone betrayed us. That woman betrayed us. I should have killed her. You Lily, you betray me. You must die. I will kill you. I will kill you all. The Fatherland will triumph.' His eyes were now quite manic. Lily looked on frightened and tearful. She was grateful to hear the scrape of a key announcing the arrival of the two orderlies. They saw the state Friedrich was in and raced over to restrain him. His delirium had consumed him. In silence they wheeled out the trolley with Friedrich trailing his free hand in a desperate farewell. Lily watched him go and waited for the inevitable arrival of Rush. She appeared almost at once, the black hood and handcuffs dangling from her hand.

A soldier in uniform removed a pair of chunky earphones from his head. He looked across to Sir Montague Daventry, who was doing the same. Their listening equipment was attached to microphones hidden in each of the lights in the room. It gave them all-round coverage of any conversation that took place. A woman stenographer stopped typing and relaxed. 'I've recorded it all, sir,' she said triumphantly.

'Good. Well done everyone,' said Sir Montague with satisfaction. 'To have got that information out of Schulz would have taken weeks.'

44

Lily's interrogator was already seated when she shuffled in the next day. She looked at Berwick to see whether she had permission to sit. She got no response, so she decided to sit. No one stopped her. Behind his inscrutable glasses the steely glint was still there, but did she detect a friendliness in his manner that she had not seen before?

'Miss Rood, good morning.' He had never addressed her like this before.

'Good morning,' she answered, a little flustered.

'I trust it was a pleasant interlude for you yesterday?' he said without irony.

'Yes sir, it was kind of you.'

'Now Miss Rood, you can do something for us.' She looked at him quizzically. 'I want you to work for us.'

'How, sir?'

'If we believe you could spy for the Germans, so can others.' She wanted to protest most vehemently, but decided it was wisest to hear him out. He took off his glasses, put them up to the light, saw where they were dirty and methodically cleaned the lens with a cloth. She watched him put them back and waited for what he was going to say. 'You may be contacted. If you are, I want you to report to me immediately.'

'But why would I be contacted by anyone?'

'Because of your friendship, you will almost certainly be known to the Abwehr.' She looked mystified. 'German military intelligence.'

'Why should I co-operate, after the way you've treated me?'

'Your fiancé was caught impersonating a British officer. In time of war that could mean the firing squad. Help us and it could go well for him.'

'Why did you take me to see him?' She looked at him closely. Did they think an act of kindness was going to soften her? She saw a flicker of a smile in his eyes. A nagging thought lodged itself at the back of her mind. Sir Montague Daventry was cleverer than that! She recalled the strangeness of the room they had been in. That it was empty and brilliantly lit. And why were those lights on the walls so precisely placed? It hit her like a bombshell.

'You were listening in!'

They had been tricked. Friedrich had told her everything, every detail of his mission, the types of explosive they used, the weapons they carried, the names of the men in his unit. She looked gutted. They had no need to interrogate her further. She was being used as the dupe in their clever game. Kindness was not in their scheme of thinking.

'Yes, we had microphones installed and heard everything. We can see now that you were not part of this suicidal mission. You have been a foolish woman, Miss Rood, although I am sure you have come to your senses and will see the wisdom of co-operating with us.'

'You will look after him?'

'I shall do what I can,' he assured her, 'if you do your part. Your indiscreet declarations of support for the enemy's way of life, if not your actual support for their political systems, could have at best landed you in prison and at worst have you branded as a traitor and collaborator. But now as a result you can be useful to us. Equally having interrogated you thoroughly I am convinced it was naivety, not malice, that motivated you and therefore I am recommending that you be released.' Lily's relief was palpable, but she reigned in her excitement at hearing the news. The last few days had been a hard lesson for her and she would now learn to keep her counsel.

'There are conditions,' he added quietly, but firmly. 'You cannot work in any office, civil or military. You cannot enlist in any of the services. You cannot write or say anything that jeopardises your loyalty to your country. If you wish to help the war effort, and I trust you do, it must be in a physical capacity. And as I repeat, if anyone at any time approaches you, you are to contact me or it will go badly for your fiancé.'

'Yes, sir,' she said in a whisper.

He waved a piece of paper in front of her. 'We've just had the news that the farmer's wife is alive ….' He paused for dramatic effect. '…. but only just. She was found bound and gagged under a tarpaulin. She had been there for two days before they found her. If this is how the enemy is going to behave if they ever get over here, heaven help us.' He gave her a long hard stare. 'I thought you might like to know.' He paused for effect. 'And Rood, although we don't use Gestapo methods here, rest assured we would have torn the information out of you and it wouldn't have been pleasant.' He turned to the soldiers, who hurriedly stopped their eavesdropping and stood to attention.

'Send this woman home.'

45

'The uniformed cows drove me back to the police station and I was bloody left there to find my own way home.' Lily took a sip from her teacup. It was Saturday after her release and she and Sally sat in the window of the tearoom looking out through the lattice work tape at the people in the street passing by. To Lily they looked so normal and only hours ago it seemed that she might never see that normal life again. And yet here she was chatting with her dear Sally.

'How awful for you? And to think they thought you were a spy.' Sally sawed away with her knife attempting to make an incision in the stale cake before her. Both remembered fondly the iced fondants and the cream topped confections they once ate, now it was unbuttered buns and rock cakes.

'I was no spy and they eventually accepted that, but not before they put me through hell.'

'Did they put you in a dungeon?' giggled Sally.

'It's no laughing matter. I was locked in a room with the light out. An iron bed with a stinking mattress and a pot to pee in. And that's after they'd stripped me and put me in these oversize pyjamas.'

'Poor Lily. How did they interrogate you? Did they torture you?'

'No. They don't do that sort of thing here. I got a few slaps from the bitch of a sergeant who stood behind me. But he just asked questions.'

'Who?'

'My interrogator. Sally, why are you asking all these questions? I don't want another third degree.'

'I'm just interested. You have to admit, it's rather exciting.'

'Well, bloody stop it.' Sally noticed how Lily's language had coarsened and hardened in the few days of her incarceration.

'I'm sorry,' she said hastily. 'It must have been a terrible time for you.'

'It was. Now I just want Friedrich to be all right.'

'Did he say anything about what he was doing here?'

'Only that they were on some sort of mission which went wrong. Someone had betrayed them, he said. He was badly wounded.' She gave no details and said nothing about the farmer's wife, nor about her meeting with Friedrich, not wanting to arouse Sally's curiosity further. Nor did she give any clue to the deal she had done with Sir Montague Daventry to protect Friedrich.

'I suppose they will send him to a POW camp,' said Sally.

'He will languish there for the rest of the war and I won't be allowed to go anywhere near him.' She looked deliberately fed up, trowelling on the self-pity for Sally's sake.

'Why? You can look for him, Lily.'

'No, I bloody can't!' She raised her voice enough to attract the attention of the couple behind her. 'They've bloody well put me in quarantine. I'm not to go anywhere near any official building. I don't think marching up to the nearest POW camp would be exactly welcome.'

'Shouting won't help either.' To deflect her friend's calculated bitterness, Sally went to order more cakes. The waitress was apologetic. There weren't any. They had used up their sugar ration.

'Oh well, one rock cake is probably enough.'

Sally smiled and asked the waitress to get the bill.

'Are you still in love with him?'

'Why do you say that?'

'Perhaps he betrayed you.'

'That's crazy talk, Sally.'

'Is it?' She looked at her friend quizzically. 'He acted strangely when he was over here. All those notes and maps. Was he using you to plan this attack?' Again Lily saw the flies fly up in front of her. She remembered what he had said in his delirious state, that he would kill her if he thought she had betrayed him. Was Sally right? Did he really love her?

'It was his duty.'

'Not when we were still at peace,' said Sally acidly.

'I know he loves me, Sally. Can we leave it at that?' She wanted to move off the subject.

'How's your job going?' she asked.

'Doing my bit, you know. But it is rather boring. I'm a secretary putting all that training to good use. Can't tell you more.'

'Can't or won't?'

'Both.' Sally grinned. 'You know, hush hush.' She put a finger to her lips. Lily found her stonewalling a little odd. Sally continued by deflecting the conversation back to Lily. 'We've got to get you back to work. Got to do your bit for victory.'

'After what I've been through,' said Lily sourly. 'I'm now branded as a collaborator.' Sally looked at her worriedly.

'Don't say that. You never know whose listening. They say they employ lip-readers to sit in public places.'

'I've no doubt they do,' said Lily with a hard edge of cynicism in her voice. 'I can't go back to the office. I thought I might try the brickworks.' The bill arrived and after they paid it, Lily watched her tousle-haired friend disappear into the Saturday crowd. She sat momentarily with her thoughts. Sally was right. Friedrich had acted oddly with his note-taking obsession, but the love he showed in his eyes when he first saw her in the hospital could not be faked. And the great thing was he was safe here in England. Now she could fight for victory certain they would eventually enjoy a future together in her homeland.

46

'Good heavens, girl, you can hardly drive a car.' Hubert exploded when Lily told him she had been given a job driving a brick lorry. Peg looked on in horror.

'I'll get instruction, Daddy.'

'But look at you,' he protested. 'A slip of a thing. How are you going to handle one of those great beasts.'

'I've met girls who've done it. And, Daddy, I'm not the slip of the girl you once knew.' She hadn't told her parents all that she had gone through during her incarceration. As far as they were concerned it had been a simple question of sorting out a misunderstanding. But hard though it was, she was now the tougher for it, more confident, more self-reliant.

Hubert reflected with a puff on his pipe. 'I think you will, old girl. I'm proud of you.'

'Won't the brickworks be a target? asked an anxious Peg. 'After all the bombs seem to be getting nearer.'

'Have there been bombs here?'

'You mother's talking about the recent bombing of the munitions factory. There was a piece in the local paper.'

'When did it happen? When I was in prison?'

'No, actually – and that was the strange thing. It seems to have happened the night Friedrich crashed in.' Lily looked at them closely. Had they seen the connection, she wondered?

'Odd no one saw any planes, but I suppose we weren't expecting them.'

'You will be careful, dear.'

'Yes, Mummy.' She pecked her mother on the cheek.

The brickworks were as vast as she remembered them, their forest of chimneys as imposing as ever. But what hit her forcibly was the absence of men. There was still the frantic activity she had seen from the train, but now the jobs were mostly being done by women. They put the bricks in the kiln, took them out, loaded them on the flat conveyor trucks and heaved them into the lorries. Lily could see as she walked to the office that it was backbreaking work. But in the event she didn't have to do it. There had been a downturn in the demand for bricks since the war started and so when she applied, the factory already had a full workforce. But she was offered a job driving a delivery lorry.

'I haven't driven much,' she warned the foreman who interviewed her.

'Don't worry love, we'll give you the once around. Not much on the road anyway. Plum job driving a lorry. Gets you to places,' he said with a wink.

Men! They're all the same, thought Lily, with their constant pestering and innuendoes.

'When can I start?'

'7.30 tomorrow. Report to the depot and we'll take you out on the road.'

Lily remembered that Lil hoped to get a job in the office, but she could see no sign of her.

'Does Lil Bates work here?' she asked.

'Day off,' said the foreman.

'Can you tell her Lily Rood is here.' The man nodded.

Back at Fenner Way, Lily found Harris tinkering with the Wolsey. After what he had probably done to shop her, she decided to exact her pound of flesh from him.

'Harris!'

He looked up from under the bonnet, his face smudged and his sleeves rolled up.

'Yes, Miss Lily?'

'I want you to take me driving. I need to refresh myself about what to do.'

'But, Miss, do you have a licence?'

'I don't need one. They've been suspended, remember.'

Lily enjoyed her lesson, with her crash course in double-declutching, mirror reversing and hill starts. By the time she had forced Harris to give her exhaustive tuition she felt moderately confident.

'Why exactly do you want to drive, Miss?'

'I've got a job as a lorry driver,' she said perkily, enjoying his dumbfounded expression as she walked back to the house.

The next day, Lily turned up at the lorry depot in a green knitted sweater, brown trousers and a scarf tied at the front of her head. With the weather turning cool she also wore a short woollen jacket. A young cheery faced woman in dungarees accosted her.

'Hi, I'm Gloria, one of the drivers. They've asked me to give you a test.' The two shook hands.

'Ever driven a lorry before?' Lily shook her head. 'These are small ones. No different from driving an old car. Get in and we'll go for spin.'

Small it may be, but it towered over Lily as she struggled first to open the door and then to climb into the cab.

'Don't make it look …. What's your name?'

'Lily Rood.'

'Lily, you have to make it look like you've done it for years or you'll be the laughingstock at any building site you go to. Let me show you.' With the lithe grace of a practised athlete, Gloria swung herself into the cab with what appeared to be a single leap. Lily looked doubtful.

'Break it into little movements,' said Gloria, repeating her action in slow motion. Lily's second attempt was better, less like a 'silly ninny of a woman' as Gloria said.

Minutes later they were both in the cab with Lily contemplating the key in her hand. Gloria gave her a quick explanation of the controls and told her to drive off. Lily inserted the key, pulled the choke and turned the engine which to her delight exploded into life. Depressing the clutch, she put the engine into first gear, took her foot off the brake and gently squeezed the accelerator. The lorry moved forward. Her time spent with Harris had paid off.

Gloria told her to drive across the depot yard and reverse into the space between two lorries parked on the perimeter fence. Lily put the gear stick into reverse and, using the mirrors as she had been taught, she nudged the heavy vehicle inch by inch into the narrow gap.

'Bravo, love. You're a natural.' Lily brimmed with pride. 'Now all you got to do is not knock anyone down, especially a copper and watch out for those one-legged romeos who want to get you under the bonnet.'

Lily laughed. 'What happens now?' she asked.

'You make your first delivery.'

'No more tests!' Lily looked alarmed.

'Can't afford the time,' said Gloria. 'Get in line behind those lorries over there and wait for your delivery instructions.' She pointed to lorries manoeuvring behind one another and lining up beside a train of trucks piled with bricks. Lily started the lorry and drove slowly over to the melee. Another lorry jumped the queue in front of her and came to an unexpected halt. She was slow to react and had to slam on the brakes. She stopped in time, but the two women careered into the dashboard.

'Silly cow,' shouted Gloria. 'She did that deliberately. Her name's Daphne. You need to watch out for her. You all right?' She pulled herself back into a sitting position.

'I think so. I've been knocked around a bit recently, so I'm used to it.' She smiled ruefully and sat waiting in line with the other lorries. She spotted a man with a clipboard handing out pieces of paper to the drivers. He was the foreman who had employed her.

'That's Mr Jenkins,' said Gloria. 'Boozy Bob we call him. He'll give you your instructions.'

'Why Boozy Bob?' asked Lily.

'He's always trying to get us girls to join him in the pub. But he's harmless.' Gloria saw the lorry in front of them had pulled away. 'Shake a leg, love.'

Lily looked at Gloria, as she moved out of neutral and closed the gap.

'You're not from around here, are you?'

'No. London Town, me, born and bred. But I got out. It was getting too hot.' She indicated to Lily to wind down the window as they pulled alongside the laden trucks. Bob Jenkins came up to the cab.

'How's the new girl, Gloria? She do all right?'

Gloria leaned over Lily towards the window. 'She's going to be a natural,' she said confidently.

'Good.' He handed Lily a piece of paper. That's your first delivery. They're building some pill boxes along the River Orme. Directions and rendezvous point are on your delivery invoice. Wait there and you'll be loaded.'

Gloria opened her door and went to get out.

'Aren't you coming with me?' asked Lily in alarm.

'Got my own lorry. You'll manage OK.' With that she slammed the door and was gone.

Lily was grateful no one could see her petrified face. She could run, she supposed. But no, what was this, but another endurance test thrown her way? She was not going to be defeated.

A sudden surge of voices made her look up. A gang of women in dungarees and headscarves and wearing thick gloves swarmed around the lorry. Lily watched in her mirrors as two of them unbolted the side gates and climbed onto the empty platform. But it was soon empty no more. With a deftness that dazzled Lily, a woman on the ground took a pair of red bricks from the truck and threw them up to the woman on the platform. She placed them carefully on the ground and instantly turned to receive another pair. Soon bricks were piled in formation on both sides of the lorry and Lily was given the signal from the foreman to set off. She turned on the engine, gave a wave to the loading gang and drove the lorry towards the entrance of the yard. She felt the engine struggling with its new-found load and she gave it more acceleration, but she was soon bowling along the empty roads, her early fears rapidly evaporating. The only obstacles in her path were military vehicles, which she gave a wide birth to and often slowed to a halt to let them pass her, invariably accompanied by a cheery chorus of wolf whistles.

Lily hated the brickyard where a fine film of pink dust covered people and lorries alike. It got on everything, clothes, face, hands, the seats in the cab. Lily found she had to wash her hair every night which left it straggly and lifeless, thankfully disguised by the scarf she wore. But once on the open road, coaxing the heavy machine along un-signposted lanes, she felt full of life. She recalled the bicycle rides she had had with Friedrich, but was less smiling now of his irritating habit of constantly stopping to note landmarks in his pocket-book. The idea that he was planning this all along continued to nag her. She wanted desperately to believe she was the centre of Friedrich's universe, but dark thoughts often crowded out such an innocent notion of love. She realised he must be split between his duty to his country and his love for her, as indeed was she.

Most of Lily's deliveries were local. Bob Jenkins, she decided, was keeping a fatherly eye on her and she was grateful for this, as now the days were closing in, it meant she could get back to the depot before dark. She even occasionally exceeded the speed limit to avoid driving in the blackout. With several weeks under her belt she always looked forward to coming into the yard and seeing the beckoning chink of light creeping through the window of the tumbledown hut that passed as a canteen and knowing she would find there a comforting mug of cocoa.

This late afternoon was no different. There was the usual group of drivers, all women, who had returned and now waited to see if they were to get a second late night delivery. They sat around a long table exchanging anecdotes, often heavily embroidered, of what befell them on the road.

'Hey, Lily, back in time to hear what happened to Gloria, today,' a chipper blonde shouted as Lily pushed open the door. She removed the old fur coat that she had borrowed from her mother to protect her in the badly heated cab and went over to the counter to order her cocoa while listening to what Gloria was saying.

'Cheeky devil asked if he could look inside my cab.' She gave a wink to her audience, who didn't miss the innuendos. 'That's after 'e'd 'ad a good look under me bonnet.'

'Did you let him in?' asked the blonde, whose name was Joan.

'Did I 'eck! I let him clamber up and just as he was straightening himself and was going for his belt, I let him have one mighty smacker on the gob. The poor boy was so surprised he fell backwards into a puddle and all I could see through the mud was my lipstick on his lips.' There was a chorus of laughter joined by Lily as she brought over her mug and sat between two of the girls.

Gloria, relishing every moment, continued her tale of the man's discomfiture. 'Just as he was getting out of the mud, I drove forward and then backed up through the puddle and gave him a second soaking.' More laughter.

'Makes you feel good,' said a girl at the end of the table, 'bringing them down to earth.'

'Did that to my Charlie once,' said another. 'Getting a bit uppity he was.' There followed a round of stories about how they shamed their menfolk.

'You got a fella, Lily?' asked Joan.

Before she realised what she was saying, his name fell off her tongue.

'Yes, Friedrich.'

'What did you say, love?' The woman who spoke was Daphne, the sharp-faced driver whom she had nearly run into on her first day.

'Frederick,' she quickly corrected herself.

'No you didn't,' said Daphne, with a surly expression on her face. 'Sounded foreign to me.'

'Isn't Friedrich a German name?' asked one of the others.

'You got a German boyfriend?' asked Daphne with a hint of menace in her voice. Oh no, here we go again. She thought on her feet and lied.

'Yes, I met him in Munich before the war. But he's a refugee now. I don't know where he is.'

'He's not a Nazi then?' asked Joan.

'No,' said Lily firmly. 'Not all Germans are Nazis.'

'What were you doing in Germany,' asked Daphne.

'I was at language school.'

'What did you want to learn that for?'

'We did it at school. I didn't know there was going to be a war, did I?'

'I hate them all.' Daphne's heavy features made her look increasingly intimidating. 'I hate their fucking goose-stepping pantomime. All that puke pouring out of them. To think you actually went there to learn that vomit.'

'Leave her alone, Daphne,' said Gloria. 'It can't be easy. War breaks people up. There must be lots like her.'

'Well, just don't ask me to sit with her.' With that Daphne got up and made a pointed exit.

'She can be a vicious bitch, when she likes,' said Joan.

The others resumed their banter and Lily's background was forgotten although it hurt her to have to lie about Friedrich. But if she was going to get through this war she had to have a cast-iron story for moments like this. Gloria suddenly leant over to her.

'You say your fella's scarpered Germany?'

'Yes.'

'And you don't know where he is?'

'Yes.'

'You could try the Red Cross. They get letters to people who have gone missing.'

'Thank you, Gloria.' Lily smiled, grateful for this small gesture.

There was a rattling on the door and Bob Jenkins put his head round. 'No more deliveries today, ladies,' he said cheerfully. 'You're released.' Chairs scraped, coats were put on and within seconds the canteen had emptied, leaving Lily with her thoughts. She got up slowly, slipped into her jacket, placed her mug on the counter, said goodnight to the woman serving behind the counter and walked out into the cool night air. It was a short walk from the yard to the railway platform and she had done it enough times for the ebony blackness to be no impediment. Tonight she was helped by a near full moon. A bomber's moon. Another raid over London, she wondered? From what she read in the newspaper it happened almost every night.

A noise behind her made her flinch, but she walked on. Seconds later it was there again. She gave a hurried look behind her. It felt like someone was following her. Nothing. She turned back. Daphne stood there. The moonlight caught her and the iron piping she held in her hand.

'My bloke died in a shit hole in Africa.'

Without warning she lunged the piping at Lily, who turned to avoid the blow, but it caught her in the pit of the back and sent her sprawling to the ground.

'And you open your legs to a filthy Kraut.' The piping flew from her hand. It missed Lily's face by inches and clattered harmlessly against a nearby wall. But Daphne wasn't finished. She flung herself onto Lily, pulling off her scarf and yanking her hair. Lily yelped with pain, but as Daphne's contorted mouth screamed 'Bitch' in her face, she summoned her reserves of strength and fought back, her nails sinking into the woman's cheeks, forcing Daphne to let go of her hair. The two wrestled in the brick dust clawing and punching each other, Daphne spitting at Lily amid a stream of abuse. But the blow to Lily's back had bruised and weakened her and little by little Daphne gained the upper hand. The iron piping had rolled back towards them and Daphne spotted it. She extricated herself, stood up, grabbed it and took aim. She never delivered the blow. An arm had come up from behind and wrestled it from her.

'Cut it out, you two.' The voice was authoritative and familiar. Lily looked up and saw Lil holding her attacker.

'Lil', shouted Lily. 'It's me, Lily.' Her friend from secretarial school hovered over her, not recognising her immediately until Lily brushed the dust from her face.

'Blimey. What you doin' down there, love. She causin' you grief?'

'She attacked me.'

'We've had trouble from her before.' Lil released Daphne but held the piping, fingering the end threateningly. 'You best clear out, Daphne, or I'll be reporting you.'

'We shouldn't be having Jerry lovers here. It 'ain't right.' Daphne shook the dust from her clothes and walked off.

'Thanks Lil,' said Lily starting to get herself up. She grimaced. Her body was wracked with pain and only with Lil's help was she able to stand.

'What was that all about? Your usual problem, Lily? German trouble, was it?'

'It follows me around, Lil.' She just managed to pick up her scarf from the ground, wincing with the effort. She looked at Lil, dressed in a smart suit under a short square shouldered coat, which gave her stubby body an unexpected authority.

'Well, it seems to have found you again. Come on, we'd better find out what damage has been done.'

'I'm fine Lil. I really am. No bones broken.'

'Well, let's have a cuppa and chat anyway. That Boozy Bob only told me today that you were here. Said it slipped his mind.' She took Lily by the elbow and together they walked back to the canteen. Lily was able to function but the bruising caused stiffness in her movements and she was grateful for Lil's support. The canteen was empty when they went in and the woman serving showed every sign of shutting up, but they were able to squeeze a cup of tea out of her.

'So what has brought you to the brickworks, Lily?' asked Lil as they sat down at the table.

'You got fifteen minutes before I lock up,' shouted the woman behind the counter.

'OK Kath. We'll not keep you.' Lil looked expectantly at Lily. 'Last I heard you were at the Food Ration office.'

Lily took a sip of lukewarm tea. How much should she tell Lil? She decided to skip her incarceration.

'I fancied some action. Office work is so boring.' Looking at Lil's office-groomed figure, she realised what she had said. 'I'm sorry, Lil, I didn't mean it like that. But I wanted to get into the fresh air.' She gazed at her friend. 'You look smart, Lil. That's a really delightful suit … and I love the jacket.'

Lil brimmed with pride. 'Thanks. Beats skivvying. So you prefer brick dust and lorry oil? I'd never 'ave believed it!' There was a note of suspicion in her voice. 'How's your Friedrich?'

'I haven't heard from him, since the war started. I don't know where he is.'

'That's hard, love,' said Lil sympathetically. 'It's all getting nasty. Could be they'll be trying to invade soon. They say they're all massed on the other side of the channel. Perhaps your fella's one of them.'

'And to think I've been delivering bricks to build gun emplacements to stop it. It's all so horrible.'

'Fifteen minutes up, ladies.'

'Come on, love. I'll help you to the station.'

They stood on the darkened platform waiting for the next train and exchanging gossip about their old typing friends. In the distance they heard the pant of the incoming train. The front of the huge engine glinted in the moonlight as it steamed into the station, the only shape that was visible until Lily glimpsed the red glow of the firebox. The coaches, a blaze of light before the war, were now blacked out and Lily took her chance that the compartment she chose was empty.

'All stations to Bletchley,' came a voice from the inner recesses of the booking hall. Lil helped her aboard with a cheery 'keep in touch.' Inside a thin blue light from the ceiling revealed two other passengers. Entombed within the blackout blinds, Lily eased herself gently into a corner seat, gritting her teeth as she felt the bruise in her back, acknowledged her fellow passengers and thought the idea of trying the 'Red Cross' a good one.

47

'Still no luck, old girl?' asked Hubert several weeks later. Lily had passed Gloria's suggestion to Sally, who took up her suggestion and made a number of attempts on her behalf to locate Friedrich through the local Red Cross centre.

'No. They have no record of him as a POW either in a camp or in a hospital.'

'Chin up, I'm sure he will bounce back.' Lily did not respond to her father's unfounded optimism and pretended to show concern. Although she did find it odd that by now there was no record of him. She could only assume that Sir Montague Daventry still had him languishing in his interrogation centre.

Word soon got around at work of Daphne's attack and Lily found that the woman was given the cold shoulder, although Lily herself kept quiet about it, not wanting to attract any further fuss. The bruising across her back made driving agony at first, but she bore it without complaint. When her parents commented on the stiffness with which she walked, she brushed it off, ascribing it to long hours in the cab. Gloria also noticed it and Lily was grateful to her for offering to take over a number of her deliveries.

Through the canteen window she watched Gloria manoeuvre a brick laden truck out of the yard and she felt a sudden pride in doing work no man thought women capable of only two years earlier.

'Our Gloria handles them things like she's born to it,' said a gruff voice beside her. She had been so rapt by the activity outside the window, she hadn't noticed a woman join her at the table.

'Thanks.' It was Daphne, her features as surly as ever, but not threatening.

'For what?' asked Lily sharply. She was surprised to see her.

'I was wrong to hit you. You could have reported me.' She looked at Lily closely. 'Why didn't you?'

'What would be the point? We need drivers and you're a good driver.'

'Yeah. Well thanks. I got you wrong.'

'I'm not the face of the enemy you know. I can't stop loving him because he's on the other side. He's a POW, God knows where.'

'Sodding war. We've both lost our blokes.'

Bob Jenkins appeared at the window and rapped a pencil against it.

'Hang on. Boozy Bob's calling. I got to go.'

Lily watched her leave and echoed to herself what she had said. 'Sodding war!'

That night she got back to Bletchley station late having been to the pub with Lil. She unchained her bicycle, switched on the shuttered front lamp and set off home. She had barely left the town when a noise made her jump. It was the air raid siren which she hadn't heard since the practices at the start of the war. The quiet night was further interrupted by shouts, sounds of feet running and whistles blown. Not Bletchley surely, she thought? It hardly had anything here that could make it a target. There was Lord Hervey's house she and Friedrich had run into. There seemed to be odd goings on there. They might be coming for that. No, more likely the munitions factory.

She decided she'd better take cover. A ditch ran alongside the road. She laid her bicycle down and clutched the steep incline to avoid putting her feet in the icy water. She crouched as much as she could and waited. Several planes flew overhead. Lily, like most people, had learnt to recognise the different types of plane from their engine noise and quickly realised these were friendly fighters scrambled to tackle a threatened raid. But it never came. The all clear sounded and shivering with the March chill she picked up her bicycle and carried on her way. The next day she learned that bombs had fallen later, one a direct hit on a house in Bletchley and one close to the big house.

But Sally assured her Bletchley wasn't a target. 'They were just dropping bombs to lighten their load on their way back to Germany', she explained, as they chatted over their weekly afternoon tea. 'Probably a raid on Birmingham.' Sally's expert knowledge was starting to intrigue Lily, but her friend continued to be evasive about her work, while Lily entertained Sally with tales of her near misses and rapacious foremen.

'You don't regret the office then?'

'I'm out on the road, Sally, away from all that grumbling. I don't think I could cope with all those bloody posters.'

They laughed. The world for most had become a daily grind of petty aggravations, overseen by a relentless stream of advice from authority. 'Dig for Victory', 'Make Do And Mend', 'Put That Light Out'.

'And don't forget,' they chorused, putting their heads together and speaking in a theatrical whisper, 'Careless Talk Costs Lives'. With their hands to their faces they stifled their laughs and hoped nobody had overheard them.

Sally was pleased to hear Lily's infectious laughter again, but she was sorry that she hadn't had more success in her search for Friedrich.

Lily smiled. 'Thank you for keeping on trying. At least I can live in hope that he's safe.'

They cut their scones. The butter barely covered the end of the knife and there was even less jam. A further cut in the jam ration had just been imposed.

48

Lily arrived at the yard several days later to be met by Lil.

'Mr Roberts wants to see you,' she said urgently. Lily looked surprised but followed Lil's stubby legs across the yard and into the brick works proper. Mr Roberts was Lil's boss and, as she was always saying, a very important person. He was, she later discovered, the senior manager of the works.

They walked across the tracks that carried the little trains from the kilns to the lorries. The dust here was much worse and the noise and heat reached unpleasant levels. Above them the tall thin chimneys belched their noxious fumes while below scores of women moved freshly cooked bricks piled into heavy wheelbarrows from the kilns to the flat trucks. Lily considered herself fortunate to be a lorry driver. Lil had a handkerchief over her face as she passed one of the kilns. It was being fired up and the great doors were open letting a blast of heat shoot into the atmosphere.

'They're controlling the temperature,' shouted Lil above the noise. Lily had put her arm up to her face to protect herself and just heard what Lil was saying. 'It mustn't go above 1000 degrees, so sometimes they have to let heat out.' Lily was relieved when they had got past the kiln and into something resembling a normal atmosphere.

The offices were housed in a two-storey red brick building overlooking the kilns. Lil led the way through a panelled entrance hall hung with photographs of the works and up a grand staircase to Mr Roberts' office. She knocked tentatively on the door to be answered by a firm but friendly sounding voice. Inside Mr Roberts sat at his finely proportioned mahogany desk. Lily recognised him, although she had only seen him once, talking to Mr Jenkins in the yard. She couldn't mistake his willowy frame. Sitting disguised the fact that he was unusually tall and he had a permanent stoop no doubt brought on by his having to continually bend down to people.

'I've got Miss Rood, Mr Roberts,' said Lil with unusual deference.

Mr Roberts invited Lily to sit, while Lil went to a small side desk where she busied herself with the typewriter.

'Miss Rood,' he began briskly, 'I've asked you here this morning because I have an important assignment for you. I understand from Mr Jenkins that you have shown yourself to be a resourceful girl.'

'I hope so, sir,' said Lily, inwardly glowing from the compliment.

'Our lorries are valuable and we don't want to lose them. We've got two stranded in London at the moment with no drivers. They were damaged by a bomb blast. One is a wreck, I've been told, but the other is driveable. I want you to go down to London to retrieve it.' Lily looked at him a little aghast. Surely there were better qualified drivers?

'I see.'

'I can't spare the others. It's a question of time.' And I'm dispensable, concluded Lily.

'Where is this lorry?'

'In a yard off Piccadilly. The lorries had just unloaded a consignment when the bomb fell. Made a pretty mess of the area. The lorry you are collecting was saved by some heavy timbers falling across it.'

'What about the drivers?' A question that occurred to Lily before any other thoughts entered her head.

'Both in hospital, but recovering,' he said. 'Are you up for it, Miss Rood?'

'I'll do my best.'

'Good.' He opened a drawer in his desk and pulled out a buff envelope. He handed it to her. 'There should be sufficient in there to cover your expenses. Travel down today, book yourself into a hotel and pick the truck up in the morning.' She could see Lil giving her a long hard stare and wondering whether she would cop out. She didn't. This seemed no great challenge after what she had already endured.

She returned home, quickly packed dungarees and sweater in a small leather case, slipped on a dress suitable for London, donned her coat, said goodbye to her mother and persuaded Harris to drive her to the station. That she found was the easy part. The local train she caught everyday did not prepare her for the ordeal of long-distance travel in wartime.

The LMS engine had shed its proud crimson livery and was now painted black. But as its great pistons steamed past Lily, making her involuntarily step back, it still boasted of power and speed. She was surprised that so many people wanted to go to London, but she remembered what she had heard on the wireless. Someone was being interviewed and had said: 'He can bomb the heart out of buildings, but he can't bomb the heart out of people.'

'Hurry up, love, we won't be getting on if we dawdle like that.' She looked round and to her surprise saw Ag behind her. She had no time to say anything as she found herself being bundled onto the train in the forward rush of passengers. Safely aboard she looked around but Ag was nowhere to be seen, nor was there an available seat. People were standing in the corridor. Some had upended their cases and were sitting on them. Lily decided she wasn't going to stand all the way to London, but she couldn't even see a space to put her case down. A sudden release of brakes shook the carriage into motion, pushing her against the woman she was standing beside.

'Sorry,' she said as they collided. The woman glared at her, but a small gap had opened up between them and Lily plonked her case in the space and defiantly sat on it.

The train was described as the express to London, but as Lily quickly found out, it was anything but. They had hardly left Bletchley when the wheels began rattling over points and the train gradually slowed and finally slid to a halt with a juddering of brakes. There was an expectant silence.

'Freight,' explained the woman beside her. 'Takes priority.' Minutes later a long goods train trundled by, carrying, Lily surmised, necessary military equipment. 'Will happen again, you see,' said the woman gloomily. It did, three times, but at least Ag reappeared to cheer things up. Her tall friend leant against the window of one of the compartments and opened up a cigarette case. She popped a cigarette out and offered the case to Lily.

'No thanks.'

'Don't smoke then?'

'Sometimes.'

'You won't mind if I do?' Lily shook her head. She watched as Ag took a lighter from her bag and lit the cigarette in her mouth. She drew on it and blew out a cloud of smoke causing Lily and the people around to inhale the fumes that gathered in the confined space. Other smokers had also lit up and soon only an open window gave relief from the fug. There was something about Ag that had changed, thought Lily. She was more smartly dressed, even fashionable, her make-up more tastefully applied. She bore herself with a level of sophistication that seemed a long way from the coarse barmaid she knew at the typing school.

'What are you doing in London, Ag?' asked Lily.

'I live there.' She gave a superior puff. 'By the way it's Agatha now.'

'Lil never said.'

'Lil doesn't know. We've gone our separate ways. You seen her recently?

'We're both at the brickworks. She's in the office. I drive the lorries.'

Her eyebrows rose. 'What a change, darling, and you the posh one, too.'

'I wanted to be active. Somehow it didn't seem right to be stuck in an office when the war's on all around you.'

'Everyone to their own, I suppose.'

'Anyway, what do you do now, Ag …. I mean Agatha?'

'I'm in showbusiness,' she said somewhat haughtily. Of the pair, Agatha was always the one putting on an act, which she was now doing with great agility.

'What sort of showbusiness? Do you act?'

'No darling, I dance.' That sounded very exotic to Lily, but the woman standing beside them could barely disguise her smirk.

'That sounds terribly clever.'

'Not really, not where I go. They always shouted for me whenever they had a knees-up at the pub. Come on Ag, they'd say.' The posh voice faded. 'Show us yer pins.' Their neighbour had by now turned her head to avoid their seeing her creased up face.

'What war does to people.'

'So why are you going to London, Lily?'

'I have a lorry to pick up.' Agatha looked her up and down, giving particular scrutiny to her arms.

'Looks like you might 'ave a bit of muscle there now. You were always a skinny one.'

'Not that skinny, I hope. But, yes, pulling those lorries around builds your arms up.'

At that moment the train which had been keeping a steady rhythm for the last few minutes, slowed again and lurched across onto another track. Lily who didn't know the route was unconcerned. But others, including Agatha, started to look around them.

'What's it doing?' she asked.

'Line's blocked ahead,' said the woman beside them. 'There was a bomb. We're having to go on a big loop.'

'Which will make us late?' asked Lily.

'Almost certainly,' said the woman.

'That's a bloody nuisance. I got rehearsals at two.' Agatha looked at her watch. It was already gone

one o'clock. The train gave no indication that lateness concerned it and trundled in stately fashion along the new route. As they got closer to London Lily saw more and more evidence of the terrible damage that had been wrought on the city. In the streets they passed whole clusters of houses had been reduced to rubble. She watched people, an old man with a stick, a woman pushing a pram, a brave soul on a bicycle, stumbling their way around potholes and piles of fallen masonry. People salvaged what they could. Lily spotted a sofa and other belongings neatly piled outside a bombed-out home. In another street an open lorry was collecting precious possessions. Some roads were untouched and in the backs of the terraced houses the distinctive corrugated curve of the Anderson shelter dominated gardens that were now neatly dug and planted with vegetables. Every so often chickens could be seen running around wire netting enclosures. There was an energy here, a determination not to be ground down, that was so different from the sedate Bletchley she had left.

The train squealed and squeaked its way into the station thirty minutes later than scheduled, but still giving time for Agatha to get to her rehearsal. As they came into the platform Lily caught sight of a large locomotive on its side and several carriages smashed and burnt out.

'Bloody hell,' exclaimed Agatha, 'take a butchers at that. Poor devils never stood a chance.'

'It was empty,' said the woman beside them getting up from the case she was sitting on. 'It happened two nights ago.' As she made to alight from the train she turned and spoke to them. 'Thankyou ladies for your entertaining conversation. You obviously don't read the posters.'

'What a bloody nerve. Who does she think she is?' An incensed Agatha stuck her thumb up to her nose, more for the good it did her than for any effect it had on the woman who had long disappeared.

'Must dash, Lily love. Watch out for those bloody bombs. Come and see me sometime.' She was off the train and disappearing in the crowd.

'Where?' shouted Lily. But she never heard Agatha's reply. She picked up her case and stepped onto the platform to be immediately swept up in a great rush of people. Everywhere she looked there were men and women in uniform all bent on going somewhere as if they were late for the roll call and faced the fall-out from their superior officer's displeasure.

Lily made her way through this seething mass of humanity, passing under a gigantic arch of sandbags guarded by armed soldiers into the station's concourse. She decided she could afford a taxi and walked towards the taxi rank she could see ahead of her. But before she could reach it, she was accosted by a man wearing a cap and jacket with a cabby's badge pinned to it.

'Are you looking for a taxi, miss?'

'Yes.'

'I've just come back on duty. My cab's parked over there.' He pointed to a black vehicle standing some yards away from the others in the rank in an area reserved for off duty cabs. Lily, for all her new-found confidence, was grateful for the offer and together they walked over to the man's taxi. There were cries from the other drivers about jumping the queue, but the man ignored them.

'Hop in love.' He reached out and opened the passenger door. Lily clutching her case climbed into the capacious interior and settled back into the roomy seats.

The cab driver, elderly and rather grizzled, but with a comforting friendly smile, looked back at her.

'Where to love?'

She wasn't certain where the lorry was parked. All she had been told was off Piccadilly, so she simply said 'Piccadilly'. The driver changed the flag on the outside of the vehicle to 'engaged' and drove off. Outside a blitzed London passed by like a macabre tableau. They drove through the shopping area and she observed the arbitrariness of war. Some shops were untouched, others had all their windows blown in. Now people were not just window shopping. They were able to feel the clothes displayed on the mannequins. Lily smiled as she watched one woman stand beside a new dress and measure it up for size. Further on a large notice proclaimed 'Grand Sale of Bombed Out Goods'. No sooner had shop fronts been blown away than hastily erected boards were put in their place. Outside one department store a young woman was up a ladder carefully painting pictures of the fashions on sale inside. Elsewhere wits had fancied their drawing abilities by scrawling slogans and cartoons across the bare board mostly directed at Adolph Hitler. It was still hard for her to swallow the idea that the man she had once admired could be so mercilessly ridiculed.

'You don't come here often, do you miss?' The driver could see through his mirror Lily's wide-eyed amazement at the sights she was passing.

'No. I haven't been since the war broke out.'

'Been some changes.'

'I'll say. Will there be a raid tonight?' she asked anxiously.

'Never know. It's like the weather. At least you can forecast the weather. You never can tell what's in Göring's mind. You going to a hotel?'

'Yes, but I haven't found one.'

'I know a nice safe one just off Piccadilly. I could take you there?'

'That would be kind.' This was not the sort of conversation her parents would be happy with, but this was war and she didn't really know where she was. She had to trust someone.

'One word of advice, love. When you get there, find out where the nearest shelter is. You don't want to be caught out if 'is nibs comes calling.'

'Thanks.' She smiled. He sounded just like Gloria at the brick works. 'Do you live in London?'

'Yes, me and me missus and me daughter. Her fella's in the army and their kids are in Devon. Turns things upside down, don't it?'

'It does.'

'What do you do?'

Lily told him. He nearly ran into a bicycle.

'Cor luv a duck. What you birds are getting up to! Be doing me out of a job.'

'I don't think so,' said Lily who couldn't see herself driving a lorry for the rest of her days. He swung the cab in front of an oncoming bus, which honked him furiously, and drove into a narrow street off Piccadilly.

'Here we are, love,' he said chirpily drawing up in front of a narrow-fronted building proclaiming itself as the Garden Hotel, although Lily saw no sign of a garden. 'Not the Ritz, but that's just across the road.' He pulled in his flag and looked at his meter. 'That'll be two bob.' Lily knew she had to give a tip, but had no idea how much. He saw her predicament. 'Add tuppence.' She gave him the extra pennies, thanked him for his help and walked through the glass and varnished doors into a drearily cramped foyer. A matronly woman stood behind the desk and looked at the approaching Lily with considerable suspicion.

'Can I help you, miss?' she asked with a tone that suggested the opposite.

'Have you a single room available?'

'How many nights?'

'One.'

'This is a respectable hotel, you know, no hanky-panky here.'

'Oh, it's all right,' said Lily brightly, 'I've got a letter of introduction.' She pulled out a folded piece of paper from the envelope Mr Roberts had given her and handed it to the receptionist along with her ID card. The woman unfolded the paper, pretended to read it in detail, huffed with disappointment at finding everything in order and asked Lily to sign the register. She pulled a key off the rack behind her.

'Room 11, first floor. Bathroom at the end of the corridor.' Lily thanked her sweetly and began walking to the spiral staircase that led to the bedrooms.

'And no smoking in bed,' the woman shouted after her as she began her ascent.

With little to unpack, Lily went to the bathroom and splashed some water over face, before beginning the task of locating her lorry. She had been given a map by Mr Roberts, but as all the street names had been removed, the only distinguishing feature on it that she recognised was the Ritz Hotel, which despite being encased in sandbags, stood in stately magnificence on the south side of Piccadilly. But several enquiries of passers-by brought her to the correct street and as she walked slowly along it she saw the lorry standing amid debris from a collapsed building. Over it and protecting it were large timbers and the remnants of a ceiling attached to them. Miraculously the angle with which the timbers had fallen to the ground created a precarious lean-to which protected the lorry. But Lily could see that the whole structure might fall down at any moment. Beyond the lorry stood its fellow completely crushed. Lily thought of the drivers and their lucky escape.

Having found the lorries, she now had to find the person who held the key. Mr Roberts said it was being kept in a small garage close by. She looked around and saw nothing that matched the description, until she spotted an entrance to a block of flats that led underground. She descended the ramp and found a parking area spread out before her. There were two or three cars parked but most of the space was occupied by camp beds with bits of bedding spilling off them. A bomb shelter.

'Can I help you?' A woman's voice came out of the gloom at the far end. Lily could see a small workshop with a pale light illuminating the figure that had spoken.

'I'm looking for a garage. They're holding a key for a lorry parked down the road.'

'You've found the right place, my dear.' The woman, in her sixties, Lily estimated, came up to her, wiping her hands on an oily rag. 'We valet and do repairs on residents' cars,' she explained. 'When they took the girls off to hospital, we said we'd hold the keys and ring up your company and let them know what happened.'

'I was told it was a bomb.'

'No, they had parked up there. It was a bombed-out lot, but the walls of the building next door must have been less sound than they thought. Anyway the vibrations from the heavy lorries caused the building to collapse. Some of it fell on the lorries. As you've no doubt seen, one was saved.'

'It doesn't look too safe. Will it fall if the lorry moves?'

'It's a chance you'll have to take, dear. When you planning to move it?'

'Tomorrow morning.'

'Dressed like that?' She saw Lily's unsuitable attire.

'I've got my dungarees back at the hotel.'

'Come here in the morning and we'll move it together.' Lily thanked the woman, but as she passed the lorry, she looked at it with some concern. Perhaps she should move it tonight? Supposing there was another air raid? But she wasn't going to be driving through London at night. No, she wasn't going to risk herself for a lorry.

49

She climbed the stairs to her room and was about to put the key in the lock, when a dapper young man, smartly dressed in civilian suit and tie, emerged from a room further down the corridor.

'I say,' he shouted, 'you're a pretty young girl. We want someone to join us for a night out.' The cheek of what he said made her stop and take a look. He waved a card in his hand. 'I've got a ticket spare. Do you fancy joining us?' Anywhere else, at any other time, Lily would have slammed the door shut and locked it firmly, but something in his voice, in his barefaced nerve made her hesitate. Now at close quarters she was beguiled by his good looks. His hair was brylcreemed. He wore a neatly trimmed moustache that followed the contours of his upper lip. He had dark features and his eyes twinkled with a rakish charm.

'Why should I accept a ticket from a total stranger?'

'Because, my darling, it's wartime and I'm back with my squadron tomorrow morning and you would make a chap jolly happy if you accepted.'

'What's the ticket for?'

'Theatre revue. Glamorous stuff.' Her eyes met his. Is this what happens in London? A strange man picks you up and you fall for it? Lily was on the point of saying no when a woman in her early thirties came out of another room and stopped beside them.

'Chloe,' said the man, 'this pretty young lady says she will come with us.'

'I never said any such thing,' said Lily, stung by his continued effrontery.

The woman, who was attractive herself, waded in. 'Will you come with us? It will make Jack's evening. You see he's been rather let down and he's back in the air tomorrow.'

Before she could say anything, he had kissed her lightly on the cheek. 'That's the ticket. See you in the lobby in half an hour.' He put his arm around the other woman and the two waltzed off. 'And wear your best frock,' he called from the head of the stairs.

'I haven't got a best frock,' she shouted after him.

Stunned by the encounter she sat on the edge of the bed and reflected what she should do. She needed Sally beside her. As that wasn't going to happen she summoned her in spirit. After their adventures in Munich, which they survived more or less unscathed, perhaps sampling for one night what London had to offer would not be so bad. And he was rather dashing, she thought. She could see Sally over her shoulder egging her on.

Half an hour later, she was standing in the lobby with Jack, Chloe and Chloe's friend Horace. The receptionist scowled at them from behind her desk. They all introduced themselves. Lily admired Chloe, dressed in what might be called wartime chic, a frock of olive-green silk with square shoulders and ruched waist. It fell just below the knee revealing shapely legs in matching olive-green shoes. To walk out she sported a jaunty brown hat and a grey tailored jacket. Lily felt decidedly dowdy in comparison, but if they wanted her they would have to take her as she was. They did.

'Right,' said Jack, 'drinks?' There was a chorus of agreement, raised eyebrows from reception and an exodus into the street, already beginning to assume its wartime darkness. They found a pub, the men downed pints and the women sipped sherries, all smaller measures than before the war.

'Where are we going?' asked Lily eventually.

'The other side of Piccadilly Circus,' said Jack, which wasn't what Lily meant. She tried another tack.

'So you're really a fighter pilot, Jack? Have you shot a German down?'

'Top secret. Hush hush, you know.'

'And Horace, are you in the RAF?'

'Ground crew. Keep the buggers in the air.' She looked over to Chloe, who gave her a knowing smile. 'WAF,' she said.

'And don't you look divine in that cute little uniform.' Horace nuzzled his face into Chloe's neck. She swatted him and laughed.

'And do you have a job, Lily?' she asked. 'We women are all expected to do our bit now, aren't we?'

'I'm a lorry driver,' said Lily simply.

'My, my,' they all chorused.

Jack brushed a finger across his moustache. 'Bet you look a treat at the wheel.' She shot him a cold glare but melted when she saw the twinkle in his eye. Jack, she had to acknowledge, was a looker.

Horace glanced at his watch. 'Hadn't we better be going, chaps?'

They set off down Piccadilly towards the Circus, dodging darkened buses and the occasional taxi. What once had been a blaze of light and illuminated signs now lay in near total darkness. People felt their way along the pavements like so many denizens suddenly struck blind. Lily was aware of Jack steering her with his hand on her arm, a light touch at first and then more firmly as his confidence grew. They braved crossing the Circus using the bollards, which had been painted with white stripes to reflect the dipped headlights of the traffic. They passed the Eros fountain now forlornly boarded up with a black tarpaulin draped over the plinth where the statue once stood. Eros, the proud heart of London, had been removed for safety, Chloe told Lily, as they looked across to what looked like a funeral pyre. On the other side, Jack led them down a side street with the outline of a theatre coming into view. There were no bright signs to entice the expectant theatregoer, but in the gloom Lily could just make out the marquee name 'Forces Fancies' and below it the slogan 'We Never Close'.

'Where are we?' she asked.

'The Windmill Theatre, darling,' said Chloe. 'You've heard of it?'

'No, I don't think so.' They climbed some steps through a darkened door into a brightly lit foyer, which after the darkness outside made Lily blink. She had been in a theatre once when her parents had brought her to a pantomime in London, but she wasn't too sure what to expect tonight. Around the walls were photographs of performers, some clowns, the occasional male in top hat and tails, but overwhelmingly showgirls with plumes above their heads and long graceful legs emerging from the clouds of feathers about their bodies. An usherette showed them to their seats. It was a box just for the four of them and sat above the main auditorium. Jack turned to the girl who had shown them in and ordered drinks, more beer for the men and cocktails for Chloe and Lily. Now on a level with her waist Lily was conscious of how short the girl's tunic was. This was not as she remembered the theatre. She leant over the balcony in front of her and gazed down into the well of the auditorium below. It was filling up fast, mainly with groups of men in uniform, laughing and joking, some in 'civvies', the occasional couple and a scattering of single men. All the services, Lily reckoned, were represented. But she sensed this was no ordinary theatre. There were women, well-dressed like Chloe, but not many. Should she be here, she asked herself?

'What sort of show is it we're going to see?' she whispered in alarm to Chloe.

'Oh, it's all very respectable, Lily. It gives the boys the chance to relax. They're under great stress, you know.' Lily looked at her oddly. Neither Jack nor Horace appeared unduly stressed. Perhaps they were putting a brave face on it. The drinks arrived and she was soon lost in savouring the flavours of her cocktail.

The band struck up a lively swing tune which got everyone tapping. The red plush curtains rolled back to reveal a blitzed London painted on a scenery back drop. A man, dressed in a suit several sizes too big for him, came on and stood in the centre of the stage. He wore a bowler hat and carried an umbrella. He was, he said, 'the spirit of London, keeping his chin up and ready for whatever Uncle Adolph was going to throw at him.' Cheers from the audience were followed by a stream of jokes mostly poking fun at the Nazis. Lily's three companions were soon doubled-up with laughter. Lily was less sure of the jokes although she had to admit they were funny. She realised that she hadn't really known anything about the men being ridiculed. Indeed her knowledge of the political situation in Germany was distinctly hazy. She was beginning to see the truth behind the jokes. Adolph Hitler was not the man she thought he was. The comic on the stage was warming to his theme.

'You know most of the top brass are so vain,' he chortled. 'Take Göring for instance. They say he has attached an arrow to the row of medals on his tunic. It reads "continued on the back".' By now he had his audience in his hand and just as they were left wanting more he broke off.

'But you're not here for me, are you boys?' There was a chorus of 'noes'. 'What you want are our young ladies.' An even louder chorus of 'yeses' erupted.

The comic signalled to the music conductor. 'Strike up maestro and let's bring on the girls.' Lily's eyes were fixed to the stage, knowing that something was about to happen. The musicians fought to be heard over the general uproar that had broken out, but they nevertheless succeeded in belting out a rousing march. To their martial beat a shapely leg shot out from the curtain followed by a lithe body in a figure-hugging military tunic. As the girl swung out onto the stage she had her back to the audience. At the opposite curtain another girl appeared. Soon there were twelve on the stage all in identical tunics. With arms linked behind their backs, they high kicked in unison to the rhythm of the music. Lily noticed they all had a strap around the back of their heads, but it was not until they turned did she see what this was. There was a gasp from the audience as a surreal and slightly unnerving tableau revealed itself. All the girls were wearing gas masks. The long line broke into a series of choreographed actions that mimicked the fighting services. At one point, half put on swastika arm bands and goose-stepped across the stage holding sticks on their shoulders. The other half played Tommies and stood firm against the advancing horde. Soon the lines broke into a melee of arms, legs and flashing sticks as the two sides fought each other, until the Nazi girls were routed and sent flying from the stage. The audience was beside itself. Hats, caps were thrown in the air. There was a crescendo of shouts and wolf whistles. Lily clapped furiously. Curiously, although she couldn't see their faces because of the gas masks, one of the taller girls reminded her of someone she knew.

'Wizard stuff, eh, Lily?' said Jack leaning across her and whispering in her ear.

'They are very well drilled,' she agreed, sliding herself away from him and determinedly concentrating on the next act, a female singer wearing a magnificent red ball gown. She sang a medley of popular songs and quickly got the audience joining in the choruses. When she left, the curtains closed and the comedian returned but his jokes were now more risqué and Lily found herself blushing at some and not understanding others. She was grateful for the dark shadows of the box, although this seemed to give Jack an un-sought for boldness. It wasn't that she wasn't flattered by his attentions but she found herself unnerved by their brazen physicality. Again she was rescued by the events on the stage.

The band produced a fanfare of brass. The curtain retreated to reveal a pastel decorated scene depicting the ornamental garden of an eighteenth century palace. Two girls in crinoline dresses, the fronts cut away at the waist, swung high above the heads of the audience. Legs flashed with the effort of keeping the swings in motion, shoes laced with diamante buckles sparkled in the light, faces heavily rouged and dabbed with a beauty spot smiled beneath white pomaded wigs. Lily was dazzled by the exotic spectacle, but the men leant forward anticipating something that Lily wasn't aware of.

While the girls on the swings continued their graceful arcs, the rest of the troupe came on wearing what appeared to be large flowing nightgowns, lightly belted at the waist through which legs would alternately appear. The music quietened and the girls moved gracefully up a staircase at the back of the stage. They arranged themselves like a tumbling fountain and, as the music started to rise to a finale, they let slip their gowns to fall in a flurry of fabric about their feet. A cascade of artful nakedness presented itself to the audience. Backs, buttocks and slender limbs flowed in a tableau of exquisite taste, which climaxed in a momentary flash of full-frontal nudity as each girl turned and froze. And in that flash Lily saw who the tall girl was that she thought she remembered. Agatha stood in statuesque magnificence.

It was over in a few seconds. The lights went out, but the uproar from the audience who wanted to show their approval of the girls' charms continued for several minutes longer.

'Great titties,' said Jack admiringly. 'What do you think Chloe?'

'I don't, my darling,' she responded evenly, 'and I'm sure Lily feels the same.'

'I thought they all looked very pretty,' Lily answered ingenuously. 'But why did they stay so still?'

'Lord Chamberlain,' explained Horace. Lily looked bemused. 'He's the censor. His rule is that any naked filly on the stage must stand like a statue.'

'Bloody difficult if you're there in your birthday suit,' said Jack.

Chloe pouted. 'Well I'm not sure I want to see a lot of wobbling tits running around the stage.' She gave them a look of disapproval. 'Come on chaps, aren't you going to buy us girls a drink? I'm thirsty.'

On the way to the Crush Bar, Lily turned to Chloe.

'Is it possible to go behind the stage?'

Chloe looked at her in surprise. 'You fancy someone, darling?'

'No. It's just that I saw a friend of mine and I would like to let her know I've seen the show.'

'Well, they don't normally let people in the dressing rooms especially during the interval. But I suppose we could try.' She looked at the press of people crowding the bar. 'It'll take the boys some time to get the drinks.' She took Lily by the arm and steered her away from the throng and led her downstairs. They got to the foyer and were about to ask directions when an usher accosted them.

'Were you in a box?' he asked.

The two women nodded, surprised.

'Is one of you Miss Lily?'

'I am,' said Lily.

'Message from a member of our cast.' He handed Lily a folded piece of paper. It read simply: 'Come and see me. A.' She showed it to Chloe, who asked the usher to take them backstage. They went through a small door behind the Box Office and found themselves in a warren of dimly lit passageways that gave onto dressing rooms and work areas. There was a constant traffic of artistes and technicians moving back and forth along the corridors. It was a bizarre mix of near-naked girls and men in dungarees not blinking an eyelid as they passed. She heard a voice call out from one of the dressing rooms and turned to see Agatha doing up a feathered brassiere ready for her next call. Lily looked in wonder at her skimpy costume, displaying an enviable figure she never thought she had.

'I got a bloody shock seeing you in that box. Gave me a right turn, it did, Lily, love.' Agatha came out of the dressing room and stood in the corridor. Chloe left them, saying she would see Lily back in the theatre.

'What you doin' here, Lily, and who's that dame and the Johnny you were with?'

'Friends, I picked up,' said Lily guilelessly. 'I met them in the hotel. They had a spare ticket for the show.'

'You got to be careful. Fellows like him are on the make, you mark my words.'

'He's nice.'

'Aren't they all! Look Lily,' she took her by the shoulders, 'don't tell Lil you've seen me. She's a bit straight about girls doing this sort of thing.'

'Don't worry Ag ... I mean Agatha, mum's the word.' Lily felt a conspiratorial excitement about keeping Agatha's secret.

'Good girl.'

'I thought you were jolly good. Are you going to have to show your ….,' she hesitated and fell back on the word Jack had used, '….your titties again?'

'Bloody men! That's all they want.'

'Chloe … that's the woman who came with me …. said they could be dead tomorrow.'

'And so could we!' Her eyes flicked heavenwards and then back at Lily. 'And so will I if I don't get on stage.' As she spoke the slow whine of the air raid siren could be heard working its way down the passage.

'Bloody hell, Lily, they're coming. And I'm dressed like some fucking parrot. Get out of here, love.' She turned and disappeared into the dressing room, the cheeks of her shapely backside, fluttering with feathers, being the last Lily saw of her.

50

Air raid! The very words sent shivers through Lily. With many others she raced along the passage and out into the foyer. The theatre was being evacuated. All doors were wide open and people were being pushed unceremoniously through them into the street. Lily stood with her back to the wall trying to locate Jack and his friends among the bubbling mass of humanity emerging from every orifice in the theatre. She kept her eye on the staircase and finally caught sight of Chloe's distinctive hat.

'There you are, darling,' Chloe cried when she spotted Lily. 'We were so worried. Stick to us now. We're going into the tube.' She threw Lily's coat at her, grabbed her hand and walked hurriedly into the cold night air, the wail of the siren propelling everyone forward with a desperate sense of urgency. Lily couldn't see Jack or Horace but then as if by magic they appeared alongside and the four walked briskly into the Circus and down the steps of the first tube entrance they encountered.

To prevent a stampede, officials were blowing whistles and directing the flow of people into the deeper arteries of the station. Jack and the others followed the sounds until they reached the top of the escalators. The moving staircases had been turned off. On all but one, two or more people had staked a couple of steps and were sitting on them. Some had unwrapped sandwiches, others drank steaming tea from thermos flasks. Several were playing cards. A couple sat with their arms around each other and were staring dolefully into space. Those sitting, Lily decided, had arrived early and were prepared. Most, she noticed, had brought blankets with them and were now in the business of turning them into comfortable nests.

She held onto Chloe's hand as they descended further down the escalator. At the bottom Horace spied a space big enough to accommodate the four of them.

'Plonk yourself down here all of you,' he said triumphantly, and Lily found herself sitting on a cold concrete floor tramped over daily by thousands of feet. But she was safe and leant against the cream and blue ceramic tiles that lined the tunnels with a sense of relief. She hoped Agatha had got away, although probably there were cellars in the theatre the cast could shelter in. It was a shock to find Agatha performing as a showgirl, but then she had always enjoyed attention, Lil had said, even as a barmaid.

Lily's thoughts were interrupted by distant thumps. People went silent.

'Bombs,' whispered Jack. The thumps were getting closer and louder. Their deep bass sound vibrated around them. Lily could hear the roar of aircraft engines now. They must be overhead, she thought. But the explosions stopped. Jack and Horace looked at each other.

'Must have shot their bolt,' said Jack.

'They've gone?' asked Lily.

'There'll be another wave soon,' said Horace.

'How long does this go on for?'

'All night,' said Jack ominously.

Chloe chipped in. 'Don't frighten the poor girl. It doesn't happen so much up west,' she said reassuringly. 'It's the poor devils in the east that get it.' But Lily hadn't heard the siren giving the all clear. In the hushed expectancy the distant notes of an accordion wafted up to her. It was a comfort to hear it. Then came the chilling drone of more planes. Wave after wave of them. But no explosions.

'The poor blighters that lot are targeting are in for a pasting,' explained Jack. 'Let's hope that's it.' It was. As the noise of the engines died away, the all clear sounded.

'Come on,' said Jack, lifting Lily up, 'let's get back to the hotel.' The four stretched tired joints and joined the exodus climbing the solitary escalator. None of those lying on the other staircases moved. Chloe could see Lily's puzzled expression.

'They're from the East End. It's safer here. They've probably been bombed out.'

'How awful.'

'They're alive.' Lily looked at Chloe's elegant clothes and wondered how that went down with the wretched people lying on the escalator. But no one seemed to notice. No flicker of resentment in their eyes, just a dull acceptance of their lot and a determination to see it through. If Chloe could walk around in a silk dress, then good luck to her seemed to be the message they were conveying.

Once again in the bustling darkness of Piccadilly people were making their way home. There were no buses or taxis, just pedestrians and the odd bicycle. Jack took Lily's arm in his, while Horace did the same with Chloe. They had just reached the two great London hotels, the Ritz and the Berkeley, and were turning up the side street that led to their hotel, when Jack stopped. He appeared to be listening for something.

'Hear that?' he said looking at the sky. None of them could, until Lily's ears picked up what Jack had heard.

'A plane.'

'In trouble. Its engines are spluttering.'

'Is it going to crash?' asked Chloe.

'Yes,' said Horace.

'Unless it can lighten its weight'

'It's a Heinkel,' Horace explained. 'It's on the return run, so it will have jettisoned its bombs.'

'Will it?' asked Jack in alarm. He urged them to move faster. 'We need to get to the hotel.' Lily could hear the engines clearly now. They seemed to stop and then judder back into action.

'It's misfiring,' said Jack as they started to race up the road to the hotel. But they never got there. Lily felt Jack's hand grab her across the chest and pull her into a porch. The other two squeezed into the tiny space with them. It was a tight fit and not a minute too soon. They heard a clear whoosh followed by an ear deafening explosion. Lily felt air sucked from her lungs and watched in horror as a whirlwind of dust and debris swept passed them. She lost her hearing and was conscious only of fine particles falling around her in slow motion. It lasted a few seconds, but seemed much longer, and all the while she felt Jack's hand pressing into her breast. Her heart missed a beat, then without warning her hearing returned and a cacophony of sounds and voices assailed her.

Jack stepped out of the porch and looked down the street to Piccadilly.

'My God!' was his shocked reaction. One by one the others emerged shaking dust from their clothes. Lily felt suddenly sick. Her hand went involuntarily to her mouth. In the distance through the dust and blackness she could just make out shapes moving, but it was the sound of screams and the cries of pain that shook her. The men stood rooted to the spot. Chloe took Lily by the hand and walked with her towards the chaos.

'People need our help Lily,' she said urgently. What help could she give, wondered Lily, but then she had helped dress Friedrich's wound. The bomb had struck a side street causing the blast to be funnelled into Piccadilly throwing pedestrians across the street and wounding them with splinters of brick and glass. Lily nearly stumbled over a man crawling towards a prostrate and motionless woman. Nearby another woman was curled in obvious agony. Confusion was everywhere. Figures were stumbling around trying to find companions who only moments ago were walking beside them. A woman screamed hysterically and grabbed at Lily's leg. 'Is that Dolores? I can't see.' Lily gently released her grip with a heartfelt no.

Men with torches were emerging from the hotels. In the flashes of light Lily could see the terrible wounds that had been inflicted. Her head whirled. She felt powerless to do anything, until Chloe shouted at her.

'Lily take off your stockings.' Lily saw at once that silk could double as a bandage and jumped to Chloe's command. She kicked off her shoes, fumbled with her suspenders and hastily rolled down the last silk stockings she owned. In her fluster to remove them she hadn't seen that Chloe had thrown off her coat, had stepped out of her silk dress and was stripping off a lace trimmed slip, which she furiously rent into strips. A wounded man lay in front of her, a stream of blood gushing from his side. Chloe threw her dress at Lily to hold, while she bent down beside the man and gently pulled up his shirt and vest. Lily gasped. The jagged wound was worse than the one Friedrich had received. Chloe rolled the fabric of her slip into a pad and thrust it into the bloody flesh holding it firm. She told Lily to tie her two stockings together and run the length round the man's back while she held the reddening pad. As Lily knelt down and did as Chloe told her, she could see the man's feverish eyes and his face twisted with pain. He was elderly, probably in his sixties. He could have been her father. As gently as she could she brought the stockings around the body and tied the ends together, holding the pad in place. The man looked grateful, but he began shaking uncontrollably.

'Use your coat as a pillow, Lily. We've got to keep him warm.' Chloe took her own coat and used it as a blanket while Lily with the tenderness of a nurse raised the man's head and deftly slipped her folded coat under it.

'Thank you,' he whispered. She stroked his brow and smiled.

'The ambulances are coming.' She could hear the approaching sirens and a growing number of official orders rising out of the confusion.

Lily looked up and saw Jack and Horace stripped to the waist tending a group of wounded. She stared at Chloe's bloodstained underwear. The whole scene resembled a macabre striptease.

'Put your dress on Chloe,' said Lily handing the silk garment back to her.

'And get it ruined? I paid a fortune for that, darling.' Lily looked at her in wide-eyed wonderment. How could a woman prepared to sacrifice her dignity to help another, still prize a silk dress above everything else?

Stretcher bearers appeared and took over. One of the men handed back the coats and replaced them with blankets.

'Here, love,' he said to Chloe, 'you'll catch your death of cold if you don't put this on.' Chloe thanked him and wrapped the coat around her.

The four stood in the foyer of their hotel, blood-spattered, half-naked and bewildered. The harridan who'd been behind the reception desk earlier had thankfully gone off duty. What she would have thought of them standing in her respectable hotel in such a state of undress Lily could only guess. The man who sat there now could only stare open-mouthed. Lily felt she was living in some ghastly tableau from the Windmill Theatre.

'I could die for a drink,' said Horace.

'Fat chance,' said Jack. 'I tried last night. You might have been asking for Hitler's balls.'

'I don't think I could get a drink down me, I'm so shattered,' said Chloe. 'I'm going up. Coming Lily? You shouldn't have been seeing what we saw.'

'Oh, I'm tougher than you think, Chloe.' The woman looked at her not quite sure what she meant. Lily didn't elaborate.

'Still, you look done in.'

'I am.' The two women went over to the reception to get their keys and climbed to the firstfloor landing. Chloe turned to Lily and touched her shoulder.

'It was lovely having you with us tonight. But I won't see you in the morning. I'm not planning to get up.' She kissed Lily lightly on the cheek, turned with a sway of the hips and clutching her precious dress, disappeared into her room.

Lily was desperate for a bath, to wash away, she hoped, the horrors of the evening. As she was putting the key into the door of her room, she felt hands on her shoulders and her body being swung round. It was Jack. He embraced her without warning and gave her what he would describe as a passionate kiss and what she saw simply as unwarranted forwardness. She pushed him away roughly.

'Jack, what are you doing,' she gasped.

'It was terrible what we saw tonight. I thought you might need a little comfort. We could share a room.' She looked aghast.

'No, Jack. You've got it wrong. I'm not that sort of girl.'

'Lily, it's war. People do this in wartime.'

'Not me, Jack. I have a fiancé.'

His tone changed. 'I've given you a night out, Lily. I'm only asking for a little feminine solace in return.'

'Then you chose the wrong woman.' She glared at him with real anger. How dare he think his pretty boy looks could seduce her just like that. 'If you'll excuse me, I must have a bath.' She gripped her key thinking it unwise to open her bedroom door and walked down the corridor to the bathroom. She locked the door firmly behind her. She could hear him outside.

'I thought you were a girl with more sense of fun. Goodnight, Lily.' She heard his footsteps receding and a key turning in the lock.

She breathed a sigh of relief. She went to the bath, turned on the hot tap and found no water coming out of it. 'Wartime restrictions' the receptionist would have said, but for Lily it was the last straw. She collapsed on the floor beside the bath and burst into tears. She was beginning to hate Germany and all it stood for. How could one country inflict so much suffering on another? The pain she had already endured, the terrible sights she had witnessed were starting to remove the scales from her eyes. Sally had been right. What they had experienced and admired during their time in Munich was only half the story. A regime that could conduct a reign of terror against innocent people and drop bombs on them night after night was doing great wrong. Surely Friedrich must come to see this. She resolved that when the war was over she would do everything she could to make him accept that what he so ardently believed and supported had turned bad.

Her sobs gradually died away. She dragged herself off the floor and looked at the splashes of blood down her coat and dress. She turned on the cold tap and a trickle of water dribbled out. She let it run while she removed her clothes and gingerly stood in the freezing puddle. She washed the dirt and blood that smeared her legs and thought of the injured man she had nursed. This was his blood that stained the water. She prayed that he would be all right. Cleaning herself as much as she could, she stepped out of the bath and then realised she had no towel. Was he still outside? She opened the door as quietly as she could and looked out. He had gone. She gathered up her clothes and ran naked and dripping to her room. She had just reached it when a voice called out.

'Goodnight beautiful. You look amazing.' She blushed and threw her clothes up against her front. No man had seen her naked before, not even Friedrich. She caught him grinning from his doorway, in his dressing gown. The arrogance of this cocky young man knew no bounds, but why did she feel strangely flattered? She pushed herself against the door and backed in, locking it with a decided turn of the key.

She found a towel lying on her bed. Her teeth were chattering and she rubbed herself vigorously to get the blood coursing through her veins. She had brought a pair of flannelette pyjamas with her and these contributed to her sudden sense of well-being. In fact as she lay in bed, it was not the destruction she had witnessed that sent her to sleep, but the thought of Jack flying fearlessly above her in his Spitfire.

51

Strange disfigured shapes groped towards her through swirls of smoke and debris. The gashed and bloodied face of an old man pleaded with her for help, but she could do nothing. 'I haven't the skills,' she told him. All she could offer was a comforting hand wiped across his brow. He thanked her. Beyond a woman stumbled blindly about her until she crashed into the old man and the two fell at Lily's feet. The woman's head rolled away. The old man's arm split from his shoulder and skidded across the road. Lily could take no more. She woke with a start, soaked in sweat. She looked at her watch. It was five thirty in the morning. Perhaps the hot water was now running. Hot or cold she had to wash away the terrible nightmare that had woken her up.

Feeling refreshed from the cold bath, she dressed ready for the drive back to Bedford. She was surprised when she entered the breakfast room to find Jack sitting alone at a table reading a newspaper, smoking a cigarette and drinking a cup of coffee.

Shaven and fresh looking, he had lost his slouched weariness of the night before. It was an empty room and he got away with a suppressed wolf whistle when he saw Lily.

'The new working gal stands before me,' he drawled in a patronising American accent. He put down his paper and opened his arms as he spoke. 'You sure look great in those dungarees, Lily. And isn't that scarf the very fetching image of our modern woman.'

'You're up early and in sparkling form, Jack,' she said sarcastically.

'Like you, couldn't sleep. Anyway I'm back on duty at mid-day.' He gestured to her to sit down. 'Join me for breakfast. I'm told it's fried bread, one sausage and powdered egg. Just what a chap needs before he throws himself at the Hun.' She caught him ogling her breasts pushing through the stretched wool of her sweater. He was irrepressible. She smiled and pulled a chair back.

'My tits do something for you, Jack?'

'They sure do baby doll.' He continued the affected drawl as she sat down.

'It must be lonely up there with no woman to sit on your knee.' What was she saying? Was this what they called flirting? He made her say these things.

'That's why I make up for lost time when I'm grounded.' He looked her over again. 'You going to drive that bloody lorry back to …. where was it?'

'Bedford.'

'Which is where?'

'Bedfordshire.'

'Of course. Don't break down. We RAF chaps won't be able to help you and there are some pretty shifty army blokes out there.' He looked around him.

'No sign of Horace and Chloe.'

'Chloe said she was going to lie in.'

'Bloody ground wallahs.'

Their banter was interrupted by the waitress asking what they wanted. Lily looked up and saw it was the sour faced receptionist of the day before.

'What's on offer, love?' asked Jack.

'Don't call me love, young man.' Jack gave a mock apology with his arms. She scowled and read from the menu. A mushroom was added to the litany Jack had already described. She solemnly wrote down their identical orders.

'You all got in late last night I hear. A bit the worse for wear, I've been told.'

'And you've no doubt been told,' said Jack, savouring his words, 'that a bloody great bomb fell in Piccadilly and we were fucking caught up in it.'

'No need to swear, young man,' she huffed importantly.

'And you were no doubt told that we were covered in blood - other people's blood when we came in.'

'Well, I'm only repeating what I was told.' She looked thoroughly discomforted and quickly left. They both laughed, although Lily felt a little sorry for her.

By the time they had finished their food, the breakfast room had filled up and they left quietly. When they reached their landing, Jack made a great play of saying goodbye as if, thought Lily, it was going to be his last.

'Safe journey, Lily ….' He paused. 'I don't know your other name?'

'It's Rood. And yours?

'Havering.'

'Goodbye Lily Rood.' He took her to him and kissed her.

'Goodbye Jack Havering,' she whispered. She felt she was playing out every wartime romance she had seen at the pictures, but the kiss nevertheless sent a warm tingle through her body.

During brief moments in this strange interlude she had lost sight of Friedrich. But as she walked to the garage to collect the key for the lorry he came back into her head. Whatever might happen, she knew she had to hold on to her love for him.

The woman at the garage accompanied her as promised to where the lorry was parked. They stood for several minutes looking at the precarious overhang that protected the vehicle from further damage but which was also the source of its possible demise.

'Do you think it will fall?' asked Lily anxiously.

'Who knows? Your one hope is getting enough acceleration to clear it before it starts falling. See if you can get it into a high gear before you move off. That way you set up less vibration.' Lily looked doubtful. She opened the cab door and climbed in. She was horribly conscious of the heavy timbers above her head. She heard the woman from the garage calling to her.

'We'll hand crank it. That way we'll be sure it will start. You need to pull the choke out.' She located the crank handle, which was inside the bonnet, inserted it into the front of the engine.

'Standby. The moment it starts, get it into gear and drive.' Lily bit her tongue. Her hands were clammy on the steering wheel. The woman gave the handle a massive yank. The engine spluttered and died.

'Close the choke. I'll try again.'

She let the handle fall to the ground and then hurled herself at it with all her strength. Her powerful action succeeded. The engine burst into life. Lily engaged the clutch, struggled with the gear stick and took her foot off the brake. The lorry started to move and she pushed down on the accelerator. An alarming high pitch whine from the high gear revs pierced her ear, but she was conscious the cab was lacking the juddering that usually accompanied starting up the engine. This allowed her to make progress until a bone-shaking crunch shook the cab. The roof had collided with one of the timbers. Lily saw it visibly move, then it seemed to stabilise itself. She exhaled air and carried on. She was almost out of the lean-to, when she heard the chilling sound of metal grinding on metal. For seconds after the collision the lean-to appeared to be in a state of suspended animation, but the impact had disturbed its equilibrium and inexorably it began to slide in the direction of the retreating lorry. The woman from the garage pointed frantically at the falling pieces, but there was nothing Lily could do except continue to accelerate. In her side mirror she saw the huge beams chasing her, getting lower as they came closer. The nearest caught the end of the lorry wrenching off the tailgate on its fall to the ground. But she was now clear of danger and stopped the lorry. As she found herself collapsing at the wheel, she caught sight in her rear mirror of the whole structure toppling into a pile of dust and debris.

'Are you all right, dearie?' The anxious garage woman opened the cab door and looked in. A relieved Lily smiled down at her.

'That was close.' As she spoke, they both heard the clanging bell of an approaching police car. It sped to a halt outside the yard and two uniformed policemen jumped out. They could see at once what had happened. The dust was still settling around the beams, now shattered into pieces.

'You the driver?' asked one looking at Lily. She nodded. 'So this lot has just fallen and missed you?' She nodded again. 'You were lucky, miss. But you shouldn't have been parked here. You must have seen that structure could have come down at any moment.'

'It wasn't like that, officer,' interjected the garage woman. 'She is just collecting it.' He looked back up at Lily.

'Would you mind stepping down, please miss.' She did as she was bid and together the two women explained the situation. The policemen seemed convinced.

'Can I drive off?' asked Lily. Neither answered, but one went around the lorry and examined the damage at the back.

'You can,' he said eventually, 'if you don't load anything on it until you get this fixed. We don't want bricks falling all over the road.'

'Where are you headed, miss?' asked the other policeman.

'Bedford.' Lily suddenly realised she had no idea of the route out of London. She decided to play the helpless innocent. 'I'm afraid I don't know my way around London much. Could you tell me the best way to go?' The older of the two men barely hesitated.

'We can do better than that, miss. We'll show you the way. Just follow us.'

Lily thanked her friend from the garage, hoping she had shown sufficient gratitude for all the help she had given her. She was sure Mr Roberts would show his appreciation later. Then she climbed into the cab, started the engine and waited for the police to move off. This took several minutes while they finished writing up their notes. She watched the police car's indicator come out and made herself ready. With a cheery wave to the garage woman, she followed the car into the road and they were away. She followed closely feeling very important especially when the police used their bell to bypass knots of traffic. Within fifteen minutes the black Wolsey had negotiated itself out of the maze of back streets and onto a main road heading north. About a mile up this road, it started flashing its lights and finally pulled into a lay-by. The driver's window came down and a uniformed arm waved her on. Lily pressed her horn in thanks and drove past, once more on the open road looking for a petrol station. In her pocket she had precious coupons given to her before she left.

52

The day was warm and sunny. Lily made good progress and quickly found herself driving along roads she was familiar with. At the rate she was going she would be back at the brickworks before the other lorry drivers had returned from their daily deliveries. She wanted to be in the canteen before they got back so she could tell them about her big adventure. She started to rehearse the story in her head, although parts she knew she would have to omit. She was happily embroidering detail, when the engine started to develop an alarming judder. Please don't give up on me, she pleaded to the spluttering machine, but it didn't listen and in the middle of nowhere on a country lane it died.

She managed to park the still moving vehicle on a grassy verge and jumped out. She waited for the engine casing to cool off and then opened the bonnet. When she checked the water and the oil levels, she found they were both reading correctly. She concluded the problem was in the engine itself, at which point her technical knowledge dried up. She had no alternative but to wait for someone to come along. She looked around her. It was the middle of the day, with not a soul in sight. The occasional plane flew overhead but they were too high up to notice her and were unlikely to be concerned even if they did. In the distance further along the road she could see a farmhouse. She would have to walk there if no one came along, but for the moment she decided to assuage a sudden hunger pang by rummaging in her case and locating a few dried biscuits. She sat down on the verge and munched happily amid clumps of primroses that the warm spring sunshine had brought into flower. Her mind drifted to Friedrich. It suddenly alarmed her that she hadn't thought of him for a while. Her time in London had been clouded by Jack's persistent presence. Why, with his odious attempts to force himself upon her, had she found him so strangely attractive? A disturbing notion entered her head. Just as she was confused over her feelings for Sally, so now she wondered whether you could fall for two men at the same time? She thought at first that it was just Jack's good looks, his debonair charm, but now, looking back on the moment, when Jack had asked to come into her room, she realised, despite her protestations, that she was on the edge of letting him in. The reality of this both troubled and excited her.

    A sudden prick in her hand broke her reverie. She had touched a sprouting stinging nettle and jumped to her feet with a painful cry.

    'Damn, that hurts. Dock leaf. There must be one here. They always grow nearby.' She hunted around and found a clump beside a hedge. Picking several leaves she rubbed them over the sting, releasing their healing juices into her skin. As the pain eased, she became aware that a vehicle was approaching. It was a tractor. She stood watching it get closer wondering whether to flag it down. She needn't have worried. The driver had seen she was in trouble and was pulling onto the verge. A cheery looking woman with a weather-beaten face in her mid-thirties sat at the wheel. She turned off the engine of the tractor.

'Are you in trouble?'

'Broken down, I'm afraid. I need to get to a garage or a telephone.' The woman slipped off her seat and came over to the lorry. She gave the engine a cursory look and shook her head.

'I'm not sure I can help you, but I know someone who can.'

'Who?' asked Lily.

'My father. He's a wizard with this sort of thing. We'll find him in a field behind the farm.' She told Lily to put the bonnet down and come with her. They walked over to the tractor. Lily wasn't sure how she was going to ride on it until the woman told her to climb onto the tailgate and put her arms around her waist as if she was riding pillion. The tractor moved off almost throwing her into the road, but she clung on as the woman drove into the farm, past the house and barns and stopped in a large field beyond, where another tractor was working.

'There's Dad.' She hollered and waved. The tractor changed course and came towards them.

Lily looked in puzzlement at the long wooden box it was pulling.

'That's a seed drill. We're planting wheat,' the woman explained. The man driving the tractor had the same cheery weather-beaten face as his daughter. He wore a moth-eaten jumper and a pair of mud-spattered corduroy trousers. On his head sat a cap, threads fraying at its peak.

'Dad, this young lady's lorry has broken down. Could you take a look at it?' Lily thought how matter-of-factly she said it. Before the war a girl driving a lorry would have been a source of much curiosity.

'Where is it?'

'Not far. You can see it from here.' She pointed to a shape in the distance.

'I'll see what I can do,' said the old man climbing down from his tractor. 'I'll take your tractor, Edith, and pick up some tools from the house. Where were you headed, miss?'

'The brickworks near Bedford.'

'Probably got brick dust in the carburettor.'

'I've also been in London.' added Lily.

'Right.' He climbed into the seat of the woman's tractor and drove off.

The woman turned to Lily. 'I'm sure you could do with a cup of tea?' Lily nodded. 'Come on then, let's go up to the house.' The woman's father had called her Edith. Where had Lily heard that name recently? As they walked side by side, a feeling that she had been here before caught hold of her. Perhaps she had driven past on one of her deliveries?

They entered an old beamed hall and the woman led Lily into a kitchen with a stone-flagged floor and a large table in the centre. It was dark and would have felt cold had it not been for the long black range that created a warm cosy atmosphere.

'Sit down, please. I'm Edith.'

'Lily.'

'Are you hungry?' Lily, who hadn't eaten properly since breakfast - and it was now nearly four o'clock - nodded.

'I've some bread and cheese. We make our own cheese here,' said Edith, picking up a blackened kettle, filling it with water and putting it on the range.

'That sounds delicious.' She looked around her. The place was spartan but tidy and well kept. Edith was clearly a capable woman. 'Do you run the farm on your own?' she asked.

'Just me and dad. We do have help from some land girls. I'm hoping to get a couple permanently. And of course there's Tommy.'

'Who's Tommy?'

' Our son. He's at school. He'll be back shortly and then he gets stuck in. He's a great lad.'

Lily smiled. 'Your husband's away I suppose?'

'Yeah. Vic's in the army. Somewhere in Africa.' She put what was clearly a freshly baked loaf on the table. Lily's mouth started to water, made more intense by the dish of cheese, newly patted butter and home-made jam that accompanied it. 'Have you got someone?' she asked looking up at Lily as she cut generous slices of bread from the loaf.

'Yes. We're engaged. He's in the army.'

'It's hard. But we make the most of it, don't we?' She pushed the bread in Lily's direction. 'Now tuck in. You look starving. I'll make the tea.'

Lily watched her go back to the range and thought what a comely and attractive woman she was. She took a slice of bread, spread butter over it, cut an accompanying portion of cheese and began to eat. What she savoured was a slice of heaven.

'Edith, this butter is the best I've tasted for months.'

'The advantage of having a farm,' her host called back, spooning tea into a teapot. Lily munched away and surveyed the room as she did so. Her eye caught a small pile of letters neatly placed at the end of the table. The top one was upside down and she played the game of trying to read it. She translated the address, Pickering Farm, Northampton. The name at the top was more difficult, but she finally deciphered it as Mrs V Lambert! She froze to the bone. The woman coming across to her with a pot of tea was Edith Lambert and it was an Edith Lambert that Friedrich's squad had tortured and kidnapped and, but for Friedrich, would have murdered. Beads of sweat broke out on her brow. Was this the same woman? Was that why she had experienced a sixth sense about the place? It fitted. This must have been the area where the soldiers got lost. There can't be any other Edith Lamberts.

'Are you all right?' As Edith put the teapot on the table she saw tears welling in Lily's eyes.

'Sorry, I've come over all emotional. It's tasting the butter. It's been so long.' She wiped her arm across her face.

'Driving that lorry has probably taken it out of you.' She poured a cup and handed it to Lily. 'Get this hot tea down you. You'll feel better.' Lily gave a wan smile and let the hot liquid work its magic.

'I saw so much destruction in London. It was horrible. Night after night those poor people.' Edith's expression suddenly changed. Gone was the warm smile to be replaced by a look of hatred.

'Those bastards. They're so cruel and hateful. What they do to people is nightmarish.' Her voice was filled with vitriol and the bitterness she expressed could only have come from personal experience. 'Lily, we have to destroy them.'

'We will,' said Lily in sympathy, but doubting her own voice as she said it. Edith sat down beside her and launched on a story that stunned her.

'We had a refugee from Belgium speak to us at our village hall. She spoke of the shootings and other cruelties the Germans inflicted on her country. She spoke of one woman, a farmer's wife, like myself, who was alone in her house when a gang of German soldiers burst in and asked the way. They were lost. She refused to tell them, so they wrapped a wet towel over her head, pulled it tight and thrust her face into a sink filled with water. She said she thought she was going to drown. They did this again and again until she told them what they wanted.'

'How awful,' was all Lily could say, looking at her with watery eyes.

'We must never let them get a foothold.' She spat the words out. 'I would rather die than be stamped on by their jackboots. But don't let's dwell on such horrible things.' Something caught her eye. 'I can see your lorry coming into the yard.' Lily swung round and to her astonishment was just in time to see the back of the lorry with its missing tailgate vanish around the corner of the house. A few minutes later Edith's father appeared at the kitchen door, a satisfied look on his face.

'All done,' he said taking off his cap. 'Dust in the carburettor, as I thought.'

'Thank you so much,' said Lily starting to get up. 'I must get on the road.'

'Stay awhile,' said Edith, 'I'm sure Tommy would love to meet you.'

'No, I must check in before they close.' This was not the reason. The truth was that Lily could not bear to be with Edith a minute longer. She could not look upon her and know what Friedrich and his companions had done to her.

'That was a mighty knock you received at the back,' said Edith's father, helping himself to the tea pot. 'Lucky it didn't take the wheels off.'

'It was bomb damage. The other lorry was totally destroyed. But thank you again for helping me.'

'Pleasure,' smiled the old man. 'Good to know I've still got a use.'

'Dad,' exclaimed Edith, putting an arm around him, 'you know I couldn't run this place without you.'

'I'll give you a lift back to the tractor,' offered Lily. The old man's eyes twinkled.

'How can I refuse?'

'Right then.' Lily thanked Edith for the tea and gave her an emotional hug. She and Edith's father climbed into the lorry. It started easily and with a last wave to Edith they drove down the drive to the road.

'She's a strong lass, my daughter,' said the old man proudly, 'and she's been through a lot,' he continued enigmatically. Lily knew what he meant. What strange fate had brought her here to bind her to victim and perpetrator of such a terrible act? War had delivered another blow to her innocence and she had to face the reality that she and Friedrich were not going to be the same people who had met each other in that ever-fading summer of '38.

53

Lily was the toast of the canteen after she recounted her adventures in London. She made no mention of Jack and his friends, of her visit to the Windmill Theatre, of seeing Agatha on the stage. She did however describe the sleeping crowds in the underground and hearing the bombs explode, but when it came to freeing the lorry she embroidered the drama and revelled in her colleagues' appreciation of her heroism.

'Lily, you were brave,' said one. 'I don't think I could have driven a lorry in that way.'

'I'd have done anything to have had the boys in blue lead my lorry out,' said Gloria.

'I certainly felt I was in safe hands,' said Lily, enjoying her new-found camaraderie.

'Did you see anything of Ag while you were up in town?' asked Lil when she and Lily had a chance to be together. Lily had been asked to write a report on how the lorry had been damaged and when she delivered it to the office she found Lil alone at her desk.

'No,' she lied.

'It's funny. I've had no letter from her. She promised to write.'

'It's a big place. What was she going to do?'

Lil snorted. 'Said she fancied herself as an actress. With that gob, I said, you'd best be keeping your trap shut.'

'I suppose she wanted to better herself. There's a lot of opportunity in London.'

'Yeah, of the wrong kind. I told her she should watch out for herself. Being a barmaid in Bedford is not like going up the greasy pole in London.'

'I'm sure Ag can look after herself.'

'You know what I think?'

'What?' Lily couldn't imagine but she was taken aback when Lil hit the nail on the head. 'I think she's aiming to hoof it.' Lily arched her eyebrows. 'Become a dancer. Have you seen her pins? Like a bloody stairway to heaven. We had the blokes falling over themselves when she did the cancan one New Year's Eve.'

'Good luck to her,' was all Lily could say. One day, she swore to herself, she would effect a reunion between Lil and Ag.

After the excitement of London, life settled down once more to the dreary monotony of wartime existence. The German U-boats tightened their stranglehold in the Atlantic, cutting off Britain's lifeblood. Shortages and privations intensified. But there were moments to enjoy.

'A dance!' exclaimed Lily.

'Yes,' said Sally, 'in a hall near where I work. They've got an RAF band, 'The Flyingaires'. They say they are very good.'

'But I haven't got anyone to go with,' protested Lily.

'You've got me,' said Sally feigning injury. 'Besides there'll be lots of fellows there.'

'Old enough to be my dad,' groaned Lily.

'No, they're planning to bus chaps in from the RAF station.' Sally gave Lily a long hard stare. 'You'll meet someone. I've noticed how flirty you're getting, Lily, with your new-found toughness.'

'Me!' Lily expressed mock outrage but was inwardly flattered. 'And what about you, Sally, have you got a fellow yet?'

Sally blushed, her face going redder than ever. 'As a matter-of-fact I have.'

'Sally that's wonderful. Who is he?'

'His name's Trevor. He works at my place, but in another department. Get your best frock out, Lily, and we'll go together.'

'Next week then?' They paid the bill at the tearoom and went their separate ways.

For Lily, Sunday was literally a day of rest. Sometimes she accompanied her parents to early morning church. Her faith was nominal and she didn't always feel the need to go. This Sunday was one of them. It was a mild late May weekend. Hubert had been puffing indignantly about the blowing up of 'HMS Hood' in Scapa Flow. The culprit had been the German battleship 'Bismarck'. Now the cry everywhere was 'Sink the Bismarck' and she didn't feel inclined to join in the vengeful voices at church. Hubert's British bulldog attitude annoyed her after what she now saw as his mild indoctrination. If he was going to change his views she wished he'd do it with more discretion.

With Harris nowhere around, she decided to spend the day in the garden. It was warm enough for shorts and a light blouse and she curled up on a seat beside the only remaining flower border and buried her head in a romantic novel. From time to time she stopped and gazed at the rows of vegetable plots spreading out before her. Whatever else she thought of Harris his gardening skills were admirable. With some help from Hubert and Peg he had achieved great productivity. The last vestige of the old garden was the peony border now ablaze with rich red blooms dotted with blue irises.

She wasn't sure why she was reading a romantic novel. It did nothing but make her think of Friedrich, languishing in some remote POW camp. Sally continued to make enquiries without success. But following the travails of the book's heroine, which seemed to shadow her own experiences in an unnerving way, gave her the solace of sharing in a kindred spirit, albeit a fictional one. About halfway through the morning she was aware of Peg gesticulating to her from near the house.

'Lily, you have a visitor,' she shouted. A figure stood beside Peg. Lily closed her book, stood up and tried to see who it was. She walked towards the house. As she got closer she could make out the figure of a young man.

'Hello Lily. I thought I'd come and see you.' Jack, to her great astonishment, was coming down the path towards her.

'What are you doing here?' she asked.

'Had to see you again, old girl.'

'Jack, please.' She tried to quieten him and hoped her mother hadn't heard. 'Mummy,' she shouted at the top of her voice, 'this is Jack. I met him in London. He flies Spitfires.' Jack turned and smiled at Peg. He held out his hand.

'I'm very pleased to meet you, Mrs Rood,' he said with a suave nod of the head. 'I can see now where your charming daughter gets her good looks from.' Peg, not normally one to be taken in by flattery, was seduced by the handsome man standing before her. Hubert, likewise, especially when he was told Jack flew Spitfires. He shook his hand vigorously.

'Well done son. Bravo. Jolly good show. You must come and tell us what it is like up there. All you brave boys.' He blustered on until Peg put a stop to it.

'Hubert, the boy's come to see Lily. Let them run along and we'll talk over lunch.' She paused and turned to Jack. 'You will stay for lunch?'

'I'd love to, Mrs Rood.'

'Good. Off you two go now and enjoy the garden.'

Lily watched them go into the house and then turned and lambasted Jack.

'What do you think you're doing coming here? You know I'm engaged. How dare you!' She spat the words out at him, making him recoil with feigned contrition. The guilt she had felt at her attraction to Jack gave way to anger that he should pursue her.

'How did you track me down?'

'You weren't difficult to find, Lily Rood.'

'I would have thought you were too busy flying your Spitfires to worry about me.'

'I've been grounded until Monday so I thought I'd come and say hello.'

'Well you've done that, so I suggest you get on your way.'

'And miss your mother's lunch? That would be rude, wouldn't it?' He smoothed his moustache and winked. She groaned. He was incorrigible.

'Come on then, I'll show you the garden.' She kept her distance as they walked around the vegetables, making sure he had no opportunity for physical contact. She hoped lunch would soon be served and when it was she let her father do all the talking. He quizzed Jack on every detail of flying a Spitfire and how he fought his way through the dog fights.

'What's your tally of kills?'

'Four, so far.'

Lily listened without comment but one thing that started to occur to her was the vagueness of Jack's descriptions. Most of what he said could have been relayed by anyone with a casual acquaintance of flying procedures. With coffee served, she asked her father whether he could take Jack to the station.

'He has a train to catch to get him back to London,' she said sweetly. Jack was about to protest but saw at once that Lily had bested him.

'Be a pleasure,' said Hubert. He did most of the driving these days as Harris was too busy with his ARP duties.

As she walked Jack to the car, she breathed a warning in his ear.

'Don't try and see me again, Jack. London was a lapse on my part and it's over.'

Jack, who was never going to take no for an answer, thrust a piece of paper into her hand.

'Telephone me on that number, Lily darling. See you soon!' He went to kiss her, but she turned away hoping her parents hadn't seen her rejection.

'What a charming young man,' said Peg as they watched the Wolsey disappear down the drive.

54

Lily put Jack behind her. Her thoughts focused on the coming dance. Several of the girls at the brickworks were also going including Lil and Gloria. There was much talk about what to wear and Lily realised that she would have to ransack her wardrobe when she got back in the evening. She wished Friedrich was coming, but she didn't think he was that great a dancer, so she would dance for him. She only had two short journeys to make and she daydreamed through both of them. She wasn't sure she had anything really suitable, but she had bought a new day dress at the beginning of the war and decided that would probably do.

Coming into the canteen she was struck by the gloomy atmosphere pervading.

'What's going on?' she asked the woman serving the tea.

'Haven't you heard? They've introduced clothes rationing.'

'Just in time for the dance,' shouted Gloria, sitting with the other girls debating the issue.

'Well it's not going to affect us this week,' said Lily bringing over her cup of tea. 'I mean, we have our dresses, haven't we?'

'I don't,' said Gloria. 'I saw this divine little frock in a window on Saturday and now I expect it will have gone.'

'How many coupons do we get?' asked one girl.

'Sixty-six for the year. A dress will cost you seven coupons, Gloria.'

'You'd better run off and get it,' said another. 'We'll cover if Booozy Bob comes sniffing around.' They all laughed. Gloria thanked them gratefully.

Lily walked out of the yard alone, thinking of how she might add some decorative touches to the dress she was going to wear. She was about to enter the station when a familiar figure stood in front of her, baring her way. Reg Fuller raised his hat and greeted Lily like a long-lost friend.

'What a pleasure it is to see you, Miss Rood.' He gave an unctuous smile.

'I'm not sure the feeling's mutual,' said Lily acidly, largely blaming him for her incarceration. What she wondered did he want? Whenever he appeared, it always boded ill.

'Can I have a little talk with you?' She could have said no, but as he was linked to Sir Montague Daventry she felt it unwise to refuse.

'What do you want?' She looked at him. He was a crumpled mess. His hat was greasy, his suit ill-fitting, his collar dirty and a button loose. She supposed it was deliberate as it allowed him to blend in with the crowd. In a pub no one would notice him, until he wanted to be noticed as on that day she first met him and Lil had warned him off.

'Can I buy you a drink? We could go to the Railway Inn over the road?' Lily nodded and followed him into the pub. He found a quiet table in the snug and sat her down while he went to get two beers. She watched his back as he ordered the drinks. Her heart sank. It had been a year since her interrogation and she had been left unmolested, but she knew that one day they would come for her again under some pretext or other. She hadn't though expected this man.

'You like beers, don't you, Miss Rood?'

She said nothing.

'Your time in Germany gave you a taste for them?'

'Can we cut the pleasantries? What do you want?'

He took a good slurp from his glass, put his hat on the table and lit a cigarette. He never offered Lily one but blew smoke into her face.

'When you were in London you met a man called Jack.' Lily coughed as the smoke got into her mouth.

'I'm sorry,' said Reg, 'that was thoughtless of me.'

'What about it?' asked Lily, ignoring his apology.

'How did you meet?'

'It was in the hotel I was staying at. I met him when I arrived.'

'Perhaps it would be best put the other way around. Not to be too delicate about it, he picked you up, would you not say?' She was a little shocked by his insinuation. He carried on. 'Don't you think it was strange that he should invite you, a total stranger, to join him at the theatre?'

'Are you saying that I'm one those easy-going girls men casually pick up?'

'Not at all. More that he was lying in wait to ambush you when you arrived. Didn't you think it an odd coincidence that you should end up at his hotel?'

'No, I thought he was just being opportunist.'

'Not at all. Think back. You were carefully taken there.'

Lily did think back, retracing her steps from the moment she stepped onto the platform in London.

'The taxi driver.'

'Precisely. He was waiting for you. Somehow they must have got wind that you were on that train. Not difficult. I expect the brickworks leaks like a sieve.'

'So what was his purpose?'

'To seduce you, not from any romantic intentions, but to obtain your confidence.'

'Why me, when there must be hundreds of girls he could get his claws into?'

'Not many have professed their love for Germany.' She balked again at his insinuation. He looked her straight in the eyes. 'He aims to turn you.' Lily looked mystified. Reg explained. 'We believe Jack Havering is a German agent and that he plans to recruit you.'

Lily laughed with incredulity. 'That's ridiculous. He flies Spitfires for goodness sake.'

'Does he? That's what he told you. But we know he has never been near an aeroplane.' Jack's vagueness when describing his exploits now made sense to Lily. She started to feel sick and betrayed. How could she have been so stupid?

'He thinks he can turn me into a German spy?' Reg watched her closely.

'Perhaps he had reason to think that?'

She laughed. 'You people never stop, do you!' She sipped her beer and reflected on what he had said. 'I don't understand. He was such a perfect Englishman.'

'He's not English. He's from Argentina. It's not difficult to acquire a cut-glass English accent in that country with all its British connections.'

'He certainly has dark good looks and charm. I fell for him, didn't I?'

'You did!'

'What about Chloe, is she a spy?'

'No. Just a friend who's been duped.'

'You know he came to my house yesterday?' Reg nodded. 'I sent him away with a flea in his ear.'

'That's a problem.'

'Why?'

'Because we want you to carry on the relationship. I assume he's not attempted to draw you in yet?'

'No.'

'He will.' He swallowed the last dregs from his glass. 'Another beer?' She declined. He got up to get himself one. What was she being drawn into? She hadn't got the stomach for this sort of skulduggery. Where was it leading? A pawn in one of Sir Montague Daventry's devious plans? If you make one slip you're theirs for life. Two years ago she was an innocent schoolgirl, now she was being asked to entrap a spy. He returned with a pint brimming with froth.

'End of the cask.' As he drank his mouth turned white. 'Will he come back?'

'A normal person wouldn't, but he's never taken no for an answer.'

He wiped his mouth on his sleeve. 'How do you think you can get him back without arousing his suspicion?' Lily thought for a moment. The answer came to her like a flash.

'I'm going to a dance on Saturday night. I don't have anyone to go with. Will he fall for it?'

'How will you contact him?'

'He gave me his telephone number.'

'Great!' Reg looked triumphant.

'I thought it was odd,' said Lily. 'It's a London number, not his RAF station.'

'Have you got it?'

'It's at home.'

'Can you remember it?'

'Not the number but the letters were ARC.'

'Archway,' he said with satisfaction. 'Get him to come. I'll be here tomorrow evening. Same time. And bring the telephone number with you.' Lily was feeling dizzy. It was going too fast.

'I want something in return.' He looked quizzically at her but said nothing. 'If you want me to do Sir Montague's dirty work you need to help me.'

'And how do I do that, Miss Rood?' he asked sarcastically.

'Friedrich Schulz. You can find out where he is and arrange for me to visit.'

'That may be difficult.'

'Then I don't help you,' she said defiantly.

'You are a determined young lady, Miss Rood.'

'You made me that.' She drained her glass. 'If that's all, I'll say good evening. I have a train to catch.' She got up from her seat and looked down on the dishevelled Reg. 'I'll meet you here tomorrow. I'll bring the telephone number, but I want your answer first.'

She went home with a lighter step. She had no qualms about betraying Jack if it would lead her to Friedrich. After all he had deceived her. She looked again at the number he had given her. She would telephone him from a public phone box when she was out on a delivery. Meanwhile there was the dress for Saturday night to attend to.

When she got home, she extracted the garment from her wardrobe and showed it to Peg. It was a simple shape which she hoped her mother could embellish for her. Its pink floral design needed help, she decided.

'Mummy, could you do things to this for me to wear to the dance?' she asked holding it up in front of her and pirouetting around the room in her dungarees.

'Give it to me and I'll see what I can do.'

'And Mummy, darling, I need a pair of stockings. It's not going to be easy getting them now we have rationing and I ruined my last pair in London.' Her pleading struck a chord in Peg. She was pleased her daughter was having a chance to enjoy herself. She was worried that her work was taking its toll on her health.

'I might have a spare pair I put aside for a rainy day.'

'You're a poppet, Mummy. I need my legs to look nice. Skirts are shorter now, they say to save fabric.'

'Who's taking you?' Peg asked casually.

'I'm asking Jack.'

'Isn't he in London?'

'He'll come. That is if he's not flying.' Which, as Lily now knew, was unlikely.

She pressed Button A and heard her coins drop into the box with a metallic clink as she was connected to the Archway number she had asked for. A woman's voice answered.

'Is that Chloe?' Lily asked.

'Yes,' a throaty voice replied. 'Who is that?'

'Chloe, it's Lily.'

'Lily, darling, how are you? We miss you.'

'I'm fine. Is Jack there?'

'I'll find him. Hold on.' She put the receiver down with a bang and left Lily listening to a distant roar that sounded like an aeroplane taking off. Where were they? If they were in London, why was she hearing what sounded like an airfield? There was scratching on the line and Jack came on.

'Wonderful to hear you, old girl. I thought you'd gone off me?'

'I'm sorry, Jack, I was rather rude.' She tried to sound as contrite as possible. She gazed over a field of ripening corn, the box she was in standing only a few feet away from her parked lorry. She listened for a trace of suspicion in his voice but couldn't detect any.

'There's a dance at our local hall on Saturday night. I was wondering whether you would like to be my partner. That's if you can get a pass again.'

'Dashed difficult, old girl. But I'll try. Love to come though.'

'I'll give you my number at home.'

'Got it,' said the voice at the other end.

'Jack, you sound like you're on an airfield.'

'I am. Chloe put you through.' Would she have believed him, if she hadn't known? Probably, as she had never doubted anything he said. He was the most convincing man she had ever met.

'I'll wait for you to call me then?'

'Lily.'

'Yes?'

'You're a darling.'

'Good-bye, Jack.' She put the phone down and stared blankly at the deep blue sky. She made no mention that men from the air base were coming. She would have to ask him to wear his uniform.

Reg was in the pub as he said he would be. Lily was late and he had already had at least one pint.

'Have you got something for me?' was the first thing she asked.

'Cooden, near Bexhill-on-Sea in Sussex. You can write to him and the Red Cross will deliver the letter. But you can't visit him. He's categorised 'black' because he was in the Waffen SS.'

'What does that mean?'

'They keep a special watch on him because he is a professed Nazi.' She winced when she heard the word articulated. It made Friedrich sound so evil and she knew he wasn't. Reg looked at her quizzically. 'Now is Jack coming?'

'Yes.' He looked pleased.

'What do you want me to do?' she asked anxiously.

'Nothing. Wait for him to make the move.' He leant over to her. She could smell the beer on his breath. 'I'll be there. Signal to me if he says anything incriminating and try to get him into a quiet place where he can be overheard.'

She looked at him in horror.

'How am I going to do that?'

'You're a pretty girl. It promises to be a warm night. I'm sure there will be a lot of canoodling out at the back.' Being interrogated was something outside her control, being asked to put a man into a compromising position using her own sexual wiles was not something she relished or had experience of.

'Can you do it?' he asked looking at her doubtful face. She nodded.

'Now, I would like a sherry.'

55

The Dance Hall at Bletchley had been built in the nineteen twenties and had some pretence to grandeur. Its entrance had the artfully arranged horizontals and verticals of an art deco design. Once it would have been a blaze of light, now two blue lamps guarded the steps up to the entrance hall. Once inside more light was allowed and in the dance hall proper a multifaceted globe sprinkled stars across the floor. When Lily arrived on Jack's arm the band was in full swing. Behind their shields depicting the wings of the Royal Air Force the bandsmen waved and jostled their silver instruments to the rhythm of the music. The band leader conducted the whole with equal vim.

'Look, Jack, Sally's already here,' shouted Lily excitedly. She grabbed him by the arm and steered him around dancing couples to the other side of the hall where Sally sat at a table with a young man. When she saw them, she gave a whoop and shot to her feet. Her hair in the flashing light seemed curlier than ever. Lily gave a stifled laugh when she saw Sally's young man. He too had curly red hair.

'Lily, this is Trevor.' She couldn't see but she felt instinctively that he had gone red in the face. They shook hands.

Lily turned to Jack. 'And this is Flying Officer, Jack Havering.' She said it with a pretence of pride that disguised her real feelings. Jack had turned up in a uniform, a white ring sandwiched between two bands of red on the sleeves of his jacket, indicating the rank Lily had extracted from him. Just turning up in a counterfeit uniform was offence enough but Reg wanted more.

The men went off and got drinks and the two girls compared notes.

'Lily, he's a dish,' said Sally in astonishment, 'where did you find him?'

'In London.'

'Well you kept that under your hat. I bet he's a mover.' I bet he is, thought Lily, with an eye for every girl in the room. As she turned around to find him, she caught sight of a couple looking in her direction. He was badly dressed in a rather loud suit and she in contrast was in a singularly drab frock. Had it not been for the fact that they were staring at her she would not have noticed them. But she saw instantly that it was Reg and the girl he had brought along to give him cover.

The two men came back with brimming pints and sherries. Jack wasted no time and had barely tasted his beer before he had whisked Lily onto the dance floor as the band struck up a lively quickstep.

'You're a picture, tonight, Lily. The Queen of the Ball.' He flattered her with his blandishments. 'And what a beautiful dress.' Her mother had certainly done wonders with decorating its plainness. She had added a wide pink belt that emphasised the waist and gave the skirt a winning flair. She had added lace on the sleeves and across the bodice and had taken Lily's hair in hand and given her a fashionable peek-a-boo hair style.

As they danced around the floor, she became aware of his roving hands, exploring the contours of her back. His fingers pressed tighter as they wove in and out of the other dancers. He was certainly fluid in his movements and he steered her own less than confident steps with great skill.

'Where did you learn to dance so well?' she asked.

'Oh, here and there,' he answered casually, with no mention of the natural rhythm he would have inherited from his South American upbringing. Weren't they born with it there? she asked herself.

'Hey, careful Jack, I can't match your exuberance.' They nearly collided with a smartly uniformed officer and his partner in a long floaty dress. The band rose to a climatic crescendo and as the couples relaxed and broke apart, applause rippled around those sitting out.

'Thank you, Jack. You certainly know how to sweep a girl off her feet.'

'Well my partner made it easy.'

'You flatter me.'

'Bravo,' said Sally as they got back to the table.

'What station are you at?' asked Trevor.

'Manston.'

'What do you fly?'

'Spitfires.' Trevor looked at Sally oddly.

'I knew someone from the Manston base. Can't remember the number of the squadron now.' Nor could Jack. Lily saw that the questions unsettled him so she hastily turned the conversation by asking what Trevor did and as with Sally she met a brick wall. The band glided into a waltz.

Sally got up and pulled her partner to his feet. 'Come on Trevor, a dance I think we can both manage.' Not to be outdone, Jack gave Lily no time to pause and had her once more in his arms. It continued like this for much of the evening, with Jack alternating between Lily and Sally.

'Your fellow is quite a dancer,' said Trevor as he sat it out with Lily. 'It's as if he frequented dance halls all the time.'

'I think he's just got rhythm, Trevor.'

During a break the RAF officer whom they nearly collided with came over.

'I hope you are better in the air than you are on the dance floor, young man.' Jack jumped to his feet and saluted as he recognised a squadron leader standing before him.

'At ease. We're off duty. But you almost had my wife's dress.' He said it half-jokingly.

'I'm sorry, sir.'

'Don't worry about it, old man. Collisions happen. You're not from around here are you?'

'No, sir. Manston in Kent.'

'Do you fly?'

'Yes, sir. Spitfires.'

'That's odd. I thought it was Hurricanes at Manston. Squadron 3 isn't it?'

'Yes, sir.' He grunted and didn't pursue the questioning. Trevor gave Sally another odd look. Lily's heart sank. She knew Jack had been caught out and hoped it would blow over. The squadron leader turned to Lily and Sally.

'Ladies,' he said graciously, 'you all look so beautiful and thank you so much for being here for my men. They do get rather lonely, you know. Now I must go back to my wife or she will be the one getting lonely.' He bowed slightly and left. Jack returned to his seat. Lily noticed perspiration on his brow.

'Jolly civil chap,' he said hastily. Lily kept her eyes on the squadron leader. He didn't go back to his wife. He went over to where Reg sat and nodded to him as he walked by. He was part of the trap, she concluded.

Jack shifted in his seat, greedily finished his beer and went to get another. He had lost his suave confidence. The band struck up a lively swing tune and Sally dragged Trevor onto the dance floor. When Jack returned, Lily could see he was grateful they had gone.

'I say, Lily, old girl, it's getting a bit hot in here. What do you say we take a spin outside?'

'I think we should wait for Sally.'

'She won't worry. She seems like a girl about town.' He gave a wink. His confidence was returning.

'Jack, you're a devil.'

'No horns, I promise.'

'Come on then.' She got up and looked for Reg. He turned away when she caught his eye, but a subliminal tilt of his head told her he had got the message. Jack held her by the waist as they walked towards a side door that stood open. It took them past Reg's table. She got another shock when she saw whom his companion was. Sergeant Berwick smiled up at her. She had no doubt Private Rush was close by.

The cool evening air felt very pleasant. They were not alone, but no one looked up from the romantic business in hand when they stepped out into what was a large yard, filled with empty boxes and beer barrels. Jack swung Lily around and began kissing her.

'Not here, Jack. It's too public.' She spotted a part of the yard at the far end that had been sectioned off with a low fence. She led him by the hand, smiling seductively or in the way she thought she had seen it done on the screen. The place had clearly been set aside for the staff. Cigarette butts littered the ground. A bench lay up against the fence. Lily went immediately to it.

They had barely touched the seat before his hands were on her breasts and he was kissing her. Her instinct was to fight him off but instead she found herself kissing him hungrily in return.

'Wow, Lily Rood, you know how to deliver a smacker.' He held her at arms-length and gazed at her admiringly. She heard a piece of wood crack nearby but he seemed oblivious. She kissed him again. But his moment of passion was over. He suddenly dropped his lover's pose and became serious.

'Lily,' he said, taking her hands in his, 'we think the same. We want the same result, don't we?'

'What do you mean, Jack?'

'I haven't got much time. I think they've rumbled me.'

'Who?'

'It doesn't matter. But I want to ask you to help us.'

'Do what?'

'To defeat this country. There is a small group of us getting information back to Germany. I want you to join us.'

'Why do you think I would do that?'

'To help your fiancé rotting in an English prisoner of war camp.'

How did he know that? Somehow he had been fed the knowledge. She was the honey trap.

'Could you do that?'

'If you help us. And help our glorious Führer to victory.'

'How do I help?'

'I'll get in touch with you shortly, but for the moment I have to disappear. Heil Hitler.'

'Heil Hitler,' responded Lily, the words sticking in her throat as she spoke them.

'Not words to be heard around here, sir.' Sergeant Berwick and Reg showed themselves from behind the fence.

'Who are you?' asked Jack with alarm.

'We are from M15 and I have the authority to arrest you Mr Havering or should I say Delgado. Planning to supply information to the enemy constitutes an act of treason.' Jack towered over Lily. His face went black with hatred.

'You fucking miserable little bitch.' She thought he would strike her. Instead he ran, pushing Reg aside, but colliding with Sergeant Berwick, who was quick enough to put a foot across his legs sending him sprawling to the ground. The two agents fell on him, but he was strong and he writhed from under them. A well-aimed punch to the face sent Reg careering across the yard. Berwick tried to hold onto a leg, but he kicked himself free, scrambled to his feet and ran. She took a whistle from her pocket and blew it with an ear-shattering screech.

'He won't get far. The place is surrounded.' The couples hovering in the shadows looked on in astonishment. Sergeant Berwick helped Reg to his feet. He was nursing a badly bruised jaw.

'Let me have a look at that, sir.' She peered closely at the swollen face. 'Can you open your mouth?'

'I think so.' Part of Lily was delighted the obnoxious Reg had taken a beating, but he looked so sorry for himself, her heart softened. She even helped brush the dirt from his jacket. He thanked her.

'You've earned your spurs, Miss Rood.'

'Will they catch him?'

'Oh, yes and he'll start squealing pretty soon. His sort has no loyalty. He goes for the highest bidder. Two weeks with Sir Montague and he'll be turned.' She looked at him bemused. 'Double agent. Germans will think he's spying for them, but in reality he'll be spying for us.'

How did she get into this world of treachery and betrayal?

'What's going to happen to me?' As she spoke two uniformed policemen came into the yard. They addressed Reg.

'He's safely in custody, sir.'

'Good.' He turned to Lily. 'I'll see that your letters get through to him.' His hand went to his jaw. 'Hell, this bloody hurts.' Berwick took him by the arm and led him away. She turned to look back at Lily. 'Keep your hands clean, Rood, I don't want you crossing my path again.' Without a flicker of emotion she led the shambolic figure of Reg out of the yard. Lily stood and watched them go. And to think, she thought, the safety of the country resided in the hands of such people.

'Where's Jack?' asked Sally when she came back into the dance hall alone.

'He got an urgent call to return to his station.' Sally was glad. She decided she didn't like Jack. He seemed a no-good cad and she hoped Lily had dropped him. The three of them sat and watched the band in silence. The trombone player was on his feet playing an energetic solo to rapturous applause. Lily was hypnotised by the way he waved his instrument and pumped it back and forth in a foot-stamping rhythm.

'I think I might have been lucky with the Red Cross, Lily,' said Sally eventually.

'That's good,' said Lily without enthusiasm. She knew Sally wanted to help her, but she knew she would have little chance of locating Friedrich. Her only hope lay with Reg and whether he would honour his promise.

56

Lily wrote a long letter to Friedrich, keeping it general in all its details, knowing that it would most likely be opened, read and censored. She said nothing of her exploits in London but repeated over and over again protestations of love. She sealed it, dabbed scent on it and wrote out the address Reg Fuller had given her. She took it to the local Post Office and asked for it to be delivered care of the Red Cross.

Foolishly she expected a reply by return of post, but of course it never came. Each day she went into the Post Office and asked whether there was a letter waiting for her. There never was. The postmistress, whom she knew well, always made a kindly denial as she must have done for countless other disappointed enquiries.

'Nothing here for you today, dear.'

Then there was. It was the day Germany invaded Russia and took the war into a deeper abyss of horror.

'This came, yesterday.' She handed Lily a buff envelope with the distinctive Red Cross marking on it. Lily thanked her and hastily pocketed the letter. She was on her way to work and she had no time to digest the contents. She must wait for a moment of privacy, which only came when she was on the road.

She parked the lorry in a lay-by and tore open the envelope. Inside were two sheets of thin rough paper with Friedrich's careful handwriting laid out in pencil. On every page heavy blue lines erased much of the text. Their opaqueness brought tears to Lily's eyes. As she read she could see Friedrich was trying to express his love but so many of the words he used were lost under the draconian strokes of the censor. He was able to say that he was in good health and was well-fed, that he was overjoyed to hear from her and that she was well. He ended, '.... please write again, dear Lily. I ~~xxxxx~~ you.' She smiled.

'How awfully wicked of you,' gasped Sally, as she listened to Lily's account of the censor's work.

'I do feel decidedly naughty.' With a lascivious wink, she gobbled a piece of rock cake. 'To think my little endearments have had the blue pencil.'

'How will you write back?' asked Sally.

'In code,' said Lily jokingly.

But in fact that is exactly what happened. She devised a shorthand for terms of affection which after several letters Friedrich eventually understood and replied accordingly. Thus love was 'reward' and kiss they encoded as 'see'. Lily might sign off with 'I hope that one day I can give you the reward you deserve' while Friedrich would answer that he 'wishes to see her'. It was gibberish but it never received the blue line.

As the weeks and the months went by, Lily began to build up a picture of Friedrich's life in the internment camp. In her weekly tête-à-têtes with Sally she relayed the many titbits she had gleaned.

'Do you think he's just putting on a brave face when he says he's being well looked after?' she asked, somehow thinking that Sally had the inside knowledge to answer the question. It was intuitive because she had never said so but she believed that Sally worked in some official capacity for the war office.

'Your guess is as good as mine, Lily, but I don't think he will be badly treated.'

'He says they have forty-two ounces of meat and eight ounces of bacon a week. Well that's more than us, Sally.'

'There you are then. Could be the Ritz!'

'Hardly! There are eighty prisoners in one hut and Friedrich says you never get a moment to yourself. Some play cards all night. Sleep is difficult. That's why he works in the fields. To get some peace.'

'Isn't it tougher for him because he is in the SS?' asked Sally.

'I don't know. He never says.' Although she knew from what Reg Fuller had said that he had to wear a black badge to identify him as SS.

One day Sally asked Lily the question which Lily herself had not yet faced up to.

'When the war's over, will the two of you live in England?'

'I don't know, Sally, we haven't talked about it. Are we going to win?'

'Tide's turning. All those victories in Africa and with America in the war. The Germans are not having it all their way.'

'It's true, you do start feeling better about things. The girls at work are getting quite gung-ho.' She stirred a minute sliver of sugar into her tea. 'I really would like to stay in England. I think Friedrich would like it here.'

'He's had a lucky escape,' said Sally. 'Getting captured and ending up here, with more meat than we poor blighters get. Must top being drafted to the Russian front.'

57

Yes, she was thankful Friedrich was where he was. Yes, he was safe, while the war ground on. 1943 dawned with much of the German army tied down in Russia, while the Allies battled their way up the spine of Italy and the RAF pounded the German heartland. The growing optimism abroad was accompanied in the early months of 1944 by a steady increase in military activity on the roads. Now it was common for civilians to have to stop to let convoys of military vehicles pass. On one chill April evening Lily found herself being pressed into the hedge as a dozen low-loaders laden with tanks and covered with tarpaulin rumbled by. It made her think something serious was happening. The next day she was to discover what.

She arrived at work as usual to find several of the drivers standing around in the yard instead of getting ready to load up. She thought this odd but ignored it and went over to her lorry. A voice called out from inside a huddle of girls. 'Lily, you're not going anywhere today.' It was Gloria.

'Why not?' asked Lily on the point of opening her cab.

'Orders. We've been told to stay here. No one's going out.'

Bob Jenkins emerged from his office, accompanied by Lil carrying a sheaf of papers. Several other girls were arriving, as mystified as Lily.

'What's going on, Mr Jenkins?' several chorused.

'Gather round, ladies,' he said, importantly. The drivers formed a tight circle around the foreman eager to hear what he was going to say.

'No one's going out on deliveries today. We've been taken over by the military.' There was audible muttering. He paused dramatically to let what he said sink in. 'Today we will be collecting troops from the army bases around here and taking them to Bedford railway station.'

'What's going on Mr Jenkins?' asked Gloria.

'Can't tell you. All I know is what I've said. You'll each get a sealed envelope. It contains instructions as to where you are to go. Only open it when you're in the cab.'

'Blimey, bloody cloak and dagger, 'ain't it?' said Daphne. The others laughed. Bob Jenkins tutted and waited for them to quieten themselves.

'Now, Miss Bates will hand out the envelopes.' Lily watched Lil with amusement as she performed her task with unsmiling efficiency.

'This can only mean one thing, girls,' said Daphne brandishing her envelope as if it were a weapon.

'What's that?' asked Lily.

'You can't guess?'

Lily could, but she wanted to appear the little mouse to Daphne. She still thought it best to keep her distance.

'The invasion,' joined in Gloria, excitedly. 'It's the start of the build-up for the big push.'

'That's right, darling. We're going to cut that jumped-up guttersnipe down to size and kick him in his pathetic little German bollocks.'

'One bollock,' shouted another of the girls, repeating a popular myth. 'He's only got one bollock.' There was an eruption of laughter.

Daphne looked at Lily. 'And you'll get to see your man. That's if the Ruskies don't get him first.' No, said Lily to herself, that won't happen.

'Wish I was going with you, Lily,' said Lil as she thrust the envelope into her hand.

'You make it sound like I'm joining up. I'm only going up the road.'

'Well, have fun with all those chaps in the back.'

There was a shout from Bob Jenkins. 'And before you go, ladies, sweep out the floor of your lorries. Can't have our brave lads sitting in brick shit, can we?'

'Thought you might have done that before we arrived,' growled Daphne under her breath. There was a general moan, then the drivers set to. Lily wrapped a cotton scarf around her face to avoid breathing in the dust, grabbed the broom attached to the lorry and began to sweep it out. She was anxious to open her sealed envelope. But she wasn't the first. An engine spluttered into life beside her. Gloria was already driving off. She wound down the window and shouted back with a great grin. 'I've got Yanks, girls.'

Lily climbed into the cab, shut the door and tentatively opened the envelope. She pulled out a thin duplicated sheet of type-written instructions. She was to go to the army base about fifteen miles to the north of Bedford and contact the commander of the American Ordnance Supply and Maintenance company. She could see Lil looking up at her.

'I've got Yanks, too,' she yelled with a laugh, making a 'V' sign with her hand. In fact it was the same base that Gloria was driving to. As they drove out of the yard Bob Jenkins yelled at them.

'Watch your knickers, girls. Remember one Yank and they're down!' Lily could see Gloria turn her 'V' sign into a suggestive fingers up! She did the same and together they accelerated away.

The roads were clogged with military vehicles moving south, but it wasn't long before she had caught up with Gloria and when she looked in the rear mirror she could see another four brick lorries behind her. They proceeded in convoy, but it was slow progress. Several times they were waved onto verges and lay-bys while military personnel directed outsize trucks along the narrow roads. Lily felt awed by the stream of heavy armour that rumbled past her cab. After months, even years of depressing news with the country barely surviving, could the end be in sight? The sense of an epic happening thrilled her and she was now part of it. The quicker the end came, the quicker she would be re-united with Friedrich and she could start the process of persuading him to settle down with her in England.

A great honking shook her from her reverie. Two trucks loaded with howitzers came towards the convoy at speed. They were in the middle of the road and while the others had time to pull over, for Lily it was too late and she was forced to take avoiding action and only narrowly missed going into the ditch as the trucks, seemingly unconcerned, carried on their way.

'Bloody road hogs,' she muttered pulling on the wheel and bringing the lorry back onto the road again.

When the others saw she was safe they carried on and together they did the final miles to the base without incident. The scene which met them when they got there was one of total chaos. But, as Lily quickly discovered, this was illusory, for behind the confusion was a well-oiled machine directing the many apparent random movements. Men and vehicles were being shepherded to their designated muster points by an army of military stewards. It was done with a cacophony of shouts and violent arm movements, underpinned by an authority that allowed no questioning of the orders. Lily kept her eyes on Gloria's lorry. She was stopped at the perimeter gate while a guard examined her papers. He shot his hand to the right, shouted some instructions to Gloria and signalled the rest of the brick lorries to follow her. Lily took her foot off the brake and eased her vehicle past the guard, who saluted, and into the maw of a great military war machine. She drove past hundreds of parked armoured personnel carriers, lorries loaded with guns, jeeps and motorcycles, tanks of all shapes and sizes, the impressive hardware designed to destroy, kill and maim. It was so awesome in its immensity she wondered how any army could withstand its assault. Finally they left the combat vehicles behind and reached groups of men standing in small clusters beside the road. Gloria was waved down beside a group at the end of the field, Lily to the next group and the others behind her.

'Hiya Ma'am.' A cheery sergeant with a clipboard came up to her cab. She wound the window down. 'You're set for Bedford station?'

'That's right.'

'If you can open up, we'll get 'em loaded.'

Lily jumped down. A chorus of appreciative shouts rose from the group as she walked to the tailgate, unbolted it and effortlessly lowered the heavy rear panel. As she did so she was aware she was presenting her rear figure to men who probably hadn't been that close to a woman for a long time. At the beginning of the war she would have been totally innocent of the effect she was having, but war was a fast educator.

'All right, boys, climb aboard,' shouted the sergeant. One by one they flung their packs and rifles onto the floor of the lorry and clambered up.

'Welcome to my lorry,' said Lily sweetly to one particularly young looking soldier.

The man, bristling with equipment, holding his pack in one hand and his rifle in the other, smiled at her.

'Lorry! Hey doll, that's kinda cute. We call them trucks.'

'Same thing,' said Lily. She gazed at his fresh well-tanned face, the webbed helmet on his head, the strap undone and hanging down, his mouth, like all the others, chewing gum and she wondered what was ahead of him.

'Get aboard, soldier,' barked the sergeant and the young man moved on. She watched the others climb up. The number had been calculated to allow most to be able to sit on the floor, while the remainder stood holding onto the sides.

'They're good to go, Ma'am,' said the sergeant when the last had found a position. Lily bolted the tailgate back into position and returned to her cab.

'Hey, baby, you look after us now. We don't want to end up in no ditch.'

'Ignore him, Ma'am. He's from New York. He don't know how to talk to no lady.'

'Don't worry, chaps, I'll get you there,' laughed Lily, pulling herself up and hearing as she closed the door of the cab voices mimicking her English accent.

The return journey was a crawl. She again followed Gloria, but they were caught in the traffic going south, which was now moving at a snail's pace. When Lily opened the window, she heard constant grumbles and jeers from the soldiers, but there was nothing she could do. Every now and again she caught snatches of familiar songs that were being sung to alleviate their boredom.

Gloria braked suddenly. Lily put her foot down hard and slew to a halt within inches of the lorry in front. The soldiers behind were thrown like rag dolls about the floor.

'Jeez honey, you trying to fucking kill us,' shouted one who had fallen on his comrade. 'We haven't even got across the dike yet.'

Lily looked out from her cab and waved apologetically.

'Sorry chaps. Bit of a jolt.' From the front of Gloria's lorry a solitary sheep emerged and wandered aimlessly across the road.

'There goes our lunch,' came a cry from the back followed by a round of laughter. When the animal had safely reached the opposite verge, the convoy moved off and carried on its halting way to Bedford station. It arrived to another scene of raucous confusion.

Railway engines steamed at the end of platforms, while troops piled into the waiting carriages. Lily was directed to a loading bay and the soldiers told to dismount. Before she had a chance to jump down from the cab, the men had unloosed the bolts of the tailgate and let it swing down, which it did with a clatter.

As they poured off the lorry they thanked Lily in various ways. She was showered with gifts, chocolates, cigarettes and a pair of nylons. Several gave her pecks on the cheek and one young man even proposed marriage.

'Wait for me, honey,' he said enthusiastically. 'I'll be coming back to marry you.'

She smiled at the handsome GI in front of her and found herself asking his name.

'Al. And hey this is to remember me by.' Without warning he lifted her up and kissed her.

Being swept off her feet in this way was not something she was expecting and she pushed him away gently. 'Just come back, Al,' she said with sadness in her voice, waving and wondering how many indeed would come back. Lost in her thoughts she hadn't heard Gloria come up behind her.

'Job well done, Lily.'

'Yes, it was good to be of use.'

'You certainly were!' she said with eyes raised.

'What do you mean, Gloria?'

'That dark haired Yank gave you quite a kiss.' Lily laughed as if it were nothing, but the young man had made her heart flutter. She looked to see if she could still see him. But he had gone.

Gloria started the engine of her lorry. 'Now we've got to get out of here and back to the yard.'

'And home.'

But that proved equally slow and frustrating and when they finally slid into the brick yard it was evening and they felt very tired. Bob Jenkins tried his luck in offering them all a drink, but no one was in the mood.

'Another day, Mr Jenkins,' said Gloria making a hasty departure, Lily in close pursuit.

'I couldn't stand an hour with 'Boozy' Jenkins trying to paw me,' said Gloria, when Lily caught up with her.

'I agree,' said Lily. 'Having him eye you up during work is one thing, but not after hours.'

'You're right there. But I say, Lily, weren't some of those Yanks heavenly?' They had reached the gate and were set to go their separate ways.

'Don't swoon too much Gloria. There's little chance of us seeing them again.'

'But you got a taste, you lucky beggar.'

'Just giving the poor boy some comfort.'

'Not from where I was standing. Looked like he was making a pass at you.'

'Well Gloria, a kiss is just a kiss,' laughed Lily, remembering the line from the popular song. But her heart told her otherwise and Gloria's emphatic wink made it obvious that she thought so too.

'Bye Lily, see you tomorrow,' she said with a knowing smile and walked off towards the shed where she kept her bicycle, while Lily walked onto the platform of the brickworks station, only to find herself with another long wait. I hate this war, she told herself, if for nothing else but the endless waiting. Her usual train didn't come. What did come, however, were the troop trains. Four in all. The last produced some familiar faces and to her delight Al was among them. The young American hung out of the window throwing kisses at Lily.

'Hi, remember you're going to wait for me.'

'Not so fast, buster.' Before Lily could respond Al's fellow GIs had pushed him to one side and began shouting after Lily.

'Hey doll, I'm your eternal sweetheart.'

'Honey, thanks for the ride.'

'We'll be kicking Hitler's balls just for you.'

The ribald laughter, the euphoric banter faded under the clatter of wheels leaving Lily a solitary figure on the empty platform. When her train finally came, it was a single coach heaving with local passengers. She opened a door to find an impenetrable wall of human flesh confronting her.

'I can't get on,' she shouted to the elderly station master who had emerged from his office to greet the train.

'Squeeze in. You're lucky there is a train. Don't you know everything's been requisitioned?' As Lily climbed up, he put his hand on her backside and pushed. She would have sloshed him for his impertinence, had it not had the desired effect and she found herself catapulted into the middle of the carriage.

'Like bloody sardines, we are,' protested a large rather irate woman, as Lily landed in their midst.

'They need the trains, missus,' retorted a sallow elderly man, holding onto a woman who appeared to be his wife. Lily, who was in an awkward crouch, pulled herself to her feet and looked around at her fellow passengers.

'Thanks,' she said, with a smile. The train lurched forward, went a few yards and then stopped. There was a cry from the other side of the carriage. Someone was trying to attract her attention. It was Yakova Marcuson.

'Lily, remember me. It's Yakova. Yakova Marcuson. We were at the typing school together.' Lily didn't want to start a conversation at a distance so she edged herself towards Yakova. She still looked as plain as ever, her black hair tied behind her head with a fraying green ribbon.

'It is so nice to see you Lily. What do you do now?' Lily told her but was equally curious to know what she did. Their last encounter when she was with Friedrich had been more than a little tense.

'I am what you say a bureaucrat. It is not possible for me to say more.' No, of course not.

'I understand. Hush hush,' said Lily wearily. 'Like Sally.'

'I work with her.'

'Do you? No, you can't tell me.'

'Sorry.' Yakova looked embarrassed. 'How is your friend?'

'I don't know.' Truthful in the sense that she hadn't heard from Friedrich for several weeks, but a lie in that she knew perfectly well where he was.

'It must be difficult for you. Not knowing,' said Yakova, sympathetically. 'I hate what they have done to people, but we don't choose where we are born. I didn't want to leave my country, but I had no choice. Maybe your man will escape one day. If he is your friend, he must be a good man.'

Yes, thought Lily, he is a good man. He is honourable and true to his beliefs. But what if those beliefs are at the service of something evil? Will he, can he change?

'It is kind of you to say this.' Lily looked out of the window. The train was coming into Bletchley station. But there was something odd happening. It stopped at the very end of the platform and they were ordered out. When they were on the platform, Lily saw that the train had come in behind another, longer one standing in the station. Ahead of them was another jostling crowd of soldiers ready to board. This time they were Tommies, all overburdened with equipment, rifles slung across shoulders, helmets on heads. The crowd of passengers started to move and were ushered out of the station by a side gate. Lily said good-bye to Yakova and was on the point of escaping, when a familiar voice called to her from the station building. Her mother dressed in her WRVS uniform was carrying over cups of tea to a group of soldiers.

'Lily, darling, what a surprise.' Hardly, thought Lily, as she was on this station every day. And today she was dog-tired and just wanted to go home. But she couldn't ignore the summons she knew was coming.

'Hello, Mummy.'

'Lily, please come and help us. We need another pair of hands.' She gave the last cup on the tray to a grateful soldier and turned to Lily. 'Trains have been coming through all day. We've been making tea and sandwiches until we're ready to drop. We're told more are coming through the night.'

'I've been busy myself, Mummy. I'm very tired,' said Lily wearily, knowing her pathetic excuse would have no effect.

'Just a couple of hours,' pleaded Peg.

It was, of course, more than a couple of hours. It was the whole night. When she finally got a chance for a brief nap in a chair, she dreamt of scrambling eggs, slicing bread, spreading butter and scooping home-made jam out of jars. Her task was to make the sandwiches and then deliver them to the eager hands stretched out from the windows of the trains as they steamed into the station. Other women carried trays of hot tea. There was a chorus of thanks from the soldiers, often seasoned with more ribald quips.

Bletchley was a junction and here carriages from branch lines were hooked up to main line trains. All night the station resounded to the noise of shunting leviathans and the banging and colliding of coaches as they were linked into the long serpents that were to slide remorselessly to the holding stations of the south coast.

After a fleeting exchange of chatter, perhaps after a hastily snatched kiss, each train was off. The women watched and waved as the engines, often in pairs, belched clouds of steam and strained at their unaccustomed loads. Wheels squealed and clattered over points and very slowly the last carriage with its waving arms would vanish around the corner. The women looked at each other, said nothing and returned in silence to the station buffet to make more sandwiches and prepare more cups of tea before the next train came steaming in.

58

Over the next few weeks the anticipated invasion of France kept Lily and her family glued to their wireless set. At work deliveries resumed, but for the girls there was no other topic of conversation. The only unanswered question was when.

On the evening of Tuesday 6th June Lily got home to find Harris in the garden deadheading the few roses they allowed themselves to grow. He had a triumphant smirk on his face. He was still in his ARP uniform and he had clearly only just come off duty.

'It's all over for you lot,' he said, snipping off a dying flower head. He looked at her quizzically. 'You haven't heard, have you?'

'Heard what?' she asked dismissively.

''Course we get information before you hear it on the wireless.'

She was getting irritated. 'What haven't I heard?'

'It's started. Our lads are on their way.' Lily didn't wait to hear more. She threw down her bicycle and ran into the house. Hubert and Peg were hunched around the wireless set, straining to catch the first words of the BBC's news bulletin. Lily shrieked as she came into the room, only to be audibly shushed by her parents. She pulled a chair up to the brown box with its amber glowing light and listened intently to what was being said. The stiff, formal voice of the announcer had started what he called 'Communiqué No. 1'. There was a deathly silence as he made his announcement, each word striking them like a hammer blow. 'Under the command of General Eisenhower Allied naval forces supported by strong air forces began landing Allied armies this morning on the northern coast of France.'

Lily looked up and saw Harris at the window, the evil smirk still on his face. She hated him for it. It made her turn back to her father and want to hug him. He had bravely rejected all that he had held dear.

'It seems strange,' she said, 'that we are welcoming the crushing of a man we all once so admired.'

'Still do,' said Hubert gruffly. 'The beggar seems to have gone off the rails a bit, but he started out the right way.'

'I'm not so sure,' said Peggy. 'Anyway Hubert you shouldn't be talking like that. If you said that in public, you could get yourself arrested. Lily can attest to that.'

'Rubbish,' he persisted. 'A man can speak freely in his own house.'

'But not in Germany,' re-joined Peggy, getting an accusing stare from her husband. 'You can look at me like that, Hubert, but I've been hearing awful stories about what's going on over there.'

'Churchill propaganda,' spluttered Hubert, getting out his pipe.

'I don't think so, Daddy. You can't keep your head in the sand forever. We can't escape the fact that the man is evil and must be destroyed along with all that he preaches. I've been blind for so long. Sally saw it long before I did.'

'She's an odd one.' Hubert puffed vigorously on his pipe. 'What does she do? Never talks about her work.'

'You know there are a lot of people like that, Daddy. Even you. We're all told walls have ears.'

Hubert grunted. 'Well, now they're going over, the sooner they get on with it the better.' They all agreed to that and lapsed into silence, each with their own thoughts on what the future might hold. Lily wondered if she might be able to tell Friedrich about it in her next letter. Probably not. Any mention of the invasion would be met with a blue pencil. It did occur to her also that it had been some weeks since she had had a letter from Friedrich. She concluded that with the big push coming there had been a clamp down on letter writing.

'Well at least you know where he is,' said Sally as they walked through the local park. 'Not like the poor devils over in France.'

'I know and I'm thankful that he is safe,' said Lily wistfully. They sat together on a bench. 'I think of those Americans I took to the station. Where are they now, I wonder?' Al's face flashed before her. 'The reports say the Yanks had a bad time getting onto the beaches. How long do you think the fighting will last?' She looked at Sally as if she knew all the answers.

'It's not going to be over quickly. The Germans are going to fight for every inch they hold.'

'What a mess it will be.'

Sally caught the anxiety in Lily's voice. 'You are not thinking of going back one day, are you?'

'Friedrich will want to. It's his home.' She hesitated, before going on. 'We want to get married in Germany. They have such a lovely way of doing it in Bavaria.'

'But it will not be safe for either of you. Such terrible things are happening there. And the Russians - we don't know how far they will come.'

'What do you know, Sally, that you are not telling me?'

'I hear things.'

'No you don't.' Lily suddenly felt irritated with her friend. 'You're told things. Are you working for the government? Remember I've had experience of their ways.'

'You know I can't say anything, Lily.'

'You always say that.'

'What?'

'You can't say.' She looked hard at her friend. 'I know "you can't say".' They stared each other out for a brief moment and then collapsed in laughter. Wiping tears from her eyes, Sally suddenly looked serious again.

'Remember Lily, if you get the chance to speak to Friedrich, persuade him to stay - at least for the moment - for both your sakes.'

Lily listened and as the days passed Sally's words resonated in her head. The landings had been successful, but the way forward was a deadly war of attrition. In the daily reports, stories began to emerge of atrocities committed against the French people. It hurt her to hear them, but she feared it was only going to get worse. Yet there were little glimpses of humanity amid the blood and gore. In one report she read, a journalist described how he had entered a house with breakfast still on the table and a note from a girl saying she would be back at 6pm. People, thought Lily, carrying on normal lives as best they could.

Throughout the winter the Allies battled their way across northern Europe, overcoming desperate setbacks, such as the Arnhem operation and the German counter offensive in the Ardennes, to reach the heartland of Germany in early February. But two events disturbed Lily's equilibrium. Firstly, the RAF conducted a bombing raid over the old city of Dresden. Thousands of high explosives and incendiary bombs were dropped creating a fire storm that destroyed the city, killing fifty thousand people. Lily had never been particularly religious, but this seemed to be revenge of biblical proportions. It could easily have been Friedrich's beloved Munich. It disturbed her to think her own country was employing the same callous techniques as the enemy.

Then a few weeks later a second event sent her spiralling into free fall. It was a Saturday night in April and she and Sally had arranged to go to the pictures. They weren't certain what was on, but as Trevor was on duty, Sally said she fancied a girl's night out. They settled down to watch the cartoon but it never came. Instead the manager strode onto the stage in front of the screen and asked for quiet.

'Ladies and gentlemen, this evening we are going to start with the newsreel. The pictures we are showing will upset you, but the management feels it is important for you to see them. If you want to leave the auditorium we will gladly refund your money.'

Lily and Sally looked at each other wondering what was coming. Nothing could have prepared them or anyone else in the cinema that night for what now appeared on the screen. Gone was the strident cockerel with its rousing up-beat musical accompaniment announcing Pathé News. Instead a frozen picture of the bird appeared silently on the screen followed by a shot of British Tommies advancing towards a barbed-wire perimeter fence. The voice which spoke over the pictures was measured and sepulchral. The troops appeared to be entering some kind of internment camp. It soon became apparent exactly what this was.

There were audible gasps from the audience, recoiling before the shocking pictures on the screen. They looked up at the emaciated bodies of hundreds of people aimlessly wandering around a dust-filled emptiness. Men, women and children from many nationalities stood naked or clothed in scraps of rags, staring at the camera. Their faces were hollow and lifeless. Many were clearly dying from starvation and disease. Everywhere bodies lay around like discarded sacks of cement. The reporter described 'the smell of decay, death, corruption and filth'. Later in the film shots were shown of the camp guards, male and female, being forced to load the dead onto lorries. Two women seized a skeletal frame by its arms and legs and heaved it aboard. For Lily the most upsetting image was a British soldier using a bulldozer to shovel bodies into a pit. As he released his load, lifeless arms, legs and torsos cascaded down the sides. One woman, barely recognisable as a human being, bounced down the heap to come to rest with a quivering jolt in front of the camera, her neck twisted and contorted, dead eyes staring out from hollowed sockets. The film lasted barely eight minutes, but it was enough for most people. There was an immediate exodus from the cinema.

Lily and Sally stood on the pavement. The air of an unusually warm April evening enveloped them. No one spoke. The only sounds were an occasional car passing and the retching of someone being sick in the gutter. Now Dresden seemed a forgivable necessity.

They turned to retrieve their bicycles from the rack at the back of the cinema.

'How could it all have gone so wrong?' asked Lily, not expecting an answer.

'I fear the seeds were there, even when we were in Munich,' said Sally. As she hauled her bike out of the slot that held it, she looked hard at Lily. 'It is imperative you don't go back. You must persuade Friedrich to stay.'

'If ever I can get to see him.'

'Well, they let you write.'

Lily nodded and put her foot on the pedal. As a parting aside she asked what the film was they had planned to see.

'It was one they were showing again.'

'Yes, I remember now. "Night Train To Munich".' As she spoke her face creased in a painful grimace.

59

Sir Montague Daventry picked up the phone and listened for some seconds to the voice on the other end.

'He's on the south coast, I think,' he said in answer to what was being relayed to him. He continued listening.

'They don't believe it?' he exclaimed finally, sounding incredulous. 'Don't worry, he'll believe her. I'll send her down. Can't have them fighting on when we have victory in our sights.' He put the phone down and picked up another.

'Get me Reg Fuller.'

Lily was coming out of Bletchley station and turning towards the bicycle rack when a policeman accosted her.

'Miss Lilian Rood?' he asked stiffly but not unkindly.

'Yes.' Her heart sank. What now?

'I would like you to accompany me to the police station.'

'I should like to retrieve my bicycle first, if I may.'

He let her and she wheeled it along-side him down the street that led to the police station with which she was so familiar. She groaned when she saw the bulky frame of Sergeant Wilks still behind the desk and she half expected to see Berwick and Rush waiting for her. Instead, she wasn't arrested as she expected, but was led into a small interview room to find Reg Fuller sitting and waiting for her. He jumped to his feet when she came in.

'Miss Rood, what a pleasure it is to see you,' he said in his usual weasel tone. 'Please take a seat.'

'The pleasure must be all yours, Mr Fuller. It certainly isn't mine,' she said icily. She sat as he requested. He put himself opposite her.

'I trust your letters are getting through.'

'You mean the blue pencil.'

He gave an embarrassed laugh. 'I'm afraid that's wartime censorship.'

'Your censorship more like. I'm assuming you're reading them.'

More embarrassed laughter, before he continued with what he wanted to say.

'Miss Rood, as you know the war is coming to an end. We expect the Allies to be in Berlin in weeks. So we can afford to begin to relax restrictions. As you have helped us, we can now allow you to visit your fiancé.' He fished into the inside pocket of his jacket and pulled out a buff envelope. 'You will find in there your pass to visit the camp.' He pushed it across the table to her. She took it and opened the flap. The flimsy piece of paper inside had a War Office stamp on it and gave her the authority needed. She did her best to sound grateful, but she couldn't help thinking there was an ulterior motive in the gesture.

'What do you think it must be?' she asked Sally when she was able to tell her.

'They've been allowing you to write. This is just an extension of that, surely.'

'Are other people being allowed visits?'

'I don't know, but take the opportunity, Lily, now it's been offered.'

Bob Jenkins wasn't too happy to let Lily go, but he reckoned he could earn a favour if he said yes. So with his reluctant blessing, Lily found herself with two days leave. She took the train to London, crossed the war-devastated capital and at Charing Cross boarded an electric train to the Sussex coast. She alighted at a small halt a few miles from the resort of Bexhill-on-Sea. The platform was built a stone's throw from the pebbly beach and the salt tang of the sea assailed her nostrils as she stepped out. She was one of a handful of passengers, who quickly disappeared, leaving her standing alone with butterflies in her stomach. At the station exit she looked around for a taxi. The only vehicle she could see was a milk float. She gave her ticket to a hand that shot out of the booth and followed it with a request for a taxi.

'Phone box outside the station,' came the not too helpful reply.

The only taxi in the area was on call, but a series of buses finally got her to the camp. The latter lay in a valley surrounded by an expanse of marshland. These were the Pevensey marshes, Lily told herself, dredging up an old history lesson from school, where William the Conqueror had first put his foot on British soil, the last time a foreign force had successfully landed in England. As the bus approached the camp she could see the corrugated steel nissen huts begin to appear. The inhospitable terrain beyond would, concluded Lily, have made escape difficult. The bus put her out at the end of a rough drive that led down to a wire fence and a guard checkpoint. She was expected, although her protracted encounter with the buses had almost made the officials at the camp give up hope that she would arrive. She was searched and her documents checked. While this was being done, she looked out on the neat rows of rounded huts and the quiet orderly progress of those internees she could see walking around. The scene was so different from the images of the German camps that still continued to haunt her.

The formalities over, she was escorted to a group of buildings that stood at right angles to the avenue of prefabricated huts that stretched into the distance. This was clearly the administrative block looking more substantial than the rest. The young soldier who accompanied her was unarmed apart from a pistol in his belt, but that was securely holstered. She was shown into an empty room with a few old chairs scattered about it. In the middle, floor to ceiling, was a wire mesh. The soldier picked up a chair and placed it in front of the mesh.

'Sit here, Miss,' he said sharply, but not unkindly. She did as she was bid. The soldier stood to attention to one side of her. Neither spoke. She looked expectantly to the door on the far side of the hut. Her heart pounded. She could hear shouts in the distance but the door remained shut. As the minutes ticked by she replayed her own incarceration and the long hours of being alone and then being questioned. She felt again the clammy helplessness she experienced of being deprived of choice.

The door banged open and three men burst in. Two were armed with rifles, while the third stood between them, hovering, uncertain what he was going to see. They frogmarched him to the mesh and stood with rifles at the ready. The prisoner stared ahead of him, his eyes sunken and vacant straining to see who was on the other side of the mesh.

Four years had aged Friedrich. That was Lily's first reaction. He had lost the boyishness she remembered. When she last saw him lying wounded on a hospital bed, he was still recognisably Friedrich. Now life seemed drained from him. His hair was less blonde, his face weather-beaten, his figure gaunt and shambling. She hoped he would recognise her. At first he didn't. He sat listlessly on the chair that had been put up to the mesh with his head down.

'Friedrich.' Her soft voice made him look up. He became aware of her presence and a thin smile began to cross his face.

'Lily, you've come.' She made to touch the wire, but her guard stopped her.

'No contact, Miss.'

'They've allowed me to come, darling. How are you?' He didn't answer but stared long and hard into her face.

'We've lost, haven't we?' he said eventually.

'No politics,' snarled one of the armed soldiers. 'You know the rules.'

'If you mean,' said Lily ignoring the order, 'has the war finished, the answer is almost.'

'And the Führer?'

'We don't know. He may have killed himself.'

'I don't believe you,' said Friedrich, his voice strangled to a whisper.

'I said, Miss, no politics.' She looked up at the surly guard half hidden by the mesh.

'It is in the papers.'

'He knows the rules,' snapped the soldier bending down to look into her face, 'and if you don't co-operate, you'll be marched out of here. Now talk about the bloody vegetables.'

'We grow sugar beet here, Lily. Fields of it. They say the English grew it to defeat Napoleon. Now I grow it to defeat the Fatherland. I show them too how to grow kohlrabi. The English spit it out. Perhaps we win after all.' He laughed at his joke. His face for a moment lost its gauntness and she saw fleetingly the old Friedrich. Then he turned serious again.

'Have we really lost?'

'Yes, the Russians are almost in Berlin.'

The guard banged the mesh with his rifle, sending the metal shivering across the room. He was about to end the conversation when the door behind Lily opened and an officer stepped in.

'It's all right, corporal,' he said, 'you can ease off.'

The corporal stood back and stood to attention. 'Sir!' he said with some irritation.

Lily, not sure what was going on, sensed, nevertheless, that she was free to say what she wanted.

'How are they treating you?'

'I write in my letters, well. As we are to our enemies. Our camps are good, no?'

'Friedrich, there have been some awful pictures on the newsreels of your government treating people they have imprisoned with terrible cruelty.'

'We see these pictures too. They show us. They are lies. They are Russian fakes. We do not believe them.' She could hardly see his face through the mesh, but the insistence of his voice terrified her.

'Our most respected reporter has visited these camps and seen everything with his own eyes. The pictures he took are not fakes.'

'My officers tell me they are fakes.'

'Darling, you are wrong, you must face the awful truth. Your government has destroyed your country. Herr Hitler and his supporters have done some very cruel things. It is all over. Soon Germany will surrender and the war will end.' As she pleaded for him to understand she realised she was wanting him to betray everything he held dear. 'You must believe me, Friedrich. While you've been in prison, I've had the scales taken from my eyes. What you so admired. What I thought I admired too, has turned rotten. What we saw uncovered in those camps was caused by evil men. You must walk away from them. If you still love me, Friedrich, you will do that.' Friedrich remained silent during all that Lily said. When she had finished, he stayed silent. Without looking at her, he got up and signalled to the guards that he wanted to leave.

On the train home Lily wept inside herself for the entire journey. Had she lost Friedrich for good? Did she still even love him? When she saw him come into the room the deep feelings she felt surged through her like a tidal wave. His rejection of what she said hurt her a lot, but it didn't affect the love she had for him. He must see sense, she told herself. It was only a matter of time. She dragged across London and went straight to her room when she got home. Hubert and Peg looked at each other. As they hadn't been told where she had been, they had no idea what ailed her. Her colleagues at work were equally bemused. It was only in Sally that she confided.

'He's in denial, Sally. He wouldn't accept the reality of what has happened.'

'Are you sure, Lily? Maybe walking off like that meant that he had understood and it was too great a shock to deal with in front of you.'

'I do hope so.'

'One day, it will all seem like some terrible nightmare.' They sat in their usual corner of the tearoom. The cakes were as bad as ever, but the talk was lighter, more animated. It was as if everyone had the sense of victory in their nostrils. Sally hoped that what she said would console Lily, but she knew that the months ahead were not going to be easy for her. She knew too that Friedrich would be devastated by the news Lily brought him.

For Sir Montague Daventry this had exactly the desired effect he was wanting. He listened with growing satisfaction to the report from the commander of the Cooden POW camp being relayed to him over the phone.

'That's most satisfactory.' He looked up at Sergeant Berwick, who stood at ease in front of him. A Cheshire Cat grin crossed his face. 'I'm sure it will go like wildfire around the other camps. Thank you for letting me know.' He put down the phone.

'It's worked Berwick,' he said exultantly. 'Apparently what Miss Rood said persuaded Schulz it was over and he's spread the word around the camp.'

'So the little bitch has been useful.'

'Very. She's stopped an outbreak of discontent that could have been most nasty. Now they know the truth, that it's not some Ministry of War propaganda, it will deflate them and they'll be much easier to handle.'

'Poor devils,' said Berwick. 'Shut up for years and now all hope gone.'

'A lot are going to be relieved. Herr Hitler didn't take too kindly to his precious German elite getting themselves taken prisoner. Worse for the SS.'

There was a knock on the door. An orderly came in holding a piece of paper. He gave it to Berwick who handed it to Sir Montague. He read it several times. It was a short note. He made a précis of its content with relish.

'Berlin has been taken. The Russians are in control of the city. The Reichstag has fallen.'

60

The nissen hut was a cheap and practical way of housing large groups of men. Constructed of two skins of corrugated steel running from ground to ground, with wooden frames at either end, the whole punctured at points along its length with window holes, it was easy to assemble and once up proved remarkably solid. It was also uncomfortable. Hot in summer. Cold in winter. And it had the added defect of being very noisy. For men cooped up for months on end against their will, this was often a tipping point. The noise to some extent was mitigated by the dampening effects of mattresses and blankets. But there was never a time when the place was quiet, even at night.

Friedrich, by nature a nervous person and quick to take offence, found the incessant activity in the hut tearing at his nerves. It was worse at night. Men stumbled and banged their way to the toilet amid a stream of oaths. All night card games often erupted into open dispute. Snores and grunts were amplified. During the day the hut became the concourse of Munich station with its frenetic pandemonium. Which is why Friedrich chose to work in the fields ploughing, planting, pulling in all weathers. He had borne the long months of incarceration with stoic fortitude, sure in the knowledge that his country would win through.

Now Lily had brought him news that was a knife-blow to his heart. Even if he disbelieved the words her lips spoke, her eyes told him it was true. Although she hadn't confirmed it, somehow in his mind he convinced himself that Hitler had committed suicide. The idea gutted him to the core, but he knew when he told the other men in his hut, there would be a different reaction from many of them. There were so many traitors in his midst and he was right. There were whoops of jubilation. Hats shot in the air, whistles were blown, bed frames banged. The whole structure threatened to collapse. It was over. They were going home.

Friedrich was aghast. 'The Führer is dead. Have you no shame?' he shouted.

'Fuck the Führer,' came a voice from the back of the hut. There was ribald laughter in answer to words that would once have earned the speaker the firing squad.

'Aye, may he rot in hell,' cried another.

Friedrich sat back listlessly on his bed. He had made few friends during his time in the camp. His inflexible correctness and his clear devotion to Hitler caused his fellow prisoners to be wary of him. He also wore the black badge of the Waffen SS which at once set him apart from the rest. The SS had brought their techniques of fear and intimidation into the camp and although Friedrich had not associated himself with the worst of the cadre, he was still viewed with suspicion. But in an instant that changed. When it sank in that

Hitler was dead he found himself the butt of jokes and barely disguised jostling. The authority of the SS melted away in a display of unbridled bravado.

'You believe what you've just said?' A fellow SS prisoner sat on the bed beside him. Horst Bülow had befriended Friedrich when he first arrived and remained his only close companion.

'I believe my fiancée,' said Friedrich. 'She has no reason to lie.'

'So it's over then?' asked Horst. Friedrich looked at his fingers and said nothing. 'The way they're reacting you wouldn't think we'd lost.'

'No.'

'You can't blame them, though. They're going back to their wives and families.' Horst looked at Friedrich's shrunken figure. 'But you've got a girl here. You should be pleased.'

'She was going to join me and we were going to follow our glorious Führer to victory.'

'Now he's gone and fucking topped himself.' It was Horst's turn to sound bitter. 'If he thinks I'm expected to follow, he's wrong.'

Friedrich found himself laughing. 'I don't think that is part of our orders.' He continued to smile. 'Remember we are reformed citizens, no longer Nazis.' They had both done the de-Nazification course, but they both knew that what they had paid lip-service to and what stayed lodged in their heads was very different.

A group arrived and took Horst off to play table-tennis. 'A victory tournament' they called it.

'Watch your words, my friends,' warned Friedrich.

'Fuck you Schulz,' snarled the leader. 'It's over for you and your gang of bully boys.' They dragged

Horst into their midst and walked off laughing to the sports hut.

Friedrich now sat alone. As he watched the table-tennis players walk the length of the nissen hut, their raucous shouts echoing around the ceiling, suspicious thoughts about Lily started to cloud his mind. Why, on her first visit, had she needed to tell him such bad news, knowing how it would devastate him? It was as if she had been sent as a messenger. Had she been turned and was working for the British? During his time in the POW camp he had become more and more convinced that she knew about the trap set for him in the hospital. Dark suspicions seized him the moment they told him how he had been tricked. These grew in intensity as the months passed. Had she even been the one who betrayed him? No, that was impossible. She couldn't have known about the mission. No words had passed between them since the time he was recruited. But it was more than possible that she was working on a plan to keep them both in England.

But that could never happen. Germany was his home. The Reich his life. He owed everything to it and to his father whose position in the Party had given him his start in life. He wouldn't - he couldn't - abandon it. He needed to know too how his parents were. He hadn't heard from them since the start of the war. He remembered when he told them how he was attracted to an English girl. They said they would only accept the relationship if Lily came to live in Germany. His mother was particularly hostile and actively sought to break up their friendship. He recalled the time when she put the phone down with such a bang that it cracked the receiver and when he raced into the hall to find out what the commotion was, she rounded on him.

'She called herself Lily.' She spat out the name in answer to his question as to who had called. 'I told her you were not here.'

'You should not have done that, mother.'

'When you get back to the army, you will soon forget the English hussy.'

He didn't, but he never mentioned their engagement. Now he needed to return with Lily to show his mother and father what a lovely girl she was and how they were going to build their life together in Germany. If Lily tried to persuade him otherwise, he would know she had been conspiring against him and it would be all over between them.

In his mind the balance between Lily and the Fatherland could never swing in her favour. His duty to his country was more important than any romantic attachment. He was relieved his parents had never found out that he had been taken prisoner. He could not bear the shame of their knowing. He had been brought up to recognise that defeat was both unacceptable and impossible. It was from his father that he learnt the doctrine of obedience and devotion to duty. He idolised the unswerving loyalty he showed to the Führer. He bathed in the benefits this brought to the family and never questioned their provenance.

'Still stuck to your bed, Friedrich?' A voice jolted him out of his trance-like-state. It was Horst, back from his table-tennis. 'You should play more. You brood too much.' For seconds Friedrich said nothing, then he looked up at Horst.

'How did it go?'

'We lost.'

61

The news continued to be encouraging for the country. But Lily saw each new development as a nail in Friedrich's heart and it pained her greatly. Almost as soon as Berlin's fall was broadcast on the wireless it was confirmed that Adolf Hitler and Eva Braun, the mistress he had married a few hours earlier, had committed suicide in a Berlin bunker. A few days later Germany signed the terms of unconditional surrender. It represented the total annihilation of everything Friedrich held dear.

'We stood and cheered as he passed. We adored him, Sally. How could we have been so naïve?'

'I don't know. But we have atoned, have we not? You, Lily, have suffered for your mistakes.'

'I was a silly girl.' They were walking together in the park, trying to sort out the confusions in their minds now the war was all but over. Sally noticed her friend had a letter in her hand.

'What are you carrying, Lily?'

'A letter from Friedrich. It came this morning. I haven't been able to open it.'

Sally put an arm around Lily's shoulder and steered her to a park bench.

'Why don't you open it now,' she said softly. They sat together while Lily carefully slid her finger through the flap. She read its contents to herself. Sally watched her friend's face. It started to change from an expression of worry to one of delight.

'He's accepted what I told him,' she said happily, holding up the letter and starting to read selectively from it. He wrote that he was sorry he had walked out, that he loved her, that together they would build a new life. She turned a tear-stained face to Sally.

'He says he wants us to get married as soon as possible.' What she didn't read out was that he wanted that to be in Germany. Nor did she repeat his continuing bitterness towards whoever it was who had betrayed him. 'One day, Lily,' he wrote, 'I will find out who did it and I will kill them.' She shuddered as she read the words. She kept silent too about his parting sentence: 'Lily, I want fuck you.' As she folded the letter and placed it carefully back in its envelope, those last words, expressed with a soldier's crudeness, aroused and scared her. If only Sally could know the depth of feeling that surged inside her. Her whole body suddenly ached for Friedrich, while Sally only heard the word 'married' and gave a great yelp of joy.

'That's wonderful. You and Friedrich married in our little church in Bletchley.'

'Don't rush us, Sally. I don't think Friedrich moves that quickly.'

'No, I don't think he does!'

In the days that followed, euphoria was everywhere. At work Lily and her colleagues took every opportunity to celebrate, but there were hidden dangers in the newly relaxed atmosphere. She and Gloria were celebrating in a pub before going home, when Boozy Bob Jenkins joined them, uninvited. Gloria looked wary and annoyed.

'Well ladies, a day for celebrating,' said Bob breezily, pleased that he had pinned down two of his female workforce. 'Will you join me in another drink?' Gloria was having none of it.

'No thank you, Mr Jenkins, I have to dash.' Lily was about to protest when Gloria was on her feet, grabbing her coat from the back of her chair and heading for the door.

'Miss Rood, I hope you don't have to hurry away.' Lily felt caught. Not wishing to seem rude, she reluctantly accepted Bob Jenkins offer.

'No.'

'What will it be?' Normally she would have said a beer, but they were celebrating and it was her boss.

'A scotch,' she said importantly. Bob Jenkins raised an eyebrow but said nothing. Moments later he was back with two whiskies.

'Well, here's to our boys.' They raised and chinked their glasses. She looked at him. He was barely forty, she thought. Why wasn't he in uniform?

'Wouldn't have me,' he said in answer to her question. 'Suffered from asthma, probably the brick dust.' As he spoke she felt his shoe brush against her ankle. He leaned forward and spoke conspiratorially.

'Miss Rood, how would you like to work permanently at the brickworks? You're a bright girl. I reckon I could swing it with the boss.' She looked at him doubtfully. He was a good foreman but for all his oily words it was unlikely that he had that sort of sway with Mr Roberts.

'I'm not sure.'

'Truth is,' he continued, 'much as I like having you ladies around me, the boys will be coming back soon and they'll be wanting their jobs back.'

'So we become the little woman in the corner again, do we? Tell that to Gloria and Daphne,' she said, with an irony that did not escape him. He leaned further forward. With the lightest touch he put his hand on her knee. She stiffened and would have kicked out had he not backed off.

'You're a friend of Miss Bates, aren't you? I'm sure she would welcome some help in the office.'

'Mr Jenkins, I appreciate your concern for me, but I don't think I shall be staying. I've got wider horizons in mind. Now if you'll excuse me, I must go.' As she got up she deliberately trod on his toe. Had she had heels it would have hurt more, but her boots had the desired effect. The foreman's face screwed up in pain, but not a sound came from his mouth.

'I'm sorry. Clumsy of me but thank you for the drink.' She gave him a coquettish smile that made his discomfiture complete.

Throughout the next day, he avoided her, but Lil did not. Her friend sought her out while she was having a cocoa after her last delivery. The canteen was empty except for the manager, who was occupied with stocktaking. Lily had her back to the door, but she was conscious of it being closed with a sharp bang. She looked round to see Lil advancing towards her wearing a storm cloud across her brow.

'How could you Lily?' she seethed, sitting down with her face only inches away. 'You knew, but you never told me.'

'Knew what, Lil?' She never answered but continued hurling abuse at Lily for betraying her.

Lily persisted with her question. 'Lil, tell me, what did I know?'

'What Ag was doing. You fucking knew where she was because you fucking went to see her.' The ferocity of Lil's words started to alarm Lily.

'Calm down Lil and tell me what's the matter.'

'I won't calm down. You went behind my back, Lily. I thought you were my friend. If you had told me, I could have seen her before ….' She stopped mid-sentence and burst into tears. Lil was a hard woman and it disturbed Lily to see her usual steeliness crumple.

'Lil, tell me what's happened,' she pleaded.

'She's dead, Lily. Blown up by one of those bloody V2 thingies. Killed outright, they said. Never knew what hit her. Apparently the house she was living in got a direct hit.' Lily handed her a handkerchief. She blew and sniffed and looked at Lily through tear-stained accusing eyes. 'You lied to me, Lily, when you came back from London.'

'Agatha didn't want me to say anything,' she said wimpishly.

'Agatha!,' she spat the word out. 'That's what they called her.'

'Who?'

'The authorities. Called her Agatha. My Ag giving herself la-di-da airs and graces. What's she say to you, Lily?'

'Let me get you a cup of tea.'

'No, fucking tell me what she said.' Lily blinked and let a tear fall from her eye. The news had hit her badly too.

'I met her on the train. She said she was dancing in a show, but never said what. It was by chance that I found out. Believe me, Lil, she never told me.'

'And what was it you found out, Lily?'

A lump formed in Lily's throat and her words formed in a strangled rasp. She didn't want to tell Lil about her exploits with Jack Havering so she said simply that Agatha was on the stage at the Windmill Theatre.

'That's that London place where they take their clothes off?'

'That's right.'

'What were you doing there, Lily?'

'It's a long story. I don't want to go into it now.'

'I bet you don't,' said Lil waspishly.

'I saw Agatha backstage. She pleaded with me not to tell you.'

'Why the heck not? She got what she wanted, didn't she?'

'No she didn't. Can't you see, Lil, she was embarrassed. Guilty even.' She looked into Lil's blood-stained eyes. 'She was ashamed. Yes, she was on the stage. Yes, she was dancing. It was the other part she hated and she didn't want you to know.'

Lil sat shiftily and fell silent.

'I'll have that tea, Lily.' she said at last. Lily lightly touched her hand and rose to go to the counter.

'I don't get it,' said Lil when Lily returned with two cups of tea, some sugar and two solitary biscuits. 'Ag was never bashful. At our New Year do her dances didn't leave much to the imagination.'

'That's perhaps because she was among friends. It's different doing it in front of strangers.'

'Or telling your friends,' replied Lil ruefully. She looked up at Lily. 'What did she look like?'

'What do you mean?'

'You know. Being starkers.'

'She looked beautiful. Like a water nymph. It was all done with the utmost of taste, Lil, believe me.'

'I do believe you. I only wished you'd told me. Ag would have forgiven you.'

'I do too. I'm sorry Lil.'

'Well, you're a hoity-toity stuck up bitch, Lily, but you meant well.' Lil had calmed down and they sat silently drinking their tea, each with their own memories of Ag.

62

The war in Europe officially came to an end on Tuesday the 8th May. At 3pm the nation glued itself to the wireless to hear Winston Churchill broadcast from No. 10 Downing Street the heart-warming words that 'the German war is at an end.' The girls in the brickworks ran to their lorries and furiously honked their horns, to be met by the shrill response from the hooters in the furnaces. It was a deafening and rousing sound. There were no more bricks made that day and no more deliveries. The entire workforce surged out of the yard and headed home for what was going to be a long and unbridled night of revelry. The weather promised to be cooler than it had been with the occasional thundery shower. But this was not going to dampen the ardour of the celebrations.

Lily put on a jersey dress and light coat and climbed into the Wolsey beside her parents and with a smug-looking Harris at the wheel drove down the drive in the dying light towards the centre of town. They were soon hemmed in by other cars making the same journey and crowded out by excited people pouring off the pavement in front of the cars. The Wolsey came to an abrupt halt.

Hubert pulled back the glass window that gave onto the driver and leaned in. 'Look, I say, Harris, you'd best stay put and look after the car. We'll walk from here.'

'Yes, sir,' said the chauffeur with a tone of distinct annoyance in his voice. Lily was pleased to see that his smugness had gone.

'Enjoy yourself, Harris,' she said cheerfully as she got out of the car and became swallowed up by the crowd, with Peg's admonishing voice urging her to be careful, ringing in her ears.

Free of her parents, she looked out for Sally. In the gathering throng this proved difficult. But she did hear cheery voices behind her shouting her name. She looked round and to her amazement she saw Lil, Gloria, Daphne and Yakova advancing on her arm-in-arm.

'This is a surprise,' she exclaimed delighted to see them. 'I thought you would all be doing the knees up in Bedford.'

'Heard you got the better fireworks,' said Gloria, 'but really we all wanted to be together.'

'Maybe for the last time,' said Lil sadly. 'Now we'll be going our own ways.'

'Don't look so glum, Lil,' said Daphne, 'you'll still have me.' They laughed, knowing how difficult Daphne could be.

'If tomorrow we die, tonight we make merry,' said Yakova, strangling the phrase she had dredged out of her English book of quotations.

'Come on then,' said Lily happily, 'we're going to the park.' Lil looked up at Lily and gave her a reassuring smile, as if to say it's OK. Lily grabbed her by the arm and squeezed it. Then linking with the others she led them into the crowd, all the while keeping her eyes strained for Sally. Eventually she caught sight of a bobbing head of red curls some distance off.

'Wait a minute, ladies,' she yelled. 'I've just seen Sally.' Before the others had taken in what she had said, she vanished and minutes later returned with an effervescent Sally. She had been on her own.

'No Trevor?'

'On duty,' said Sally. Always on duty, thought Lily, which was odd, but she didn't press the matter. They joined the others with squeals of delight from Lil and Yakova. Lily introduced her to Gloria and Daphne.

The noise around them became deafening. Everywhere there were shouts and gales of laughter. The emotional relief people felt expressed itself in outrageous ways. Whistles were blown, rattles shaken and anything individuals could lay their hands on banged with gusto. Boys climbed trees and threw firecrackers into the crowd, sending the girls scampering across the grass. Groups formed impromptu choirs and gave raucous renderings of popular songs, songs which had buoyed the nation through the war and to which people now danced with uncontrolled frenzy.

Gloria spotted a conga line coming their way and they all ran to join it. Soon they were weaving in and out of trees, around park benches filled with necking couples and over bridges that crossed the serpentine lake. Lily held onto Sally's waist as she kicked her legs out to the rhythm of the dance. Firm hands clutched her from behind and she realised it was Daphne holding her more tightly than she would have liked.

'Your bloke will be free now to go back to Germany,' she whispered with a hissing breath in her ear.

'Yes.'

'All I got is a sodding stone in the desert.' Yes, thought Lily looking around her, so much joy now, but under it all deep sorrow. Daphne had lost her man. Lil had lost Ag. Yakova was a refugee. And Sally? Perhaps the happiest of all, quietly going out with Trevor. Or was she? She must probe a little more in that direction. And she? Ahead of her lay a process of healing, of bringing back a deeply hurting man to a world of normality.

'Blimey, look at that!' Lil's cackling voice made them all strain their necks in the direction of the lake which they were crossing for the umpteenth time. Squeals and cries came from a group of partygoers frolicking in the lake. The girls were young and the men much older but they had all stripped to their underwear and were splashing each other with great cascades of water.

'They'll catch their death,' said Gloria. 'That water must be bloody cold.'

'Hey, what the hell's going on,' shouted Lil in alarm. The conga line had come off the bridge and was snaking itself round and moving straight towards the water. Everyone was staring in horror at the lead man who showed no sign of deflecting the line.

Lil's voice rose to a squeak. 'He's bloody going in the water.' He was. What to do? Break the line or show this was VE day? No one dropped out.

'Can you swim Lil?' asked Daphne with a laugh, knowing she was the shortest of the group.

'Don't worry, Lil,' shouted Lily over her shoulder, 'it'll only come up to your tits.' There was more laughter, but now of the nervous kind. The water was getting closer.

'Kick your shoes off,' shouted Sally, always the practical one. Lily thought of the new nylons she had put on, but Sally was right, walking in the water wasn't going to be easy in heels. She stepped out of her shoes, just as cries ahead told her it would soon be her turn to take the plunge. She felt Sally judder and yelp. Her friend was in and then water struck with an icy smack. Breath seemed to be sucked from her lungs. Soon the freezing water had crept up her legs and was circling her waist. But there it stopped. It was now just a question of forging forward to get to the other side. Daphne, the hard one, had made no sound, but she could hear Gloria giggling with hysterical laughter.

'They should have warned us, then we could all have been in our scanties,' she cried.

Lil was struggling. 'Keep going, darling.' Gloria had her by the waist and part hoisted her up as they surged through the water.

'Fuck me,' cried Lil, 'I'll soon be getting icicles up me fanny.'

'You'll have worse than that, if you don't keep going,' retorted Gloria.

Cheered by the half-naked girls in the lake, the conga snaked its way relentlessly and drunkenly across the water. One of the men emerged under the surface beside Lily. He spluttered and spat water as he righted himself.

'You should take that coat off, miss. It'll drag you down.'

'I'll manage,' said Lily. 'We're almost on the other side.' She looked at him and decided he was no great specimen. The water had streaked his hair leaving large bald patches and a large belly floated on the surface. A huge wave of water suddenly engulfed him, brought about by Daphne's left leg.

'Tosser,' she hissed.

By now the lead dancer was on dry land, but he showed no sign of stopping. Like some demon minstrel he danced on twisting and turning his seemingly never-ending wave of humanity. Eventually he ran out of steam and he led his followers into an open area of grass where he wove them into a diminishing and ever tightening spiral. When the last stragglers had caught up he gave an exultant whoop and the whole body of revellers fell exhausted to the ground in a frenzied tangle of arms and legs. Everyone was intoxicated with high spirits. Even Daphne had a smile on her face, which vanished when two worsted trouser legs strode across them. They belonged to Bob Jenkins.

'Hello ladies. Thought you might like these.' He dangled three woollen blankets in his hands. 'If you don't dry yourselves, you'll catch a chill.' The five women looked up at him in astonishment.

'Why have you got those, Mr Jenkins?' asked Lil.

'To sit on the grass,' he said, as if it was obvious.

'Just you?' asked Lily in surprise.

'Well, I thought I might find some of my workers here to share them with me.'

'He's bloody followed us here,' whispered Gloria under her breath.

'Can't say the blankets won't come in useful,' said Lil getting up and wrapping one around her shivering body. The others did the same. Lily and Sally shared one, as did Gloria and Daphne. Only Yakova was left out until Lil took pity on her and invited her in.

'Thanks Mr Jenkins,' they chorused.

'What do you say to a drink to celebrate. On me.'

Why not, they thought? A warm pub, Boozy Bob was buying and there was safety in numbers.

63

With the war over, the immediate thought in Lily's mind was when would Friedrich be released? For Hubert and Peg this was also a question uppermost in their minds.

'Are we going to hear wedding bells?' asked Peg, hoping it would prompt some information.

'Mummy, you're getting ahead of yourself.'

'Surely they're going to want to get rid of those fellows back to Germany as quickly as possible,' said Hubert, puffing reflectively on his pipe. 'I hear they're bringing our chaps back into civvies in their droves,'

'Friedrich does say in his last letter that we may have to wait some months before they will consider him for release. After all he must be one of the few German combatants actually captured on English soil and being in the Waffen SS will go against him.'

'And what are you going to do now, dear?' asked Peg. 'I expect the men will want their jobs back at the brickworks.'

'I expect they will, Mummy, but I have no intention of staying there.' She paused. 'I don't know what I'm going to do. Nothing, probably, until Friedrich gets out.'

'The lassies at my place are getting a bit worried about what's going to happen to them,' said Hubert.

'I bet they are, Daddy. This war has changed us women, you know.' Hubert grunted and Peg raised an eyebrow. 'Now, if you'll excuse me, I have a phone call to make.'

Next day she sat alone in the pub near the brickworks and waited. She was early and he was late.

'At last. I thought you had stood me up.'

'A pretty girl like you, Miss Rood. Never.'

'Before you sit down, I'll have another half of bitter.'

Reg Fuller went to the bar, ordered the drinks and quickly returned.

'So, what is it that I can do for you, Miss Rood?' he asked as he sat down.

'I assume my visit to Sussex was not arranged out of the goodness of your heart?' He gave a smirk and said nothing.

'I trust the result was to your boss's satisfaction. Sir Montague was it?'

Again, he said nothing.

'What do you want, Miss Rood?'

'Well, as I've been of further help to you, I would like you to do something for me in return.'

He drained his glass. 'If I can.'

'Two simple requests.'

'Which are?'

'Release SS Sturmmann Schulz.'

'If he co-operates I see no reason why this can't be done. And the other request?'

'Now the war is over, who was it who told the authorities about the raid?'

He laughed. 'That, Miss Rood, will stay classified information for a long time to come.'

'Friedrich will return to Germany and I shall go with him.' That was the truth as far as Friedrich was concerned. She didn't intend to tell him that she planned to change his mind. 'We will be disappearing.'

'So why do you need the information? Even if I could get it, which is doubtful.'

'Curiosity.'

He looked at her in disbelief.

'After all,' she continued, 'whoever was responsible for betraying us, caused me a great deal of pain.'

'Me?' queried Reg. 'Are you now admitting you knew about the raid.'

'I was implicated through my association with Friedrich. No, I knew nothing about the raid.'

'So you want this information for revenge?' He picked up his empty glass. 'I must get another drink. Do you want one?' She nodded in the affirmative. At the bar he looked back at her and scratched his head. She could see the expression of puzzlement on his face.

'Look,' she said when he returned, 'I'm curious, yes, but I don't need to go beyond that, but for Friedrich it's different. He feels his betrayal more deeply. If he doesn't find out how it happened, it will eat him up, eventually destroy him. In the old days they used to exorcise demons. I need Friedrich to confront his demons so we can move on and the only way of doing that is for him to be in full possession of the facts.'

'You have thought it out, haven't you?'

'I've had time.'

He swallowed half his glass. He was a drinker that's sure, thought Lily.

'I will see what I can do, on one condition.' She eyed him suspiciously. 'That you have dinner with me on Saturday? I know a nice quiet little restaurant where no one will overhear us and we can discuss this further.' His words had his familiar oily slur. Her skin prickled.

'Dinner, but no more.'

'Good. I look forward to it. I'll pick you up from your home at 8pm.'

'No,' she said hurriedly. 'I'll be outside the railway station at eight.'

'As you wish. Now, my dear, I must go. 'Til Saturday.' He gave her a parting smile and left.

Lily watched him with foreboding. What had she got herself into? He was a slippery and ruthless man. What guarantee had she that he would stop at a simple meal? How far was she prepared to go? And how likely was it that he would deliver what she wanted. She sat for some minutes turning it all over in her mind. The only encouragement she had was that in the past he had done whatever she had asked him. She picked up her cardigan that was on the back of the chair and wearily made her way home.

64

It had been a fine day and a crimson sunset cast a golden glow over even the most mundane of settings. She stood in the forecourt of the railway station to catch the dying warmth of the sun, waiting for the odious Reg Fuller to make an appearance. All day she had asked herself why she was doing this, but she had learnt, over the few bitter years since her innocent days in Munich, that men could be manipulated. Women had their sexuality which they could use or withhold as they wished and there, that evening, lay the problem for Lily. Be too forward and he would take advantage and want more. Hold back and he wouldn't give her what she wanted.

She had ransacked her wardrobe for a suitable dress. She chose the one she had worn in London, now a little careworn and out of fashion, but alluring enough in a discreet sort of way. Despite the soaking her nylons had got on VE night, they had survived. She applied a minimum of make-up and just a dash of scent. She told her parents she was out with Sally and hoped they wouldn't ask too much when she got home.

The quiet little restaurant that Reg Fuller had boasted of knowing was tucked away in a narrow street on the edge of the town. Called 'The Gay Corsair' it had pretensions to the exotic. Tables were candlelit and decorated with a single rose. They were escorted to a corner that gave them a view of the restaurant but shielded them from the prying eyes of other diners.

'This is nice,' said Lily sweetly in a voice she hoped would relax him. 'Have you brought other girls here?'

'Don't laugh, if I say Sergeant Berwick. And I have been here once or twice.'

'So, you've had a chance to reconnoitre the table lay out.'

'Very shrewd, Miss Rood.'

'Oh, call me Lily, please.'

'Lily, that's a lovely name, when it's not being written down in some police station log.'

'It's short for Lilian.'

'Lily, I prefer.'

'Was it business or pleasure?'

'What?'

'Your coming here with Sergeant Berwick.'

He laughed. 'Two of your nastiest people getting it off together!' Exactly that, said Lily to herself.

'Mavis is a charmer when she's off duty.'

'She never was when we were having our little chats.' He chuckled.

'You have a dry wit, Lily. I'm glad we're getting to know each other.' A waiter hovered close by. They ordered cocktails, Lily deciding to be daring and ordered a 'Mary Pickford' with its combination of white rum, pineapple juice and grenadine.

'Takes me out of this drab world,' she said laughingly.

The settings promised the exotic but the menu hardly lived up to that promise. Wartime restrictions were still in place and, as people had started to notice, food rather than becoming more plentiful had become more scarce.

'Why do you think that is?' asked Lily looking down at the uninteresting list of choices.

'All the extra mouths to feed,' suggested Reg. 'We're responsible for Europe now, not just ourselves.'

A spiced onion soup arrived served with a flourish. Lily decided she was hungry.

'Are you married, Reg?' she asked casually between slurps of soup. She suspected the answer as she had never seen a ring.

'I was. Me and me missus never hit it off, especially in my line of work.'

'You don't look like an obvious spy.'

'That's because of all those penny-dreadfuls you read. Suave, debonair types who sweep a girl off her feet.'

'Well, you're not going to do that Reg.' It was the wrong thing to say. Lily knew it at once. His face glowered.

'You're a bit stuck-up, Lily, aren't you?' he said sharply.

She looked at his badly cut suit, with its herringbone stripes, and thought how common he looked, but she needed quickly to massage his ego.

'Sorry, forgetting my manners. You must be very good at your job. Unsung hero and all that.'

'Well, I shan't be getting the VC if that's what you mean.'

'But you must be proud of all those traitors you've sent to the gallows.'

'You don't like me much, do you Lily?'

'Remember, I've been threatened with the hangman's noose. What do you call it – the drop?'

'All part of my job, Lily.'

'That's right. So I forgive you, Reg.' She sipped the last of her cocktail and gave him what she thought was her sweetest smile. He waved to the waiter and ordered two more cocktails. The rest of the meal went smoothly and he started to show his funny side which she had never seen before as he told her tales of the many compromising and unlikely situations he had been in. Then about halfway through coffee he announced that Friedrich would be released within six months.

'That's if he doesn't turn up on parade giving a Nazi salute. Some of the buggers still do that, you know.'

'I think Friedrich has more sense.' She got up from her seat, leant over and gave Reg a kiss on the cheek.

'Thank you, Reg. You're a swell guy.' She mimicked a Hollywood film star. He ignored her, knowing she was playing with him.

'But the other matter? That may be more difficult.'

'But not impossible?' Her voice was a simpering whisper.

'You must stay in touch with me. Let me know where I can contact you. If you disappear into Germany, that won't be easy.'

'Where do I contact you?'

'As always, my phone number or Bletchley police station.'

'I will stay in touch. I will make sure of that.'

He looked pleased. Knowing he had a pretty girl dangling gave him pleasure. Lily looked at her watch.

'Oh my,' she said in mock horror, 'look at the time. You must take me home, Reg. I will tell you the way.' He made no attempt to delay and asked for the bill.

'Thank you for a lovely evening. It was delightful.'

He bowed with a sycophantic smile. When their coats came he helped her on with hers and thanking the restaurant owner, he led her to his car, a green Austin 10 saloon. He helped her in and as she swung her legs into the well of the car she caught a worrying smirk on his face. He climbed into the driving seat, closed the door with a bang and drove off down the lane. She assumed he was planning to turn around somewhere as there was no room outside the restaurant. But the obvious place at the end of the lane he drove past and to her alarm he stopped the car in a darkened yard. He reached over and locked the door on her side. His hand fumbled with the buttons of her coat and slid it off her shoulders.

'No, Reg, I just said dinner.'

'For what you want me to do? Don't you think I deserve more?' He pressed himself on her and kissed her while his hand continued its exploration. She felt fingers compressing her breasts. She tried to push him off, but he was too strong and in the confines of the tiny car they were locked together. He fumbled with the hem of her dress and was on the point of pulling it up, when there was a loud thump on the driver's window. Both looked up and saw a police constable shining a torch into the car. Reg stopped his groping and wound the window down. Lily had the presence of mind to turn her face away.

The policeman's threatening attitude changed when he saw who it was in the car.

'Mr Fuller. I'm sorry I disturbed you.' His voice quivered in a fluster of embarrassment. 'We've been having some trouble in this lane .... so I thought ....'

'That's all right, constable, we were just leaving.' Reg had recovered his equilibrium and gave the policeman an oily smile.

'Have a good evening, sir.' He gave a wink as the window wound back up. The policeman had saved the day for Lily. Reg, thankful too that she had stayed hidden, let his ardour melt away.

'You're an iron-willed bitch,' he said, watching her smooth out her dress. 'No wonder Sir Montague recruited you?'

'What do mean?' She looked at him oddly. 'You mean I wasn't a suspect and needn't have gone through all that interrogation?'

'Oh, you were, but when we found you were clean, he ran you through the war.'

'So I've served my country. But like you I doubt I'll get a medal for it. Now will you take me back to the town.'

'I'll take you home.'

'No, the railway station will be fine. I'll get a taxi from there.' She kept her voice matter-of-fact, fearing to say anything that might arouse him again. He snorted and settled himself into the driving seat. He did as she asked him and drove to the station. He leant over and unlocked the door for her.

'Your Kraut is a lucky sod. Nice knowing you, Lily Rood.' He all but pushed her out and spun off. Lily wondered how much damage she had done to her plans. Perhaps she would never know.

65

Odious though he was in many ways, Reg Fuller had a thieves' honour and regarding Friedrich's release he was as good as his word. Which is why Lily sat with Friedrich on a stone bench one cold February morning six months later, staring out to sea and wondering what their future held.

Friedrich had been released with papers to travel back to Germany. These Lily knew could be converted into a pass to return to England. But this was not what Friedrich had in mind. He sat in his demob suit and overcoat with his arms around Lily, on the upper level of the Colonnade that decorated the seafront at Bexhill-on-Sea. Lily's eyes were fixed on the white balustrade and domed cupola, now somewhat shabby from wartime neglect. It reminded her of Agatha in her classical tableau at the Windmill. She smiled and for a moment felt at peace.

'It's nice here isn't it?'

He squeezed her more tightly in reply.

'How is your room?'

'It is good.' She had secured a room in a boarding house on the seafront for him to stay in after he had been released while more permanent plans were made.

'Friedrich.' She turned to him and looked earnestly into his eyes. 'You mustn't think of going back to Germany. We will be happy here. We can get married. Mummy and Daddy want it to happen very much. You can get a job. I have a little money. It will be safe for you here.'

'No, Lily, I must return. I need to know what happened to my parents.'

'But it is very dangerous for you. I read so much about the terrible conditions there. Everything is destroyed. You could be arrested.'

He smiled and took her hands in his. 'I must see for myself, Lily. We've been told so much. How do I know if it is all true unless I see it with my own eyes? I believe in the greatness of the Fatherland. I must go to help rebuild. We will be new Germans together.'

'But I'm not German,' protested Lily.

'You will be when we marry.' She shivered. The sea breezes had got under her coat.

'Please say you will come, Lily.' She found herself melting under the gaze of his clear blue eyes, still bright despite the weather-worn face. How could she resist him?

'I will come Friedrich, but only for six months. Then you must return with me to England.' Friedrich's face darkened. It worried him, she could see. He wasn't used to making compromises.

'When do we marry?'

'When we come back to England. And ….' She wiggled his chin, '…. I'll find the perfect log for us to cut.' He laughed and gave her a kiss.

'You promise, Friedrich. Six months?'

'I promise.' They gave each other another hug and kiss but pulled back guiltily when they found themselves attracting the attention of passers-by. Friedrich knew he had made a promise he wasn't going to keep.

Lily's heart pounded to the rhythm of the train as it sped homewards. She and Friedrich had agreed it would be best that for the moment they did not disclose their plans to her parents. She would let them know when they were in Germany as she didn't want any tearful partings.

'How is Friedrich?' asked Peg as she came in through the door. 'I thought he would be with you.'

She put her suitcase down in the hall and kissed her mother.

'He's in a boarding house in Bexhill, waiting for his papers to be finalised.' This was not true, but she doubted either her mother or father would query it. While she didn't mind spinning a yarn for her parents, she did resist seeing Sally whom she felt sure would see through her plans at once.

Over the next few days she quietly gathered together the few clothes she felt she needed and neatly folded them in a case which she stowed under her bed. She had given in her notice at the brickworks, although it had been made clear to her that she wouldn't have the job for much longer anyway, and said good-bye to her friends. It was strange she thought how the war had held people together and now it was over everything was in a state of flux. Lil had decided to stay, Gloria went back to London, Daphne vanished and Yakova returned to secretarial school. Sally remained in her secretive and, from what Lily had been able to extract from her, lucrative job.

She planned to meet Friedrich in a small hotel in Dover before catching the cross-channel ferry to Calais. She told her parents that she would be going back to Bexhill for a few days and this allowed her to pack more into her case.

'I hope the boarding house you have found is a nice one,' said Peg, giving Lily a farewell hug.

'Yes, Mummy. It is very smartly kept and Mrs Brown is a very respectable woman.'

'And Friedrich is in the same boarding house?'

'Yes, Mummy, but in another room. So don't worry. I'm twenty-six. I know how to look after myself.' After all that had happened to her, it irked that her mother still treated her as a young girl. Peg sensed her daughter's irritation but still gave her another kiss as she helped her into the taxi that was to take her to the station.

'Mummy,' she protested, 'I'm only going to Bexhill!'

Hubert had offered Harris and the Wolsey, but she had cleverly avoided this by stating that her train's departure coincided with Hubert's golf. Getting to his club on time took precedence and the last thing she wanted was to have Harris nosing around the station and finding she was buying a ticket to Dover and not Bexhill.

She wondered, as the taxi drove down the drive, what was in store for her and when she would be returning to Fenner Way. At the station she rang Friedrich in Bexhill and told him the time she would be arriving in Dover.

'Are you sure you're happy about getting a train to Dover?' She spoke anxiously to the voice at the other end of the telephone. 'If you aren't sure, Friedrich, just get Mrs Brown to write down the stations.' She was nagging, but it had the desired effect. Friedrich was standing on the platform as the London train steamed into Dover station. He was still in his grey herring-bone demob suit. The small brown case he carried held all his earthly possessions. He waved when he saw Lily, ran to the carriage door, put down his case and before she could alight he had swept her into the air and landed her onto the platform. He then ran back to retrieve her case. It was heavy.

'You have much in here, Fräulein Lily. Enough for us both?'

'If you want to wear a dress,' she laughed.

'Ja, I look good, no?' He minced around the platform to the consternation of the other passengers. They both laughed. The intoxication of freedom had gone to his head. But the moment quickly passed. He cleared his throat in embarrassment, picked up the two cases and with a sober step made his way down the platform. They ate supper in the station restaurant and then found a hotel in a crumbling Victorian terrace that had escaped Dover's devastating bombing but had still seen better days. The proprietor asked no questions when they signed themselves Mr and Mrs Smith. This was a port in the aftermath of war and the only concern of management was the money that came in and not where it came from.

The room they were shown was as decrepit as the outside. But it mattered little to them that the wallpaper was peeling, the basin in the bathroom was cracked, that the chairs were unstable or that the carpet was threadbare and the curtains torn. What mattered was that they were together. Although the question of where each was to sleep taxed them. The cramped wooden bed with its bile green satin coverlet was barely large enough for one person and Friedrich, much as he desired Lily, felt his customary sense of propriety hold him back.

'I'll sleep on the sofa,' he said. Much as she desired him, she was grateful for his restraint. She strained her body up and kissed him on the neck. She then opened her case, removed her toilet bag and nightdress.

'See if you can find a blanket, Friedrich,' she said as she disappeared down the corridor to the bathroom. When she returned she found Friedrich in his underpants and holding a tattered rag that doubled as a blanket. Pyjamas were not part of his demob issue.

Lily laughed. 'Tomorrow we must buy you some proper clothes. I'm not sure we will find them in Germany.'

'You make joke of me, no?' he asked sharply. She stood in her nightdress and gazed at his naked torso. His work in the fields had developed his muscles and he had lost the dejected look he had had when she saw him in the POW camp.

'On the contrary, I adore what I'm looking at.' But his quickness to take offence continued to alarm her. She held out her arms. 'Come here.' He relaxed and walked over to embrace her. As their bodies came together, she hoped that whatever might happen their love for each other would not fade.

'Come to bed', she whispered and led him across the room. Pulling the satin coverlet off, she folded down the sheets and slipped into bed, dragging Friedrich with her. She was wanting him to cuddle up beside her, but there was little room in the bed to do this and before she knew what was happening he had rolled on top of her and was pulling up her nightdress. Instinctively she wanted to say no, but now it was happening and, with five years of war depriving them of getting married and little chance of marriage in the months to come, it all suddenly seemed right.

At breakfast the next morning, the young couple sat with their backs to the other residents. But they had a conspiratorial grin on their faces most of the time. They felt like husband and wife. Whatever the future held they would face it together. Friedrich felt that Lily was now his to take to Germany to share his life.

They had no desire to linger in the hotel and they were soon out around the town on a shopping expedition. Lily took care to buy clothes that eschewed any hint of uniform. That was in the past. Casual shirts, light trousers, pullovers, the very essence of Englishness, all packed into a new and larger suitcase. And for the ferry a smart blouson jacket. On the top deck they stood hand in hand and watched the white cliffs slowly recede. It was their last glimpse of England, but only, vowed Lily, for six months.

66

In Calais they sensed the first signs of the upheaval that had visited the continent. The plush boat train Lily had travelled on when she first came to Europe had gone. In its place the carriages were corridor-less and utilitarian. Darkness had fallen when they left the port and Friedrich quickly fell asleep. Lily sat in a warm glow of contentment as she looked across at the recumbent form of her husband-to-be. There were few lights to be seen as they rushed through northern France but occasionally she caught glimpses of a smashed and uprooted landscape. But even Lily, happy though she was to stay awake, finally succumbed to sleep, lulled by the wheels' rhythmic clickity-clack.

The passengers were rudely woken by a sudden braking as the train arrived in Aachen on the German border. There were shouts from outside. Lily looked through the window expecting to see the station platform, but they had stopped several yards down the line. Everyone was ordered out by guards in French uniform. With no platform it was a long drop to the ground. Friedrich went first and took the cases and then he gave a hand to Lily. Safely beside the train, they saw at once why it had stopped short of the station. The rails ahead were twisted and buckled and in parts had disappeared altogether. They were herded together and then escorted in single file along the track to the platform. Here the French guards handed them over to British soldiers who inspected their papers. They were told there was no train to Germany that night and that they had to wait until morning for a train to take them on.

It was three o'clock and a chill air crept over what remained of the station. The waiting room lay in ruins and all other buildings, if surviving, were firmly locked. There was a feeling of gloomy resignation among the passengers as one by one they hunkered down to await the morning train. Friedrich found a wall and put their two cases against it to form a seat. He sat Lily down, kissed her forehead and fished out of his coat pocket the remains of a sandwich which he started to break in half. As he did so a skeletal arm came around his trouser leg and pushed its hand towards the sandwich. Lily sat up with a fright. Friedrich looked down and saw a blonde-haired child clutching at his legs. The face was shrunken, the rest of the body as skeletal as the arms and dressed in tatters. The child spoke in German and asked for food.

'Do give it to him, Friedrich,' said Lily pleading. 'He looks so hungry.' Friedrich proffered the half he was giving to Lily. The boy snatched it and hungrily devoured it. As he did so, another child appeared and soon they were surrounded by more than a dozen.

An armed soldier came around the corner, saw what was happening, levelled his rifle and gave a loud bark. The children raced off.

'Feral kids,' said the soldier, shouldering his rifle. 'If you give something to one, you'll be pestered forever.'

'It's so sad to see them,' said Lily.

'Breaks yer heart, I agree, but nought to be done about it.' The three lapsed into silence for the moment. For Lily and Friedrich it was their first encounter with the depths to which German life had sunk.

'You going far?' asked the soldier, breaking the silence.

'München,' said Friedrich.

'You'll probably have to walk most of it.'

'That bad,' said Lily.

'And worse,' replied the soldier gloomily. 'But don't worry the track from here isn't too bad. Well, sweet dreams.' With that he marched off leaving them to a fitful few hours until morning.

The soldier was right, the track out of Aachen was much better, but the carriages were even more uncomfortable than the French train. Again they had no corridor and only had wooden seats. They were, thought Lily, little better than cattle trucks. Before they left, a trolley was wheeled onto the platform that had bread and cheese for sale, which everyone pounced on and emptied within minutes. Lily saw that armed soldiers surrounded the trolley keeping off a horde of children who stood like expectant pigeons in the distance.

For a few miles the train made good progress, then, what was to become the routine for the rest of the journey, it was shunted onto a loop that by-passed damaged or destroyed track. As they got closer to

Cologne the devastation became more widespread. The great cathedral city had been flattened but miraculously the cathedral itself had been spared. As the train edged past its soaring spires, Lily could see in Friedrich's eyes a welling up of bitterness. The carriage lurched and swayed as it eased itself into the station that lay in the shadow of the great Gothic building. The platform was pitted with bomb craters and from the window Lily watched people looking for a train door that did not teeter over a large hole.

'So different from when we were last here,' she said sadly. As in Aachen the station was haunted by gangs of desperate children, their faces ashen, their hair a tangle of dirt, their hands held out for a passing coin or a crust of bread.

The other passengers in their compartment alighted at Cologne. Their excited activity roused Friedrich. 'I will go and find food.' He opened the door and jumped across a large crack in the surface of the platform. She watched him disappear. Then her eyes caught sight of a group of women in the distance standing on a mountain of rubble. She had to strain to see what they were doing, until she realised they were a human conveyor belt, moving masonry piece by piece down a line to waiting trucks. The enormity of their task appalled Lily and she thought back to her own long hours at the brickworks. But Germany was one huge wasteland which had to be cleared before rebuilding could begin. These women were making a start. While Lily sat there, the fruits of their efforts, the laden trucks, trundled by on a specially constructed narrow-gauge railway.

How could a country she once so admired come so low? She felt desperately sorry for the ordinary people, but then how far had they been complicit in all this? A noise outside interrupted her reverie. A gang of young men was passing by. Demob soldiers in high spirits she thought. The last of the group was just disappearing when he caught sight of Lily alone in the compartment. He called his companions back and the entire group poured into the carriage. In her shaky German, Lily pointed out that the seat opposite was taken. The one who seemed to be the leader took no notice and laughingly sat down in the seat Friedrich had occupied. When she looked at him, she involuntarily recoiled, a reflex that didn't go unnoticed.

'You don't like what you see, Fräulein?' One eye was missing and a large part of his cheek was a livid mess of repaired skin.

She stuttered nervously not knowing what to say. 'I'm sorry. I didn't mean to stare.'

'Not a pretty sight is it?' Before she could say any more the man's companions had made enough commotion to divert attention. They left a space beside Lily. Minutes later Friedrich returned clutching two paper bags. He saw at once what had happened but said nothing and sat down in the gap.

Lily kept her head lowered and concentrated on unwrapping the contents of the paper bags. In silence they ate the sausage sandwiched between two stale chunks of bread.

'Looks like you were lucky, sunshine,' said the man with the damaged face.

'What?' grunted Friedrich between bites.

'No mark on you. Where did you serve?'

'I was a POW. In Britain.'

'That so?'

Friedrich looked up as he demolished the last of the sausage.

'What's that supposed to mean?' Lily put a hand on his knee. The train shuddered and began to move forward.

'They look after you over there, did they?' Ahead the engine blew its whistle. 'Nice warm cell, while we froze to death in that eastern hell-hole.'

'We all fought for the Fatherland,' said Friedrich flatly, hoping to defuse the man's growing anger, but it had no effect. He leaned over the compartment and all but thrust his nose into Friedrich's face.

'Fuck the Fatherland and fuck you. I pissed ice for the Fatherland and when I get home, what do I find. My house flattened and a wife who opened her legs to any fucker who fancied her. This,' he pointed to his face, 'is my iron cross.' Lily clutched Friedrich's arm tightly. The man's aggression frightened her and he sensed it.

'She for sale?'

'Calm yourself, Helmut,' said the man sitting next to him.

'When every woman in Germany's been whoring while we've been away doing our duty, why should she have been any different? You ask her what she's been doing while you've been tucked up in your nice cosy prison hut.'

'I think you are being offensive and you should listen to what your friend is saying and calm down.'

'You don't like what I'm saying.' Friedrich could smell the man's breath. He had been drinking. A lot he suspected.

'No I don't and if you speak like that about my fiancée again, I'll …..'

'You'll what, my friend …. ?' A knife flashed across Friedrich's face forcing him back against the hard wooden seat. Lily gasped. Friedrich felt the sharp edge of the blade across his throat. For several seconds he thought he was going to be cut. The man's one eye burnt into him with a deep self-loathing. No one spoke. Finally it seemed the man had exhausted himself and he sank back into his seat. A tense silence followed, the only sound being the grinding movement of the train as it lurched and clattered over uncertain track. At the next station the group left without a word.

'That was horrible,' said Lily. 'What a brute.'

'I feel for him,' replied Friedrich. 'He has suffered much and his world has been destroyed.' He looked out of the window at another half-demolished station. 'We could have achieved so much. We nearly did. If our raid had been successful we would have proved our ability to attack England on the land.'

'But you weren't successful, Friedrich. You must put all that aside.'

'No, Lily, we were betrayed and I will not rest until I have found who betrayed us. I will hunt them down and I will kill them.'

'Please don't speak like that, Friedrich. I couldn't live with you if you really felt like that.' She took him in her arms and looked him in the face. 'You mustn't hold this bitterness inside you. I love you desperately but if you keep this hatred in your heart we will never be able to live together.' The kiss he gave her in response did nothing to assuage the coldness that had seized her. She knew more than ever now that she must be the one to unmask his betrayer. Whoever it was she had to get to them before Friedrich.

67

There was a knock at the door. Peg opened it.

'Sally, how nice to see you. I'm glad you've come.' Peg showed Lily's friend into the drawing room. She thought how her freckles were even more pronounced than usual.

'You said on the phone that you had a letter from Lily? From Bexhill, I presume?'

'No, my dear, Dover.'

'Dover?' echoed Sally. 'They're going to Germany?'

'Going,' repeated Peg. 'Gone more like. Here read this. I'll make some tea.' She handed over a single sheet of paper. Sally read the short message that had been written on it.

'Dear Mummy and Daddy

By the time you read this Friedrich and I will be in Germany. We didn't tell you before as we didn't want to worry you. Friedrich is desperate to see what has happened to his country. We plan to be here for a very short time, six months

at the most, and then we will come back to England and get married. Don't worry about us. Lots of hugs and kisses.
Love from your darling Lily
PS please tell Sally'

Peg returned with a tray of tea as Sally was putting the letter on a side table. 'Did you know she was planning this?'

'She told me she was considering it.'

Peg motioned Sally to sit down and placed the tray in front of them.

'Sugar?' Sally shook her head.

'Did you think she'd do it?'

'I told her it would be an unwise thing to do. But you know Lily, once she is set on something, there is no stopping her.'

Peg handed over the cup accompanied by an offer of a biscuit. Sally took both.

'I like Friedrich,' said Peg. 'He's a nice boy, but he is a little serious and he did rather take this Fatherland business to heart.' She then asked Sally what the latter thought was a strange question. 'Is Lily in danger being with him?'

'How do you mean?' asked Sally munching her way through the biscuit.

'Those who are Nazis are being arrested, aren't they?'

'Friedrich has already been in prison. I don't think they will arrest him again. Anyway I'm not sure Friedrich was that much of a Nazi.' Sally said this to reassure Peg, but she knew it wasn't true.

'You're a bright girl, Sally. Can you find her for me?'

'I'll try, Mrs Rood. Is there any forwarding address on that letter?'

'No.'

'I'm afraid we must wait for one to come.' Peg nodded. Sally accepted the offer of another cup of tea. She could see Lily's mother was agitated. She twitched and moved around the room.

'Is there something else on your mind, Mrs Rood?' she finally asked.

'Yes,' said Peg. She went to a bureau in the corner and pulled out another letter. 'This,' she said, holding up a blue envelope, that looked to Sally like an airmail letter. 'It's come from America. It's addressed to Lily.' She handed it to Sally, who examined the cover with its US Post stamp. 'Do you think I should open it?' Sally thought for a moment and it dropped into place who might have sent it.

'Yes, I think you should,' she said.

Peg took a paper knife and slit the envelope, pulling out a flimsy sheet, written on both sides. She did a quick scan of its contents. Sally took a sip of tea while she waited expectantly for Peg to hand over the letter. She didn't but précised what had been written.

'It's from someone called Hartmann.'

'Berthold and Magda Hartmann,' said Sally, an expression of pleasure crossing her face. 'That's wonderful.'

'You know them?' ask Peg somewhat mystified.

'Yes. Lily and I met them on the train home from Germany. They were Jews fleeing the country. They had lost everything. They said they were coming to England to get a boat to America.' Peg's eyebrows rose. She shared her husband's views about Jews and was disturbed to hear her daughter had associated with them.

'I see,' she said disapprovingly.

'But they were dear people,' said Sally.

'Of course it is horrible what has happened to them, but ….'

'But you don't want us to have befriended them?' interjected Sally.

'No. I just meant ….' Sally could see she was flustered and embarrassed, so she reassured her again that they were very nice people.

'I'm sure they were, if you and Lily liked them.'

'Lily met them again at Bletchley station. They were being interned on the Isle of Man. We felt sorry for them as they had escaped from Germany only to be rounded up here.'

'Well they seem to have got where they wanted to go.' She looked down at the letter. 'They're writing from a place called ….' She stumbled with the pronunciation and showed Sally the word.

'Frankenmuth.'

'Yes. They say it is in Michigan, not far from the Great Lakes.' She stopped and decided to read the rest. 'It is like Bavaria. Some people speak German. The buildings are like home. We are happy. Fräuleins, you must come and visit us.' She stopped again. 'The rest is in German.' She handed the letter to Sally to translate.

'They're signing off with "kind regards".'

Peg huffed. 'Well, you won't be going there, I'm sure.'

'One day, perhaps,' said Sally, lightly. 'I've always wanted to go to America.'

'You'll be better off going and finding my daughter, Miss Deeprose.'

'I *will* try, Mrs Rood.' But she knew they could do nothing until Lily contacted them with an address.

68

Lily and Friedrich's train pulled into Munich station a day late. The pair had been subjected to endless delays, re-routings and enforced stops in remote sidings. Sleep on the wooden seats was impossible, but when Lily finally managed to doze off, she was abruptly wakened by a series of severe jolts. Through barely opened eyes she saw a railway locomotive on its side and several half-standing carriages come into view. Beyond this destruction the remains of a railway terminus emerged and, in the foreground, a mangled sign with the letters M Ü N C still intact. She felt a weary exultation. They had arrived.

She went to stand up, but her legs wouldn't support her. A sudden movement sent her back to her seat. Friedrich laughed and held out his hand.

'Come, Lily, we're here.'

'Friedrich, I'm so tired.'

He gave her a sharp tug. 'You will be better, when you are out.'

'Out' meant negotiating a crater-riddled platform along with all the other passengers. Wearily she followed Friedrich circumnavigating piles of rubble to the main concourse. Lily looked up to see the great arched roof that she remembered when she was last here. It was now a tangle of twisted metal frames, with girders hanging by little more than a rivet. Most of the glass had been blown out. Shards still lay like snow on the railway tracks.

'Where are we going, Friedrich?' asked Lily breathlessly as they stood at the entrance vainly looking for some form of transport.

'We find my house.'

'Your parents' house?'

'Ja.' Since stepping onto German soil, she noticed how he was speaking almost always in German, even to her.

There were no taxis. The tram system had been completely crippled. There was the occasional bus. They found one that was going in the direction Friedrich wanted to go. Squeezing aboard its crowded interior, they were given glares from other passengers who noticed with distaste their English clothes and large cases which knocked ankles and legs. Friedrich handed the conductor a dollar note, a currency that was universal throughout the city now the Americans were in occupation.

Like the train, the bus spent most of its journey avoiding obstacles in the road. Munich had been heavily bombed. Its historical heart had been torn out. Everywhere buildings Lily had gazed at in raptures during her first visit lay in ruins. She looked out at the Glyptothek where she had stood and admired the male torso and gasped at the huge gash in its side. One wall had completely collapsed exposing an interior gallery.

Remarkably a statue of a Roman general stood un-toppled amid a mass of debris and broken columns. Lily felt sad at seeing so much destruction. She could not imagine what Friedrich was feeling.

Germany had been divided into three Allied sectors. Munich lay within the American sector. On the streets this occupation was graphic to behold. GIs swarmed over everything. On foot, aboard lorries, driving gun carriages, riding jeeps with legs hung jauntily over the side and provocatively perched on armoured cars. Most distressing for Friedrich was the sight of American soldiers escorting long lines of German prisoners to detention camps outside the city, even though the war had been over for twelve months. He stared at their dejected faces and their humiliation in having to walk with hands on their heads.

The bus put them down some way from Friedrich's old neighbourhood and like everyone in the city they had to proceed on foot, carrying their heavy cases until their arms were stretched beyond endurance and they were forced to halt. Lily looked around her. This area had suffered badly. Few buildings had escaped the destruction. Most were grim skeletons of themselves, their half-demolished frames creating a surreal landscape of desolation. Lily was suddenly aware of the silence, contrasting with the military urgency they had left behind. While she stood resting and shaking her arms to get the blood moving again, she caught sight of a small cart sitting abandoned by the roadside.

'We could take that for our cases.'

'It's not ours,' said Friedrich.

'But it's been left. There's no one here. We could return it.'

Reluctantly he agreed and together they loaded the cart. When they went to push it, they saw why it had been discarded. One wheel was broken, which caused the cart to run lopsidedly. But it was still preferable to carrying the cases and after slow and painful progress they reached the area where Friedrich had lived. It occurred to Lily seeing the houses in front of her that Friedrich had never talked about his home. These were modest dwellings compared to the mansion where the Grubers lived. Her fiancé had never said much about his upbringing, but he was clearly from a humble background. She sensed keenly the mismatch between what she was looking at and the trappings of power she experienced the day they drove to see Adolph Hitler.

'Your father. He was an important person in the Party?' Friedrich saw in her eyes what she was thinking.

'We were not – how you say it in England – connect …. ?'

'Connected.'

'Ja. We were not connected. The Party looked after my father. He was loyal. We had good life, but it was not always so.' He stopped, then pushed the cart around a half-demolished house.

'We are here,' he said excitedly. 'This is our street.' He looked down the length of ruins, the eagerness on his face giving way to anguish. He stood staring ahead in silence.

'It's gone, hasn't it?' said Lily softly. 'Your house?' He didn't answer but she could see what he was looking at. Most of the buildings in the street were badly damaged, but between two of them was a mountainous pile of rubble. Weeds and shoots of buddleia now grew there softening its starkness.

'Friedrich, I'm sorry.' She put an arm around his shoulder and tried to share his pain. They moved closer to the gap taking in every disturbing detail, until they stood opposite the ruin. The click of a door opening behind Lily made her turn. A small wiry woman had come out of the house they had their back to and was coming down the front steps.

'It was terrible,' she said as she joined them. 'It happened four years ago during the worst of the raids. Most houses were knocked about, but that one took a direct hit.' The woman stood beside them and said nothing more. She was in her sixties. Her hair was white although Lily thought it had once been of a silvery colour.

'Are you from around here?' the woman asked, curiosity getting the better of her.

'That's my house,' said Friedrich flatly. 'I lived there.'

The woman gave him a keener look.

'You're Adlar Schulz's son.' She gave him a smile of recognition. 'You're Friedrich.'

They shook hands. 'I didn't recognise you. You've changed.' She corrected herself. 'You've grown.' She bubbled with excitement and her sudden enthusiasm roused Friedrich from his melancholy.

'I remember, now,' he said. 'You moved in just before war broke out. I remember. We talked when I was back on leave.'

'That's right. I'm Frau Jager.' She gestured to her front door. 'Please come in. I have a little tea.' They were pleased to accept and started to follow her up the steps.

'Bring your cases. Everything gets stolen now. It wasn't like that before the war.' They heaved their cases out of the cart, hid the lopsided vehicle and followed Frau Jager into the house. They left their cases in the entrance hall and proceeded through to the drawing room. They were not expecting what greeted them. The room was normal at one end but at the other the wall had been blown away, leaving the room opening onto a spectacular vista of the broken city. Lily gasped audibly. A makeshift curtain had been put up to provide protection.

'Welcome to my al fresco living room.' Frau Jager gave a dramatic gesture with her arms and laughed with a desperate irony. 'Here I can sit and feed the birds.'

'Did it happen at the same time?' asked Friedrich.

'Yes, but I was lucky. I was out.'

'And my parents?' he asked nervously, knowing the likely answer. 'Were they in the house?' The woman looked at him with sorrow in her eyes.

'They were,' she said slowly. 'I don't think they ever found the bodies.' Lily recalled the mountain of rubble. Were they still lying in that, she wondered?

'You're not German?' Frau Jager asked of Lily.

'No, English. We met in Munich before the war.'

'Ah, what a gay city it was then.'

'I loved it,' said Lily.

'Sit down, my dears, while I go and find that tea.'

She scuttled out. Friedrich held Lily tightly, fighting back the tears. The two sat without saying anything gazing out at the scene before them. People picked their way through the ruins. Fires burned with figures squatted around them for warmth. Nearby some boys baked potatoes from sticks held over the flames.

In the distance a line stood patiently beside a standpipe, one by one filling buckets with water.

'It is like a vision from hell', mused Lily, 'but one where no one speaks. When I was last here the city was bursting with gaiety. There was so much to live for ….'

'And now we live to survive, dear.' Frau Jager returned bearing a battered tin tray on which sat three chipped cups all with different patterns and two missing their handles. There were no saucers, sugar or milk. The tea pot had lost most of its lid and the glaze was badly crazed. She caught Friedrich looking at the tray and its pathetic contents.

'This was all I could salvage after the bombing.'

Friedrich, who had been strangely silent for the last few minutes, suddenly exploded in anger at what he called 'the stench of defeat'.

'How I hate these people cowed and wallowing in their own self-pity. We should be holding our heads high. We were not defeated. We were betrayed at every turn.' Lily watched his face contort with vitriol. It was an outpouring of outrage and incomprehension she knew she had to exorcise, but now was not the moment. The discovery of the likely deaths of his parents had awakened his bitterness.

'Our glorious leader led us to greatness and he was knifed in the back.'

'This is what you believe is it, young man?' As Frau Jager poured the black tea she looked around her. 'I see all this and I ask myself what was it all for?'

'Our Führer was betrayed. The Communists. The Jews. They let the enemy in.' Frau Jager gave a scornful laugh.

'Have you seen a Jew recently? You've been away too long. Everything has changed and none of us know where it's going.' She handed a cup with a handle to Lily and cradled a handleless one in her hand. 'But I do know this, Friedrich, that if you say any of that in public you'll get your throat cut.' Lily shivered and not just from the cool air coming in from outside.

'Have you anywhere to stay?' They looked at each other and shook their heads.

'There's some sort of hostel at the end of the street. It's in a derelict tenement block. They may have a room.'

After finishing their tea and thanking Frau Jager for her help, they heaved their cases back into the cart and trundled its squeaking and wobbling wheels down the road. The building Frau Jager had described was barely standing. The front door was off its hinges and there was no glass in the windows, although several of the occupants had hung sacking from the frames. A burly man with an unshaven face and wearing a black leather coat over a collarless shirt answered their knock. He said nothing but waited for them to speak.

'We are looking for a room,' said Friedrich.

'You got money?' Friedrich rummaged in his suit pocket and brought out some German Reichsmark.

'No good, chum. Dollars or cigarettes?'

'I have some cigarettes,' said Lily, remembering she had packed some for just such a contingency as this. She rarely smoked herself but the war years had taught her how valuable cigarettes were.

'How much for the night?' she asked.

'Fifty,' said the man.

'Too much,' said Lily, not knowing whether this was true or not, but probably thinking it was. 'Fifty for two nights.' The man nodded and held out his hand. Lily knelt down beside her case, snapped open the catches. She hoped that what she had put on top was decent. Fortunately she had laid a skirt the full length of the case. Using this to shield her actions from the gimlet glare of the man, she burrowed into her clothes until her fingers felt the hard edge of the cartons. She pulled out five packs and handed them over. Snapping the case shut again Lily stood, only to be handed a rusting bucket. Friedrich was also given one.

'One for water,' said the man curtly. 'The standpipe's round the corner. The other's for pissing in. You crap outside. Follow me.' He led the way up five flights of stairs. Despite the man's exhortation to use buckets, the smell of urine and faeces was everywhere. As the stairwell got gloomier the dark and the overbearing stink reminded Lily of her first night in the police station and the growing realisation that life had now become one incarceration after another. They finally reached the top floor and were shown into a tiny room that just accommodated two small mattresses. The window had no glass and above their head the roof was punctured with holes.

'The management are planning repairs soon, but you got to hope it doesn't rain.' The man guffawed at his own joke. Friedrich looked at the door.

'Do you have key?'

'You must be fucking joking mate. But you need to keep a tight grip on your missus there. There's a good market in fanciable women.' He left laughing down the stairs. Friedrich took a walk to the window. As he stared out at the ruins below, there was a scream from Lily. He turned to find two men standing threateningly in the doorway.

'What do you want?' asked Friedrich. Both men held sticks in their hands. Lily had her hand to her mouth.

'You're not one of those Nazis, are you?' asked the largest of the men menacingly speaking in the low German of the north. Lily hoped Friedrich would remember what Frau Jager had said.

'No,' said Friedrich quickly.

'Only that's a nice piece of cloth you're wearing and she's pretty dolled up.'

'They're fucking Nazis. I know they are. I can smell them,' said the other man nastily.

'No,' said Friedrich, 'this suit was given to me when I was released from the POW camp in England. And she's English.'

'I say we duff up these two fuckers, Jörg,' said the second man, ignoring what Friedrich had said. 'Parading here in their fancy rags.' The two levelled their sticks and advanced on Friedrich and Lily. The pair had nothing to defend themselves with. They retreated to the window. Friedrich saw that his only chance was to make a sudden frontal assault. Before the men could raise their sticks above their head, he cannonaded himself into the nearest one.

'Kick them Lily, wherever you can,' he shouted as he and the other man careered through the door and onto the stairs. The man hit his head hard against the stairwell wall, his stick flying from his hand. Friedrich kicked him hard and sent him tumbling down the stairs. He turned back to see what was happening to Lily. She was poised to fend off a blow aimed at her head. He grabbed the fallen stick and hurled himself at the second man thrusting the stick between his legs unbalancing him so the blow to Lily was deflected. Floored the man suffered kicks from both of them before he too was thrown down the stairs.

'Hey, my friends, careful with my décor.' The man who had rented the room to them had come up the stairs to find out what the fracas was about. He looked with disgust at the two bodies lying in a heap at his feet.

'Were these two reprobates troubling you? I'll throw them out but be careful when you leave tomorrow.' With that he picked them up by their arms and dragged them down the stairs.

'Are you all right, Lily? Did he touch you?' asked Friedrich anxiously.

'I'm fine, but I don't want to stay here.'

'Tonight we must. But tomorrow we find something better. We must, too, find work.' He let her head nuzzle against his neck while he bent and kissed her on the head.

'We do not sleep together,' he said. She wasn't sure what he meant, but he made it clear. 'It is too dangerous for us both to sleep at the same time. One person must stay awake, like army watch.' She understood.

'You, Lily, sleep first.' She looked down at the mattress.

'I'm not sleeping on that,' she said in disgust. 'It'll be full of fleas and bedbugs. And goodness knows what else. I'll sleep in my coat on the floor.'

'Then let's use these to protect us,' suggested Friedrich. She agreed. They heaved the filthy mattresses into an upright position and let them fall against the door.

Lily rubbed the dirt from her hands. 'Now I need to pee,' she said brightly. 'Hand me the bucket.'

'Lily I ....' He started to protest.

'Don't be so bashful. I've been in prison too you know. Just turn away.' As she squatted over the bucket the deep sadness she had felt earlier overwhelmed her once again. But she was conscious of another thought. She adjusted her dress and turned to Friedrich.

'Where's the rest of your family?' she asked casually.

'I have no family,' he said blankly.

'No aunts and uncles or cousins. What about your friends?'

'I have no friends,' he stonewalled. His voice was cold. In the darkness she couldn't see his face.

'What happened, Friedrich?' He said nothing. She applied gentle persuasion. 'You must tell me what is troubling you. We must have no secrets.'

He spoke, but he was barely audible.

'They – how you say it – they cut us off.'

'Who cut you off? The family?'

'Yes.'

'Why?'

'They were opposed to my father joining the Party. They couldn't see it was the way forward. They tried to persuade him not to, but when he went ahead, they threw him out of the family. I lost everyone. My friends as well.' He seized Lily by the shoulders. 'But our great Führer saved us. I found strength in the Fatherland.' Help, thought Lily, he will end up with a noose around his neck and me with him if he doesn't soon clear all this out of his head.

'Where is your family now?'

'I don't know. Dead possibly.'

'Why do you say that?'

He was silent for a moment and then he spoke with a chilling intensity that scared her.

'Do you really want to know, Lily? You probe like a dentist who hasn't used ….' he struggled for the English word and spat out the German translation, '…. narkose.'

She understood. 'Anaesthetic.'

'Ja.'

'Friedrich, sometimes it's better for the poison that's causing the pain to come out.'

'I heard my father talking to my mother.' He had resumed his whisper as if he were afraid of someone eavesdropping. 'That afternoon he had signed a number of deportation orders, among them his own brother and sister.' Lily shook with horror. She sat pole-axed by the terrible words he had just spoken.

'That's awful.'

'No!' The word came out of him with a ferocity that scared her. 'It was noble and brave to do this. They were cowards and had to be stopped.'

'But didn't your parents show any compassion. It must have been terrible for them.'

'It was their duty. It would be weakness not to do it.' Lily didn't know how to respond. She was grateful that the black opaqueness of the room hid her face and the tears that were starting to moisten her eyes. She was frightened by Friedrich showing no remorse in what he was saying.

'Where were they sent?' she asked.

'Dachau.' Where we rode our bicycles, she gasped to herself. No wonder Friedrich turned around when he saw the towers. It must have been a shock to come on the place where his uncle and aunt were languishing.

'Now Lily….' He was digging his fingers into the flesh of her arms.

'Friedrich, you're hurting me.' His fingers relaxed but his voice became as hard as steel.

'Lily, I have more to tell you. We have work to do.'

'No more, Friedrich. Please. I'm tired.' The physical hardships and the emotional strain had broken her will to question further. She pushed him away and lay down. She was so fatigued that she drifted off the moment her head hit the floor. Woken in the early hours by Friedrich she was still bleary with tiredness. She envied him his chance to sleep, but he failed to take it, tossing and turning in fitful wakefulness. She sat in a corner and watched the outline of his body move in the darkness. It scared her that his mind was becoming ever more feverish and twisted, dwelling continually on scenarios of revenge. His country was in ruins, his parents were dead and his leader had killed himself, yet it chilled her to think that he was still bent on tracking down the person or persons who had betrayed his mission and if necessary execute them. At the first available opportunity she must contact Reg Fuller.

The hours passed slowly. Once she heard a scratching at the door. Another time she thought she saw the door move or was it the darkness playing tricks with her? Fortunately the mattresses held fast. Gradually the stars through the window started to fade and the sky began to change colour. Reluctantly she woke Friedrich who had finally slipped into a deep sleep.

'It's dawn. We must go,' she said urgently.

Wearily the two of them pulled back the mattresses and cautiously looked around the door. All seemed to be quiet. They crept down the staircase with their cases and were almost out of the building when a voice called from the shadows.

'Running out, are you?' It was the burly landlord.

'We paid for two nights,' said Lily indignantly.

He hurled abuse at them. 'Good riddance. Your kind aren't wanted here.' They ignored him and walked off. Friedrich said no more about what they had been talking about in the night. Lily was thankful for this and hoped to steer clear of the subject until she could come to terms with Friedrich's revelations. Meanwhile she had a more urgent objective. Friedrich said she was going the wrong way, but she persisted until she reached the water standpipe.

'It may not be safe to drink,' he said.

'I need a drink.' She was starting to feel delirious from lack of liquid. She turned on the tap. The water flowed clearly, so she raised her cupped hands to it and sipped it. She took a chance and drank. It made her feel instantly better. Friedrich declined saying that if one them was going to get ill the other should stay fit. You are a prig at times, Friedrich, thought Lily to herself.

They stumbled on their way through the ruined entrails of the city until they miraculously arrived in an area that had escaped the bombing. American jeeps passed up and down it. One, driven by a solitary GI, saw them struggling with their cases, stopped and asked them whether they wanted a lift. Their faces said it all.

'Where'd you wanna go, bud?' Lily thought on her feet. Before Friedrich could get his words out, she answered: 'American headquarters.' Friedrich gave her a scowl.

'Sure, lady,' said the soldier with a grin, 'jump in. Just fling your bags in the back.' They did as they were asked and climbed into the seats at the back of the jeep. Lily eyed the rifle that sat beside the driver.

'What you doing in these parts?' he asked as they drove off.

'We lost our way. There is so much destruction,' said Lily, 'and we couldn't find a taxi.'

'Yeah, those flyboys sure laid a few eggs. You a limey?'

'A what?' asked Lily not too familiar with the man's American jargon.

'English.'

'Yes'. She couldn't get over how casual the American military man was. This one spoke through a mouthful of gum. His helmet was unstrapped and sat jauntily on the back of his head. His whole body, despite his broad shoulders, spoke of a relaxed easiness.

'Your pal a Jerry?'

Friedrich was half picking up what was being said, but he understood the word 'Jerry' and it made him bristle.

'I am a German, yes,' he said in his careful English voice.

'Not a Nazi, then?' The soldier pronounced Nazi with a short 'a'. Lily was quick to refute any suggestion of this. She couldn't see the man's face, but she guessed he was grinning.

'No offence, lady. Don't find many of them around now.'

They were passing a number of large buildings. The soldier brought the jeep to a halt in front of a high protective fence topped with barbed wire. A checkpoint with a barrier and armed guards provided the centrepiece. Beyond, a large edifice rose up with a sign that described itself as 'Office of Military Government, United States'.

'Here we are, guys,' said the soldier breezily, opening the door of the jeep. They threw their cases onto the ground, thanked the driver and climbed out.

'You have a good day now,' he said as he thrust the jeep into reverse and sped off.

'What are we doing here, Lily?' asked Friedrich, at last able to question what he considered to be Lily's high-handed decision. They stood on the pavement under the watchful eye of the guards opposite.

'We need work, somewhere to live. The Americans can give us that.'

'You think so?'

'We'll only find out if we try.' She picked up her case, walked across the road and up to one of the guards. She showed her English passport.

'We're looking for work. We were told we could apply here.' It sounded limp, but to Lily's surprise the guard responded.

'You could try Major Norris's office. I heard they're looking for people.'

69

'What makes you think you've got something to offer us?'

Lily and Friedrich sat in the well-furnished office of an officer of the American army.

'I type. He translates,' said Lily briefly. 'I'm sure you need both skills.'

'We do, Ma'am.' Major John Norris looked at her with keen eyes. He was in his forties, smartly dressed and wearing a beige shirt, matching tie, the dark khaki double-breasted jacket of his rank and contrasting beige trousers. It was a fetching combination that took Lily's fancy. Like all Americans he didn't sit but lounged in his chair. Lily had bluffed her way through to this point and now hoped the bluff would continue. To her surprise, the major stopped talking to her and turned to Friedrich addressing him in what she considered more than adequate German.

'Judging by the suit you are wearing you are a demobbed POW. That's a limey issue. Am I right?' Friedrich nodded. 'Why are you in Munich?'

'It is my home. I come back to my family.' He turned to Lily. 'And this is my fiancée.'

'Papers.' Friedrich rummaged in his pocket and handed them over. Major Norris took some minutes to peruse the contents. The two watched anxiously. Without looking up he asked the question they knew was coming.

'SS?'

'But only a fighting regiment,' said Friedrich. 'You see I have done the de-Nazification course and passed.' The major grunted.

'It says here you were captured while on a raid in England.'

'Yes.'

'That must have been quite something. What happened to the rest of your unit?'

'I don't know sir,' said Friedrich. 'Perhaps they get back to Belgium.'

'Yeah, something to find out.' He handed the papers back. 'So, you're free of all that Nazi poison, are you?'

'Yes, sir,' said Friedrich calmly. Lily was impressed by Friedrich's refusal to show any emotion in answering the questions.

'Well,' said Major Morris, 'if we can't hang every sucker who signed up to Hitler, we can sure turn them into useful citizens in this new Germany. I can use you Schulz in one of our translation offices. We are busy issuing newspapers and booklets to help wean the populace off their old ways.' He lapsed back into English and addressed Lily.

'You are right, Miss ....' He looked at the passport in front of him. '.... Rood, I need typists. Yeah, we can employ you both. Army wages. Can you start at once?'

Their faces lost the gloom of the last few days, but Lily chanced her luck with one more request.

'We can,' she said, 'as soon as we can find somewhere to live. Can you help us?'

'Speak to my adjutant, Miss Rood.' This was a dismissal and Lily took the hint. They left thanking the major and went in search of the adjutant.

Within days they were settled into a work regime that for the first time gave them stability in their lives as a couple. With the help of the adjutant's office they were able to rent a small apartment on the first floor of an undamaged building, a few streets away from the American HQ. At work they were both assigned to the new propaganda department responsible for publishing material designed to steer Germany back to democratic values. Lily found herself not only typing copy but checking it, as much of the writing started life in English. It then went to the translators which is where Friedrich came into the picture.

They often left work together and shared a home life they had never had before. Food was scarce and tightly rationed but Lily found she could scrape enough together for them to eat frugally. They also enjoyed the benefits that came from working for the Americans and they never went short of chocolate and, most usefully, cigarettes. Lily found it strange buying a new dress and using cigarettes to purchase it. She also never went short of nylons. But Friedrich, despite this new-found normality, continued to chafe at the many minor irritations that they met in their daily life.

'They say that they are teaching us the ways of democracy,' he said one evening as they ate a modest stew that Lily had prepared, 'but it is not democracy as we know it here in Europe.'

'What do you mean, Friedrich?'

'Well I was working on an article for the next issue of their paper. Translating I mean.' Lily chewed on a piece of stringy pork wondering what was coming.

'It's American propaganda,' he continued. They're trying to impose their way of life on us. You know the paper they're producing is filled with stuff about American film stars, fashion.'

'And you think it should have German writings?'

'People want to read about their own country.'

'Maybe the Americans think they have something to offer.'

'The details of some film star's divorce? We're not stupid, Lily. People will soon see through it all.'

'Your job is to keep your head down and not sound off about such things or we will be out.'

He grunted and took a mouthful of stew.

'This is good, Lily.' He swallowed appreciatively and then put his cutlery down. 'Soon we must get married. In Munich, no?' He looked at her as if food and marriage were inextricably linked, which was not a romantic connection that appealed to Lily.

'If you had said England, I would have said yes at once. But, darling, I'm not ready to say yes to Germany. You must give me time.' She laid her hand on his. He didn't look happy. She knew she had to make haste to write a letter to her parents and one to Reg Fuller.

'I have to let Mummy and Daddy know we are safe and well. Perhaps they can come and see us and see how well we are getting on.'

'Then we decide.'

'Perhaps.' They finished the stew in silence. That evening Lily wrote home and the next day arranged for the department they worked in to act as a 'post restante' address. During a break she composed a note to Reg Fuller giving the address and hoping he had news.

Her fingers flew across the keys and she barely noticed the beige trousers that passed by. They belonged to a young GI who was on the point of leaving the room, when the temptation of saying hello to the pretty girl sitting at the typewriter, whom he had only seen from behind, got the better of him. He hovered at the door and looked in her direction. Seeing Lily, a mystified expression crossed his face.

'Hey,' he shouted, 'don't I know you?' Lily's fingers stopped mid-sentence and she looked up. She was puzzled at his quizzical attention and then she recognised him.

'You're one of the soldiers I carried back in England.'

'Sure was. I'm going to marry you, remember.'

She laughed. 'Too late. I'm engaged.' She held up her ring.

'Gee, honey, couldn't you wait?' he said with mock disappointment. He walked over to her and held out his hand.

'Al Powalski.'

'Lily Rood.' They shook hands.

'What you doing here, Lily?'

'My fiancé's from Munich. He's working here too …. in the translation department.'

'No kidding.' He looked at her with a great grin. 'Say you got time for a coffee?'

Seeing him unnerved her. In her mind flashed that moment he held her in the air. She could still feel his strong hands sinking into her waist. Then she wondered whether he would survive the war. Now here he was alive and well.

'Give me five minutes and I'll see you in the canteen,' she said happily. He gave her a wink and walked off. She hurriedly set to to finish the letter to Reg Fuller.

'I hope I'm looking a little more presentable than when you last saw me.' They sat at a table in the large canteen with two mugs of coffee in front of them. As they were in a little bit of America, such luxuries were readily available.

'No more dungarees,' she said, 'or greasy head scarf.'

'You looked swell then.' Lily smiled. She was now wearing a skirt and tight sweater which made her feel decidedly more feminine.

'How did you get here?' she asked.

'Walked. Well, most of the way.'

'Was it awful? When we waved you good-bye that day we wondered what you were going into.'

'The beaches were the worst. Sitting ducks we were until we got cover. I lost several good buddies there. Crossing France was a doddle, but when we got to Germany the Krauts …' He stopped himself. '…. I mean the Germans threw everything at us. That was hell.' She studied him as he spoke. Back in England she hadn't really registered what he looked like, only that he had kissed her. Now sitting across a table she couldn't miss his willowy frame, dark features and black curly hair. Gloria had said he was good-looking. She was right.

'Where's home?' she asked.

'A small town in Michigan, not far from Chicago.'

'I know someone who was hoping to go to Michigan. It was a German family – they were Jews – escaping from Germany.'

'I hope they made it.'

'I don't think they did. It was funny, I met them in England on their way to an internment camp. They may still be there.'

'Gee, this war is crazy,' said Al draining his coffee. 'Turns everything upside down. Like meeting you again, Lily. Guess we're sort of working together.'

'What is your work, Al?'

'I was a writer before I got drafted, so I suppose that's why I'm here. I do the Hollywood page.' Lily's eyes started to widen.

'Were you in Hollywood?'

'Not exactly. I used to write the movie stuff for our local paper.' Lily looked disappointed.

'But I did meet Clark Gable once. When he was on location in the area.'

'What's he like?'

'Big man. But I didn't talk to him. Saw him in the distance.' Lily's hopes of some inside gossip faded. Sally was next on her list to write to and it would have been fun to have a few film star names to drop in.

'My fiancé doesn't approve of all this film stuff you put in the newspaper. He says there should be more German material.'

'I guess he's got a point. It'll change with time. Well, I gotta go, Lily.' He pushed the metal chair he was sitting on with a nerve-jangling squeak and stood up. 'Guess we'll be seeing each other around.'

'I imagine we will. And Al if you need a typist ….' Was she flirting?

He laughed. 'I know where to come, baby.'

Sally. Her friend reared up in front of her. She felt suddenly guilty about not having written to Sally. She would make it up with the sweetest letter.

70

About two weeks later, Lily was handed a buff envelope from the messenger boy. It had come in the military despatch bag rather than the ordinary post. Although the latter was fitfully operating, it could not be relied on for a speedy delivery. Lily tore the letter open. It was, as she suspected, from Reg Fuller, but alas contained no positive information. It did however have one nugget of hope. *'I'm waiting for some classified access to be approved,'* he wrote, enigmatically, *'If that happens I will be closer to getting what you want.'* She felt a thrill inside her. If she could once and for all commit Friedrich's ghost to oblivion, they could go forward.

Life now settled into a routine. Shortages, disrupted services, chaotic transport still ruled everyday activity, but they subsumed it into a semblance of normality. Lily saw little of Friedrich at work, but they did manage to meet for lunch in the canteen. One day she waved a letter in front of him.

'From Sally,' she said.

'How is she?' asked Friedrich, showing little sign of interest.

'She wished we had told her, but she wishes us well.'

'She would have tried to stop you,' he said sourly.

'Why are you so bitter towards Sally, Friedrich? She's my best friend and is only trying to look after me.'

'I look after you,' he said defiantly. Yes, he would. She was all he had.

'Friedrich, what you said about your family.' They sat together on the sofa later that evening and she felt relaxed enough to tackle him again on what he had told her in the ruined house. 'Do you not think your father was wrong to do what he did?'

'How could he be wrong when it was his duty?'

'But would you have done that?'

'Of course.' Again his certainty frightened her. 'I look after you, Lily, my father look after his country.'

'But times change, Friedrich. What happened then, should not happen now. You have to change your views, darling.' He looked into her eyes and she thought for a second she saw hesitation in them.

'Oh, Friedrich.' She took him in her arms. They lay there, no more words spoken, for over an hour and then fell into bed together and made love.

The next day she sat and laughed with Al in the canteen, reminiscing over their favourite films. She looked up and saw Friedrich had come in. He showed surprise at seeing Lily so relaxed with a strange man. He walked over, a cloud on his brow.

'Friedrich, darling, this is Al. I do some typing for him. You remember I told you we met back in England. He was with the troops I was taking to the station.' If Lily had ever said this, and even she was doubtful, Friedrich gave no indication of it. He just stood there. It was Al who made the move to ease the tension. He got up and shook Friedrich's hand.

'Glad to meet you, pal. Lily's told me a lot about you. What a great guy you are.' Friedrich continued to stand stiffly. He went to make a bow. Oh, please, Friedrich, said Lily to herself, don't click your heels. But the bow was all he offered.

'It is pleasing to meet another friend of Lily's.'

'I said to Lily, you and I must take her out to the beer garden they've just opened around the corner. I hear you Munich guys like your beer.'

'We invented it,' said Friedrich, sharply.

'Yeah, no kidding.' It probably wasn't true, thought Lily, but if it made Friedrich feel better, she wasn't going to question it.

'I think we drink you Americans under the table.'

'Say, bud, I'll hold you to that. Come and join us for coffee.' Al pulled up another chair and went to the counter for more coffees. Friedrich with some reluctance sat down.

That evening they had their first row.

'Pal, guy, bud. I do not welcome to be called that, Lily.'

'Oh don't be so stuffy, Friedrich. Relax. That's the way they talk.'

She flew at him when he made another sarcastic remark about Al.

'The trouble with you, Friedrich, is you are too bound up with yourself. If you came down off that high horse of yours, you might start to see how we ordinary people live.'

'And you, Lily, at times, are a flirtatious slut.' Lily slapped him hard across the cheek.

'Don't you ever talk to me like that again, Friedrich. If that is how you feel about me, you can take your jealous self off and get out of this house.' He rubbed his hand over his face, turned smartly about, clicking his heels and did just what she said, banging the door behind him.

Lily felt angry. His outbursts far from subsiding were becoming more frequent. It angered her that he was starting to cling to her in a suffocating way. Equally it frightened her that he showed no regret or remorse for what his parents had done. What, she wondered, was he capable of doing when aroused? She still loved the Friedrich in between, but could she live with the other Friedrich? For the first time in their relationship, she was scared.

Friedrich walked the streets confused and angry. He had never felt before the intensity of jealousy that now overwhelmed him. Could it mean he was afraid of losing Lily, that he loved her deeply and needed to possess her at all costs? She was his. Not another man's. This she must learn. He felt his mouth dry. He decided he needed a drink. In the dying light of the evening he spotted a small bar and walked into it. It showed all the signs of being reconstructed from rubble. No tables matched, chairs were of varying heights. The bar itself had pieces of old wood inserted into it. The wallpaper on the walls was peeling and stained. Hastily filled holes dotted the floor. But they were serving beer. Friedrich asked for a large flagon, took it to a table in the corner and sat listlessly staring into its foaming head.

He was on his third glass when a voice made him look up.

'Sturmmann Schulz! Fuck me, I thought you were dead.' Standing over him was the imposing figure of Sturmbannführer Helmut Weber, the man who had led the espionage raid in England. 'I didn't think I'd see you again.' He held a glass in his hand and sat down. Friedrich nearly choked on his beer.

'You got out,' he stuttered in equal surprise.

'Just. If it hadn't been for my markings we'd never have made it back to the reeds.' What was the man saying? While they were escaping he bloody well saved their skins! They must have known he was likely to be dead meat!

'You were lucky,' he said simply.

'And you? I often wondered what happened to you.'

'I was hit, but managed to get away.' He made no mention of his being captured. As he sat opposite the man, he saw Weber's face properly for the first time. A livid scar crossed his right cheek disfiguring his already hard face.

'Looks like you ran into trouble too?'

'Took a bullet, but it was only a flesh wound.'

'Did anyone try and come back for me?'

'Couldn't. We'd never have got back to the coast. If we'd delayed, the country would have been swarming.' He looked across at Friedrich and saw in his eyes what he was thinking. 'You did well to hold them off for so long.'

'I took the flack, Sturmannführer. Did you know I ended up in a POW camp?' He could see from his expression he did not. He went on. 'I was interrogated for days. I said nothing.' He made no mention of being tricked. Weber saw Friedrich felt let down and went out of his way to mollify him.

'That's rough,' he said, 'but what you did saved us and we are all grateful for that.' Pleased to bathe in Weber's belated praise, Friedrich's ire subsided. They sat silently for a few moments and took in what each had said.

'Did you find out who betrayed us?' asked Weber eventually.

'No, but I'm trying to find out.'

'Good man.' Weber looked hard into his eyes and kept his voice to a whisper. 'You're still devoted to the Fatherland, then?'

'Of course,' said Friedrich, almost indignantly, 'that's why I must find our betrayer and then I will kill him.'

'Take care what you say, but I'm pleased to hear of your loyalty.' Weber got up holding his empty glass. 'Another?' Friedrich nodded. He watched the big German walk to the bar. What a chance meeting! A curious excitement began to stir in him. Was Weber suggesting there was something afoot? That he could be of use? When he returned he waited for him to speak.

'Can you come here on Monday night?' Weber handed him a scrappy piece of paper. It had an address scrawled on it. Friedrich looked at it once and deftly pocketed it.

'Yes. Are you ….?' Weber cut him short.

'Not here.'

They both drank deeply.

'What happened to the others?' asked Friedrich.

'When we got back to France we were all redeployed separately and told to keep our mouths shut. I went to France. The others I think all ended up on the Russian front. Dead most likely.' He emptied his glass. ''Til Monday, Schulz.' With that he left, leaving a now tipsy Friedrich alone with his befuddled thoughts. As he eventually wove himself out of the bar, he was too drunk to see the two American soldiers eye him with more than casual curiosity.

Friedrich never came back to Lily that night. The next day she sat at her typewriter seeking solace in the rhythmic clatter of the keys. She barely saw the text through her tear-stained eyes. She wanted to go to the canteen for a coffee but was afraid of bumping into Al. She couldn't face him this morning. She was on the point of asking a passing colleague to fetch a coffee for her, when she felt a hand gently placed on her shoulder and a voice whispering in her ear.

'Lily, I'm sorry. Will you forgive me?' She didn't turn but stayed facing the keys.

'I can smell your breath, Friedrich. Go away and clean up.'

71

Al was true to his word and that weekend he asked Friedrich and Lily to show him the rituals of the Bavarian beer garden. The couple were enjoying an uneasy truce. Lily had half forgiven him but she was still alarmed by his sudden violence. However, she vowed she would enjoy their time with Al and she was pleased to see Friedrich was looking forward to it too. For the last few days he had returned to his old self.

With the city erupting from the ruins in blisters of pleasure, any place of entertainment that established itself was heavily patronised. When the three got to the beer garden in the warm early evening it was already in full swing. Friedrich found a small space on a bench at the end of a table. They all squeezed onto it. This time, Lily noticed, no one moved up for Friedrich.

Al's eyes popped out of his head when he saw the huge tankards brimming with foaming beer.

'They drink from those?' he gasped. 'At home one of those would last the night.'

'I thought you Americans drank a lot,' said Lily.

'Not in that way. We've had Prohibition remember. Don't want it returning.'

Friedrich ordered a Maßkrug all round. Al eyed the waitress who served them with an appreciative look.

'I dig your get up, Ma'am,' he said with typical directness as he took in her embroidered blouse and dirndl skirt. The girl, who probably didn't understand him, smiled and left to get the order.

'The dames here make our women look like pygmies.'

Lily laughed. She took Friedrich's arm and gave him a friendly clutch. 'It's good to see people enjoying themselves. It's like the old Munich.'

When the beer came, Al drank greedily. Friedrich was more circumspect. As the evening progressed Lily began to see the game he was playing and it worried her.

'What's Michigan like, Al?' she asked trying to direct the conversation away from drinking.

'Big. Kinda like here in some ways. A lot of trees. And the lake. That's pretty. It's so big, it's like a sea. You can't see the other side.' His eyes lit up in the way they do with anyone talking about their homeland. 'We get a lotta snow in winter. Boy, it's cold sometimes, but not as cold as Minnesota and Wisconsin. Been up there several times and you step outta your car and your breath freezes.'

'Sounds awful,' said Lily.

'Man, it's fucking beautiful.'

They lapsed into silence as the accordionist, who had stopped for a while, struck up another tune.

'You get snow here, Friedrich?'

'Sometimes.' It was now his turn to enthuse about his home. 'But we have more snow in the mountains. We go skiing there in winter. It too is beautiful.'

'Is that where friend Adolph had his eagle's nest?'

Lily jumped in with a warning. 'It's not good to speak his name in public here, Al.'

'Gotcha, Lily. Another round?'

'My turn,' said Lily. 'I think we should go for smaller glasses.'

'Can't have a lady ordering her drink,' said Al and before Lily could say anything he had summoned a passing waitress in the imperious way only Americans have. The girl was even taller than the last, with blonde-braided hair and an infectious smile.

'Two small glasses and another of those big ones.' He made a sign with his hands. The girl nodded. She turned to leave when Al spoke again. 'Say babe, what's your name?'

She understood. 'Helga.'

'That's a pretty name.' She smiled and left.

'That chick reminded me of Ingrid Bergman. Did you dig that voice?' He gave a poor imitation of the Swedish star's husky accent. 'Do you like Ingrid Bergman, Friedrich?'

'Ja, I like her.' As he spoke an American officer passed and tapped him on the shoulder.

'Easy how you go, pal. Remember the uniform you're wearing.'

Al looked momentarily chastened. 'Yessir.' He watched the officer go, but his voice stayed slurred. 'Must find the rest room,' he said.

Friedrich looked mystified.

'*Herren,*' said Lily. Friedrich pointed to the toilet block.

Al rose from the bench in an unsteady motion and swayed uncertainly towards his destination. He had to hold on to tables at several points on his way.

'There goes one of our conquering heroes,' said Friedrich sarcastically.

'You're deliberately getting him drunk, Friedrich. Please stop it.'

Friedrich looked indignant. 'He chose to get drunk.'

The waitress delivered the new round of drinks. She spoke to Friedrich in German.

'Your friend should be careful.'

'I'll tell him, thank you.'

Al returned, more upright.

'These broads are amazing. I could watch them all night.' His words blurred into each other. 'Gee, they got muscles on them that would do credit to any guy.' He picked up his glass and sunk his lips into the froth on the head of the brightly amber liquid. 'They carry four of these at one time. Must develop their tits too.'

'That's enough, Al,' said Lily sharply, worried that things were getting out of hand. 'I think it's time we went home.'

'You look neish, Lily.' Al made a lunge for Lily, lost his balance and fell headlong to the ground, knocking over his glass as he did so. The beer swept across the table and cascaded onto his inert body sprawled in the dirt. Friedrich looked pleased with himself. He had his revenge.

For a moment there was a general uproar as people raced to help Al to his feet. Lily was concerned he had hurt himself, but like most drunks he had fallen softly and appeared unscathed when he was lifted up.

'Al, speak to me,' urged Lily.

'Thasst's quite a tumble,' he said with some surprise. Lily went to take his arm when two burly GIs elbowed their way into the group and grabbed Al by the shoulders.

'It's all right, Ma'am. We'll take him from here.' She let go and watched them part drag, part walk the drunken Al away.

'He is,' observed Friedrich, 'what you say in English, legless!'

'I hope you are happy, Friedrich.' He could hardly contain his glee.

The waitress, Helga, came over with a bucket, scrubbing brush and cloth to clean up the spilt beer. Friedrich and Lily stood back as she was doing it, but she turned to Friedrich and spoke in German.

'These Americans are arrogant bastards. They think they can come into our country and lord it over us. I spit on them.' A well-aimed gob of phlegm landed in the middle of the beer and swirled around until it got swept into the bucket. Friedrich watched the buxom girl finish the clean-up with a flicker of pride.

On Monday morning a sheepish and apologetic Al Powalski appeared at Lily's typing desk. He had lost his bravado and was clearly suffering from a pulverising hangover.

'That was a pretty gross scene last night.'

'If you mean you made a bloody great fool of yourself, yes it was.'

He made no attempt to offer a coffee as a peace offering, for which she was grateful.

'They didn't arrest you then?'

'Caution. Next time the slammer.'

'You need to be careful.'

Your fiancé made a sucker of me, didn't he?'

'Yes, Al, he did.'

'Guess I deserved it?'

'Yes, you did.'

Lily smiled. Al was the sort of person you could quickly forgive. His open and cheerful nature was in marked contrast to Friedrich's frequent gloomy disposition. The next day she succumbed to his offer of coffee. She felt in a good mood. She had heard from her parents and from Sally. She was particularly pleased to read that they had received a letter from the Hartmanns and that the couple were now safe in America.

'A place called Frankenmuth,' Lily explained. 'It's in Michigan. Isn't that where you live, Al?'

'Yeah. Saginaw. Towns are close. Frankenmuth's kinda quaint. Must feel like you're back home. They speak German there.'

'That will be wonderful for them.'

'Hey, Lily, you must take a trip. Come over and see the folks.' He spoke with his usual exuberance. She laughed, knowing how unlikely that was.

'One day, perhaps.' She could dream, but she had the much more pressing matter of Friedrich's mood swings to deal with, although like her he was in good spirits when he joined Lily for lunch in the canteen. He told her that he had met an old acquaintance and that he had arranged to meet him that evening. To his surprise, she made no objection saying that she had letters to write home. She was pleased he had found someone he knew and was happy for him to go.

72

The house was the only one in the street that had survived the bombing. He knocked on the door.

'I'm Friedrich Schulz,' he said to the man who opened it. He was led along a darkened hallway, lit by a single naked bulb, and, at the end, ushered into a small anteroom.

'Wait here,' his host said curtly. He could hear distant voices in another room. After several minutes, he was summoned back down the hall and into what once must have been the drawing room. Wallpaper still clung to the walls, but the paper was split by large jagged cracks. Like the hall, the room was dimly lit and in the shadows sat a small group of men, their features largely hidden and made more opaque by a miasma of cigarette smoke.

'Gentlemen, this is Sturmmann Schulz.' It was Weber, his old leader, who spoke. 'Somehow, he's managed to find his way to Munich.' Friedrich heard chuckling from the others.

'I'm from here,' he said quickly.

'Welcome, Schulz,' said an older voice. 'Take a seat.' Friedrich looked around him for somewhere to sit. There was nothing except a plank on two metal drums. He perched on this.

'Sturmmanführer Weber tells me you fought well during their mission to England, but ended up in a POW camp.'

'Yes, sir.' He added the sir. He couldn't see the man speaking, but his voice conveyed the authority of an officer.

'I'm sure it wasn't easy.'

'I never talked, sir.'

'Well, you're here because Sturmmanführer Weber has vouched for you.' Friedrich remained silent. He waited for someone to explain what the group was and who the figures were lurking in the shadows, instead he got only questions.

'You say you were betrayed, but you don't know who did it?'

'No.'

'Have you any suspicion?'

'Yes.'

'Have you pursued it?'

'I have. I believe it is my fiancée and her friend.'

'If when you do find out, what will you do?'

'I will execute them on behalf of the Fatherland.' His voice had the coldness of steel.

'Thank you, Sturmman Schulz.' Friedrich felt baffled and confused. He hoped to be taken further into their confidence now he had spoken out.

'Is that it?' he asked. 'Who are you?'

'The less you know, the less you can tell,' said a disembodied voice.

'Suffice to say, we all have a grudge against someone who has betrayed Germany. We will all take revenge. When you have carried out your execution, report back to Sturmmanführer Weber. After tonight this house will not be used again. Thank you for coming.' The man who had opened the door emerged from the shadows and handed Friedrich an object wrapped in cloth.

'You will need this,' he said softly and before Friedrich could say anything he escorted him out into the street and shut the door.

Outside it was still light. After the darkness inside his eyes blinked. He felt a strange elation. He had stumbled by chance on a group bent on cleansing Germany of those responsible for its cowardly capitulation. He was no longer acting alone. He was part of something much bigger. He cradled the object he had been given and without unwrapping it traced with his finger its hard outline. Dark troubled thoughts boiled up in his mind. His love for Lily seized him like a sharp pain. But he knew he was losing her. He had long begun to feel she was moving away from him. She refused to understand how he felt. It was her duty to support his vision, not resist it. She claimed she knew nothing of the plan to entrap him, but he never believed her. Love or the Fatherland. It was a stark choice. If Lily and Sally had betrayed him, they must die. Somehow, he must find proof. But Lily must never suspect He walked home pondering the part he would play in the rise of the new Germany. He failed to notice the figure trailing him at a distance.

When he got back to Lily he found her still engaged on her letter writing.

'I've asked Sally over to join us,' she said without looking up. Friedrich frowned.

73

The summer in Munich brought rising heat making the city a cauldron of dust and pollution. Rubble was the big problem. As bomb sites were cleared, dangerous walls pulled down, clouds of dust were released into the atmosphere. On some days it got so bad that people walked along with scarves around their faces. Friedrich came into Lily with what he thought was the answer.

'I've heard they're starting to allow swimming in the Feringasee again. They clear the lake. Make it safe. We go there on Saturday, Lily.'

'That would be lovely. But I haven't anything to swim in.'

'You buy from the Comm…. How you say it?'

'Commissariat.'

'Ja.'

Lily had been in the Commissariat once to deliver some typing. She thought it was military supplies only, but when she went there during her break she found it stocked every type of goods, civilian as well as military. It was a supply base for occupation. When she asked one of the clerks on duty whether they stocked ladies swimwear she was to her surprise given an affirmative.

'Latest styles from America, Ma'am. You follow me.' The clerk led her through a veritable cornucopia of fashionable clothes which ended at a rack of swimming costumes.

'Can't get these anywhere else. Got to have our personnel looking their best when they are out and about.' And flaunting American superiority, thought Lily to herself.

'Thank you,' she said sweetly. 'I'm sure there's something suitable here.'

She browsed through the rack of brightly coloured garments and pulled out a yellow two-piece that took her fancy. To her surprise there was even a changing room.

The Feringasee was in the north of the city in an area that had not suffered too much damage. Transport was still difficult and so the two of them had managed to acquire bicycles.

'This is just like my first days in Munich,' Lily shouted to Friedrich as they set off to find the lake. But it wasn't quite. Now there were potholes to be negotiated and the sadness of seeing whole areas blackened and desolate, but gradually they emerged in streets that still had trees, where flowers still grew in gardens and houses still had their windows. Feringasee was a large expanse of water, tree-lined in parts and with grassy swards rising out of the lake in others. They stood their bicycles against a tree trunk and laid out towels in the sun. They were sweating from the exertions of riding and the sight of the water dappling in the sunlight hastened their disrobing. Friedrich hadn't seen Lily's costume and when she revealed it, he yelped with a puppyish pleasure that surprised him. How could he do what was in his mind? When she was like this, he adored her.

'You like it? It's the height of fashion from America.' America again! But this time there was a benefit! He adored what he saw and gazed for some moments at the bright yellow costume with its large bows on the bosom and across the waistline.

'What's the matter, Friedrich, cat got your tongue?'

'What?'

'An English saying.'

'Lily, you look beautiful.'

'You're not bad yourself,' she said. With the sunlight highlighting his tall blonde figure, she was as admiring of him as he was of her.

'Come on, race you to the water.' She played the trick she used to do with Sally of starting off as she was speaking. But this time it was to no avail. He instantly gained on her and dived into the water first. As she plunged in more tentatively she gave a great shout as the cold water hit her hot body.

'Help, it's icy.' The water came up to her thighs and she hesitated about submerging herself. But she had no choice. Friedrich advanced on her. She could see what he was going to do.

'No, you don't Friedrich.' She tried to retreat. But he was too quick. He swept her up in his arms, gave her a wet kiss and threw her bodily into the water. She screamed with delight and soon the two of them were swimming like dolphins around each other. He glided through the water with long leisurely strokes. Her swimming technique was less developed. She let him show off and revelled in their moment of togetherness.

In the clean and reviving air, she clung once more to her love for him.

They swam and played with each other, shouting and screeching like children. Every now and then Lily looked up to make sure they weren't worrying any one and on one occasion she saw a solitary man staring at them from the shore, but she was too far away to identify him. Finally, exhausted, they stumbled out of the water and flopped down on their towels, letting the sun warm their wet bodies. After a few minutes, Friedrich got up and with some urgency said he needed to relieve himself.

'You'll need to go across that field,' said Lily pointing behind her from her recumbent position. I saw some bushes on the far side when we arrived.'

'I do it here. It is OK for German man to do that.'

'You will not,' said Lily sharply. 'When I'm around you'll do it the English way and find a bush.'

Friedrich grunted and walked off in search of his bush. Lily turned over to let the sun dry off her backside.

When she felt a hand on her back, she decided Friedrich had not done as she had told him to. He had probably just gone behind the tree. But she forgave him as the hand gave her a delicious feeling. She purred contentedly until it began to go where she didn't want it to. She turned over.

'That's enough, Friedrich.' But it was not Friedrich staring down at her, it was Al. Lily shrieked. 'What are you doing?'

'Saw you here. Thought I'd say hello.'

'Are you stupid Al, Friedrich's around.'

'Sure. Saw him go off. He's on the other side of the field.'

'You can't touch me like this?'

'You liked it. I could sense it.'

'Just go away before Friedrich comes back.'

He bent down. 'Come on Lily, give me a kiss.'

'Please Al, for all our sakes, don't!' Her words had no effect. His lips pressed against hers and she found herself responding. What was she doing? She made to break away when a voice bellowed in their ears.

'Let go my wife, Al. What the fuck you doing?' Friedrich had come back. Above them he wielded a stout piece of wood. He must have seen them as far back as the tree and had picked up a fallen branch. He jabbed Al in the neck with it.

'Easy, man. I was just giving Lily a friendly kiss.'

'It looked more than a friendly kiss.'

'No, Friedrich, it's true.' said Lily with little conviction in her voice. 'Al was just trying to be friendly.'

'I don't believe you.' He swung the branch at Al's head. The American put his arm out to deflect it and instinctively moved his head away. The blow struck him hard on the shoulder. Friedrich raised the branch for a second strike. This time Al rolled with it and in a flash was on his feet with his hands up.

'Hey buddy, back off. I don't want to fight you.' Friedrich snarled and advanced on Al with the ferocity of an angry bear. Al turned and ran. Friedrich let him go and went back to Lily.

'If he touches you again, I kill him.'

'He won't. Come sit with me.' He threw down the branch and joined her on the towel. The sun had warmed her on the outside, but she felt cold within. Friedrich had justification for his violence, but still so easily resorted to it. He had called her 'his wife' in a way that sounded frighteningly possessive. Perhaps it was just an exaggeration of the moment, but she doubted it. She examined her own feelings. Al was wrong to do what he did, but she couldn't deny that she found it pleasant. She liked Al. She enjoyed his company. But was it more than that? Was she beginning to have real affection for him? If that was so, Friedrich had a right to be jealous. But once again he had resorted to violence all too quickly. She wanted him to put her arms around her. But he didn't. Instead he just sat and stared at the water of the sun-baked Feringasee.

74

As summer began to slip by, Lily despaired of ever hearing again from Reg Fuller. Despite autumn approaching the hot weather continued and on a particularly hazy Saturday she rode across to the small market where she knew she could buy her favourite Bavarian cheeses. On the way back she stopped at a standpipe and drank copiously from it. Friedrich had told her many times not to do this. So far she had suffered no harm. Today, however, her luck ran out.

Some two hours after getting home, she started to feel cramps in her stomach. She paid little attention to them and went to prepare their evening meal. It was a simple dish of spaghetti and vegetables, helped down with bread and Bavarian wine. She ate what was in front of her but began to feel nauseous soon after. She retired to the bathroom and threw up the entire contents of the meal.

'Friedrich, I must go to bed. I don't feel well. I've just been sick.' It was too early to have been affected by what they had just eaten.

'Lily,' said Friedrich in a scolding tone, who knew exactly what had happened, 'have you been drinking from a standpipe?'

'Yes.'

'Ah, I told you, you would suffer. Yes, you must go to bed. If it gets worse we will find a doctor.' It got worse. Lily was prostrate with headaches. She had diarrhoea and further vomiting and became weak. Friedrich had no idea where he was going to get a doctor.

'Try the American base,' whispered a frail Lily. He rode in on his bicycle and explained what had happened. A doctor came straight away. He prescribed rest and plenty of clean water.

'Come by the Commissariat and pick up bottled water, young man.' He rummaged in his case and handed over two bottles of pills. One for the headaches, the other for dehydration. 'No food, just dried biscuits when she starts to feel a little stronger.' Friedrich saw the doctor out and then went to sit beside Lily. An hour later he rode to the Commissariat for the water.

By Monday Lily was starting to feel more like herself again, but she was too weak to return to work so Friedrich went in on his own. He sat down at his desk and carried on working on a translation he had started the previous Friday. It described the democratic process of local government and how elected officials had to be answerable to the citizens who elected them. He hated this American propaganda. From the cubicle where he sat, he could see Al Powalski talking to his editor. He had stayed clear of him since the incident for fear of not controlling his actions should they meet. He still felt a hatred towards him for what he saw as his attempt to force his unwanted attentions on Lily. He broke a pencil thinking about it.

'Mr Schulz?' He looked up to find the messenger addressing him. 'I was told you know Miss Rood.'

'I live with her.' The man raised his eyes but said nothing.

'This came for her today. Could you deliver it to her?'

'Of course.' The man handed him a small buff envelope. It had come from England. It was typewritten and looked official. He laid it on his desk and carried on with his work. Through the morning curiosity started to gnaw at him. Who could be writing to Lily like this? Possibly a throw-back to the time she was being interrogated. But that he thought was unlikely. That was long over. Maybe it was something Lily needed to attend to urgently? He would be doing her a favour by opening it. He put the letter in his pocket and went for a coffee. But he found he couldn't open it in such a public place. He returned to his desk. He lifted a paper knife that sat beside his pad and very carefully slit the buff envelope. He teased the letter out. The few type written words on the flimsy page exploded in his head. He read and re-read them. He took a sharp intake of breath as the import of the contents began to sink in. He clenched his fists until his knuckles drained of blood and then he put the letter in his pocket and never gave it to Lily.

Lily was feeling much better when he got home and was able to eat some biscuits and a little rice. Friedrich had gone to the Commissariat and had managed to buy some eggs. This cheered Lily up immensely and she tucked into a plate of scrambled eggs with relish. By the middle of the week she was back at work. Waiting for her were letters both from her parents and from Sally. She had hoped to find one from

Reg Fuller, but she enjoyed reading of life back in Bletchley. She was delighted to read in Sally's letter that she was planning to come out to Munich. She didn't tell Friedrich this as she didn't want to upset his current amiable mood. He seemed more relaxed and she had hopes of persuading him to return to England.

75

Sally entered the hall where visitors were placed, an elegant room with panelled walls, a hammer-beamed ceiling, dotted with comfortable armchairs, the whole giving the appearance of a gentleman's club. The man she presumed she was meeting had his back to her when she came in, but as he was the only person in the room, she assumed he was the one. She introduced herself. The man turned and stood up to confront her.

'Miss Deeprose, thank you for seeing me.' Sally stared at the man before her. He was in his forties, hair smarmed down, his posture slumped, and his clothes dishevelled. He wore a grubby raincoat, frayed at the cuffs, an equally grubby shirt, with its collar button missing and a tie hanging from it like rope. She didn't look at his shoes but assumed they were scuffed. He hardly seemed the man to frequent a place like this, thought Sally.

'Please, sit down.' He didn't introduce himself but merely gestured to a chair opposite. Mystified by his cloak and dagger attitude, she did as he bade.

'You are about to go to Munich?'

'Yes.' How did he know? But then, thought Sally, in the world she worked, that was never a question that needed to be asked.

'Who are you?'

'Someone who has your welfare at heart and that of your friend Lily.' Of course, this must be one of Lily's sleazy acquaintances, whom she had a habit of dropping into the conversation from time to time.

'Do you work for the government?'

'In a manner of speaking,' continued the man enigmatically. This was beginning to annoy Sally.

'Speak what you've got to say.'

'I've come to warn you and Lily, who I will be contacting, that you may be in danger in Munich.'

'Who from?'

'From Miss Rood's so-called fiancé.'

'Friedrich?'

'Yes, Friedrich Schulz.' Finally the man elaborated. 'Schulz has got into some very bad company. An organisation of former Nazis bent on revenge.'

'That's ridiculous.' said Sally vehemently, her freckles almost dancing with indignation. 'How do you know this anyway?'

'My organisation has been in talks with our counterparts in the American sector in Munich. Schulz's name has come up in signals between us.' He looked at the growing alarm on Sally's face. 'Don't worry, we will look after you. When you get to Munich you will be met by someone who will take care of you.'

Sally gave a watery smile. 'Why are you so interested in Lily, Mr ....?'

'Fuller.'

'.... and me?'

He didn't answer but got up from his seat.

'Take care, Miss Deeprose.' He shook her hand and left, his scruffy figure shuffling through the hall door, leaving Sally with mouth open and head filled with alarm bells. What in her mind was to be a trip filled with happy and nostalgic reminiscences had become one that promised the opposite.

76

Lily was mystified as to why she hadn't had a communication from Reg Fuller, but at least she had heard that Sally was on her way. She so wanted to see her dear friend again. Friedrich had become his affable self once more and she hoped he wouldn't feel too affronted to see Sally again. In fact he was displaying an excitability that was out of character. On an unusually warm autumn Saturday, he proposed they spend it in the English Garden. The leaves were turning colour giving the park land a golden glow. They walked arm-in-arm along the extensive paths, had lunch in the beer garden and watched the few brave souls struggle in the fast-flowing waters of the Eisbach.

'It means icy water,' said Friedrich.

Lily stooped down to let the stream flow though her fingers.

'Ouch, it's cold.' She looked at two boys struggling to stay upright in the raging current. 'How do they endure that?'

'Germans enjoy a physical challenge,' said Friedrich.

They got home around 4pm. Lily went to the kitchen to make a pot of tea. When she returned she found Friedrich staring out of the window. Lily put the tray down on the small table in front of the sofa and joined him. A car was parked outside and a man in an American uniform was closing the door. He had his back to her. The occupant or occupants of the car had clearly just got out. She caught sight of a coat flapping as it disappeared behind a tree. Her heart pounded with excitement.

The doorbell rang. Friedrich went to the door. She heard the familiar voice. There in the shadows, with her freckles and her mass of wild curls as pronounced as ever, stood Sally. When she saw Lily, a great grin crossed her face. The two women embraced each other in warm exuberant hugs.

'It's so lovely to see you Sally.' They nuzzled each other and let tears run down their cheeks. Sally saw Friedrich looking at them with an expression of confusion on his face. Their affectionate greeting seemed to go beyond a warm welcome. Watching them hug each other, they seemed like lovers. He was now convinced that Lily was complicit in his betrayal.

'Hello, Friedrich, good to see you.'

'And you Fräulein Sally.'

'What about a drink? After that bloody journey I need one.'

'Of course,' said Friedrich quickly. 'I get. Please sit down.' He took from her the small overnight bag and went out to the kitchen while the two women sat together on the sofa.

'It's good to be together again, Lily,' said Sally. 'It was naughty of you running off like that. You upset your parents you know.'

'I know,' said Lily regretfully, 'but it was for the best.'

'Are you coming home?'

'I hope so.'

'You still drink beer, Sally?' Friedrich's voice came from the kitchen. 'American beer?'

'Wonderful,' said Sally. She looked around her. 'You look very comfortable here.'

'We've been lucky. Getting jobs with the American Military has meant we can get all the supplies we need. You've seen what a mess the city's in.'

'God, it was awful driving through all those ruins.'

Friedrich came back with four bottles of Miller High Life. 'You drink from bottle?' he asked.

'From anything as long as it's liquid,' said Sally picking up a bottle and greedily quaffing its contents. For a few moments they sat in silence enjoying being together, then Friedrich pulled out of his pocket the buff letter addressed to Lily.

'When you were ill, I was given this.' He handed it to her. Lily took it and read the contents. It was from Reg Fuller. It was brief: *'I have the information you wanted. The person who alerted the authorities to the raid that we intercepted was Sally Deeprose. I cannot tell you more. You must ask her. Reg Fuller.*' Lily stared at the paper, uncomprehending. Sally twitched nervously. Friedrich looked triumphant.

'She, your friend, Lily, betrayed me,' he said with venom in his voice.

Lily ignored the accusation. In her mind, there was a greater betrayal. What Friedrich did in opening the letter was to destroy the trust between them. Whoever was going to be revealed as the informant was information for her alone, information she would use in her own way.

'You had no right to open that letter, Friedrich. You have destroyed everything.'

'No, Lily, she destroyed us.'

'She was doing her duty,' snapped Lily. 'We were fighting a war and we were on different sides. That is something you have not come to terms with, Friedrich, and I don't think you ever will.' Sally put her hand on Lily's knee.

'Lily's right,' said Sally. 'It was a mess. Before the war, we were young, confused, uncertain where our loyalties lay. When war broke out Lily was torn between love for you, Friedrich, and loyalty to her country. I had no such worry. I knew where my loyalties lay.'

'So,' he said icily, 'tell me how you knew of our raid?'

Sally took another swig of beer. She looked at Lily, avoided Friedrich and breathed deeply. 'I have been sworn to secrecy and in telling you this I shall be breaking my oath and probably committing treason.' She looked pointedly at Lily.

'You know, Lily, how I was unable to tell you what I did. Well, I worked at a very hush hush establishment. It intercepted enemy signals and decoded them. I was employed as a translator in the German section. A message landed on my desk that hinted at a likely raid on the east coast. Yours, Friedrich, was one of the names encrypted. I immediately alerted my superior.' She allowed herself a quick glance at Friedrich. His eyes had hardened.

She went on. 'Other messages came through and the military were able to prepare themselves for an attack.'

'You could have, how you say it, sat on the information.'

'And let you and your comrades go rampaging around the English countryside. You were doing what you saw was your duty and I was doing mine. But it wasn't just coded messages was it, Friedrich? You were working for your country long before war broke out?'

Lily looked mystified. Sally went on.

'I remembered those maps you so meticulously marked. I know you Germans have an eye for detail, but what I saw when I interrupted your work that day went beyond casual record. I now realise you were creating reconnaissance maps for the Wehrmacht.'

There was a violent scrunch on the floor. Friedrich had pushed his chair back and stood glowering over Sally.

'I rotted in a POW camp for four years and you say you didn't betray me.' He turned on his heels and walked into the bedroom.

'He's angry,' said Lily. 'I had wanted him to confront this in a different way.'

'Are you angry, Lily?'

'No, just upset that it had to be you.'

'I just happened to be in that place at that time.'

'I know.' Lily took Sally's hand in hers. 'Then, it would not have been easy to forgive you, but we've moved on and I see that if I had been you, I would have done the same.' Jack Havering reared up in front of her as she spoke, the man she herself had betrayed. But she hadn't realised that Friedrich had included her in the list of his betrayers.

He came back in. Lily looked up. Had he been crying? There was sadness in his eyes. One arm, shielded from her, hung limply at his side.

'Lily,' he said calmly, 'please stand up.' His voice was so icy Lily looked alarmed. Sally could see no reason why her friend should do what he said, but he repeated the request.

'Stand up.' There was a tremulous quiver on his lips. Sally sat bemused until she caught sight of what he was holding. Lily saw it at almost the same instant. His arm came up and the barrel of a Walther PP handgun sank into the back of Lily's head. She froze. The words she wanted to shout never came.

Sally screamed. 'Friedrich what are you doing?'

'You betrayed me. You must both pay the price.'

Lily found her voice. 'Friedrich, you're insane.'

'Don't call me that, Lily.' He flashed his eyes furiously. A frightened Sally sat rooted to the sofa.

'Lily, I shan't say it again, please stand up.' He jabbed the gun into her skull. Her body shaking with fear responded. Slowly she rose from the sofa.

'Place your hands on your head and kneel.' She did his bidding.'

'Friedrich, stop this.' Sally was half off the sofa pleading with her eyes. He pushed her back with his free hand, the gun never moving from Lily's head.

'Sit down and keep quiet.'

'She's innocent, Friedrich, she never betrayed you. It was me. You saw the note.'

'She knew of the plan to trap me in prison. I spoke things I would never have done, because of her.'

Lily knelt whimpering in front of him. With her hands on her head, she couldn't see him, but his untrue words cut through her with devastating hurt.

'I did not know. They tricked us,' she whispered with halting words that were barely audible between the sobs.

'I do not believe you and now you must pay – and your friend too.' He looked in Sally's direction and, without moving the gun, motioned her to join Lily on the floor. He had worked out that Sally might have resisted, but with his gun firmly at Lily's head, he knew she would obey without hesitation.

Lily took comfort from the closeness of her friend's body sinking down beside her.

'Please Friedrich, Germany is changing. You can do so much to help your country recover. The bad times are all in the past.'

'No, Lily, they are not. You asked me once if I would have done what my father did. This ….' He pushed the barrel deeper into her flesh, causing her to flinch with pain. '…. is my answer. You will never understand that I cannot forget. You must die.'

'Remember Edith Lambert, Friedrich,' she beseeched him, making one last desperate effort to save them. 'You were the one who let her go.'

'She was innocent. You and Fräulein Sally are not.'

They heard the click of the gun being cocked. Lily broke into sobs again, torn apart by the realisation that Friedrich could sacrifice her for some insane ideology. No-one can tell how they are going to face death when the moment comes, but for Lily facing that reality, it was the loss of all those she loved, and that included Friedrich.

She wanted to hold Sally in her arms, but even if she could it would not have been possible. Her arms and legs had turned to jelly. Her bladder was about to burst. Out of the corner of her eye she could see that her friend's freckles had vanished into an ashen whiteness. Momentarily Friedrich eased the gun away from Lily's head, the more to make sure the first bullet hit both of them. Neither moved.

Then Lily heard them. Flies. Swarming around her. Flying up from the ground in their hundreds. In the buzz of their wings she heard a cry of 'Schulz', then a blinding flash and an explosion that shook the house. The gun spun from Friedrich's hand and curled across the room. Both women crumpled and slumped to the floor, both only vaguely conscious of the many booted feet running towards them. Kindly hands took them over and started to get them on their feet. Lily lifted her tear stained face just in time to see Friedrich being led away. Behind him stood the imposing figure of Al Powalski, holding the gun he had just fired.

77

'I thought I could love him whatever happened, but now it has just drained out of me. He may be alive, but in my heart he has gone.'

Tears streaked down her face. She wore a fur-lined black coat. The trees were bare and lifeless. It was now mid-winter. Sally stood beside her, holding her around the shoulder. They waited for Major Norris to come down the steps of the courthouse.

Today was the day the sentence was being announced. The trial had lasted five months and at the end of it, Friedrich had been found guilty of planning to shoot Lily and Sally in a military style execution. Throughout the proceedings neither women attended and only gave evidence behind closed doors. Now they stood waiting for details of the verdict.

'He has been given life imprisonment,' said Major Norris. 'Had he co-operated, he would have got much less. As you know we believe he was not acting alone, but he never divulged any information about any others involved.'

Lily was silent as she listened to Major Norris, but Sally was curious.

'Will he ever be let out?'

'Possibly, especially if he changes his mind and is prepared to give us information.' He looked at soulful Lily. 'Can we give you a lift back to your apartment?' They accepted gratefully.

Sally had stayed in the apartment with Lily during the long months of the trial. Both women suffered sustained shock from their experience, but Sally recovered more quickly and was able to get typing work to fund her stay. Lily could never forgive Friedrich for what he had put her through and even though she returned to work, she could find no point in life. In their weeks together Sally and Lily often returned to their old haunts in Munich, those, that is, that still stood. But it was a bittersweet time for Lily, for on every street they walked she saw Friedrich on the other side of the road, and she hated him for destroying her happiness.

But with the trial over, Lily began, little by little to work out a new life for herself. For years she had met betrayal and mistrust, her misguided affection for an evil regime embroiling her against her will in the dark practices of intrigue and espionage. She had met a succession of people who were not who they said they were and it made her once open and trustful character resentful and cynical. She had flirted with and become attracted to Al Powalski but now in her mind he was just like the rest of them.

'Who are you, Al?' she asked one day while they were having coffee together.

'An ordinary guy.'

'No, you're not. You're like the others. Living double standards. You're no better than Friedrich.' She stirred a spoonful of sugar into her coffee. Before the war she never took sugar, but its scarcity had made it a desirable luxury to be indulged. 'How did you get into this business?'

'What business, Lily?'

'Tricking people.' He didn't answer immediately. She waited.

'Seems I'm good at being buddies with folk.' He gave one of his infectious grins. 'So I guess they thought I could be useful. Go undercover for them. Sniff out the Nazis.'

'But what I don't understand is how you knew Friedrich and I would turn up here?'

'That's an easy one. We didn't.' He watched her sip her coffee. 'But you don't think we'd give you jobs without doing checks. A quick call to the Brits and it all came out what you'd been up to back there.'

'And so you were asked to get friendly with us?'

'That's about it.' He paused and looked Lily in the eye. 'But I really didn't know it was you until I saw you at the typing desk. That's the honest truth.'

'But the kisses …. they were all a sham, were they?'

'Hell, no. They were real, Lily.' He moved his hand to take hers. She recoiled.

'No, Al. It's too soon.'

'Falling for you and getting Friedrich all riled were not part of the plan. But it didn't matter. He wasn't smart enough to cover his tracks.'

'And it was you who met Sally at the station?'

'Sure was. Met her, took her straight to your place. We had a good idea what your guy was gonna do, so I hung around.'

'It's as well you did,' said Lily grimly.

'He was never gonna shoot before I got to him.'

Sally was not convinced when Lily told her what Al had said.

'I agree,' said Lily. 'He didn't feel that steel against his temple.'

'I was pissing myself. I don't remember a thing of what happened after I put my hands on my head.'

'Little wonder,' said Lily, 'you blacked out.'

'You like him, don't you?'

'Who?'

'Don't be coy with me Lily. You know who.'

'Al?'

'I've seen the way you look at him.'

'I've told him, it's too soon. I've got a lot in my head to sort out.'

Sally leant over and hugged her. They were sat on the sofa. Lily luxuriated in the close embrace of her friend. Soon they would be returning together to England and Lily looked forward to putting the tangled past behind her.

Al took them to the station in his jeep. They protested, but he insisted and from the open rear seat they took a last look at the city that had been so much part of their lives.

They boarded a train that now had corridor compartments, an early sign that Germany was starting to rise from the ashes. Al came on the platform and would have come into the carriage had Lily not stopped him. But she didn't protest when on the steps he quickly kissed her.

'Remember, Lily Rood, I have promised to marry you.'

As the train pulled out, he shouted: 'You're no longer engaged!' She watched his tall lively figure with its black wavy hair slowly shrink to a dot and felt a warmth spread through her. The first thing she had done when she had started to recover was to throw her engagement ring down the drain.

The mist had come down when she went on deck, but she preferred the fresh air on her face. The ferry's hooter blasted above her head. She shivered a little and wrapped her coat and scarf tightly about her. She thought now of the future, of rebuilding her life, of seeing her friends again, Lil, Yakova, Gloria, perhaps even Daphne. While she was staring into the white veil ahead, she became conscious that it had started to lift. Very gradually indistinct shapes emerged from the gloom. Soon they had sharpened and become cliffs. She felt a hand on her shoulder. She didn't look round. She knew Sally was behind her.

'The White Cliffs,' she said.

'Yes, Lily, we've come home.'

Lily returned to her old room in Fenner Way and took comfort in the familiar objects around her. In the same way Sally and her wartime friends gave her assurance that a normality had returned. She often saw Lil and Yakova and in fact got an administrative job at the brickworks, where she shared the same office as Lil.

'Bloody hell, for a toff you don't 'alf live a dangerous life, Lily,' exclaimed Lil, when Lily gave her an expurgated account of what had befallen her.

'Not as dangerous as having to fend off Boozy Bob.'

'You're right there, Lily. Poor man's bereft with the loss of all his lovely ladies.' She gave a snigger.

'What are you giggling at?'

'He's got one, though.'

'What do you mean?' asked Lily mystified.

'Daphne. She's come back. We were short of one or two drivers and Mr Roberts took her on.'

Lily laughed. Of all the women Bob Jenkins had worked with, Daphne was the least fanciable.

'Poor bugger. Don't rate his chances if he tries anything.' Lil gave one of her throaty cackles.

At weekends, she and Sally had their regular get together at the tea shop. Their bubbling conversation was in marked contrast to the quality of the fare on offer, still subject to draconian rationing. Now Lily knew where Sally worked, she could ask in conspiratorial whispers what she was doing.

'It's the Russians keeping us busy.'

'You don't know any Russian, Sally.'

'No, I'm now on the machines.'

'What machines?'

'Can't say.'

'I know, hush hush!' They collapsed in laughter, cut short by Lily's sudden horrified expression. She had her head out of the window. Sally turned around to see what she was looking at.

'What's he doing?' whispered Sally.

'Passing by, I hope,' said Lily anxiously. On the other side of the road, they could see the shambling figure of Reg Fuller walking along the pavement. He stopped briefly and stared at the tearoom. If he had seen them, he gave no indication, and, after his momentary pause, continued shuffling down the road, soon to disappear, Lily hoped, out of their lives forever.

Over the next few months, life consisted of picking up the pieces after the war, until Peg started to notice the number of letters for Lily coming from America and, as she astutely observed, coming from two different addresses. She said nothing and waited for Lily to explain, which she did one evening when they were having coffee after dinner.

'Mummy and Daddy, you've probably seen the airmail letters. They're from the Hartmanns. You remember.' Peg and Hubert nodded. 'They've invited me to stay with them for a while in their new home in America. It's in Michigan.'

Hubert puffed on his pipe. 'That's a long way away,' he said.

'Not today,' assured Lily. 'Boat to New York, then train to Chicago. It can't be any worse than crossing Germany.

'And the other letters?' enquired Peg.

'They're from Al Powalski. He's an American soldier I got to know in Munich.' Fortunately she hadn't said who it was who had shot Friedrich. She knew her mother had found it hard to reconcile the Friedrich she knew with the twisted man he had become, but equally it disturbed her to know that he had been shot. She shivered visibly when Lily told her how close Sally had come to being killed.

'Is he a nice man?'

'Very nice. Great fun. He lives in Michigan too.'

'So you will be seeing him?'

'I expect so.' If there was a huff from her mother, she missed it.

Sally was thrilled and wished she were going too. The weeks ahead were filled with preparations and farewells. Lily's whole being throbbed with excitement as she wrote out the luggage labels. This was a new start which she hoped would wipe away the horrors of the war. Sally had agreed to come with her to Southampton. From the towering mass of the liner she looked down on the diminutive figure of her friend. She could still make out her curls, but her freckles blurred in the space between them. She would have to imagine them and wait for the time she would return. But would she return? As the great liner edged its way into the Solent, that question hung over the water, unanswered.

About the Author

Keith Sheather spent most of his life in the BBC, where he made documentary programmes for BBC Bristol. One of these was 'The Wartime Kitchen & Garden', which, with its accompanying book by Jennifer Davies, has provided him with valuable source material about the Home Front in the Second World War. 'Lily at War' is his first novel. He is now retired and lives with his wife in Bristol.